ROTHERHAM LIBRARY & INFORMATION SERVICES

This book must be returned by the date specified at the time of issue
as the DATE DUE FOR RETURN.
The loan may be extended (personally, by post or telephone) for a
further period if the book is not required by another reader, by quoting
the above number / author / title.

CL/132/F14

Ciara Geraghty lives in north County Dublin with her husband and three children.

BECOMING SCARLETT

In Scarlett O'Hara's life, everything goes according to plan. Until now . . . Scarlett has returned to her childhood home, her plan in tatters and a baby on the way, while John Smith — Scarlett's boyfriend — has left her to join an archaeological dig in Brazil. Worse still, she's unsure who the baby's father is . . . even though she's slept with exactly four-and-a-half men in her entire thirty-five years. Scarlett throws herself into her job as a wedding planner, but even that's not going smoothly, because she has growing feelings for her most important client's husband-to-be . . . In the end it's the person she thought she knew best — herself — who surprises her the most, as she tries, for the first time ever, to navigate life without a plan.

CIARA GERAGHTY

BECOMING SCARLETT

Complete and Unabridged

CHARNWOOD
Leicester

First published in Great Britain in 2010 by
Hodder & Stoughton
An Hachette UK company
London

First Charnwood Edition
published 2011
by arrangement with
Hodder & Stoughton
An Hachette UK company
London

The moral right of the author has been asserted

Extract from *The House on Pooh Corner* by A. A. Milne
© The Trustees of the Pooh Properties. Reproduced with
permission of Curtis Brown Group Ltd.

British Library CIP Data

Geraghty, Ciara.
  Becoming Scarlett.
  1. Single women- -Fiction. 2. Pregnant women- -
  Fiction. 3. Weddings- -Planning- -Fiction.
  4. Chick lit. 5. Large type books.
  I. Title
  823.9′2–dc22

  ISBN 978–1–44480–540–6

Published by
F. A. Thorpe (Publishing)
Anstey, Leicestershire

Set by Words & Graphics Ltd.
Anstey, Leicestershire
Printed and bound in Great Britain by
T. J. International Ltd., Padstow, Cornwall

This book is printed on acid-free paper

For Frank MacLochlainn
Who still holds my hand when the plane
takes off

'I don't see much sense in that,' said Rabbit.

'No,' said Pooh humbly, 'there isn't. But there was going to be when I began it. It's just that something happened to it along the way.'

The House on Pooh Corner, A.A. Milne

1

The missed period happens on a Friday. It is due at 11.23 a.m. By 11.30 a.m., I am worried.

Now it is a quarter past two in the afternoon and still no show. Fear grips me like a vice and for a moment I struggle for breath and wonder if I am hyperventilating, the way Maureen does.

'Are you all right, Scarlett?' It is Elliot, my boss and the company's closet Westlife fan, because there's always one. His head curls round the edge of the door.

'I have to go out,' I say, getting up.

'You're like a cat on a griddle these days,' Elliot says.

His concern is like a bowl of noodle soup and I nearly tell him. But I don't. Of course I don't. He will not see the seriousness of the situation. He will tell me that a delay of — I check my watch — two hours and fifty-two minutes cannot be described as 'late'.

'Anyway, you can't go out. It's time for the monthly meeting.'

'I'm not going.'

'You have to. You know I can't go on my own.'

'You're forty-bloody-two. Of course you can go on your own.'

'I'm not forty-two till next month. You *know* that.'

I can't look at his face. If I look at his face, he'll persuade me to go. I stare at my computer screen. 'I'm too busy.'

'You're not. You're playing backgammon. I can see the reflection in the window behind you.'

Dammit. I should have pulled the blinds down.

'Fine,' I say, snapping off the game. 'But you shouldn't bring me to these meetings. It makes you look bad.'

'Bringing you to the meeting makes me look good,' Elliot insists. 'Everyone knows I won't be able to answer any of Simon's questions if you're not there.'

'Tell me again why you're my boss?'

'Because my mother is a media mogul who makes Rupert Murdoch look like a paperboy,' recites Elliot off by heart. 'Not to mention the fact that she owns stackfuls of shares in the company.'

'Don't you mind?' I've often wondered but I've never asked the question before. My discretion seems to have fled, along with my boyfriend.

Elliot pauses before answering. 'Well,' he says eventually, 'I might mind if she owned stackfuls of shares in a morgue and she got me a job embalming corpses or something like that.'

'I don't know,' I say. 'A morgue would be a lovely, quiet place to work.'

'Upbeat, aren't we?'

'What's there to be upbeat about?'

'I think we need a little hug, don't we?' Elliot moves in my direction.

I stop him with my stare, the unblinking one with eyebrows in the shape of London Bridge high on my forehead. 'If you hug me, I'll bite your ear until you cry like a girl.'

'Temper, temper.'

'And I won't go to the meeting with you.'

Elliot stops walking and lowers his arms. 'Fine, fine, fine. I was just trying to cheer you up.'

'I know,' I say, doing my best to smile at him.

'Do you have toothache?' he asks, concerned.

'No. Why?'

'You just looked like you were in pain there.'

I stop trying to smile and sigh instead. I am exhausted. Probably because of my period, which is on its way. Any minute now.

'Fine. I'll come. I just need to go to the loo first.' To see if it has arrived without my noticing. Although that's as likely as Filly missing an episode of *Home and Away*.

★ ★ ★

The management meeting happens on the last Friday of every month. I'm not technically management but Elliot insists I go with him. He's a little nervous of Simon Kavanagh, our MD, which is understandable, given the peculiar bulldog-ish disposition of Simon's face and his tendency to shout (he's deaf in his left ear and refuses to get a hearing aid on the grounds that it will attract attention to his ear hair, which is thick and dark and in direct contrast to his head hair, which is thinning and grey). I know this because Simon's long-long-long-suffering PA tells Filly everything, who, in turn, tells me.

3

The fact that Simon insists the monthly meetings be held on a Friday afternoon is really all you need to know about the man. I never want to go and I am more adamant than usual on this particular Friday. The absence of John is something I am learning to cope with from Monday to Thursday but I haven't got the hang of the weekends yet. I get a heavy feeling in my stomach on Friday morning (as if I've eaten a sausage sandwich, which I have not, because I'm a vegetarian) and the feeling only really starts to lighten on Sunday evening with the prospect of a return to work on Monday.

It seems impossible that we had our last conversation *three weeks ago*. In John's flat. Already I am calling it John's flat.

'I'm leaving,' he'd said.

'No, I heard that bit. What did you say after that?'

'The bit about . . . ?' His voice fades away.

'The sentence directly following the one where you said, 'I'm leaving.' '

'I said . . . I said . . . What I said was . . . ' He glances at my face. 'I've decided to join an archaeological dig in Sao Paulo. Well, near Sao Paulo. About seventy-five kilometres away. That's in Brazil.'

I know that Sao Paulo is in Brazil. I am a woman who knows things. Except this. I am — and I hate this word but I'm going to use it anyway — *flabbergasted*.

'But you don't even speak Portuguese,' I say. For a moment I wish I had older brothers. *Huge* ones. Hairy. I'd ring them — they'd all live

4

together in a big converted stable somewhere — and I'd tell them about John and they'd say nothing, just nod at me down the phone (they're a taciturn bunch, strong, silent types) and then they'd go and *sort him out*. But there are no brothers. Or sisters. There's only me.

'I can learn. It's a derivative of Latin, as most of the modern languages are.'

'But you've never studied Latin,' I point out, like this is an argument I can win.

Somewhere inside me I know this is not a normal break-up conversation. People don't discuss languages when they break up with each other. They shout. Sometimes they break things — like plates or the other person's big toe when they drop something heavy on it, like an iron. Sometimes they throw things — like the other person's clothes out of a window, preferably a top-storey window. But we do none of these things. We are not that sort of couple. I stand there looking at his familiar face and his mouth is moving and I know this mouth so well. The way the top lip is half the width of the bottom one, the fleshy colour of it, the way it is careful to cover his teeth when he smiles because of the braces that march across them like a heavily armed platoon. I almost smile at him but then he opens his mouth and the sunlight catches the metal and glints against it so hard I almost have to shield my eyes.

'We can still keep in touch,' he says.

'No we can't,' I say.

He doesn't say anything to this. He just looks at his shoes. They are sensible brown leather lace-ups and nothing about them suggests that he is going to leave me and sift muck in Brazil. He shifts from one foot to the other.

And that's when I know. That he is leaving.

★   ★   ★

I move along the corridor towards the boardroom, concentrating on placing one foot in front of the other. This Friday is particularly bad. This third Friday. It feels like the thirtieth Friday. The weeks are like weeks in Lent when you're eight and you've given up sweets and crisps and Catch bars.

2

The meeting is held in the boardroom on the fourth floor. Simon is already there, sitting at the head of the table drumming his fingers, even though the meeting is not scheduled to begin for another five minutes. He is a stout man with small eyes. It is impossible to say what colour they are. A pale colour. But they never miss a beat. They follow me into the room with radar precision. I slip into a chair between Elliot and Duncan, our mild-mannered accountant, it being furthest away from Simon's line of vision.

Gladys Montgomery arrives in a clatter of heels. Her hair, piled as usual on top of her head, leans like the Tower of Pisa. With her lanky frame, her high heels and the swell of her hair, she looks about seven feet tall. She sits on the other side of the room, nods at us and sets out her stall: leather-bound diary, notebook — a stern black hardback — Parker pen, BlackBerry, mobile phone, glasses case.

'What is she doing here?' I write on a piece of paper and slide it over to Elliot.

He scribbles on the page. A gigantic question mark surrounded by a series of exclamation marks. Elliot is her boss and he doesn't know why she's at the meeting. Something is *up*.

Simon Kavanagh clears his throat. 'Ah, Scarlett, good of you to join us. Heard you weren't well. I've been away so I didn't get a

chance to speak with you. Are you all right?'
When he's not shouting, Simon's voice is thin,
although he prides himself on his diction and has
no problem making himself heard.

Everyone at the table leans forward and looks
at me.

I pulled a sickie the day after John dropped his
bombshell. Because I haven't pulled a sickie
since that Monday back in 1998 when I had to
be removed from the office by ambulance
(meningitis — the non-fatal strain), it made
front-page news on the office grapevine. This
time, I had slept on Filly's sofa bed the night
before. I only noticed it was still a sofa and not a
bed when I woke up the next morning.

'But you're not sick,' said Filly, when I told
her I wasn't going to work. 'You're hung-over.
You can't not go into work just because you're
hung-over. If everyone in Ireland did that,
there'd be no one left to run the place.'

'No,' I say, 'I really am sick. My head aches
and I might throw up. Plus I could go back to
sleep, even though it's after nine o'clock in the
morning.'

'Classic hangover symptoms,' Filly insists.
'Look at me.' She sticks out her tongue and
points at it. It is the colour of bacon fat,
surprisingly long and fleshy. I feel my stomach
heave.

'I'm not going to work today,' I say again. My
voice is as firm as a bodybuilder's biceps.

'But the last time you missed work was so
legitimate. I mean, you nearly *died*.'

'So? I'm due another sick day, aren't I?'

'I suppose so,' says Filly, conceding the point grudgingly. 'What are you going to do?' she asks, peering at me like I'm an interesting exhibit in a museum. 'I mean, you're welcome to stop here as long as you like.' She sweeps her hand around the room and suddenly I want to be somewhere I can call home.

Filly tugs at my sleeve and I realise that I slept in my coat. I straighten up and ease my legs over the side of the sofa until my feet reach the floor. I press them against the floorboards, assessing their ability to take my weight. Leaning on the arm of the sofa for support, I stand up and, apart from a shooting pain up my back, pins and needles in both legs, a queasy rumble in my stomach and a searing pain in my head, I feel OK.

'Right,' I say. 'I have a plan.'

Filly looks relieved and I realise how worried she is about me. I smile at her in what I hope is a reassuring way.

'First up, I'm going to the bathroom to vomit,' I say, 'and then I'm going to John's flat to pack.'

Back in the boardroom, everyone is still looking at me and I realise I have to say something.

'I'm fine, thank you, Simon.'

The silence in the room is expectant. Like a pregnant woman. It's the sympathy on their faces that kills me.

'I've managed to get the Martello Tower for the Smithson-Carling wedding vows,' I say. There is a collective intake of breath from around the table. I press on. 'And I'm meeting

9

Edward Smithson-Carling there for a recce at twelve o'clock tomorrow.'

'But tomorrow is Saturday.' Duncan is aghast. He likes to spend Saturdays lying on his couch in his pyjamas, eating dried figs and apricots. He loves fruit, especially the dehydrated variety.

'Well, you've missed a couple of days this month, haven't you?' Gladys pipes up. 'You probably need to catch up, don't you?'

I look at her until she has the grace to look away. I launch into my plans for the vow-renewal ceremony.

'What about the budget, Scarlett?' says Duncan, his cherubic face split in two with the smile that stretches across it. He asks the question simply so that his contribution to the meeting is recorded in the minutes.

I give him a breakdown of projected costings for the event, as well as the estimated cost of the contingency plan I've come up with, in case the Martello Tower finally crumbles into the sea or is attacked by Vikings, or some other eventuality.

When I finish, Simon spends the next five minutes explaining the consequences of underestimating the importance of the Smithson-Carling wedding-vow ceremony, which is doubling as a family reunion. He loves pointing out the obvious, mostly because it is the easiest thing to point out.

Now, he's talking about some AGM that Corporate are planning for a supermarket chain whose managing director was pictured on the front page of a tabloid this morning in his underpants perched on the balcony of one of Dublin's finest hotels, with his nose in a rolled-up €100 note.

I take the opportunity to check my diary. It's definitely due today. But lots of people have periods that come late, don't they? Proper late, I mean. Like days. Maybe even weeks. Can't stress cause a delay in the cycle? And isn't this my first period due since John left me? I shy away from that thought. I don't want to be someone who has been left. Like a paperback discarded on a plastic seat at the airport. Not something you'd go back for.

A pain arrives in my belly and I reach for it, hoping. But it is just a hunger pain. I realise I haven't eaten anything other than a banana all day.

I zone back into the meeting. Simon is still talking. The drone of his voice has the effect of sun through a window in the afternoon and I feel myself drift. Thoughts of John seep in, like blood on a tissue, dodging the hefty bouncers on duty at the door in my head. I've told them that John-related thoughts are the equivalent of pimply youths wearing white socks and are not to be let in under any circumstances. But sometimes they get in anyway.

I can't make sense of it and this is what kills me. I did everything by the book: I made sure he didn't know how much I needed him; I never whined if he worked late or had to go to a conference on a weekend; I paid my way; I never complained when he got me exactly what I needed for Christmas instead of surprising me with a piece of jewellery or a weekend in Paris. I had been good.

Gladys does one of those fake coughs ('Ah-hem, ah-*hem*'), which brings me back to the room. She fixes Simon with a look that can be described as meaningful. I sit up straighter in my chair, on full alert now.

Simon looks confused before his face clears. 'Oh, yes, there is one other thing.'

Silence roars around the room like static electricity. I clock Gladys smiling like smugness himself. It is Simon who gets the full force of her smile but instead of shielding his body from it, like a normal person, he laps it up like a cat with a bowl of cream and smiles back at her. And in that moment I am certain they are having an affair. I recognise the signs. Simon — married for fifteen years with three children — has affairs like other people join gyms: usually in January, with the horror of the family Christmas still fresh in his mind, and usually for about three months, when the novelty fades and he grows tired and can't remember why he started it in the first place. He applied to my gym once.

'I'll be very brief,' says Simon. 'I'm sure you all want to get home soon.' He turns and smiles at me now. 'We're creating a new position on the management team.' He pauses to allow the significance of the statement to sink in. He picks up the end of his tie, examines it — perhaps making sure he didn't dip it into his boiled egg that morning.

My internal antenna is erect and twitching

12

now. I've heard nothing about a new position. And why is Gladys here, smiling at Simon? I want to grab him by the lapels and shake him until he tells us what is going on. Instead, I sit on my hands and say nothing. Simon — loving the weight of everyone's rigid attention — takes his time, setting his narrow chin on to the bridge he makes with his hands and smirking at us. My mobile chooses that moment to squawk and, with the silence in the room, everyone jumps.

'Sorry,' I say. I check the text. It is only from Maureen, my mother, wondering if I have collected her tap shoes from Dance World. I have them in my bag. 'Sorry, Simon, it's a text from Edward Smithson-Carling, confirming our meeting tomorrow. I'll just be a second.'

I text, 'Have shoes. New taps very tappy. [Smiley face.] Home soon.'

'If you're quite finished, Scarlett,' says Simon. The tip of his long, narrow nose is white. This happens when he is annoyed, which is most of the time. He shuffles the papers on the desk in front of him, trying to retrieve his moment of gravitas. 'The board feels that the wedding-planning element of Extraordinary Events International has grown exponentially over the last twelve months and projections for the next twelve indicate a further surge.' He smiles conspiratorially at Gladys, who licks her lips and sits up straighter in her chair, her chest pushed out and straining against the thin fabric of her shirt.

I feel excitement pounding in my chest like a drum and I hold my breath, sure that if I exhale,

13

the sound would be a pant or even a yelp that may be difficult to explain away in the circumstances. I force myself to listen to Simon's droning monotone.

' . . . separate position. In fact, a separate department, concentrating solely on weddings. We haven't come up with a title for the position yet' — another smiley glance at Gladys — 'but the position will be a managerial one, with all the trappings that entails.' I know these trappings. They will include a punishing work schedule, long hours over Saturdays and Sundays and holy days and bank holidays, testy, hysterical clients ringing for comfort at four o'clock in the morning, impossibly high targets pulling like chains around my neck and no time for a personal life. It is *perfect*. Already my head is raging with plans. I will promote Filly, make her a wedding planner, and then poach Mary-Lou — Gladys's assistant — who is hands down the best administrator in the company after Filly. We'll be like the Three Musketeers, conquering the world, stamping out singledom and exuding success and efficiency up and down every aisle in Ireland. No! The World!

'Did you say something, Scarlett?'

Everyone looks at me expectantly. Is it possible that I squeaked or gasped out loud? I'm pretty sure I didn't. But still. I cough with my hand over my mouth. 'Sorry, Simon. Think I may have swallowed a fly.'

'A fly?' He frowns at the interruption, especially given the incongruity of the reason. Elliot tells me later that I sort of snorted.

'A small one. Probably just a flea, really. Nothing to worry about. Sorry to interrupt.' I nod at him, smiling, encouraging him to continue.

'Well, yes, that's all really for the moment. The position will be advertised within the company first, as is the normal practice, and then, if we don't find someone suitable' — another intangible flicker of his eye towards Gladys — 'we'll seek an external candidate.'

I do the sums. Gladys and I are really the only two people in the company eligible for the role. Gladys has worked the position longer, is better connected and — if I'm right about this, and I think I am — is doing the hokey-pokey with Simon at the apartment he keeps in the city *for convenience*. But I have the best clients. The Marzoni sisters, for example. And I generate more revenue than any of the company's planners by a mile. Surely that should swing it. I feel my confidence falter and wane in a way that I am unused to. I don't have time for a crisis of confidence. I need this job. I can pour it into the void left by John. It will cure me. Or at least leave me so busy that I won't have time to think about anything else. Like my missed period, for example. I look at my watch. Three o'clock. Three hours and thirty-seven minutes late. I'll take a test. A pregnancy test. That way, I can stop worrying and start concentrating on getting this promotion. I get up from my chair so quickly it falls away from me and lands on the floor with a clatter.

'Sorry, Simon, I have to go.' I can't even think

of any good excuse for leaving so abruptly.

Because it is unheard of for anyone to leave one of Simon's meetings before he says we can, he doesn't know what to say and so he says nothing.

I wave at everyone, which is weird because I don't wave, as a general rule. I fight an instinct to break into a run and force myself to smile as I back out of the room. Once outside the door, I run on my tiptoes so the click-clacking of my heels will tell no tales.

3

I walk towards the pharmacy on the corner. I know this is ridiculous. Unnecessary. But I continue, now pulling Blue — unused to being walked so far — along behind me. I call him Blue mostly because of his coat, which is such a glossy black it is almost blue. Also, he has a tendency to mope. I take Blue to the office with me every morning. He's been unsettled since I moved back to my parents' house and I am afraid he might run away if I'm not there. I can't cope with anyone else running away. Blue is none too pleased at this new routine, which includes lifting him from his bed (my bed) at six in the morning. He is not a nocturnal creature, as he is supposed to be. In fact, he's not much of a daytime creature either, preferring to stay indoors most of the time, eating fish and chocolate, licking his fur and snoozing. He doesn't bother himself with any of the cat toys I buy him and he never exerts himself with balls of string or whatnot. Some people might say he's lazy but I prefer to call him *discerning*.

With my free hand I rub my face. My jaw hurts. Maureen says she can hear my teeth grinding through the bedroom wall at night.

We are nearly there, the pair of us. I walk more slowly now. Just because I am nearly at the pharmacy doesn't mean I have to buy the test. I can refill my prescription for the Pill. I've been on the Pill for the past four years. Am still on it, in fact. In the last few weeks, the taking of the tiny white tablet every morning after breakfast has become symbolic, like a silent hope, a wordless prayer that I send out that things may return to the way they used to be.

Or I could buy something else. Maybe some paracetamol for the pain in my face. Or some nice, gloopy liquid in bright green or blue, to pour into the bath. Or maybe a tonic. People often take tonics at this time of the year. Something to perk me up a bit, help me dodge the tiredness I've felt for the past few weeks. Nobody says I have to buy it. Nobody even knows I am here. I can just turn round and head back to the office. Maybe even pick up Blue and carry him back. He has done enough walking for one day. My legs feel heavy now, as if they know there is no turning back.

I am at the door of the pharmacy. A buzzer sounds when I push the door. Heads of customers and staff turn and look at me and I nearly run away. But then they turn back to their lives, ignoring me, and I pick Blue up and move towards the counter, just another customer in just another chemist on just another ordinary Friday afternoon.

'How may I help you today, madam?' The woman has a heavy hand with the make-up and, in the harsh light of the shop and the reflection of her white coat, the dark brown make-up — probably expertly applied in the soft light of the morning — is beginning to slide down her face in such a slow, sad way I think I might weep.

18

Instead, I hand her my prescription.

She nods and points at a row of chairs, all empty. 'You can sit there while you're waiting,' she says, smiling gently at me like she knows everything.

I fold myself into one of the chairs, trying to make myself as unnoticeable as possible. Blue does the same, curling himself into a tight black ball on my lap.

To keep myself from thinking about anything, I time the pharmacist. It takes her exactly three minutes and forty-five seconds to fill the prescription. When she returns, she looks at me and then back at the prescription in her hand, the familiar confusion spreading across her face. Her mouth opens and I can see the shape of my name forming on her lips. I jump out of my chair but it's too late.

'Scarlett O'Hara?' she says, shaking her head slowly like there must be some mistake. She has one of those voices that carries. It rings out like a church bell on a Sunday morning.

The other patrons of the pharmacy look at her and wait for her to correct herself. To say, 'Sorry, I meant Soairse O'Hara.' Or Scarlett O'Herlihy. Or Dympna Gibbons. Or something like that.

But there is no mistake.

'The amazing thing is,' the pharmacist says as if we are in the middle of a conversation, 'you're such a dead ringer for Vivien Leigh.' Her head twitches this way and that, examining me.

I take a deep breath and nod. There's nothing else to be done. Because it's true. I have the lot. The dark curls. The heart-shaped face. The

19

small, pointed nose. The green eyes. I am even the same height. Exactly five foot three and a half inches. My mother told me that and I believe her. Maureen's knowledge of the minutiae of films and film stars is legendary.

'Thank you,' I say, taking the packet of pills from her and smiling. The resemblance is not as marked when I smile.

'Is there anything else you need?' she asks.

'Yes, I just . . . ' I whip my head from left to right, scanning the shelves. I can't see any. I'll have to ask her. I check behind me, making sure there is no one from the office. There isn't.

I turn back to her and she leans towards me with an expectant smile. 'Could I have a . . . ?' From the corner of my eye, I see a basket of cat collars, red ones, with tiny bells hanging from each of them. Blue could do with a new cat collar. I'm sure he could. ' . . . a cat collar, please?'

'Oh. Right. Sure.' The pharmacist seems a little wrong-footed as she reaches for a collar and hands it to me.

And then I see them. Row upon row of them, in long, thin, rectangular boxes, lined up in a display case right at the front of the counter. With pertinent names like Clear Waters and To Be Sure, To Be Sure (an Irish brand) and Testing, Testing 1, 2, 3 (American). The woman stands at the cash register, smoothing out the barcode attached to the collar with long, pale pink nails. While she is distracted, I make a grab for one of the boxes and slide it on to the counter beside the cash register. She doesn't

20

even look up from what she is doing.

'The Clear Waters has two tests in it and it's cheaper than that one.' She taps the barcode on the collar manually into the keypad of the register.

'Oh,' I say. 'Fine. OK. I'll take it. In fact, I'll take them both. And that one as well,' I say, pointing to a test in a fluorescent-pink box called It's a Girl!!!!

In the end, I take one of each of the tests available in the pharmacy. She piles them one on top of the other. It takes her quite a while but she doesn't comment and I am grateful for that.

'For best results, place the end of the stick into the mid-stream, all right?'

'Mid-stream?'

'Yes, the mid-stream of your urine flow,' the pharmacist confirms with the voice of a woman who has said that exact sentence as many times as Filly has said, 'I'll be ready in two minutes.'

And then the sound of the buzzer, squawking like a seagull who's just spotted a discarded bag of chips. Heads swivel towards the door. Mine too. I hold my breath but it is no one I recognise. I turn back to the pharmacist, willing her to conclude the transaction and put the collar and the tests into a lovely brown paper bag that no one can see through.

She looks at Blue and then back at me. 'You know about cats, don't you?'

'Eh . . . yes.' I am confused now. I wonder if the pharmacist is perhaps a little unhinged. Maybe the smell of Calvin Klein over a prolonged period of time? Or perhaps a worrying

21

tendency to seek refuge in a bottle of cough medicine? 'I've had Blue since he was a kitten,' I say, although I'm not sure why. 'He's had all his shots, if that's what you mean.'

'No, dear, I'm talking about the possible dangers that cats present for women in pregnancy.'

My head surges with things to say.

Like the pregnancy tests are not for me. I'm just getting them for a friend.

Like my period is only *technically* late but not really late. Not like normal people's version of late. Only minutes late, really. Maybe a few hours. Nothing to worry about.

Like how I can't be pregnant because my boyfriend has just left me.

Like how I can't be pregnant because it's not in my plan. It never has been. On this point John and I were united.

Like how I can't be pregnant because . . . if I am . . . if I am . . . then . . .

I can't be sure who the father might be . . .

I can barely contain myself. I want to grab the tests and run back to the office. I can barely breathe with the need to pee on a stick. If there was a toilet in the pharmacy, I'd be on it, despite my golden rule about the use of public conveniences.

She is still talking, oblivious to the panic that is setting like cement in my head. ' . . . a condition called toxoplasmosis. It's more than likely that you're immune to it at this stage but if you are pregnant and you do get it, it could cause you to miscarry, or cause mental

22

retardation or blindness in the baby.' She smiles at me like she's just told me that the Clinique face mask comes as a free gift with the tests.

Blue hisses and I realise I'm clutching him like a rugby ball. I set him down on the floor.

The woman smiles indulgently at him and leans across the counter, lowering her voice. 'Now, there's just one thing I simply must ask you before you go, if I may?'

I know what she is going to ask. Everyone does. Sooner or later. I wait.

'Are you related to Declan O'Hara, by any chance?'

'Yes. He's my father.'

'I *knew* it,' she says, banging the flat of her hand against the counter. 'I loved him in that movie. What was it called again? The one where he plays the vegetarian butcher?'

'*Meat and Two Veg*,' I say automatically.

'That's the very one. Tell me . . . is he still making films?'

'No, he's . . . He retired.'

'Pity that.' She shakes her head. Then she tosses her hair, collecting herself. 'Still, it's great to see one of our own above in Hollywood all the same.'

'How much do I owe you?' I ask, desperate to get out of the pharmacy.

'Let me see. That's a total of sixty-seven euros forty-five. The advice is, of course, free.' She allows herself a little laugh. 'Seriously, though, dear' — she leans towards me — 'don't hesitate to come back to us. You know' — at this she nods towards the tests, now safely encased in a

23

brown paper bag — 'if you have any questions or you need any, you know' — she touches me briefly on the hand — 'advice.'

For the second time that day, or it could be the third or fourth, I feel the threat of tears. It could be the kindness in the woman's voice or the fact that Blue could cause such harm to an unborn baby. But I don't cry. I accept the heart-shaped lollipop — 'We give one to all our customers,' the pharmacist assures me — and leave the pharmacy as quietly as I can.

4

Peeing on a stick — even in mid-stream — turns out to be easier than it sounds. The difficult bit is the three-minute wait afterwards. I am in the ladies' on the third floor, last cubicle on the left. Not my regular toilet — I always use the one on the second floor, second cubicle on the right.

There is nowhere to set the stick down once I pee on it so I hold it between my fingers and wait. There is nowhere to sit other than on the toilet so I pull the seat down and sit on the hard plastic. It is cold. After a while I can't feel my bum. I check my watch. Thirty seconds down, a hundred and fifty to go. The bathroom door opens and I can hear the steely plink of high heels — two pairs. It must be Eloise and Lucille from Accounts. They always travel in pairs.

' . . . to a kibbutz or someplace like that,' Eloise is saying. 'That's what I heard.'

'But I thought it was somewhere in South America?' Lucille says.

'Yeah, Peru or somewhere.'

'Where Paddington Bear is from.'

'Who?'

'Sorry. I forget you're younger than me. Anyway, I heard he joined one of them religious cults down there.'

'He never seemed the type.'

'It just goes to show you.'

A lull as the pair select suitable cubicles:

adjoining ones. I reef my feet up on to the toilet seat and roll myself into a ball. Eloise and Lucille select the two cubicles nearest the door.

One and a half minutes to go. Ninety seconds sounds better. Shorter.

I can hear the scratching of zips along metal teeth and the static of tights against skin. Then the creak of bums on seats and they are off again, still talking but now peeing as well.

'As far as I know, kibbutzes are only in Israel. You don't get them anywhere else.' Lucille is an authority on the subject, it seems.

'Oh.' Eloise is either digesting that particular nugget of information or concentrating on the business at hand.

Even with my hands held against both ears, I can still hear them, fainter now. They are unfurling long lengths of toilet paper from the dispenser. In spite of everything, I admire their synchronicity.

' . . . not a bother on her. You'd think nothing had happened.' Eloise lifts herself off the toilet seat. I hear the rustle of her skirt.

'Yeah, but she *is* a cat person.'

'That's true.'

I look at my watch. Fifty seconds to go.

' . . . definitely a dog person.' This from Lucille.

'Me too,' says Eloise. They are at the sinks now, reapplying lipstick. 'Although I wouldn't be mad about dogs, per se. But if I had to choose between dogs and cats, I'd definitely choose dogs.'

'That's exactly how I feel about it,' says

Lucille. 'They're just not as . . . What's the word?'

'Nasty.'

'Yeah, that's it. Nasty. They're not as nasty as cats.'

'Cats kill for pleasure, you know.'

Through the slit at the edge of the door, I see the two heads — a honey-dew blonde and a caramel blonde — nodding in unison. I clench my fists. Cats do *not* kill for pleasure. They are natural hunters. I look at my watch. Thirty more seconds. I steel myself not to look at the stick before the full three minutes are up. It is much more difficult than I thought it would be. I push the stick up the cuff of my jacket and sit on my hand. Not even when the pins and needles arrive do I release the hand from the bony prison of my right buttock.

Twenty seconds. Eloise and Lucille are finally leaving the ladies', their voices harder to hear now over the roar of their heels against the marble floor. As far as I can tell, they are now discussing the new girl in the IT department.

' . . . could be quite pretty, really.'

'If she dyed her hair and wore nice clothes.'

'Do you think a fringe would suit me?'

And then blessed silence as the door shuts behind them and I am alone again.

I lift myself off the toilet seat with my hands and unfold my legs. They cramp, sending shooting pains up and down my thighs. I sit back down, leaning against the cistern and pushing my feet against the cubicle door to encourage the blood to flow again. I look at my watch one last time.

Five more seconds.

Four seconds.

Three.

Two.

One.

The silence is thick and heavy, like Maureen's one and only attempt at homemade soup. I pull my hand from under my bum. It is a strangled purple colour, like somebody else's hand. With my other — normal, recognisable — hand, I pull the stick down from my cuff and see it immediately. The tiny pink plus. I do not have to reread the instructions to know exactly what it means. I reread them anyway. I stare at the pink plus, willing it to change. While it blurs a little around the edges, it endures my visual onslaught, retaining its shape and colour and *message*.

I tear the wrapper off the second test and start again. What I am looking for is doubt. Even just the faintest trace of uncertainty. There is none to be found.

In the end I take all the tests. Even the one made in Kazakhstan with the warning in the smallest small print I have ever seen: Results may be compromised if test is taken on day 7, 18 and 21 of your menstrual cycle.

I take the test.

It is the last one.

It is positive.

5

I arrive at my parents' house with no recollection of the journey from Dublin, which is worrying because the trip is an hour and a half in heavy traffic at this time of the day. I get out of the car and stand there for a moment, shivering. It is February. The miserable part of February. The part before the daffodils begin their struggle through the frozen ground. The part when spring seems like a politician's pre-election promise. On either side of the avenue leading to the house, endless rows of trees with their bare branches stretch like varicose veins against the heavy blue of the darkening sky.

The house is in darkness, the thick stone walls glinting like steel through the gloaming. I look at my watch. It's 7.03 p.m. Maureen will be in the kitchen pouring herself her second glass of wine. Declan is probably down in Hugo's house. It is only when the wind blows my skirt up into my face that I realise I'm still standing there. I brace myself and move towards the house where I grew up.

It is a place of extremes. There were times — long ago — when you couldn't hear yourself breathe with the crowds in the long reception room, talking and eating and singing and dancing. At other times — like now — my footsteps echo down the long hall from the front of the house to the kitchen at the back, bouncing

29

against the thick walls festooned with photographs of Declan and Maureen at one function
or another, accepting awards (Declan) and
airkissing (Maureen).

It is a house that is hard to heat. The kitchen is
the warmest room, where the heat from the Aga
— lit in September and doused in May — wraps
around us like hands.

Maureen alights on me in the hallway before I
even get my coat off.

'Oh, it's only you, Scarlett. I thought it might
be Cyril Sweeney.' Cyril Sweeney is one of the
founding members of the local Amateur
Dramatic Society, which means he was probably
born when Shakespeare was a slip of a lad. He
nearly always directs the performances put on by
the society and my mother adores him.

I open my mouth to say something but the
mechanism feels sluggish and I realise I haven't
spoken to anyone since I took the tests. Maureen
examines the reflection of her face in the glass of
one of the photographs hanging on the wall.

'Where have you *been*, Scarlett?' she asks.

'At work,' I say.

'Work?' says Maureen, as if it's something
she's heard of but can't quite place. 'And *there's*
Blue. I've been looking for him everywhere.'

Blue is in the cat cage. I have to incarcerate
him when I'm driving. Otherwise he sits in the
driver's seat with his paws on the wheel. He
hates being a passenger. To make it up to him, I
put him into his favourite room in the house,
which is the hot-press. I give him his blankie, a
chewed, frayed, discoloured bit of material he's

30

had since he was a kitten. He arranges it around his head with his paws until it looks like a bandana. Then he settles himself on a pile of warm towels and is asleep in seconds.

When I return to the kitchen, Maureen is at the counter, poking the fillets of salmon I brought with a long fork.

She looks up. 'These have gone a funny colour, Scarlett. I think they're off.'

'No, they're fine.'

'But they're orange.' Maureen sniffs the air above the fish and wrinkles her nose.

'That's the colour they're supposed to be,' I explain.

'Well, they've always been a lovely pale pink colour anytime I've eaten them.'

'That's when they're cooked.'

'Oh.'

'Don't worry, they'll only take twenty minutes,' I say. 'Why don't you sit down and relax?' I ease her towards the chunky kitchen table that can seat fourteen at a push — and often did, in its heyday.

'Where's Declan?'

'Oh, he's probably still in the den. With Hugo. The pair of them have been closeted in there most of the evening.' Maureen sniffs.

'What are they up to?' I ask, although I know that they are probably just laid out on the two opposing couches, reminiscing about the good old days when movies were called *fillums* and Declan had to beat plum roles off with a stick.

'Well,' Maureen says, lighting one of her

reed-thin menthol cigarettes, 'they said they were rehearsing.'

'Rehearsing?'

'Yes, well, apparently a script arrived today,' says Maureen. 'By post,' she adds with a note of contempt, probably remembering when scripts used to arrive by white-gloved hand, delivered by directors mad for Declan to star in their latest project.

'A film script?' I ask.

'Yes.'

'From who?'

'From whom, Scarlett, dear, from whom.' She takes an enormous pull of her cigarette, her lips disappearing into her mouth with the effort. She waves her hands in front of her face when she exhales, distributing the smoke as evenly as she can around the kitchen. I hold my breath and wait for the smoke to dissipate. She heightens the drama by not answering immediately. Instead, she concentrates on smoking.

I look at her. She is a cornucopia of accessories. Today she is wearing two long, trailing scarves tied round her neck. I can tell that she spent ages this morning, arranging them so they look *jaunty*. Also so that they cover the wrinkles on her *décolletage*, of which she is deeply resentful. She jangles when she moves, like a cat with bells on its collar, because of all the bangles and bracelets and trinkets and necklaces and dangly earrings. Also, her right knee clicks every time she sits down or stands up or curtseys, which she does a lot when she is rehearsing for a play. A long, flowing top over a long, flowing skirt completes the outfit, giving her a terribly *busy* look. You have to look carefully to actually see her underneath all the *stuff* she carries around. Her hair is the busiest of all. It would remind you of Grand Central Station, it's that busy. Piled on top of her head like a haystack, and riddled with grips and clips and two knitting needles that poke out at the top like an aerial. Still suspiciously black, although she denies dyeing it.

'Oh, some writer I've never heard of.' Maureen has already lost interest in the conversation, tipping her ash into a nearby pot housing a — half dead — busy Lizzie. The plant has been half dead for days, maybe even weeks. I place an ashtray on the table and remove the pot from Maureen's reach. Maybe George will know how to revive it. I'll ask him tomorrow.

'Remember when Martin Scorsese called to the house and Phyllis wouldn't let him in? Said she'd never heard of him.' Maureen's eyes suddenly light up.

'Oh, yes,' I say. 'Although I wasn't there that day. Phyllis told me about it after.'

'And his eyebrows . . . ' Maureen rushes on. 'She said something about his eyebrows, didn't she?'

'She said his eyebrows were *suspiciously* bushy,' I remember.

Maureen laughs her gorgeous tinkling laugh. 'Those were the days, weren't they?'

'Eh, yes.'

'I don't remember you being there that day.' Maureen turns to me, frowning.

33

'I was in hospital, remember? Getting my appendix out.'

'You got your appendix taken out? Whatever for?'

'It burst, remember? The day before. When I was in town with Phyllis. Buying my school shoes, I think.'

'Oh my God, yes,' says Maureen, the clouds of confusion clearing from her eyes. 'I think I must have repressed that memory.' She takes a huge drag from her cigarette before adding, 'It was a very painful time for me, you know. You were so tiny, lying on that operating table. Only five years old, you were.'

'I was seven and a half.'

'You *looked* five,' she insists. Her voice wobbles and I back away from the subject before she makes herself cry.

'So you were telling me about Declan. Rehearsing.'

'Oh, yes,' says Maureen, yawning. 'Although . . . I haven't seen him this excited about a part since he played the cowboy in that martial-arts film. What was it called again?'

'*Cowboys and Ninjas*,' I supply automatically.

I turn on the oven, prepare the fish, toss a salad and rinse some rice.

'I'm going to say hello to them,' I say. 'Can you keep an eye on dinner?'

'I'll take care of it, Scarlett, darling,' says Maureen, lighting another cigarette and taking an almighty slug of wine.

★ ★ ★

I hear my father before I see him. He is crucifying a song on the piano in the study. Hugo sings along in his usual tuneless way. I see them in my mind's eye. Hugo, standing behind Declan, one hand on his shoulder, the other conducting an imaginary orchestra. At the end of the song, both men will bow to an imaginary audience. A packed house, no doubt.

Hugo is Declan's agent. He is older than Declan, maybe seventy. Unofficially retired. Has to be, really, seeing that my father was his only client and Declan hasn't done any real work in about ten years. Hugo, originally from New York, retired to Ireland. To Wicklow. Maureen maintains that he would have moved right into the house, had he been let, which he had not. Although he spends so much time here, it wouldn't seem unfair to charge him rent.

I stand at the door of the study and watch them. The bottom of a champagne bottle pokes out of an ice bucket. There is what looks like red wine in a milk jug on the top of the piano, which the men take turns to swig from. Declan plays with only one hand when he drinks the wine but it makes no difference to the quality of the performance.

After a long drawn-out and dramatic finish, I clap and they look up and see me. Hugo acknowledges my applause with a small bow from the neck and his quiet smile. Declan's response is more flamboyant. He does his best to bend from the waist, the long strands of his charcoal-grey hair sweeping the yellowing floor-boards. He straightens and steadies himself with

35

a hand on the lid of the piano.

'Scarlett!' He reaches me in two strides, his arms spread as wide as the smile on his face. Instead of removing the cigarette from between his fingers and setting it in the ashtray as I would normally do, I find myself walking into the circle of his arms, bending my face into the folds of his neck. He smells like the inside of a bar on a Sunday morning. His skin is soft and warm and scratchy in places neglected by the edge of his razor that morning. I close my eyes and try not to think about the tests. The positive tests.

He pushes me away then, holding me at arm's length. 'Darling girl,' he says, examining my face. 'Whatever is the matter?'

'Nothing,' I say, rearranging sheaves of papers on top of the piano. 'Just . . . not a great day at work.'

'Work? That's where you've been all this time?' Declan is as confused as Maureen with the notion of a Monday-to-Friday, nine-to-five type of existence.

A pause while Declan looks at Hugo for a reasonable explanation. Hugo often has reasonable explanations for questions that perplex Declan.

'Don't look at me, old fellow. I haven't worked for years,' Hugo says cheerfully. Hugo, like most Americans, loves everything English, especially the accent, which he acquired on day two of his ten-year stint in London, where he met Declan.

'Hello, Scarlett, old girl,' Hugo says, sidling up to me. Even I have to bend slightly to hug Hugo. He can be summed up in the word 'dapper'.

'This calls for a toast,' says Declan. In his world, even the most benign of events calls for a toast. He splashes red wine into two coffee cups, handing one to Hugo and the other to me. He lifts the milk jug and holds it aloft. 'To Scarlett, who has come home to us.'

'Jesus, Dad, I was only at the office. You're such a drama queen.'

'But such a great drama queen,' Hugo pipes up. Notwithstanding his retirement, he will always be Declan O'Hara's agent.

'Well, not great. I wouldn't say great now.' Declan makes a stab at modesty. 'But it's paid the bills around here.'

'It has indeed, my good man.' Both men clink their cup and jug together and roar, 'Olé,' at the same time, as they always do for reasons long lost in the dulled mists of time.

I have to move a leaning tower of papers from the couch so I can sit down. I look for somewhere to put them but every available surface is occupied, with papers and books and scores and overflowing ashtrays and dirty glasses and two plates with the remains of what looks like a bacon and egg lunch. In the end, I put them on the floor. I look at my watch; the fish will be OK for another five minutes.

'I should be going,' says Hugo, standing up.

'Stay,' I say. 'There's more than enough fish for supper.'

'No, I really should go. I've been here all afternoon.' Hugo lifts his eyes towards the door, as if expecting to see Maureen there with his hat and his coat and a stick to hasten his departure.

He and Maureen have always vied for Declan's time and attention, and even though Hugo often wins, he gives her a wide berth, not wanting to rub her nose in it.

He and Declan hug like brothers who are going to war and may never see each other again. He smiles at me and leaves, muttering something about Sylvester (his goat), who he has to untether from the gate at the top of the driveway. Sylvester is Hugo's alternative to a security alarm and somehow he has proved an effective burglar deterrent, despite looking as intimidating as a calendar kitten.

'So,' Declan says, lowering the lid of the piano so he can sit on it, 'what news of the outside world?' When his eyes finally settle on me, with their soft green light, it's like he knows and I feel the panic circling like wolves, pressing against the barricade of my mind.

I pull the sleeves of my jacket down so he can't see my hands, curled into fists. 'Nothing much,' I say, and I am surprised at the tone of my voice, which sounds the same as it always does. 'Maureen tells me you got a script today.'

Declan stops what he was doing — editing some part of Bach's Fifth Concerto by the looks of it. 'It came by post,' he says in a small voice. 'From someone I've never even heard of.' He sighs. 'I used to know everybody in the business.' His hand gropes along the top of the piano. I get up, locate his packet of cigarettes, take one out, light it and hand it to him.

'What's it like?' I ask, returning to the couch.

'What's what like?'

'The script.'

'The script?'

'The one you got in the post today.'

'Oh, yes.' Declan scratches the top of his head with the heel of the hand holding the cigarette. The tip of the cigarette burns dangerously close to his hair and when I look closely, I see some hairs at the top of his head crinkling in the heat. To my left, a glass vase of — wilting — flowers stands on the windowsill with two inches of greenish water at the bottom. I can always throw that on top of him if his hair goes up again.

'Dad?' Declan drags his eyes from the window and turns to me, smiling.

'It's good.'

'Good?'

'Maybe very good.'

'Oh.'

Very little has been 'good' and absolutely nothing has been 'very good' for most of the last ten years. It is the excuse he uses for not working.

'In fact . . . '

'Yes?' I wait for him to continue.

'It's magnificent.' Declan looks suddenly sober. He crushes his cigarette against a rasher rind and jumps up, looking around him. 'It's here somewhere. I'll show it to you.' He begins to rummage through the piles of paper teetering around the room.

'Who wrote it?'

'Donal somebody. He's an actor, I think. Out-of-work one, of course.' He is on the second pile, throwing bills and envelopes and what might be a tax disc on the floor beside him.

I eventually find it on the floor of the downstairs toilet, where Declan likes to repair to read and smoke and listen to Maxi on the radio, despite the fact that her show starts at the ungodly hour of 5.30 a.m. He *loves* Maxi. He calls her 'my girl', which infuriates Maureen no end.

The script looks like it has been typed on an actual typewriter. The title sits halfway down the cover page. It's not quite centred but I like the fact that someone has made the effort to try to centre it. It is called *The Jou ney*.

'*The Jou ney*?' I say. I'm worried. According to ScrabbleIreland.ie, I'm the third best Scrabble player in the country and yet here's a word I've never even heard of.

'It's called *The Journey*,' says Declan. 'There's no 'r's anywhere in the script.

'No 'r's?'

'Not a single one,' Declan says. He sounds proud, like this is something the scriptwriter has painstakingly achieved.

'And you managed to read it?'

'Twice.' He looks different. There is life in him. I can see it moving behind his eyes.

'Scar-lett.' Maureen's voice shoots down the hall in a screech like a car in the Monte Carlo Grand Prix.

'Yes?'

'I think the salmon might be done.'

'Did you check it?'

'No, but there's a sort of a fishy smell coming from the oven.' I recognise the panic in

40

Maureen's voice; she often panics when left unsupervised in the kitchen.

'Don't move. I'll be right there,' I say. I smile a conspiratorial smile at Declan but he looks worried at the prospect of a fishy smell permeating the kitchen.

'Go and help your mother, like a good girl.'

It's the funny thing about returning home. You regress just a little, no matter how old you are or how long you've been away. I do as I'm told and don't even mind Declan calling me a 'good girl'. In fact, a part of me likes it. Maureen is using the kitchen window as a mirror to practise her famous pout. That's the great thing about her panic attacks. They don't last long. I turn off the oven and set three places around the table.

'I suppose you'll have to set a place for Hugo,' says Maureen sourly.

'He's gone home,' I say.

'Hmph,' Maureen sniffs. 'I'm surprised he didn't ask for a doggy bag for himself and that ridiculous goat of his.'

I locate a pair of oven gloves and lower the oven door. I unwrap one of the parcels of fish and poke at the pink flesh with a fork. 'Declan seems interested in that script.' I have to raise my voice to be heard over the roar of the extractor fan.

'Hugo shouldn't encourage him.' Maureen stabs her cigarette out in the ashtray, making sparks fly around her hand.

'Why not?' I turn round, the fork in my hand. A piece of salmon falls on the floor.

'Why not what?' Maureen is already lighting

41

up another cigarette.

'Why shouldn't Hugo encourage him? Someone should,' I say. 'It's not like he hasn't got any talent. He won an *Oscar*, for God's sake.'

'Yeah, about a hundred years ago,' Maureen says, dismissing this achievement with a wave of her hand. 'And what has he done since then? Nothing.'

'He's done some ads,' I say.

'For God's sake, Scarlett, the last ad he did, he played a fecking tomato.'

That is true. Embarrassing but true. I let it drop but Maureen is on a roll. She took the tomato role very badly. Almost as badly as Declan played it.

'And now,' Maureen says, 'if he were auditioning to play the fecking donkey in the local school's nativity play, he wouldn't get the part. He wouldn't even get a call back.'

'Has he been offered a part in this film? *The Jou ney*, or whatever it's called?' I hold my breath and wait. Maureen allows the moment to stretch. She *loves* dramatic pauses. Very effective, she says. I realise how right she is.

'He has to audition.' She whispers it but even so I can hear the bitterness in her voice, like lemons. It's not about the money — they still have buckets of that. It is the life less ordinary that Maureen misses. Being the wife of a big fish in a small pond. It is the captions beneath the photographs. 'The beautiful Mrs O'Hara.' And she *had* been beautiful. In a tempestuous, doe-eyed, big-haired kind of way.

42

'Maybe he'll get it. The part, I mean,' I say, eventually.

Maureen looks at me as if considering that possibility for the very first time. 'Do you think he could?'

I consider the question. It doesn't matter what I think, what I plan, because all my carefully laid thoughts and plans have brought me to this place where nothing makes sense any more.

'I'll dish up,' I say.

'I'm not hungry.' Maureen is as petulant as a seven-year-old who asks for a pony for Christmas and gets a gerbil instead.

'I'll just put tiny bits of everything on your plate, OK?'

Maureen refills her wine glass and sighs a deep sigh, which is her version of yes.

We take our usual places around the dinner table: Declan at the head of the table, Maureen at the other end and me at the side, equidistant from both.

Declan gets the carving knife out of the second drawer and begins to sharpen it against a piece of flint he keeps in the garage.

'It's fish tonight, darling,' says Maureen.

'It'll still need to be carved, won't it?' Declan says. He got the block of knives from Hugo a couple of Christmases ago and he's mad about them. He considers the carving of a joint of meat as a type of DIY and he's terrible at DIY but not bad at carving meat. This is his way of being good at DIY.

'Well,' Maureen says, 'it's fillets. They don't need to be carved as such.'

43

'Oh,' says Declan, prodding a piece of fish on his plate. The pink flesh tumbles easily from the bone, mocking his hopes of carving duty.

A howl pierces the house like a pin.

'It's Blue,' I say. 'He must have woken up.'

'Is he in the hot-press?'

'Yes. I'll go and get him.'

'I'll go. You eat your dinner.' Maureen loves cats and Blue more than most. He is such an eccentric creature, maybe he reminds her of herself.

'No, you have your dinner,' I say. 'I'll go.' I leave the kitchen at a trot, allowing no room for argument. I have to keep busy. Keep moving. Leave no space for any random thoughts, which all lead back to the tests. The positive tests.

★   ★   ★

'Give him here, Scarlett. I missed him today.'

I settle Blue on the table beside my father's dinner plate. Declan cuts the salmon darne in two and moves half of it — the bigger half — towards Blue. The cat bends his head to the plate and sniffs the offering, pushing it around the plate with his paw like a child with a floret of cauliflower.

'Declan!' Maureen is appalled. 'Poor Blue might choke on a fish bone. You have to make sure it's completely filleted before you feed it to him.'

'Christ, yes. Sorry, Blue.' Declan lowers his face to the piece of fish and dissects it into tiny crumbs, not stopping until he is completely

44

satisfied that it is hazard-free. Then he pushes the plate back over towards Blue and the pair of them bend their heads and eat. Blue is finished in seconds.

'I'll put him out,' I say.

'But, darling, he'll catch his death out there.' Maureen emphasises her words by pulling one of her scarves around her neck.

'Yes, but it's a quarter to eight,' I remind them.

'Great Scott, he *still* does his business at the same time every day?' Declan's tone is almost reverential. Since he brought Blue home (he was a kitten, only four days old, and a local farmer had plans for him that included a bag, a rope, some heavy stones and the fast-flowing river that runs through the village), Blue always insists on repairing to the garden (or the balcony, in John's flat) to attend to his toilet at *exactly* 7.45 p.m. every day, even on weekends and holidays.

When I return to the table, everyone is busy eating and the silence is like a loud noise that I want to smother.

'There was no need for you to cook dinner, Scarlett. I was going to make something tonight.' Maureen has the grace to look a little pink around the cheeks.

'I know that,' I say. 'I didn't know what you had planned for dinner so I brought some . . . just in case, you know?' I don't add that, with Phyllis away, I knew they'd be either eating out or having a Findus crispy pancake from the freezer.

Also, Maureen kind of panics when she has to

feed me, on account of my vegetarianism. I turned vegetarian when I was twelve — after watching a documentary on battery hens — and Maureen never quite got over it. She loves the *idea* of it. The eccentricity of a twelve-year-old vegetarian back in the 1980s in Ireland appeals to her sense of unconventionality. It is the logistics she objects to. To be honest, it is cooking in general she objects to. When I lived at home, Maureen lumbered Phyllis with the responsibility of feeding me. Phyllis — who thinks vegetarianism is some sort of cult, up there with scientology — used to try and sneak meat into my food at every turn until, inevitably, I began to cook my own meals.

'Phyllis hardly ever cooks fish,' Maureen says. 'In fact, she doesn't do a lot of cooking any more but she refuses to retire. You know what she's like.' Phyllis still lives in the granny flat above the garage, still calls herself the housekeeper, still answers the phone with her imperious 'O'Hara residence. How may I help you?' She is in her sixties now and spends most of her days playing bingo on her laptop and swatting at corners with her feather duster. But she is as much a part of the family as any of us, including Ozzie, the Oscar won by Declan back in 1995, which now double-jobs as a doorstop to prevent the bathroom door banging against the wall on stormy nights.

'When is she back from Lourdes?' I ask. Phyllis goes to Lourdes every year. She prays by day and drinks too much sherry by night, sometimes breaking into a spontaneous version

46

of the theme tune from *Watership Down*, unprompted and in a voice as sweet as the sherry she drinks.

The house doesn't feel quite like home without Phyllis.

'The end of next week, I think,' says Maureen.

I delay going to bed for as long as I can. When you're an insomniac, going to bed is like drinking cod-liver oil. You do it because you know it's good for you but it doesn't make it any easier to swallow.

The insomnia has been worse since John left. My bed is like a boxing ring with me in one corner and my thoughts in the opposite one. They hit me like fists. Before John left, my nocturnal thinking centred around my five-year plan. Then, when I first moved back to my parents' house, my nocturnal thinking centred around the fact that I am a thirty-five-year-old woman living with my parents. A thirty-five-year-old single woman living with my parents and my cat. It doesn't matter that Blue is a sort of super-cat or that he's more intuitive than a lot of people I've met. People just look at him and think, Cat. Full stop. This kind of worrying takes me deep into the night and makes time tick in slow motion so that when I look at the clock on my bedside table, it seems impossible that only fifty-four minutes have passed.

Tonight, sleep will be more elusive than usual. I do everything as slowly as I can manage, washing the dishes by hand instead of using the dishwasher, rearranging the larder so the labels on all the tins and the packets face out front like they're supposed to, changing the message on the answering machine so that our names are now all in alphabetical order ('Declan, George, Maureen, Phyllis and Scarlett cannot come to the phone . . . '). I look at my watch. Only 11.34 p.m. In desperation, I insist on a game of Scrabble before bedtime. This kills three-quarters of an hour. Maureen loves Scrabble — so long as she wins. We usually don't allow Declan to play on account of his inclination to make up words and then insist that they are real, actual words, which will result in further words — and not nice ones — between him and Maureen, which might include the throwing of crockery (Declan) and the pulling of hair (Maureen).

Afterwards, I make myself a mug of Ovaltine and do a lap of the garden. Sometimes this works. I check my watch. It's 00.19 a.m. I check myself for signs of tiredness. None. And then I ring Bryan.

'Can't sleep?' he says.

'Sorry,' I say. 'I tried not to phone you tonight but . . . '

'Don't worry about it. I wasn't asleep. What's up?'

'Nothing. Just . . . a bad day is all.'

'Do you want me to come over? It'll only take me forty-five minutes at this time of night.' The temptation is huge and I feel myself wavering towards it. Bryan is my cousin although he is what I imagine a brother would be like. Or a sister. People say we look alike but it's only our colouring, really. Or lack of it. We both have the milky-white complexions of people who have never seen the outside world. The same green eyes. Identical sets of lips that are too big for our faces — a gift from our uncle Colin, who is a bit of a black sheep, on account of his insistence on writing unauthorised biographies of Declan that sell by the truckload all over the world. We have the same hair: unruly and thick. I tame mine with a trim precisely every six weeks, weekly frizz-control treatment and a daily application of a sterling serum I order online from New Zealand. Bryan's is the environmental equivalent of Alaska: wild and free, mostly untouched by human hand. Rather than growing down, it grows up and out, defying gravity and spurning hair-tending accessories like brushes and combs. Even I have given up trying to organise it.

'No,' I say at last. 'I just . . . '

'Do you want me to read you a few pages from the dictionary?'

'You're probably tired.'

'No, I'm fine.'

'Well, if you're sure you don't mind.'

'I'll just go and get it. We're on the 'm's, I think.'

'No, it's the 'n's,' I say. 'We stopped at 'nuptial', remember?'

When we get halfway through the 'o's ('order: the condition in which every part, unit, etc., is in its right place . . . '), he stops.

'You know, Scarlett, it's not always going to be like this,' he says.

'What do you mean?'

'I mean it'll get easier. Eventually. Things will work out.'

'Something awful has happened,' I blurt out, lowering my voice.

'I know. But you're going to get over it. You'll get over John and meet someone else and . . . I know it doesn't feel like that now but you'll see. I mean, look at me. How many times have I been dumped?'

It's true. Bryan gets dumped as regularly as I get my hair trimmed. Filly says it's because he's too *nice*. Bryan says he can't help it. He's tried one-night stands but he says they make him feel *used*. He's tried not ringing women the day after he eventually sleeps with them. He's tried arriving on dates late. Leaving early. He's even tried pretending to like David Lynch films. Nothing works. They always get a sniff of his *niceness* eventually and, like a David Lynch film, it's over and you're none the wiser.

' "Organisation, uniformity, regularity, system, pattern, symmetry — " '

'It's OK, Bryan, you can stop now,' I say.

'Why? Are you tired?'

'No, but you are. I can hear you pretending not to yawn.'

'I could go another page or so,' he offers. His voice is like a fleece blanket wrapped around me.

'No,' I say. 'Go on. Go to bed.'

'OK, then. If you're sure . . . '

'Goodnight, Bryan.'

'Goodnight, Scarlett.'

'Bryan?'

'Yes?'

'Just . . . you know . . . '

'I know,' he says. 'Now go to bed. Try to get some sleep.'

★   ★   ★

Eventually, when I can think of nothing else to do, I climb the stairs with Blue. He settles himself in the bend of my legs, just behind my knees. His breath tickles my skin but it is warm and comforting, like a bowl of Ambrosia creamed rice. I set my phone for 5 a.m., punch the pillow and slot my head into the indentation it makes. I fill my mind with sheep in a pen and begin to count them. Not that this works. It's a habit I've attained. Besides, I like sheep. Especially the ones I imagine. They're like that one in the nursery rhyme, with fleece as white as snow.

But the sheep escape through a hole in the fence and before I can round them up again, I'm thinking about the tests. The positive tests. There's one thing I know for certain. Something I've always known. I can't be somebody's mother. I don't know how. I don't know what a mother does. What a mother is supposed to do.

Downstairs, I hear Declan and Maureen arguing. I wait for the argument to die of natural causes like any argument about the uncorking of a bottle of wine should. When it does not, I get out of bed, walk down the stairs, move into the kitchen, open the bottle of wine (turns out to be a twist lid) and set it on the table in front of them. The argument stops then, with Maureen

51

picking up the bottle and offering to top up Declan's glass.

'I really shouldn't. I have a lot of work to do in the morning,' Declan says.

'Oh, go on, darling, it's early yet,' says Maureen. (It is 1.34 a.m.)

'Thanks, darling,' Declan said. 'Just half a glass, mind.'

Back upstairs, I see that Blue has taken up most of the middle of the bed and I have to content myself with the edge, where it is cold and daunting, given the considerable drop to the floorboards. I sit on the edge of the bed and press my hands against my belly. I only realise I am biting my lip when I taste blood, sweet and warm, in my mouth. I ease myself down along the edge of the bed, careful not to wake Blue. I shut my eyes tightly and start listing all my brides in age order. This will take some time. After that, I'll think of something else to do. I reach down and put my hand on Blue's soft fur. He twitches his head twice but allows my hand to remain. I practise breathing deeply, as if I were asleep. The day has wrung me out but even so sleep will be like a bus to Clonee: a long time coming.

6

People say, 'She's in denial,' like it's a bad thing but for those first few days denial is my crutch and I bear down on it with both hands. Denial hauls me out of bed in the morning. It pushes me into the shower and shovels food down my throat. Denial allows me to ignore my breasts, which are as hard as stones and spill over the top of my previously more-than-adequate 32B cups. Denial is my friend. I rely on it utterly and, somehow, it gets me through.

My office door opens and I look up. It's Filly, my assistant. Of course, that's not her real name. Her real name is Felicity but she's Australian — home to kangaroos and abbreviations — and, besides, the shortened version suits her much better than the full title ever could.

Filly arrived in Ireland two years ago for a five-day stopover on her round-the-world trip, met Brendan, a butcher from Marino, and that was that.

She arrives with her usual 'GoodmorningsorryI'm late', two skinny lattes, sausage rolls (for her) and a fruit salad (for me). I point out that, technically, it is the afternoon but she counters by telling me that it's the middle of the night where she comes from, which is above and beyond the call of duty, considering the pittance we're paying her.

'It's not the middle of the night. It's only nine

o'clock in Sydney,' I can't help telling her. She ignores me and unwraps the first of the three sausage rolls from the grease-sodden paper, demolishing it in two bites.

She wears her hair short and spiky, still in the colours of the flag since Australia Day last month. She sits down and tucks her legs into the chair, the tips of her Doc Martens barely visible below the hem of a long, tasselled skirt. She wraps her skinny little arms around her narrow frame and leans forward. She looks about thirteen years old.

'Will you forgive me if I give you an interesting piece of news?' she says when she's washed down her breakfast with most of her coffee.

'I might.' I pour two sachets of sugar into my coffee and she looks up. I don't take sugar in coffee and she knows that but she doesn't mention it. I drink from the cup and it's so sweet I wonder how I ever drank coffee without sugar before.

'Well,' she says, getting comfortable on the chair and releasing the last of the sausage rolls from the bag, 'there was an interesting piece of news in Anna Barlow's column in the *Herald AM* today. Did you read it?'

'No.'

Filly looks at me but doesn't comment. She knows something is up. 'Sofia Marzoni announced her engagement.'

'Sofia? Are you sure? She's never even brought a boyfriend to any of the weddings, as far as I remember.'

'I'm positive. She's the only one left. You've

married off all the rest.'

'Who's she marrying?'

'Some artist or other. Ronan Butler, I think. Or Donald. Something like that. No one I've ever heard of.'

I don't care who she's marrying. I don't know why I even asked the question. A Marzoni wedding. It's *exactly* what I need. Like the time John bought me the dual-control electric blanket for our — his — bed. My face feels funny and I realise I am smiling.

'You know what this means, don't you?' Filly's smile is half grimace.

I nod slowly. I've already planned the weddings of Sofia's four sisters for Extraordinary Events International. The five women are the apples of their father's eye. Heiresses to a fortune in the form of a couple of hundred fish-and-chip shops dotted around Ireland and England. Their mother abandoned them when they were kids. Ran off with the bloke who delivered the oil for the deep-fat fryers in their very first chip shop, in Finglas, if the stories are to be believed.

I was the chief wedding planner on all four Marzoni weddings, each one more outlandish than the last. In fact, the fourth one — Maria and Riccardo's one — was held underwater in Howth, where the first cod ever served in her father's very first chip shop had been caught and gutted (when it was still OK to catch and gut cod). There had been a near-fatal incident involving two overweight and curious-bordering-on-aggressive sea lions. The Aston Martin wedding, I christened it, because I bought the car immediately after the wedding. A gift to myself.

'I betchya a pound of rashers Sofia will ring tomorrow and book you.'

Even though I don't eat rashers, I take the bet. Filly calls it unsporting if you don't. Then silence as I wait for her to leave so I can get back to my denial.

She looks at me sideways. 'So,' she says, leaning against the filing cabinet instead of leaving, 'how are you?' The question is as loaded as a gun.

'Fine. Grand. Never better,' I say, turning away from her and walking over to the couch. I make a great show of running my hand along Blue's — still sleeping — form.

'I'll take him for a walk when he wakes up,' Filly offers, and her voice is so gentle I have to clench my entire body to stop myself turning round and telling her everything.

'We should probably stop walking him,' I say when I gather myself again. 'He's getting confused. Yesterday he sniffed at the lamp-post outside the building. Next, he'll be cocking his leg.'

'So?'

'He *is* a cat, Filly,' I remind her.

'He's got four legs, hasn't he? Why should dogs get all the fun?'

'Anyway, I can't find his lead,' I say.

Filly reaches into the pocket of her jeans and pulls out a length of yellow ribbon. 'I'll use this,' she says. The ribbon is about fifteen inches long.

56

There is no way it can double as a cat lead. But still. The exercise seems to calm him, makes him a little less likely to spit at clients and rip holes in another pair of my tights.

When Filly leaves, I Google 'Marzoni, Ireland, chips' in hope of a phone call from Sofia before the end of the week. There is an article in *OK!* about the family.

Entitled 'From Cod to Caviar', it details the rise and rise of one Valentino Marzoni, a penniless cobbler from a cul-de-sac in Sicily. Valentino argued with his father when he was seventeen and walked out of his family home. He didn't stop walking until he reached the north of France, where he took a boat to Cork, hitched to Dublin, stumbled upon Finglas and got involved in a poker game with three men, all called different variations of the name Patrick (Paddy, Pat and PJ, which stood for Padraic James). Valentino — a bit of a card sharp on account of a grandfather, who let him hide in his coal shed on schooldays and taught him poker — beat the three Patricks hands down and emerged from the four-day card game the proud owner of the run-down chip shop on the corner, which was then called Clarkes, only with the 'e' missing. With the first bit of profit he turned, he changed the sign to Marzoni's and never looked back.

I read on. If anyone comes into my office now. I'll look as I always do. Busy. Productive. Like I'm thinking important things about wedding organisation. Nobody would ever know that I'm rooting through the personal files in my memory bank. Strangely, since the tests — the positive tests — I've allowed myself to think more about John. Being left by an actuary for an archaeological dig in Brazil doesn't have the same resonance somehow since everything else that's happened.

Now, I'm going over the conversation. That last one. I'd been so calm. Why hadn't I slapped him across the face? Pushed him even? Made him trip over his brown leather laceups? And later, in the flat. Packing up. Nothing unreasonable. Did I lift one single cup or plate or glass and dash it against the cold ceramic tiles on the kitchen floor? No. Did I empty the contents of the brown bin on the bedclothes? No. Did I leave the taps running? Take the batteries out of the smoke alarm? Rip his original Jack Yeats painting from its frame and cut it into miniscule pieces? No, no and no. For Christ's sake, I'd even reset the bloody burglar alarm when I left. This rational behaviour stings me now like nettles. I am *consumed* by the injustice of it. And I keep thinking irrational thoughts and I hate John for turning me into this irrational person whom I barely recognise. I never want to see him again. But, at the same time, I want to see him more than anything else. I want to hurt him, maybe get the abacus his mother bought him when he was five and break it. Well, maybe not break it. Maybe just hide it somewhere. I want him to beg my forgiveness on his hands and knees in the middle of O'Connell Street. I want to watch him doing it while I turn my back and walk away. I want him not to want to leave me. I want to be enough for him.

These thoughts leave no room for the pink pluses and the blue lines and the smiley face (the Kazakhstan test) that skulk in the suburbia of my brain, only allowed to enter my thoughts at the weekend, with taxis booked for 1 a.m. to take them back to wherever they came from. Further out, in the midlands, is the man from the bar. I can't even remember his real name.

Although I did ask him. At least I had the wherewithal to do that.

I was standing at the bar trying to remember the names of the drinks we were drinking by then.

'Are you OK?' The voice comes from somewhere over my head. A gin-and-cigarettes voice. Some people would call it sexy.

'Yes, of course I'm OK. Why wouldn't I be OK?' My tone is waspish.

'No, I didn't mean, like, are *you* OK? I meant, are you *OK*? As in would you like me to serve you a beverage? Because I happen to be a barman. In this very establishment.'

'What?' I have to shout to be heard over the music.

'Do? You? Want? Something? To? Drink?'

'Oh,' I say. The man is on the other side of the counter, as most good barmen are. I find my wallet and look at him. He is very long. My head moves up and up until my eyes reach his face. It seems to take ages.

'The same again?' he suggests, pointing down to the table where Filly is sitting, waiting.

His hair needs cutting. A good two inches off the fringe, back and sides. But it is the colour of

59

it that draws my attention. Even in the gloom of the club, it roars red, like an angry sunset. Or a fire brigade scorching to a blaze.

'Your hair . . . ' I say. I am appalled by my rudeness.

'Yeah, I know. Shocking, isn't it?'

'What's your name?' I don't know why I ask him. Maybe if I'd never asked him, everything might be different.

'Everyone calls me Red,' he'd said. He looks resigned and a little apologetic at the predictability of the nickname.

'Red.' I pick it up and try it out. 'Red what?'

'Butler. Red Butler,' he says, before adding, 'but it's Red because of my hair, not that guy in that movie. Besides, his name wasn't Red. It was Rhett.'

'Yes, I know,' I say in a low voice, turning the cocktail menu the right way round so that it makes a bit more sense.

'Oh. Not many people know that.' He grins at me then and I remember this grin. Wide and a little quizzical. The kind of grin that makes you want to grin back. And I do. I remember that. Even though I don't grin as a rule, I grin back.

★ ★ ★

Anytime Red Butler creeps into the capital city of my head, I douse him by conjugating a particularly vicious French verb. Like *mettre*. Or *vouloir*.

I concentrate on the Marzonis, gathering any information on Sofia I can find. Not much, as it happens. Sofia seems to be the most elusive of the Marzoni women. I email what I've collected to Filly with a request to open a file on the Sofia Marzoni wedding. I'm 97.5 per cent certain she will ring. I write down the percentage and circle it until the nib of the pen scores a hole in the page. If I get the wedding, my chances of getting the promotion increase. Not to 97.5 per cent, of course. No, nothing like it, what with the Gladys Montgomery situation. But still. I concentrate on the phone and will it to ring.

When that doesn't work, I walk to the photograph, framed and mounted on the far wall of the office. It is a photograph of the Marzoni sisters at Maria Marzoni's wedding last August. It is my call to prayer. My Mission Impossible statement. A monument to brute force and bullheadedness and a dogged refusal to accept defeat, even when defeat seems not just inevitable but almost welcome.

The picture was taken after dinner. The dinner where Isabella Marzoni — the eldest of the sisters — announced that her husband of two years was a lying, cheating, carousing son-of-a-whore and that she was leaving him. That very day. She made the announcement from the head table, waiting until she'd eaten her dinner and drank the best part of a bottle of the prosecco her father imports on the side. She used the microphone that I tried — too late — to snatch from her, her eyes a set of flashing knives that she threw at me as if I were the *stinking, philandering, wine-soaked pig* and not Paul, the husband, who cowered in his chair at table number six, a speckled bread roll held against his heart as if to protect himself from the slings and arrows of the outraged Isabella.

In the photograph, Isabella smokes a thin cigarette and even manages a slight smile, thanks in no small part to the two Valium I made her take after I persuaded her out of the dining room and away from the open-mouthed horror of the Irish guests; the Italian ones seemed not at all put out by the drama. In fact, they appeared to enjoy it.

The Marzonis stand in a line in age order. Sofia is there, in the middle, looking away from her sisters with the kind of look people get in their eyes when they are someplace else. They are as Italian as macaroni and cheese, these sisters, with big hair and big teeth. A healthy-looking line of women, glossy as a fashion magazine. Their skin is the colour of Italian coffee, with a dash of milk. Maria is the youngest, although there isn't much more than nine months between any of them. His 'steps', their father calls them. Sofia is the third oldest or the third youngest. Either way, she is the middle child.

I force myself to sit at my desk and look at some emails. There's one from Bryan with a recipe for break-up pavlova. I write the ingredients on a yellow Post-it, using my left hand so that it takes longer. I memorise the method and then I save the email into my 'Recipes' folder but I don't give the recipe its full title. I just call it 'Pavlova', in case hackers break into my system. I don't want everyone knowing my business. When I check my watch, four minutes have passed.

★ ★ ★

'Did Sofia ring yet?' Filly asks me later in the kitchen.

'No.'

'What time is it?'

'Five past five.'

'Early yet,' Filly says. 'For the chip business.'

'Sod it. I'm going home.'

'Already, Scarlett? You working part-time now? Heh, heh, heh.'

Filly and I spin round even though I know who it is. I recognise the high-pitched breathy voice. It is Gladys Montgomery.

'You look tired, so you do.' Gladys eases a Rennie out of a box in her bag and pops it into her mouth. She moves towards us. 'Do you want one?' she says, shaking the box under our noses. Her breath is chalky, a nod to the four Rennies she's already taken today. She's always at the Rennies, on account of her biliousness. We shake our heads. I look at my watch and make a bet with myself that she will mention Tanya Forsythe's wedding within the next fifteen seconds.

'I can't believe Sofia Marzoni hasn't rung you yet,' says Gladys, trying her best not to look delighted.

'She will,' says Filly, and I can see her tiny hands curling into fists inside the front pockets of her jeans. 'She only announced her engagement today.'

'Anyway, I can't stop. I'm up to my eyes with Tanya Forsythe's wedding plans.'

I check my watch. Twelve seconds. Not bad.

'What's the name of her girl band again?' wonders Filly out loud. 'Eight, is it? Or Nine? I can never remember.'

'It's Ten,' says Gladys, looking closely at Filly, trying to work out if she is mocking her. 'They may not be a household name in Ireland yet but they're *huge* in Norway, so they are.' She sweeps out of the kitchen, leaving us gagging in the wake of her scent, which is a peculiar mix of Rennies and hairspray.

'You could always ring Sofia,' suggests Filly, not quite looking at me.

'Ring her? No way. That would look way too needy,' I say.

'But you *do* need her,' Filly points out.

'I don't. I have loads of other stuff to do. I'm working on Jane Browne's wedding and there's the Smithson-Carling vow renewal. I'm busy.'

'But not busy enough,' says Filly. 'You need something that will consume you. Something that will eat you from the inside out, like a maggot. You need Sofia Marzoni.'

Filly is right. Despite the denial, I know I am clinging on to the remains of my life by a thread, a threadbare one. If I didn't have to get up every morning to give Blue his breakfast (sardines on wholegrain toast), it's just possible that I mightn't get up at all.

But I can't ring a client with a begging bowl in my hand. Especially not a Marzoni sister. Things aren't that bad. Not yet anyway.

7

Denial stays for another few days and then, like all good houseguests, it leaves before I want it to. It's been six days now since I took the tests — the positive tests — but, with denial sprawled all over the couch in the front room of my head, I've managed to hobble through the days so far.

Now fear arrives in its place. Great dollops of it. It's one of those houseguests that never lets you forget they are there. Leaves stuff strewn all around the place. Never cleans up after itself. Walks into the bathroom when you are clipping your toenails. It's a horrible thing, to be afraid. It consumes you. Digs into your stomach like a tapeworm. Fear hunkers down, gets itself comfortable. I can feel the façade I have been hiding behind begin to crack like a thin sheet of ice beneath the glare of a wintry sun.

I take out my organiser. I open the section where I keep my five-year plans. The current one is so far off course there's no way I can amend it. I'm going to have to rewrite it completely.

The decision I make doesn't feel like a decision, because I don't feel like I have any choice in the matter. Besides, it's so early. It would almost be like taking the morning-after pill. Wouldn't it? And I've always been pro-choice. Haven't I? But it's easier to be pro-choice when it's not you making the choice.

I chew the top of my pen until it splinters in my mouth. Then I reach for the telephone. I still have the number of the clinic in my BlackBerry since the Charlotte Crosby wedding. We called her BrideZuki. Just as fearsome as a BrideZilla but very, very small. Not quite five feet. Charlotte got pregnant six weeks before her wedding. I remember it as one might remember having a limb amputated without the benefit of an anaesthetic. She didn't care who knew. She just wanted the situation *dealt with*. And I dealt with it. The clinic had been discreet (BrideZuki was marrying one of Ireland's top jockeys), efficient (the appointment was made on a Friday for the following Monday) and reassuringly expensive (Charlotte was Brand New Money and insisted on paying over the odds for everything).

'Good morning, Davenport Clinic. May I help you?' The receptionist sounds like the same one I spoke to about Charlotte.

'Eh, yes, please, I'd like to . . . I'd like to make an appointment.' There is a shake in my voice. I clear my throat.

'Certainly, madam. Do you have a preferred consultant?'

'Is Mr Ashcroft available?'

It is one of those clinics where you shop by name rather than product. Mr Ashcroft is the man I need. The receptionist knows what I want without me having to say it.

'Yes, he is. I'll just get his diary out.'

I hear papers rustling. My hands tighten around the phone. I wait.

66

'When would suit you?' The receptionist is back. She sounds kind, like someone's granny.

When would suit me? Right away. Immediately. Today. Fear and panic are jostling for position. They fight for space at the back of my throat, making it hard to breathe.

'Eh, tomorrow?' I try to eliminate the tremor from my voice but the days ahead seems as long as a funeral procession and I know I can't make it through another weekend.

'Oh, I'm sorry, Mr Ashcroft is out this afternoon and he doesn't usually work on a Friday.'

Panic is the forerunner now, thundering down the inside track of my mind.

'Isn't there anyone else?'

'Have you been here before, madam?' the receptionist asks.

'Not myself, no, but you might remember I made a booking with you a few months ago. For one of my clients? My name is Scarlett O'Hara.'

'Oh, yes, of course, Ms O'Hara. I thought I recognised your voice. I'm going to see what I can do and ring you straight back, all right?'

Maybe the receptionist thinks that I have a whole stable of clients in need of the clinic's services, or maybe she is just a kindly soul who can sense my desperation. I thank her profusely ('Thankyouthankyouthankyouthankyouthankyouthankyousomuch'), hang up the phone and resume biting the thumbnail on my left hand, a habit I cured myself of when I was eleven years old with the aid of mustard powder, cod-liver oil and the wooden stick of a

Loop-the-Loop, which I bit to a splint after applying the mustard and oil to the thumbnail.

The phone on the desk buzzes and I fall on it, picking up the receiver with both hands. It is only Filly.

'Who were you calling just now?' Filly usually makes all my calls for me, mostly because she likes to know what is going on at all times.

I feel like I've already done it. Guilt gathers on my skin, like sweat.

'Eh . . . no one . . . I was just . . . '

'Was it Sofia?' I can hear Filly holding her breath, willing me to tell her I've got the Sofia Marzoni wedding in the bag.

'No,' I tell her. 'But it's only been three days . . . ' I taper off, knowing how lame this sounds. Three days is much too long, especially for a Marzoni wedding. Lucia Marzoni — the second eldest of the Marzoni girls — phoned me the moment her boyfriend (Giovanni) popped the question. Before she gave him her answer, I mean. Just to check I was available. Only when I said yes did she say yes. With me still on the line.

'Who then?' asks Filly.

'What?'

'Who were you on the phone to?'

'Oh . . . eh . . . Bryan,' I say.

'No,' Filly corrects me. 'He rang while you were on that call. In fact, we had a chat about you.'

I can't think of anything to say to that.

'He says you've been acting very strangely this week. Not returning his calls or responding to his texts. He says he even sent you an email

68

about a potential client and you never got back to him.'

'I meant to. I . . . I must have forgotten.' I never forget about potential clients. 'Who's the client?'

'No one,' Filly admits. 'He made it up. He just wanted you to ring him back.'

'Oh,' I say. I want to say something else — anything really — but I can't think of a single thing.

'So?' Filly prompts. 'What gives?'

'Nothing really,' I say. 'Just my boyfriend of four years left me to go and play in some sandpit in Brazil.'

'Apart from that?' Filly is nothing if not abnormally perceptive.

'Sorry, Filly, I have to go. I have to phone Maureen. Her horoscope this morning said that she has to be strong and face up to things and she's in bits about it.' I hang up before Filly can respond. I hate doing this to her. Although it *is* true about the horoscope.

I can't talk to Filly. I can't talk to anyone. Not today. Later maybe. Afterwards. Just not now.

The phone rings again and this time I check the caller ID before answering it.

It is the clinic.

8

The airport is full of people. Laughing, clattering people with oversized bags and wide-brimmed hats; busy, important people with laptops and briefcases and mobile phones coming out of their ears; faded, worn-out people standing in front of flight-information displays with glazed eyes and unkempt hair.

I stand still for a moment. The crowd swarms around me and it feels like I'm not even there. I set my overnight bag on the ground beside me and take a tissue out of my handbag. I rub at the sweat that gathers on my forehead and along the ridge of my top lip.

When I bend to pick up my bag, white spots dance at the edge of my vision and I hunker on the floor, pretending to adjust a strap, closing my eyes against them. This has happened a few times over the past couple of days and, because it's never happened before, I know it is something to do with the baby. I shake my head. It's not a baby. Not yet. It's a clump of cells. Invisible to the naked eye. Barely there at all.

'Are you all right, love?' A hand grips the soft, fleshy skin of my upper arm. I can feel it through the thin fabric of my jacket. It warms me.

I snap my eyes open and stand up. 'I'm fine, thank you,' I say, but I sway a little and the woman in front of me touches me again, both hands this time, on my arms.

'You're white as a ghost, so you are,' she says.

I notice her mouth first, then her nose and cheeks and eyes and forehead, like a camera zooming out.

'I stood up too quickly, that's all,' I say, taking a step backwards.

The woman is older than her voice suggests. Her gaze is unsettling. Like she *knows*.

'Bovril,' the woman announces.

'Sorry?'

'It's great for shock.'

'But I'm not in shock or anything. Just . . . just a little dizzy.'

'Great for dizziness and shock and all manner of things.' The woman lowers her hand into a mother and a father of a shoulder bag, until her whole arm disappears. I wonder if she has a jar of Bovril in there but when the hand reappears, it holds nothing other than a mobile phone.

'Well,' I say, taking care to bend my knees this time when I pick up my bag, 'I'd better go. My flight is — '

'I'm telling you, love. Bovril. With two spoons of sugar. That's what you need.'

'You're not supposed to put sugar in Bovril,' I say. 'I mean, as far as I know,' I add, because the woman is being kind. Odd. But kind.

'You're not supposed to do lots of things, love,' says the woman, punching a number into her phone. 'But people still do them, don't they?'

Before I can think of a single thing to say, the woman begins talking — shouting, really — into her mobile. 'Ellen? Is that you? Ellen? Can you hear me? Ellen?'

I stand there, unsure of what to do next. It might seem rude to just walk away from this woman without thanking her for her help and the Bovril advice.

'Can you hear me? Yes, I can hear you. Ellen? Ellen?'

I gather my belongings. I decide to wait until the woman looks at me. Then I'll smile my thanks at her and leave.

'No, Ellen, hang on there a minute. There's a slip of a girl here beside me about to faint. Yes, of course I told her about the Bovril. Yes. And the sugar. Hang on . . . ' The woman lowers the phone from her ear and looks at me.

'Eh, I'm fine now. Thanks.'

'Don't forget the — '

'No, I won't forget. Thanks.'

The woman, belted and buttoned into a beige coat two sizes too small for her, waves at me, mouths the word 'Bovril' and returns to her phone. 'Ellen? Ellen? Are you still there? Can you hear me? Ellen . . . '

I keep walking until I can't hear her any more. I look at the flight display screen. There is a flight leaving for Sao Paulo in fifteen minutes. The gate is closing and a voice over the tannoy announces the last call for flight EI231. For just a moment, I picture myself buying a ticket. Skipping a queue. Running. Arriving at the gate, breathless, red-faced. But even if I run all the way there, I won't make it. And even if I make it, what good will it do?

I check the flight to London. It is on time and departing in an hour from gate 32. I have time

72

for a cup of coffee. Or Bovril? No, coffee. I have already checked in online. I check through my papers again: passport, booking reference number and a printout of directions from the clinic's website. My stomach clenches and I think it's nerves, although it feels more like a cramp. I wait for the pain to pass and head for the café.

★ ★ ★

The coffee is lukewarm and the gingerbread man is stale, one of its Smartie eyes gone, giving it a lopsided, neglected look. It lies there, on the plate, looking at me with its one good eye. In the end I turn it on to its stomach and push the plate away.

I check my phone. Three missed calls. Two from Bryan and one from Filly. I told them I was going to Newry to see a dentist.

'But you have perfect dentition,' Filly said, suspicious.

'I . . . I need a filling.'

'But you have a dentist. On Morehampton Road.'

'He retired. Last week.' I wonder when I got so good at lying.

'I'll come with you if you like. Keep you company,' says Bryan. 'I have to find a film location anyway. Somewhere with mountains. Northern Ireland is falling down with mountains, isn't it?' Bryan works for a film production company and even though he has a job title (I think it's Post-Production Assistant Manager. Or Pre-Production. Or something like that), he seems to do a bit of everything. Finding locations is one of those things he does.

I reel off the names of all the mountain ranges throughout the six counties, which goes some way towards reassuring Filly and Bryan that I am all right.

'Thanks, Bryan, but I need to do some shopping and you won't want to be tagging along after me.'

'Are you shopping for clothes?' Bryan *loves* clothes shopping. And accessories. He is the only man I know who buys manbags and, because he is chunky and short, he can carry it off.

'No, I need to buy a microwave.'

'For Blue?' Blue is a cat who loves his dinners heated up. And his milk. And cream (which he only gets on Sundays as a treat because of his cholesterol levels, which were a little high on his last check-up).

'Yes.'

'So, do you have a toothache?' Filly doesn't let it go.

'Um, yes,' I say, cupping my cheek with my hand for emphasis.

'You never said.'

'I did. You mustn't have been listening.' Filly can't say anything to that because it might be true. She zones out when people talk about certain things (like toothache, the Axis of Evil and gardening) and thinks instead about things like coconut snowballs, Brendan's buttocks — generous and soft, like hotel pillows, she tells me — and *Countdown*.

Another cramp brings me back to the café. I

sit there and count backwards from ten, waiting for it to pass. It is like a fist in my belly, squeezing. I stop when I get to five, the fist unclenching, the pain subsiding. I dismiss it, putting it down to the fact that I haven't eaten much over the past few days and lack of sleep, which is normal for me but maybe, in these straitened conditions, assumes a greater importance than it normally would.

I try to think about work. Lobbying for the new position. The continued silence from Sofia Marzoni. Instead, I close my eyes and wish for things to be the way they were before. When I knew what was going to happen. And when. When I had plans that worked out. My old life. I wish for it so hard, it is like a physical pain — backache or groin strain.

I think about the first time I met John. Nothing dramatic. No fireworks or fuss. A calm meeting of minds. It was a golf outing that I organised for one of our most important clients, an insurance company. Normally, I work exclusively as a wedding planner. Organising golf outings is the sausage and chips of the event-management world. Anyone can do it. But Elliot had begged.

'Help me, Obi-Wan Kenobi, you're my only hope,' he says, clasping his long fingers together in a prayerful manner. He's also a *Star Wars* fan, although not a closet one. He leans across my desk with his begging eyes that are too big for his narrow face.

'Why can't Cecile do it?' All our golf events are organised by Cecile. I regret asking the question because there is a story. Of course there is a story. And because it is an Elliot Friel story, it is a long and dubious one. Elliot is unable to say anything in five words or less. Apart from his name, which is Elliot Francis Columbanus Friel — I swear to God. Elliot tells the Cecile story but, instead of listening to it, I use the time to try to come up with a credible excuse as to why I can't do it.

'It's a bloody golf outing. A stray dog could do it.'

'But you *know* about golf. You're great at it.'

'I've never played golf,' I say.

'But that doesn't mean you don't know how to.' Elliot is on his feet now, his arms stretched towards me, palms upwards in his traditional pleading position. 'You're the only person I know who knows how to do everything.'

'Elliot, I . . . ' I am about to agree to take the bloody job — mostly to shut him up but also because of my crippling sense of duty — but he is on a roll and sweeps on, ignoring me.

He hands me the manila folder. 'This is what Cecile has done so far.' The folder is as flat as a golf scorecard.

'But there's nothing in here,' I say.

'No, wait, there's a telephone number in there somewhere, I'm sure of it.' Elliot takes the folder back from me, opens it, turns it upside down and shakes it. A torn and dirty piece of paper falls out of the folder and flutters gently on to the desk. Elliot hands it to me. He is right. It is a telephone number.

'OK, OK, I'll do it. Just don't hug me.' I cross

my arms in front of me but it is too late. Already he is off his chair and racing round the edge of the desk to get at me.

'Gerroffme.' My voice is muffled against the shoulder of his jacket where he holds my head in a vice-grip.

'You know, this could work out well for you,' says Elliot, finally releasing me. I smooth my hair and straighten my jacket back on to my shoulders. 'The MD of the insurance company has a daughter who's getting married next year. If you do a good job on this, he might ask you to plan it.' I look up to gauge the truthfulness or otherwise of this statement. Elliot is not beyond telling what he calls 'white lies' when he is in a tight spot. He presses home his advantage. 'She's his only daughter. It could be a society wedding.'

'What makes you think that?' Elliot thinks every wedding could be a society wedding.

'She knows Bono.' He lays the sentence carefully on the desk, like a card player with a full house.

'Bono?'

'Or Edge. One of them anyway. The short one.'

'That's Bono,' I say. 'Although it could be Edge. Neither of them are what you might call lofty.'

Elliot slaps my shoulder in what he probably thinks is a comradely gesture and takes to his heels before I can change my mind.

★ ★ ★

77

John was an actuary at the insurance company and, as such, not normally exposed to the clients. But he was there that day.

Some people would call it fate. John Smith. That's his name. It is one of the millions of things I love about him. John Smith. The fabulous plainness of it. Not even a 'y' in the middle of the Smith to lift it from obscurity. Just the wonderful predictability of the unobtrusive 'i'. The mundaneness. The sheer forgetability of it. Except people never forget it because it is so bland. But lovely. Like rice pudding.

The first thing I notice about him is the book tucked under his arm, *The A–Z of Golf*. This is when I feel it. The initial frisson of recognition. I look at him again, more carefully now. If you didn't know he was an actuary, you couldn't really tell, although he blinks a lot, as if his eyes are unaccustomed to daylight.

'Have you read that book?' I ask, hardly aware of a coquettish note that has crept into my voice.

'I only had time to speed-read it in the car on the way over here,' he says. 'Although it was a twenty-minute journey through five sets of traffic lights on red,' he adds.

'So how much of it did you get to read?' I ask.

'I'm up to 'A birdie in the hand',' John says.

'How many pages?' I hold my breath, hardly daring to hope.

'A hundred and twenty-four,' he says. 'Oh, and I read the glossary of golf terms at the back of the book as well. But I only skimmed those.'

And there it is. The meeting of minds. The click that the last piece of a difficult 1,000-piece jigsaw puzzle makes when you slot it home. And while there are no fireworks, there is a gorgeous glow in my sky, like the sun coming out after a long, dull day.

John isn't either tall or short. And he's not fat or thin. Average, some people might say. But as my eyes slide south, I decide that I like the look of his bum in the dark brown chinos. Round and snug. I find myself wondering if his bum is hairy or smooth and hoping it is the latter.

I like his economy with words. The way he only speaks when he has something sensible to say.

When he asks me out for dinner, I accept.

His reasons for being a vegetarian are the same as mine. We are both animal lovers and between us have three and a half cats — one of his cats is pregnant — but neither of us are *fanatical* about it.

While his taste in music is uninspiring (mostly jazz and classical), we enjoy reading books of a non-fictional nature and sipping small amounts of full-bodied red wine from big-bellied glasses.

When he tells me he loves me — on the first anniversary of the golf outing — I tell him I love him too. It feels like the right thing to do.

On the night of our second anniversary, he asks me to move in with him and I say yes. There is no reason not to.

Neither of us wants to get married. Neither of us wants to have children. Neither of us wants to invest in a property together until the housing market regains some semblance of normality.

We are happy with these decisions. I accept

John into my life the way some people might accept delivery of a sofa. But that doesn't mean I didn't love him. I did.

And even though his bum turns out to be hairy instead of smooth, I get used to it until, after a while, I don't notice it any more.

9

'Is there anyone sitting here, love?' I look up and the babble of the airport rushes at me like a train. A woman leans towards me over a double buggy.

'No,' I say, standing up. 'I was just leaving.'

'But you haven't touched your bun. Or your drink. Latte, is it?'

'Eh . . . I . . . '

'God be with the days when we drank Maxwell House and loved it,' she says, unhitching a child from her backpack. 'And the price of them. Shocking, it is.' Now she begins unstrapping what look like twins from the pram.

'They're . . . lovely,' I say, nodding at the children. It's only when the woman straightens that I notice the sling. Clamped to her chest. The infant looks brand new, a line of dark hair running along the centre of his — or her — head, like a mini-Mohican.

'Holy horrors, the lot of them,' the woman tells me, slapping plastic beakers and Tupperware containers on the table.

I smile to show that I know she is joking, although I'm not entirely sure that she is.

The next thing on my to-do list is getting through security. This is how I've been coping recently. I assign myself one task at a time. Nothing too strenuous. I know that getting through security at Dublin Airport is not without

81

its challenges but it is something I can do. Difficult, yes. But not impossible. And while I'm doing it, I don't have to think. About the appointment in the clinic at one o'clock that afternoon. About the cells. The clump of cells. Multiplying and multiplying and getting bigger and bigger and becoming a baby. And there it is. That word. That four-letter word. I will not be able to get through this day if I think about that word. I quicken my pace and reach the queue for the security check.

★ ★ ★

'Scarlah! Scarlah O'Hara! Over here!'

I look — as does everyone else in the lengthy security-check queue — in the direction of the yelling. It is Sofia Marzoni. She looks taller without her sisters. More striking. Teeth as white as an American actor. Big, black hair. Long, red nails. Today, she is in a suit. It is pale yellow, not unlike the colour of a cooked chip.

'Hello, Sofia. How are you?' I say.

'Come here to me.' Sofia grabs me in a Canadian bear hug, squashing me against her vast chest. The smell of Chanel No. 5 makes me want to throw up over Sofia's shoulder but the long crowd of people in the queue are too close, pushed up as they are against each other. Then, when I think that I might actually pass out with the heat and the smell, Sofia thrusts me away, although I am still close enough to see the pinprick of a tiny hole in the side of Sofia's nose where the skin has been pierced for a ring, years before.

'You look terrible, Scarlah. What's wrong with ya?'

Everyone in the queue strains to get a glimpse of my face. Am I imagining it or are some of them nodding their heads in agreement?

'I'm . . . fine,' I say, pulling at my jacket, which has slipped off my shoulders during the vigorous embrace. 'A little tired, that's all.' I speak quietly in the hope that Sofia will follow suit and lower the volume on her voicebox. She does not.

'I'm gettin' married, Scarlah. Did you hear?'

'I think Filly read an article about it,' I say. I can't let her know how desperate I am.

'Sorry I haven't called you yet. I've been up to my tits in chip business recently. A crisis about the cost of oil or some shite. I'm on my way to a board meetin' now. In London. They're like babbies, so they are, those directors. Still need someone to hold their dicks for them, wha?'

I look around to check who's listening. Everyone. Then again, it can be very boring standing in a security-check queue. Especially at Dublin Airport, where the queues are as long as Good Friday.

'I thought you were going to the dentist today. In Newry.'

'Why did you think that?' I ask.

'Filly told me. When I rang. This morning.'

This morning? I look at my watch. Christ, it's only 9.22 a.m. What the hell time had she rung the office? And how on earth did she manage to speak to Filly, who hasn't been up before nine in the morning since they stopped showing *Skippy the Fecking Bush Kangaroo?*

Sofia seems to read my mind. 'I rang her on her mobile. Told Brendan it was an emergency and he agreed to haul her out of the bed.' Sofia laughs at this, a big, wide belly laugh.

A gigantic group of Japanese tourists join the end of the queue. One of them films the sweet counter at the kiosk with a tiny hand-held camera.

'Listen, Sofia, I'd better join the queue or I'll never get through security. Why don't you come into the office after the weekend and we can have a good chat about it?'

'What day?'

'How about Friday?' I need to buy myself as much time as possible to come up with a suitably impressive plan.

'How about Wednesday?'

'Eh, OK,' I say, backing away. The pain is back. Low in my belly. Two fists this time.

'What time?' Sofia is relentless.

'How about after lunch? Say two o'clock?'

'How about after breakfast? Say nine thirty?'

'Fine,' I say, nailing what I hope is a smile on my face. It feels more like a grimace. I bend down to pick up my bag but Sofia isn't finished with me yet.

'It's a show I'm after really. Not just a weddin'. I want it to be *huge*. A spectacle.'

This is great news; it means the budget will have to be *huge* too.

'But the budget will be tight. What with the fecking oil crisis and that.'

I barely hear the end of that sentence. Another

84

pain, stronger this time, doubles me over like a kick. Quite without meaning to, I grab Sofia's arm and lean, waiting for the pain to subside, trying to catch my breath.

'Jaysis, Scarlah, what's the matter?'

As I force my head up, a couple of things happen at the same time. I can see Sofia's mouth moving but I can't hear her — which is pretty worrying considering the timbre of her voice. And Sofia — along with everyone else in the queue — seems further away now, fainter. The sounds of the airport fall away and in the silence I hear the low grunt of someone in pain. Someone crying. Someone stumbling. A gush of something warm and sticky down my legs. Vomit on the polished, patent shoes of the tall, thin man in the queue behind Sofia. And then the ground. Rushing up to meet me. Hard but mercifully cold. It is filthy, the floor. I can see chewing gum. Chewed-up, spat-out chewing gum. And people's shoes. Boots and pumps and wedge sandals and one — unfortunate — pair of Hush Puppies, last seen in Ireland in 1982. It is peaceful down here in the silence and I let it pull me by the hand until the world dims and darkens and I can't feel anything any more.

10

The world comes back slowly at first. Shadows and shapes. Sounds like the ones you hear underwater. Whispers in slow motion, gentle as a warm breeze. For a moment, I allow myself to float in this quiet landscape.

'I think she's waking up.'

'How do you know?'

'I saw her eyes move.'

'But they're closed.'

'I still saw them move. You know how observant I am.'

'Christ, I hope she'll be OK. This weddin' isn't going to plan itself.' A frosty silence greets this particular gem, and then, 'I'm *joking*. Of course I'm joking. Just trying to lighten the mood. Kerr-ist, one near-death experience and everyone's sense of humour evaporates.'

'She didn't nearly die.'

'She did. You weren't there.'

'Stop it.' A third voice. 'Filly, go and get someone and tell them Scarlett's waking up.'

As soon as I realise that Bryan is there, I allow myself to open my eyes. Just a chink. My worst fears are confirmed: Sofia Marzoni is here, a fiercely protective look on her face, like a lioness with a brand-new clutch of cubs.

I want to know where I am but I don't want to say, 'Where am I?' like some C-list actress in a made-for-TV film on TV3. Instead, I say, 'What are you all doing here?' My mouth feels dry and it is hard to get words to come out of it.

Bryan hands me a glass of water. 'Filly phoned me,' he says.

'And I phoned Filly.' This from Sofia. 'Right after I phoned for an ambulance.' Sofia smiles at us, her chest puffed out even more than usual.

Filly strides towards us and that's when I realise that I am lying in a corridor. I lift my head. I'm not the only one. There's lots of people lying in this corridor. Surrounded by groups of people — tired, fidgety people, shifting their weight from one foot to the other and looking up and down the corridor every so often, like people at a bus-stop, waiting for a bus that never comes. And that's when I figure out where I am.

'I'm in A&E, aren't I?' I say.

The three nod their heads.

'On a trolley.'

Again, the heads nodding in unison.

'Oh shit.'

It is a whisper and Bryan leans over and squeezes my hand. 'Don't worry,' he says, 'it's Tuesday and the nurse told us that Tuesdays are generally their quietest time.' He has to shout to be heard over the wails and moans and death rattles coming from the other — I do a quick head count — fifty-seven people on trolleys in the corridor.

'Ah, we're awake, are we?' The four of us jump when a nurse appears, unannounced, at the side of my trolley. Her voice is cheerful and sounds out of place in the war zone of the corridor. We're all awake so we all nod our heads and wait for her to say something else, in a voice that is like a warm fire on a cold night in November. The first thing I notice about her is her name badge (Dympna, a solidly reassuring name) and the fact that she carries a clipboard with a pen at the top, attached by a sturdy-looking cord. I smile at her. She looks like a woman who *knows* things, a woman who can *get things done*.

Dympna consults her notes, holding the pen between her fingers without chewing the top of it. 'Well, the good news is that you've stopped bleeding . . . '

'Bleeding?'

Dympna lowers the clipboard and looks at me. 'Did you have any pains before you collapsed?'

'I didn't really collapse,' I say. 'I just felt a bit weak.'

'You did collapse,' Sofia interrupts. 'She did,' she says again, this time to Filly, Bryan and Dympna, not wanting anyone to think she'd summoned an ambulance for a woman who just felt weak.

Dympna ignores Sofia and leans closer to me. 'Well? Did you?'

This morning seems like a long time ago now. Then I remember. 'Yes,' I say. 'Kind of like cramps.'

'In your abdomen?'

'Yes.'

'Low down? Here?' Dympna places her hands just above my pubic bone and I nod. 'Could you be pregnant?' Dympna continues, brisker now, writing something on the clipboard.

'NO!' Filly and Bryan say the word at the

same time, both as emphatic as each other, then smile sheepishly, the way people do when they draw attention to themselves in a public place. And no place is more public than the A&E corridor on this Tuesday morning.

'Eh, well . . . ' I say, with no idea of what I will say next. You can't *lie* to a medical professional. What is the point? But the truth is messy and complicated and not something I am ready to blurt out. Especially with an audience.

I am saved by an arc of vomit that erupts — really unexpectedly — from my mouth. Dympna catches it in a bowl she whips from a pouch at the front of her uniform. I can tell she's done that before but even she cannot resist a small smile of satisfaction at her efficiency. She sets the bowl on the trolley beside me because she knows — even before I do — that there will be more.

As I retch, Filly speaks to the nurse in a loud whisper. 'Her boyfriend left her. A few weeks ago.'

Dympna looks confused. 'And . . . ?' She waits.

'You see, Scarlett wouldn't have an unplanned pregnancy. She doesn't do anything unplanned,' adds Bryan.

'She's a wedding planner.' Sofia puts in her tuppence worth, not wanting to be left out. 'My wedding planner, actually.'

'Oh,' says Dympna. 'I thought you were all part of Scarlett's family?'

'We are,' says Filly, louder than necessary, perhaps sensing an eviction order in the offing.

'I'm her cousin,' Bryan explains. Dympna looks at him from underneath a pair of busy eyebrows crying out for a good plucking. Dympna looks like a woman who has no truck with beauty salons. 'Her *first* cousin,' he adds.

'And I'm practically her sister,' says Filly, thrusting her chin up in the air, which is her defiant, not-backing-down look.

'An' as I said, she's my weddin' planner,' says Sofia, although even she has to concede that this link — at least from an outsider's point of view — might be considered tenuous at best.

Dympna puts a full stop at the end of whatever she had been writing on her clipboard. She looks like someone who has reached a decision and we crane towards her, to hear what she might say next.

'Right, Scarlett, I'm going to find you a bed and then we're going to run some tests, OK?' Before anyone has time to ask what kind of tests or marvel at Dympna's optimism (finding a bed in an Irish hospital is up there with spotting a dodo or an empty seat on a commuter train in Dublin at eight o'clock on a Monday morning), two skinny, ageing porters materialise on either side of the trolley and begin inching it along the corridor without speaking.

'Bryan, you can go with Scarlett if you like,' says Dympna, smiling — gently but firmly — at Filly, who trots along behind the trolley.

'Come on,' says Sofia, placing a hand on Filly's shoulder. 'Let's go to the canteen and play Russian roulette with some hospital food.'

Filly lets go of the trolley, her hand slowly

lowering. She smiles at me although the smile fades when Sofia adds, 'We can talk about the wedding. It'll take your mind off things.' Sofia curls her arm around Filly's elbow in an old-fashioned link and frog-marches her down the corridor.

I can hear their heels growing fainter and nearly smile at Filly's fate. I lie on my back, my eyes open now, watching the long tubes of fluorescent lights passing overhead. Bryan slips his warm paw of a hand into my cold, clammy one as he walks alongside the trolley. He never mentions Newry, how I am supposed to be there having my teeth drilled like a road.

The pain is gone. The baby is probably gone too.

I place the hand that Bryan isn't holding on my belly. I feel tired. And empty. This is what I'd wanted. What I'd planned. The thought brings no comfort and I close my eyes and try to think of nothing at all.

11

The day seems as long as a jazz concert. I sleep through a lot of it, without really meaning to. Bryan sits beside my bed and doesn't ask any questions. He is like an armchair: big and soft and comforting. People come and go, taking my blood pressure, my temperature and samples of blood and urine.

'When was the last time you ate?' Dympna asks, hooking me up to a drip.

I think about the one-eyed gingerbread man, discarded on a plate at the airport. 'Yesterday. I think. Tuna fish.' I'd eaten it straight out of the can, dishing most of it into Blue's bowl. I think about Blue then, lying on the back of the couch in the den, occasionally lifting his head to scan the driveway, waiting for me to come home. I think about Mr Ashcroft, checking his watch, sighing and shaking his head as he realises his one o'clock is a no-show. Thinking about the nine holes he could have played instead. I meant to phone the clinic earlier. To explain. But somehow, with all the lying around, there's been no time.

Dympna enters the ward sometime after three and walks towards my bed. The one by the window. 'Where we put the celebrities' daughters,' Dympna jokes. I know what she is going to say. I see it in her gait. Slower now. More careful. I can tell by the smile on her face, a half-smile, a trying-to-be-a-smile smile. I know it in the way she holds her clipboard now: no longer bet up against her chest but hanging loosely from a hand, the bottom of it touching her knee, the pen now trailing on the ground behind her, still attached by the cord but struggling to keep up. At least, that's how it seems to me. When Dympna reaches me, she pulls the curtain all the way round the cubicle and sits down on the edge of the bed, the springs creaking and moaning beneath her weight. She looks at Bryan first.

'I need to speak to Scarlett,' she says.

Bryan nods and gets up from the chair.

'No. Wait,' I shout, my hands outstretched like the hands of a clock, in a sort of 'ten to two' formation.

Dympna and Bryan look at each other and then at me.

'I . . . I mean . . . I don't mind if he stays,' I say. 'I'd . . . I'd like him to . . . Bryan, will you stay?'

Bryan nods and resumes his seat. Dympna looks at him and then turns back to me.

'I've had a miscarriage, haven't I?' I say suddenly, wanting the conversation to be over so I can get back into my clothes and my life as soon as possible. My hands grip the bars at the side of the bed, my knuckles straining white against the skin.

'It's a possibility, yes,' says Dympna.

'A possibility?'

'Well, it might be what we call a threatened abortion,' explains Dympna, consulting her notes.

93

The word hits me like a slap. Dympna hurries on. 'The pregnancy test is still coming up positive but the cramping and bleeding are textbook symptoms of miscarriage.'

'I was on my way to London today,' I whisper at her, 'to have an abortion.'

'Look, Scarlett,' says Dympna, setting her clipboard down on the bed, 'let's get you sorted out first. We need to give you an ultrasound scan and then we'll know what's what and we'll go from there, all right?' The nurse's tone holds nothing but kindness and compassion, which I feel I do not deserve.

At least there is a plan in place. It is like a banister that I can hold on to. I grip it with both hands.

★　★　★

The room with the scanner is quiet and dark, like a church on a winter's afternoon. My breathing thunders into the silence, despite my best efforts to still it.

'Now, Scarlett . . . ' The radiographer — 'Call me Pete' — is a thin, fidgety man and speaks in the high, excited tones of a teenager whose voice is about to break.

Bryan, still there, tightens his grip on my hand. The doctor squeezes gel from a tube and smears my belly with it. The coldness is shocking and I clamp my lips together to stop myself from gasping out loud.

'So your old man is Declan O'Hara, is he?' Pete says. He lowers his hand to my belly again

94

and moves the Doppler across it, in what feels like a figure of eight. An image jumps on to the screen. A grainy image. Like looking into the mouth of a cave on a moonlit night.

'Eh, yes,' I say. I've had this conversation many times but it feels different, wrong somehow, to be having it here, in this room, at this moment.

'I loved him in that film. What was it called again? The one where he plays the soldier who goes AWOL?'

'*Absent Without Steve*,' I say.

'Ah, yes, that's the one. *Loved* him in that. And . . . ' Pete stops talking and bends his head to the screen. 'Aha!' he says.

I crane my neck to see what he sees. I can't see a thing.

'What?' says Bryan. I take comfort from the fact that he can't see a thing either. 'What can you see?'

Pete looks at the pair of us as if we are both deranged.

'Is it a . . . ?' Bryan begins.

'Yes, of course it is,' says Pete, nodding at the screen.

'But the nurse said . . . '

'Nurses aren't always right,' says Pete with an injured air. 'They just think they are.'

'But I . . . '

'Yes, Scarlett?' asks Pete.

'I can't see anything. There's nothing there.'

Pete sighs the long, inevitable sigh of a genius who is surrounded by half-wits. 'Hang on,' he says. 'I'll zoom in.' He worries at some dials on the machine and the image jumps closer.

I lean closer. And then I think I see something. A pulsing blob of jelly with an oversized head. Jerky. A bit like a mini-Michael Jackson in the 'Thriller' video.

I point at it. 'Is that . . . ?'

'That's the embryo, yes,' says Pete. 'About an inch long, I'd say. When did you have your last period?'

'On 14 January.'

'That's what I thought,' says Pete, rather smugly. 'I'd say you conceived this baby about four weeks ago.'

I do the maths, although there's no need. I already know. John left four weeks ago. I went out with Filly on that stupid, stupid night four weeks ago. Four weeks ago, I had a life. A lovely one. Four weeks ago, there was no such thing as men in real life called Red Butler.

'Is everything all right?' asks Pete, looking at my face.

'Yes. Why?'

'You just sort of squeaked there.'

'Squeaked?' Four weeks ago, I was not a woman who squeaked in public. Or indeed anywhere. 'I'm fine,' I say.

I wipe the goo off my belly with the tissue that Pete hands me. He pushes a button on the scanner and the image fades until there is nothing but a black screen.

'So,' I say, 'you think the . . . the embryo . . . is . . .'

'You can call it a baby if you like,' Pete offers. 'I call it an embryo because I'm a professional. That's what we call them at this early stage.'

I can't think of anything to say to that.

'Is the baby all right?' asks Bryan, which is what I wanted to say.

'Looks as it should at this stage,' says Pete.

'What about the cramping and the bleeding?' Bryan says in a low voice, as if he's afraid the baby might hear him.

'I could theorise,' begins Pete, sitting at his desk now, making a pyramid with his hands. 'Of course I could. But I'd prefer Scarlett to speak directly to her doctor.' Pete bends his head and writes something on a piece of paper.

Bryan and I look at each other and then back at Pete. When he looks up again, he seems surprised that we are still in the room.

'You can go now,' he says. 'If you like,' he adds, perhaps considering his earlier tone a little abrupt.

'Eh, grand so,' says Bryan, beginning to wheel my bed towards the door.

'You'll have to wait for a porter,' says Pete, pointing his pen in Bryan's direction.

'OK, I'll . . . ' begins Bryan.

'Just park her out in the corridor,' Pete says, as if I am a car being brought in for a service.

'Wheel me back to the ward,' I hiss at Bryan when we are out in the corridor with Pete's office door firmly closed.

'We're supposed to wait for a . . . ' Bryan begins. After one morning in the health system, he is already institutionalised, not wanting to interfere with the hospital hierarchy, which greets us like a stone wall at every turn.

'Those porters are like a fecking lunar eclipse

of the sun, they're that rare,' I remind him.

Bryan puts the brake on the bed and looks down at me. 'You look terrible,' he says after a while. There is such tenderness on his face I am afraid I will cry.

'It's only because my make-up has evaporated off my face with the heat in here,' I say.

'We need to talk,' he says eventually.

I nod. I know this is true but I can't think of where to start.

'Say something.'

'Nothing's worked out the way I thought it was going to,' I say eventually.

'Sometimes things don't,' says Bryan. 'That's not always a bad thing.'

'How is that not a bad thing?' I am confused, as if Bryan has suggested that the Black Death had its moments.

But Bryan's response will have to wait. Two porters, ancient and thin, possibly the same two from before, materialise at either side of my bed and begin pushing me down the corridor, not talking but breathing heavily with the effort of it all. Bryan follows behind and I can hear him fiddling with his mobile phone.

'You're not supposed to use your mobile in the hospital,' I tell him. He ignores me. 'Who are you phoning anyway?' I ask, pushing myself into a sitting position, twisting my neck towards him.

'Maureen and Declan,' Bryan says.

'What on earth for?' I can't *believe* it.

'They're your parents. They should know you're here. Just in case . . . you know . . . '

'What? In case I die?'

'Well, no, not die exactly but . . . come on, Scarlett. You know it's the right thing to do.'

'Well, yes, in the normal course of things, I'd agree with you. But this is Maureen and Declan we're talking about.'

Bryan thinks about this for a moment. He is probably imagining my parents in the ward: Declan signing autographs and performing Hamlet's soliloquy even though nobody asked him to; Maureen wringing her hands, wailing like a banshee and telling anyone who will listen about the time she had a ruptured hernia and she'd been rushed to hospital, given forty-eight hours to live and defied all doctors' expectations when she not only survived but lived to star in the Amateur Dramatic Society's production of *At Death's Door*, which she co-wrote with her close friend and mentor Cyril Sweeney.

'OK, then,' Bryan says, slipping his phone back into his pocket. 'But we still need to talk.'

12

The doctor is one of those people bursting with good cheer, bonhomie and general loveliness. Everything about him is round, even his elbows and his nose. His face is like a football, it's that round, and his smile stretches all round his head. Even his laugh is round, a fat chuckle with no beginning or end. He chuckles a lot, even with his head bent between my legs, as it is now.

From beneath the sheet covering my legs, I hear him say something.

'Sorry. What did you say? I . . . I can't quite hear you.'

Dr Goodman's round face — reddened now with the downward angle of his head — reappears between my knees and he smiles his round smile at me. 'Just saying how lovely your cervix is,' he says, a little out of breath.

'Oh,' I say. 'Eh . . . thanks.'

'Well, the good news is that your lovely cervix has stopped dilating.'

'What's the bad news?' I ask, holding my breath.

'Ah, yes, I was just getting to that.' Dr Goodman is a man who doesn't like to be rushed. He peels off his latex gloves, places them into the bin and washes his hands for a good two minutes, then dries them until they are like the Sahara Desert, they are that dry. While I appreciate his dedication to hygiene, I have to bite my lip to stop myself asking him what the bad news is again. Eventually, he is finished and even I have to admit that you could eat your dinner off the palms of his hands. He opens the curtains round my bed. Bryan is still there. I don't think he has moved since Dr Goodman pulled the curtains in the first place. He nods at Bryan and looks down at me with his round brown eyes.

'Scarlett . . . ' He pauses.

'Go on,' I say, having worked out that Dr Goodman is a man who needs prompting after all.

'Well, the thing is . . . ' Another pause.

'Yes?' This is excruciating, like Clare Coleman's wedding day, when everyone turned up at the church except for the groom.

'We think you were pregnant with twins.' Dr Goodman takes a step back and puts one of his immaculate round fingernails into his mouth.

'Twins?'

'Eh, yes. Twins. Two babies.'

He waits for me to say something and, when I do not, he asks me a question. 'Do twins run in the family?'

'I was a twin,' I say then, in almost a whisper. I'd never told anyone that before. There was no need, with Maureen around. 'My mother miscarried my twin when she was eight weeks pregnant with us.' Before today, I had accepted this fact about myself the way one would accept being left-handed or double-jointed. Just one of those things. But now it seems like such a sorry little story. I've never given any consideration as to how I might have felt, in my mother's precarious womb, suddenly on my own in the dark. If it were any other day, I would dismiss this thought and get on with things. But because it is today, and not any other day, I think about the baby in my belly, alone now in the space that is suddenly bigger than before. Emptier. I feel tangled up and the feeling is unfamiliar, like I've lost something and gained something at the same time.

Dr Goodman is still talking and I struggle to pay attention. ' . . . a congenital condition. That would not be unusual.'

'Is there any other reason that this might have happened?' I ask.

'We don't know,' he says and then, as if he can read my mind, 'it's nothing you did or didn't do. That much I know. Sometimes these things just happen.'

I nod.

'What about the baby?' Bryan asks softly. 'The other one, I mean?'

Dr Goodman takes a breath and smiles his wide, round smile at Bryan, relieved that there is someone else he can talk to. He consults his notes, rustling the pages importantly.

'All the signs are good,' he says, running his finger down a page. 'There's no reason to be pessimistic. This baby's a fighter, I would say.'

'A fighter?'

'Well, yes, I mean, this type of miscarriage does happen but it's much more common for the mother to lose both babies. When one hangs on, I like to think of the baby as a fighter.' Dr

Goodman reddens as he speaks, perhaps thinking that he has said too much.

And that's when it happens. Something shifts in me, like soft sand beneath bare feet. I can't see it but I can sense it. I lean forward and put my hands across my belly.

'Are you all right, Scarlett?' the doctor asks.

'Can the baby . . . ? Is she aware . . . of . . . of . . . the situation?' I feel foolish even asking the question but Dr Goodman responds as if it is a perfectly reasonable enquiry.

'No. Absolutely not. There's no need to worry on that score.' He scribbles something on a piece of paper. 'And we can't tell the sex of the baby yet.'

'It's a girl,' I say to no one in particular.

'Woman's intuition?' Dr Goodman says with a small smile and a raise of his eyes at Bryan.

'I'm going to call her Ellen,' I continue, this time looking up at the doctor.

'Ellen?' says Bryan.

'After the Bovril-and-two-sugars lady,' I say. 'She was lovely to me.'

'Did you meet Ellen at the airport?' Bryan asks, clearly confused.

'No, I don't know what her name was.'

'So why are you going to call the baby Ellen? If it's a girl, then?'

'Because her friend's name was Ellen. And it *is* a girl. I'm not sure about anything else at the moment but I know the baby is a girl.'

Dr Goodman chuckles. 'Well, you've got a one in two chance of being right, I suppose.'

The pager on Dr Goodman's belt emits a

beep. Ignoring it, the doctor continues to write on my chart, his handwriting large and childlike, with loops on the bottoms of the 'y's and curls at the heads of the 'h's. I manage to hold back for thirteen seconds before speaking. 'Your beeper went just there.' Maybe he hasn't heard it.

'Oh, yes, I know. It's always going off,' he says, not lifting his head from the chart.

'Aren't you going to answer it?' I feel patches of sweat breaking out on my forehead. An unanswered pager makes me anxious. Even someone else's unanswered pager.

'I will in a moment,' says Dr Goodman, the tip of his tongue caught between his teeth as he continues to write.

'It might be serious.' I can't let it go.

'Maybe you should answer it,' suggests Bryan, probably thinking about the time he left his pager in my office one afternoon. I couldn't ignore it and ending up fielding Bryan's messages, firing an actress (for snorting coke on the set of a remake of *Little House on the Prairie*), finding a dog who could bark the theme music of 'Don't Worry, Be Happy' for an ad for Caribbean rum and sourcing the perfect location for a new Irish film *Two Pee or Not Two Pee*, in which the action takes place in or around the time of the euro changeover. I know I shouldn't have done any of that but, really and truly, I couldn't help myself. An unanswered pager is up there with a poster on a lamp-post for a lost kitten. It upsets me.

'Oh,' says Dr Goodman, finally looking at his pager. 'It's a cardiac arrest in outpatients.' He

104

clips the pager back on to his belt and smiles his fabulous smile.

'So . . . you should probably get down there,' I tell him, swinging my legs out of the bed.

'I suppose I should,' says the doctor, putting the lid on his pen and slipping it into his pocket.

It's all I can do not to force the doctor into a wheelchair and push him all the way to outpatients, bouncing him down stairs if I have to.

'First of all, I want to tell you — '

'I'll take it easy, don't worry,' I say.

'And you really should — '

'Yes, I'll get myself an obstetrician. It's at the top of my list of things to do when I get discharged.'

'And don't forget to get some — '

'Folic acid, yes, I won't,' I say. 'Forget, I mean. To get some.'

'Right, well, you seem to have everything covered, Scarlett.' Dr Goodman finally gets up to go and I am giddy with the relief of it. 'You'll need to stay in bed for a while.'

'How long?'

'Well, it's hard to say really. Maybe a week. No excitement, no activities and, of course, no sexual intercourse.'

'That won't be a problem,' I say, mostly to myself.

'Well, maybe not for you but for the father here . . . ' Dr Goodman smiles across the cubicle at Bryan.

'Oh . . . no . . . no . . . Bryan is my cousin,' I say quickly.

The doctor's face darkens. 'Your cousin . . . ?'

'Yes . . . but, no . . . I mean, he's not the father of the baby. He's just . . . my cousin.'

'Her *first* cousin,' adds Bryan, in case the doctor asks him to leave because a) he is not the father and b) he isn't sufficiently related to me to warrant being here.

Dr Goodman looks relieved. 'Now, what was I saying?'

'You were telling Scarlett not to have sexual intercourse,' offers Bryan, in his usual helpful manner.

'Ah, yes,' says Dr Goodman, scratching the tip of his ear with the end of his pencil. 'Some medical evidence suggests that the contractions of the vagina achieved during orgasm could — '

I have to stop him there. 'It's OK, Doctor. There won't be any sexual intercourse.' Dr Goodman opens his mouth to say something but I press home with a curt 'None whatsoever.'

'OK, then, Scarlett,' says the doctor, and I can tell he is miffed at not being able to finish his spiel about the orgasmic and treacherous properties of the vagina. Maybe he has written a paper on it. A thesis, perhaps.

'And if I do all that?' I ask.

'I'm not going to lie to you, Scarlett, there are no guarantees with this pregnancy. We don't really know why this happened. Your cervix dilated and now it's stopped. But it could start again. Or it might not.' As an answer, it is most unsatisfying. 'Sometimes these things just

106

happen.' When Dr Goodman stops smiling — as he does now — his face looks empty, like a boarded-up house. 'But all the vital signs are positive and the baby is, for the moment' — he pauses for gravitas — 'intact.'

13

Bryan doesn't ask me to tell him everything but I do anyway. In the car on the way to Tara. It's a relief. To tell someone. I don't know why I didn't do it sooner.

'You should have told me,' is what he says when I have finished.

'I know,' I whisper, and he lifts one hand off the steering wheel and finds mine and squeezes it tight.

★　★　★

It's not as easy to tell Maureen. In the end, I just tell her.

'I'm going to be a . . . a . . . *granny*?' The last word is a whisper and the horror etched on Maureen's face — usually static with Botox — adds years and years. For a moment, she looks like she *could* be a granny. I am glad we are in the hall, where only one mirror hangs, a small one at an awkward angle that Maureen has to crane her neck to look in.

Maureen sinks into a chair, conveniently located beside the front door, where I have imparted the news. Maureen fumbles in the pouch-like pocket at the front of her dress.

'Here.' I reach into the pouch and withdraw the smelling salts she carries about her person for emergencies. Although — in fairness — the emergencies are usually less dramatic: the non-arrival of an invitation for Declan to officiate at Local Heritage Week; the absence of Maureen's hairdresser from the local salon due to an unexpected bout of scarlet fever. Maureen presses the bottle under her nose and inhales long and loud. The smell of the salts comes to me, wrapping around me like tentacles.

'I'm going to be sick,' I suddenly say, to no one in particular.

'I'll get a paper bag from the kitchen,' says Bryan.

'I don't need a paper bag — I'll go to the toilet.'

'No, I mean for your mother. I think she may be hyperventilating.'

'Oh.' I run then, leaning over the toilet just in time.

Afterwards, I sit on the cold floor and press my forehead up against the wall, closing my eyes. I think about the baby I have lost, running down my legs at the airport in bloody clots. I didn't want that baby but now that he is gone — I feel sure he was a boy — the loss of him stabs me like a knife. I think too about the baby I have — quite unexpectedly — found. Ellen. A fighter, the doctor called her. And in the cold quietness of the bathroom, where I sit on the floor, in the dark, I lie my hands across my belly and whisper her name like a prayer.

It is Bryan who comes to get me in the end. He knocks on the door so gently that I don't hear him. When he opens the door and sees me sitting there, on the floor, he crouches down

109

beside me, lifts one of my hands off my belly and holds it between both of his.

'It'll be all right, you know,' he says.

'I don't even know which one is the father.'

'We'll find out. There are tests . . . '

'I'm going to be a single mother.'

'Yeah, but think of all the lolly you'll get — single mother's allowance and rent allowance and butter coupons. Loads of stuff.' Bryan smiles at me, jollying me along. I am not ready to be jollied along yet.

'You don't get free butter for being a single mother,' I say.

'Sure you do. And a house. People are always banging on about single mothers getting houses.'

A smile tugs at the corners of my mouth, pulling them up. 'I don't know why I didn't do it years ago,' I say, and the smile on my face feels good now. It feels real.

'Now,' says Bryan, standing up and pulling me up with him. 'How do you feel?'

I think about it. 'Starving,' I say, surprised.

'Rightio,' says Bryan at once. He is the only man I know who says, 'Rightio.' He is also partial to the phrase 'Ups-a-daisy.'

'What would you like to eat?'

My mouth waters. 'A steak,' I say. 'A really big one that hangs over the edges of a dinner plate. You have to serve it on a platter, it's that big. Crispy on the outside, pink in the middle. Oh God.'

'But you don't eat meat,' says Bryan, confused.

'I know.' I bite my lip and force myself to think

110

about a calf — a cute one — with a glossy black coat and a bell round its neck. A pink nose — twitching — all pink and wet.

'OK, then, I'll have a burger. A quarterpounder. With cheese. And a chocolate milkshake.' I can barely get the words out, there is that much saliva in my mouth. I swallow and look at Bryan, who stares back at me as if he has no idea who I am. 'There's hardly any meat at all in those burgers,' I say in a sort of plaintive whine.

'Get into bed. I'll bring something up to you, OK?'

He goes into the kitchen and I move into the hall. I am heavy with tiredness. I sit on the chair in the hall, before tackling the stairs.

Luckily, there isn't a scrap of meat in the house. In fact, there's hardly any food in the fridge, what with Phyllis still away.

'You can't possibly be hungry at a time like this,' Maureen screeches at Bryan as he rummages around the deserted-looking fridge. She is draped across her favourite armchair, one hand pressed limply to her head, the other holding the smelling salts to her nose like they are the only thing between her and imminent death.

Bryan backs out of the fridge, armed with a withered chilli pepper, two speckled eggs, a sad-looking scallion and the remains of a Cheddar cheese, hardening around the edges.

'Scarlett needs to eat something,' he says.

'I need to drink something. I think I'm in shock.' Maureen manages the walk to the fridge and extracts a bottle of white wine.

'I'm going to make her an omelette. She likes omelettes.'

'I won't have any,' says Maureen, trying to pull the corkscrew from the cork of the bottle, which she has trapped between her knees.

Bryan takes the bottle from her, pulls the cork out, pours her a glass of wine and hands it to her.

'Where's Declan?' he asks.

Maureen allows herself a generous swig of wine before answering. 'He's gone out. With Hugo.' She spits the words out. 'He's never here when I need him.'

Bryan, sensing tears in the wings, wisely decides not to pursue this line of conversation.

'I'm going to bring this up to Scarlett,' he says instead, nodding at the pan, where the safe bits of the chilli pepper and scallion are sautéing in a knob of butter.

I get up from the chair and head for the stairs, stopping when I hear Maureen's next question.

'I wonder what John will do when he finds out?' says Maureen, inserting a cigarette into a long, slender holder.

'John . . . ?'

'Yes. When Scarlett tells him he's going to be a father.'

The step I am standing on creaks like a barn door and I move to the next one and wait. They are still talking; they haven't heard me.

'Oh . . . yes.' Bryan says.

I will him to decide that Maureen has had enough excitement for one evening. To leave the tale of Red Butler for another day. A quieter day.

He does and relief pours through me like rain in a drought.

'I'll make her some tea,' says Bryan, almost to himself. 'With sugar.'

'Scarlett doesn't take tea. Or sugar,' says Maureen, and I can hear the flare of her lighter and her deep breath as she pulls the smoke down inside her.

'She does today. She's had a rough day.'

'Haven't we all?' Maureen says, blowing billows of smoke from her mouth and nostrils at the same time.

'And, Auntie Maureen . . . ?'

Something about Bryan's quiet tone makes Maureen stop examining her nails and look at his face.

'Yes?'

'I . . . I'm not sure you should be smoking around Scarlett any more. I think it might be bad for the baby.'

I stop on the stairs again. I have to hear Maureen's response to this.

'Oh God,' she says, stabbing the cigarette out on an empty plate. 'I'm going to be a granny *and* I can't smoke.'

'You can smoke outside,' says Bryan. I can tell that he is relieved — and surprised — that she hasn't gone into one of her huffs about the smoking. 'And you'll be a fabulous granny. A glamorous one.'

'You think so?' Maureen looks dubious as she opens the kitchen door.

'I know it,' says Bryan, flipping the omelette expertly in the pan until both sides are a fluffy golden brown.

'Mention Helen Mirren, for God's sake,' I whisper to myself.

'Look at Helen Mirren, for God's sake.'

'Is she a granny?' Maureen is suddenly interested.

'Of course she is.' Bryan knows nothing about the familial status of Helen Mirren. Neither do I for that matter. 'And she's fabulous, isn't she?'

'Well . . .' Maureen is coming round.

'And glamorous,' Bryan adds, on the home stretch now.

Maureen looks into the middle distance and I can tell she's imagining herself with a blonde bob and a clipped English accent.

'Tell her she bears more than a passing resemblance to Helen Mirren,' I whisper, staring at the back of Bryan's head, willing him to say it.

'You know,' begins Bryan, and I know he's going for it, 'you're quite alike, you and Helen. Especially around the eyes.'

Maureen tells him not to be so ridiculous and flounces out of the kitchen into the back garden to smoke. I know for a fact that she is examining her reflection in the garage window, paying particular attention to her eyes.

I continue upstairs, where I am met by Blue, who is poised in the landing. I hunker down in front of him. 'Blue,' I whisper, 'I'm sorry for leaving you behind today. I had to.'

Blue is not interested in my attempts at conciliation. He turns his back and lifts his tail,

114

exposing the pale pink cheeks of his bottom. This is his catty way of saying, 'Up yours.' I remember then what the pharmacist said about cats. Instead of lying on the ground beside him and pushing my nose into the soft fur around his neck — as I normally would when he's in one of his moods — I pick him up, holding him at arm's length and run into my room, depositing him in the ancient wardrobe. I turn the key, locking it. Blue is so surprised at this he doesn't even begin howling until I am in bed with my pyjamas on.

★ ★ ★

'What have you done with Blue?' asks Bryan, setting the tray on the bed.

The sight of the food distracts me. I pick up a fork and prod the omelette with it. 'Is there any meat in that?' I ask.

'Sorry. I couldn't find any,' confesses Bryan, tucking a napkin into the neck of my pyjama top.

Another of Blue's howls rent the room.

'I had to put him in there,' I say. 'He might give me or Ellen toxoplasmosis and I could miscarry her or she could be mentally retarded or blind or something awful.'

Bryan hands me a mug of tea. 'Take a drink of that.'

'God, that's gorgeous. How many sugars did you put in it?'

'Three.'

'Oh.' I bend my head to the mug and drain it. I don't say anything until the omelette is gone. I mop the plate with a slice of bread until it's clean enough to be put back into the press.

'Bryan,' I say when there's nothing left to eat or drink, 'what am I going to do?'

'Nothing,' he says, lifting the tray off my lap and placing it gently on the floor.

'But . . .'

'At least not tonight,' he says, tucking the sheets around me so tightly I can barely breathe.

'But . . . but I don't know anything about babies. I don't even know what they eat or what age they're supposed to be when they crawl. Or walk. Or anything.'

'They drink milk,' Bryan says, as if it's as simple as that.

'Yes, but not for ever. I mean, at some point they're supposed to eat something. But I don't know what. Or when. Or . . .'

'Ssshhh,' Bryan says. 'We can find out tomorrow. We can Google it.'

'But . . . but I have to amend my five-year plan . . . again . . . I'm running out of space on the page.'

'You can get another page,' he says, turning off the lamp beside my bed. 'You need to rest now. That's what the doctor said, remember?'

'I was going to have an . . . an abortion.' I make myself say the word.

'But you didn't,' says Bryan, tucking a strand of hair behind my ear.

'Only because I had a miscarriage instead.'

Bryan knows there is no point in disagreeing with me. Especially since I am right. He waits for me to continue.

116

'This morning, I didn't want to have a baby,' I say, almost to myself. 'Now, everything is different and I don't know why. Now, I'm worried about the baby being blind. Or mentally retarded. That doesn't make any sense, does it?' There is a packet of Minstrels poking out of Bryan's shirt pocket and I reach for it and rip it open and eat a fistful of them before even thinking about offering one to Bryan. I can't ever remember feeling so hungry. 'And are you even supposed to say mentally retarded any more? I mean, you don't call blind people blind any more, do you? It's visually impaired, as far as I know.'

'Let's not worry about the political correctness or otherwise of congenital disorders for the moment, OK?' says Bryan, releasing Blue from his wardrobe prison. The cat leaps out, freezes us both with an icy glare and a flick of his long, imperious tail and leaves the room, no doubt for the sanctuary of the hot-press. 'Anyway, you're probably immune to toxoplasmosis by now. Plus, as far as I know, once you keep away from his litter tray and don't let him lick your face, you should be fine.'

We both smile at the thought of Blue licking anyone's face. Scratching maybe. Or hissing. But no public displays of affection. And not many private ones either, come to think of it.

'I wish you hadn't told Sofia.'

'I had to. She was still in the canteen when I went down to tell Filly. She was worried about you. I couldn't not tell her.'

'I have to tell John.'

'And Red . . . eh . . . Butler.'

'He can't be the father.'

'But he could be.'

'Oh Christ, what a mess.'

Bryan puts his hands on my shoulders and waits until I look at him. 'It's going to be OK, Scarlett.'

I do my best to smile at him. His psoriasis tends to play up when he is anxious.

'Of course it is,' I say. But I am not sure of anything any more and it feels like a foreign country, this feeling. Like somewhere I have never been before. It feels like Kazakhstan.

14

I feel a little more myself the next morning. A little less Kazakhstan. A little closer to home. Jersey, maybe. I cup my belly with my hands. Yesterday, there were three of us. Now there are two. And if things had gone according to plan, as they usually do, there would only be one. Just me. I think about the baby that I never knew about. The one I will now never know. I want to make a promise. To Ellen.

'I promise you, Ellen . . . ' I whisper, and then I stop. I don't know what to promise her. I am wary of promises. They are fragile things, promises. Easily broken. Instead, I think about her and I smile, without meaning to. I have about fifty-four other things to think about but I think about Ellen. And smile. And in the half-light of the world between sleeping and waking, I imagine what Ellen might look like and how she might smell and what her first word will be and the weight of her warm baby arms wrapped round my neck.

Then the world comes back into focus, in the guise of Maureen carrying a tray into the bedroom.

'Good morning, darling. How are we feeling today?' Maureen wears what actually looks like a nurse's uniform: a white dress with a navy cardigan and sensible, low-at-heel shoes. She is *in character*.

'I've been to the butcher's,' she explains, setting the tray down on the bed in front of me.

'The *butcher's*?' On a massive full-moon of a plate lies most of a pig, in the form of rashers, sausages, pudding (both colours) and chops. I feel my stomach coming up to meet my throat and I look away and the feeling subsides. 'Thanks, Maureen. But . . . I'm a vegetarian. Remember?'

'Yes, but yesterday . . . '

'That was . . . a momentary lapse. I don't know what came over me.'

'Oh. I thought maybe because of the pregnancy, the doctor might have recommended meat.'

'No.'

Maureen is gearing up to say something. I can read her like a storybook with pictures.

'Scarlett, I — '

'Oh, sorry, I'm going to have to vomit.' In spite of the emptiness of my stomach, I manage to charge to the bathroom and heave what looks like a quart of bile into the yawning mouth of the toilet bowl.

'I think that was morning sickness,' I say, coming back into the bedroom, beaming, like I've just invented time management.

Maureen sets the tray on the floor and pushes it with the point of her shoe under the bed. 'I think I may have sympathetic morning sickness,' she announces, lying one hand across her forehead.

'Here, why don't you get into my bed and I'll go and make you some tea?' I offer.

'Camomile?' Maureen asks, her voice now a sickly whisper.

'Of course.'

'With Sweet'N Low?'

'Two tabs.'

'Thank you, Scarlett,' says Maureen, leaning back against the pillows, her brief experiment with nurturing officially over. 'I'm thinking about getting reddy-gold highlights in my hair, Scarlett. What do you think?'

'Well, I . . . '

'Cyril Sweeney says it would suit me. Says it would bring out the sallowness of my skin. The silly old sausage. Still, worth thinking about, wouldn't you say?'

'What does Dad think?'

'Him? Sure he wouldn't notice if I shaved all my hair off and did a sun dance on top of the dining-room table.'

I wonder briefly what a sun dance is.

I kneel on the floor, reach under the bed and pull the tray back out. I hold my breath when I lift it. It's heavy; there must be about two pounds of meat on the plate. From the bed, a low whine.

'What did you say?' I ask, holding the tray as far away from my body as possible.

'I . . . I'm not sure if I'm ready to be a grandmother,' says Maureen, her face barely visible among the pillows and the sheets she has pulled up around her.

I am unsurprised at this admission. As far as I can tell, Maureen is still not ready to be a mother. I put the tray back on the floor and sit on the edge of the bed. I find Maureen's hand under the bedclothes and hold it, relieved now with my decision not to tell her about the other baby. The one I lost.

'Did you tell Dad?' I ask.

'No, I . . . *Ow*, Scarlett, you're squeezing my hand.'

'Sorry.'

Maureen lifts the injured hand up to her face, blowing on it and flexing her fingers slowly as if she is afraid one of them might be broken. I sit and wait for the scene to end. There is no point in prompting Maureen to tell me anything before she is ready. Maureen gets a cushion, plumps it with her good hand and gently lays the injured one on it before settling herself back against the pillows with a deep sigh.

'I haven't told your father yet,' she says eventually. 'He stayed with Hugo last night.'

'I'll tell him myself,' I say, wondering how Declan will react to the news.

The phone rings then, an old-fashioned *der-ring, der-ring* that is as much a part of the house as the Aga stove and the sash windows.

'I'll get it,' I say, lifting the tray again and moving out of the room. 'I'll bring your tea up in a minute.'

'And some toast, perhaps? I think I could manage a slice or two. With honey on it. And maybe some sliced avocado . . . '

'That's an unusual combination,' I say, walking carefully down the stairs now.

'Sympathetic cravings, I'd say,' Maureen shouts after me, which makes me smile. Although, now I think about it, avocado and honey on toast sound like a marvellous combination and I wonder why I've never considered it before. I reach the phone on the seventh ring. It is Filly.

'How did she take it?' Filly pounces on the conversation like a cat on a mouse.

'Very well, considering. She's got sympathetic symptoms, which are distracting her, thank God.'

'What kind of symptoms?'

'Oh, you know, nausea, cravings, exhaustion, that type of thing.'

'Jesus,' Filly says, exhaling loudly. Even Filly — whose mother describes herself as a 'white witch' in the 'Occupation' box of any form she fills in — knows that Maureen is not what you might call your common-or-garden mother.

'How about you? How are you feeling?'

I sit on the bottom step of the stairs and wrap my dressing gown around me. It is cold in the hall. I think about Filly's question.

'Well, I keep throwing up, even when I haven't eaten anything.'

'That'll be the morning sickness,' says Filly, who is an authority on everything, from tedious tiddlywinks rules to recipes with chickpeas in them, to fluctuating interest rates and their relationship with the cost of the frock in the Coast shop window (although she rarely shops in Coast, preferring to spend her money in Oxfam and Fred's Fashions, where she says she can 'give something back', although really what she should be giving back are the clothes that she buys in these establishments).

'Apart from that, though, I'm fine. Much better than yesterday.' Guilt pushes at me and I shut my eyes against it.

'You know,' says Filly, 'what happened would have happened anyway. Regardless of . . . of anything else.' Filly has joined the dots on my plans yesterday. But she doesn't bring it up. I don't know how I feel about that. Grateful, I think.

'Could Red Butler be the father?' Filly asks.

'Yes.' There is no point dressing it up or down. Not with Filly.

'Or John?'

'Yes.'

'How the hell did this happen?' says Filly, almost to herself.

'I don't know. I've always been so . . . '

'Careful,' Filly supplies, and I agree. 'I mean, you used a condom,' she says. It is a statement rather than a question.

'I'm on the Pill. You know that.'

'With Red, I mean,' she says. 'You must have used a condom then.'

A pause. 'Yes, well, it's just . . . it was all a bit last minute.'

'It's like you're talking about a completely different person,' says Filly, and her voice is a concoction of disbelief and something that could be close to admiration.

'I know,' is all I can say. And then, 'Oh Jesus,' as I try again — and fail again — to come up with a plan that will make things less complicated.

'We'll work it out.' Bryan used that word as

124

well. 'We.' Their concern is like a warm blanket and I wrap it around me.

'How did Sofia take it?' On this point, I am curious.

Filly considers the question. 'Melodramatically,' she says eventually. I think this is an apt response, given the Marzoni women's penchant for drama.

'Does she still want me to plan her wedding?' I squeeze my eyes tightly shut and wait for Filly's response.

'She was talking about postponing it. Till after you come back from maternity leave maybe . . . '

'Postponing her own wedding? Christ, no, we can't let her do that.'

I need this Marzoni wedding. I need this promotion. They will be my D-Day landings. The thing that will go according to plan. And if I lose Sofia Marzoni, I might as well climb up out of the trenches waving a white flag and hand Gladys the job like a head on a plate and there is just *no way* I am going to do that. I simply do not have the capacity for that kind of surrender.

Panic grips me. 'I've got to ring her. Today. Now. Persuade her to go ahead with the wedding. Ellen's not due till October. We could do it in August. The world looks gorgeous in August.' It sounds easy when I say it like that. But I know only too well the trauma of a Marzoni wedding. How it gnaws at you from the inside out until you are a crust of a woman with crazy hair and nails bitten down to the quick. Filly is talking now and I force myself to concentrate.

125

'. . . supposed to be resting. I'll contact her. But not today. She's gone to that board meeting in London.'

'But it's Saturday.' I sound like Duncan now.

'She rang the other directors and postponed it till today.'

'Jesus,' I say, thinking of the disruption that must have caused.

'Yeah, there were directors over from Sicily and they had to stay the night in London.'

'I don't know why she came with me to the hospital. There was no need.'

'She was worried about you. We all were.'

'I'll ring her anyway. Leave an urgent message on her mobile. We need to get this sorted. There's no way I'll get this promotion without that wedding.'

'You're going to get the promotion because you're the best candidate.' God love Filly and her sense of justice. It seems almost quaint, like a china teacup.

'What about Gladys Montgomery?'

'She'll never get that job,' says Filly, loyal as a Labrador.

'She's sleeping with Simon Kavanagh,' I hiss down the phone. 'Elliot says she's great in bed and Simon's a sucker for extramarital sex. You *know* that.'

'She slept with *Elliot*?' I can't believe Filly doesn't know that.

'Years ago. He hadn't slept in three days. It was our first Marzoni wedding and he'd had two glasses of wine on an empty stomach. You know the way he can't hold his drink.'

'Jaysis,' is Filly's response. 'That Gladys, she'd get up on a nettle for a sting, wha?'

I have to agree. The coupling of Elliot and Gladys was akin to an anaconda wrapping itself round a newborn lamb and Elliot had been full to the brim afterwards, with regret and remorse and self-loathing.

'The details of the job went up on the internet,' says Filly. The words squeeze themselves around my heart like a hand.

'Jesus. When?'

'Yesterday.'

'Why didn't you tell me?'

'You had other things on your mind,' she says.

I stand up and grip the banister. I am breathless, like I am running a race where all the runners are so far ahead of me I can't see them. Like I am running with two left feet. In a pair of flip-flops.

'OK, that's it. I'm coming in on Monday.'

'You can't.'

'I have to. I have to get that job, find somewhere to live, book an obstetrician, organise Sofia's wedding and amend my five-year plan. Again.'

'Well, I suppose if that's all you have to do, you could come in for a half-day, then,' says Filly.

'You're making fun of me, aren't you?' I say.

'A little,' Filly admits before she changes the subject. 'I'm thinking of a ball theme for Sofia's wedding. What do you think?'

I consider the idea. 'Have you mentioned it to Sofia?'

'Yeah, I just ran it past her as a possibility. She seems quite keen.'

Relief floods me like a burst dam. The wedding is In Hand. 'What about a venue?'

'Sofia wants a castle. With a moat and a drawbridge and maybe a fire-breathing dragon. She says she's only getting married once and she wants it to be a fairytale wedding.'

'Well, that's what we'll give her,' I say. I resolve to give Sofia Marzoni the wedding of her life. It will be the most fairytale of fairytale weddings. As sweet as a jam doughnut.

'I'll ring Milly and Billy. See if their place is free,' I say, taking my mobile out of my dressing-gown pocket. Lady Margaret and Lord William Wright-Armstrong — Milly and Billy for short — are the owners of Clemantine Castle. I've used it many times and it's got everything Sofia wants. I feel something that might be optimism's distant relative. Then I remember Simon.

'You know how he feels about working mothers,' I say.

Filly's silence is a nod of acquiescence. Working mothers are on Simon's top-three list of 'Things He Hates', the other two being foreign nationals (*spongers, wasters, skivers* are just some of the adjectives he uses) and builders (he recently had his house in Dalkey renovated, not in the two months promised by the contractors but rather over the course of a long, long year during which time he behaved like Margaret Thatcher with PMT).

'I'd better go,' I say. 'Think I may throw up

again.' Also, I can hear Maureen calling from upstairs. In her weak-from-hunger voice.

'I've got a friend who's an airhostess,' Filly says suddenly.

'So?' I ask, wondering if I have missed some vital part of the conversation.

'I'll get her to send me a stack of sick bags. They're dead handy, so they are. You can fit them into your handbag and then you can throw up wherever you like.' Filly sounds pleased with herself.

The doorbell rings then, the sharp noise of it zipping through the hall and making me jump. It might be Declan.

'Filly, I've got to go. Talk to you later, OK?'

'Take care of yourself, Letty.' Filly calls me Letty and I let her. In fairness, I can't stop her. She shortens everything.

'I will. Oh, and Filly . . . ?' I stop, not sure how to say what I want to say.

'It's OK, Letty, I know,' Filly supplies. But I want to say it myself.

'Just . . . just . . . thanks, you know? For yesterday and . . . and everything.'

'Jesus, how hormonal are you? Next you'll be telling me you love me,' says Filly.

There's a sensation at the back of my throat. Like the one people get just before they cry. It feels strange because, you see, I haven't cried since I was six and a half, when my first milk tooth fell out. I put it under my pillow and went to bed straight after dinner, hardly able to wait till morning. I woke at dawn and lifted the corner of the pillow, holding my breath. But there was no shiny silver fifty-pence piece. The bloody stump of the tooth had spotted the sheet with a pale pink hue. The tooth itself was immaculate in its whiteness. I was proud of that tooth. No one told me that you had to tell your parents when you left a tooth under your pillow. And my parents were away, some film festival as far as I remember. It was only George and Phyllis and my imaginary friend (Anne) and me. I left the tooth under the pillow for four nights. On the morning of the fifth day, I picked up the tooth and held it between two of my fingers over the toilet bowl. I waited before I let it drop, perhaps still hoping for something to happen. It sank to the bottom of the bowl, a white speck against the porcelain. I pulled the chain and watched it churn in the water before disappearing. I sat on the edge of the bath. By the time Phyllis called me downstairs for breakfast, I knew. That there was no such thing as a Tooth Fairy. Or Father Christmas. Or the Easter Bunny. Or guardian angels. I knew that there was no magic.

I don't say *I love you*. It's not a thing I say. Not out loud. I blink hard and pinch the end of my nose. It works; I don't cry.

Filly finds her voice at last. 'Now, stop being soppy and get your skinny arse into bed and get some shut-eye.' She hangs up and the doorbell rings again. I see the flamboyant silhouette of one Cyril Sweeney, Esquire, through the dappled glass. I know it is him because of his hat — a bowler — and the cape he favours. He bounds into the hallway

130

when I open the door, like a puppy off a lead.

'Good morning, Scarlett, darling.' He registers me with a deep bow from the waist and I can hear bones creaking in his hips as he straightens. 'I simply must speak with Maureen. I bring *tidings*.'

'Of great joy?' I can't help asking.

'Well, not joyful exactly. No. Certainly not.' He drops his voice to a stage whisper and leans towards me. 'It's Olwyn Burke,' he hisses. 'She's been taken ill.'

There is a shriek from above and Maureen appears at the top of the stairs, still in her dressing gown but now with a full face of make-up. 'How ill?' she shouts down the stairs.

This year's Amateur Dramatic Society's main production is *Romeo and Juliet: The Musical* — or *Romeo and Juliet Lite*, if you like. Maureen has landed the plum role of understudy for the part of Juliet's nurse. Olwyn Burke got the actual role but, because Olwyn is inclined to 'suffer with her nerves', as Phyllis puts it, Maureen harbours great hopes of getting to play the part. She is an optimist, as irrepressible as a rubber ball.

'Oh, darling, it's terrible. Truly terrible.' Cyril arranges his face into a suitably sorrowful expression. 'You know how that magazine *Country Homes and Garden Gnomes* were supposed to be covering her annual garden fete?'

'Yes, of course I know,' says Maureen impatiently.

'Well,' says Cyril, drawing himself up to his full height — five feet eight inches in his cowboy boots, which have a sly wedge heel. 'They've only gone and cancelled on her.' He pauses for dramatic effect. Maureen and I wait for him to continue. We know there is more to the story. Even I find myself holding my breath, although, in fairness, Cyril can spin a good yarn. 'She's taken it very badly,' Cyril says.

'How badly?' Maureen wants to know.

Cyril looks around the hallway before replying. 'She's gone into St John of Gods. For a rest, Maurice says.' Maurice is Olwyn Burke's long-suffering husband. A skin-and-bone used-to-be-a-man type of a man. A saint, in my opinion.

Maureen covers her face with her hands — no doubt to hide a jaw-cracking smile — and gives a little shriek of pure joy scantily disguised as upset. 'How long will she be kept in?'

'Maurice didn't know but a few weeks at least, he thinks. He seems relieved, to be honest with you. Says she's been very agitated recently and could do with a good rest.'

I want to guffaw — as Cyril would say — when I hear this. If anyone can do with a rest, it is Maurice and I picture him, sitting on the couch in the drawing room, as Olwyn calls it, feet — still in shoes — up on a pouf, football on the box, can of lager in one hand — not even poured into a glass — remote control in the other and a grease-stained brown-paper bag full of chips balancing on his belly.

'So we need to get to work, my darling,' Cyril is saying to Maureen. 'Get dressed now like a good girl and we'll work in the study. Declan's

132

not here, is he?' He peers behind the curtains at the front door as if Declan might be crouched behind them.

'No, he's down at Hugo's, I think,' says Maureen. 'Rehearsing for that audition thingamajig. We have the whole place to ourselves,' and do I imagine it or is there a coquettish note in Maureen's voice now? I glance up the stairs to remind my mother that her daughter — i.e. me — will be here but Maureen has gone, although I can hear her in the bedroom, pulling out drawers and emptying the contents of her jewellery box and dragging boxes of shoes out from under the bed and generally dismantling the place in a bid to gather a suitable ensemble.

'Are you going out, Scarlett, darling?' Cyril asks with an indecent amount of hope in his tone.

'Eh, no, but I'll be upstairs mostly,' I tell him.

'Oh good,' says Cyril, heading for the study. 'I mean, it's good that you're following doctor's orders and getting enough rest. Maureen told me about your . . . eh . . . *condition*.' He makes it sound as if I have contracted a fatal strain of genital herpes and I wish — and not for the first time — that Maureen was a little more discreet. A little more like Bryan's mother and less . . . well . . . less like herself.

I make tea and toast (there are neither avocados nor honey in the kitchen), and climb back up the stairs. I meet Maureen on the landing.

'Oh, thanks, darling, I'm absolutely famished. Must be all the stress, what with you and now poor Olwyn.' She shovels a piece of toast — which I have cut up into soldiers — into her mouth and waits until she swallows it before speaking again. 'Scarlett, darling, could you possibly arrange for a bunch of flowers to be sent to the hospital for Olwyn? Just say, 'To my darling Olwyn, all good wishes for a speedy recovery. Lots of love, your dear friend Maureen O'Hara. Kisskisskisskiss.' OK?'

My mother is already halfway down the stairs, followed by a long piece of silk the colour of an angry sunset, which is looped round her neck. As she descends, she sings the play's finale song, 'Love Is All Around Us', interspersed with great bites of toast and slugs of tea.

I think about going back down to the kitchen to make more tea and toast but the cloying trail of Maureen's perfume (her trademark Femme Fatale) has dulled my appetite and leaves me feeling lightheaded. I head instead for my bedroom, stopping to check that Blue is still sulking in the hot-press, which he is. He turns his head from me when I open the door and doesn't even look round when I place three of his favourite cat biscuits on the stack of towels beside him. I know he'll deign to eat them just as soon as I close the hot-press door. Back in my room, I phone the local florist and organise the flowers for Olwyn, fill a hot-water bottle, check my phone for messages — none — and sit on the edge of the bed, wondering what to do next. I know I won't sleep but I think I might lie down for a few minutes. Maybe rest my eyes. I pull the covers over my head the way Blue does. And then a strange thing happens. Maybe it's because of Ellen. Or the warmth of the hot-water bottle pressed against my belly. Or maybe it's just because it's the daytime and not the night, when I usually conduct my game of hide and seek with the elusive sleep. Whatever it is, I am asleep in seconds and, for the first time in a long time, I sleep a deep and dreamless sleep and don't even wake up when Cyril and Maureen begin practising their version of the can-can and knock over and break the standard lamp — a monstrosity of a thing — in the hallway.

15

By the time I get round to thinking about telling Declan, it is the following day, at dinnertime, when Declan returns from Hugo's house for a change of clothes, a hot shower and some food that isn't either takeout Indian curry or sandwiches (Hugo does a mean cheese-and-onion toastie but its tastiness has diminished over the years in direct proportion to the regularity with which Hugo serves it). Hugo also has a dreadful habit of forgetting to pay his electricity bill (and gas bill and phone bill) so the house is often cold and dark and soundless when the utility companies eventually disconnect him from their various services.

'I've run you a warm bath,' I tell Declan, who stands shivering beside the Aga. 'Here's a glass of brandy to bring with you. It'll warm you up. Oh, and I've made a vegetable lasagne. It'll be ready in twenty minutes.' When Declan doesn't respond, I stop what I am doing (emptying the dishwasher, setting the table and changing the voice message on my mobile phone) and glance towards my father.

'Shouldn't we be taking care of you now?' he says. 'For a change?'

He looks straight at me, not moving and not speaking, just looking at me with a kind of tenderness that makes him seem older, a little jaded. I know at once that he knows.

'Who told you?'

'Harry Fields.'

'Who told him?'

'Sally-Anne Campbell.'

'Who told her?'

'Michelle Wellington-Smythe.'

'Who told her?'

'Angelica Sweeney.'

'Kerr-ist,' I say, sinking into a chair. I can join the dots from there. Gossip seeps from Cyril Sweeney's pores like sweat. And as for Maureen, well, they don't call her Loose-Lips O'Hara for nothing.

'Don't worry, you'll be yesterday's news by tomorrow.'

We both know that's not true. Roskerry depends on the O'Haras to provide entertainment; we are like Roskerry's personal PlayStation that way.

'What did John say?'

'I haven't told him yet.'

Declan moves towards me then and pauses before reaching over and patting me on the shoulder. It is an awkward gesture, Declan unsure of himself in this new role. 'It'll all work out in the end,' he says, like this is one of the hundreds of films he has worked on where happy endings are expected and delivered, despite all evidence to the contrary in real life.

'How do you feel about being a . . . a grandfather?' I am curious on this point.

Declan gives it due consideration. 'Actually,' he says, 'not bad. Not bad at all.' He looks into the middle distance and I know he is picturing himself in a huge rocking chair with a pipe and one of those watches that hangs from a gold chain and lives in the silky folds of a breast pocket in a waistcoat. 'I'll have to get one of those sterilisers,' he says, almost to himself.

'Oh . . . right,' I say, wondering what he needs a steriliser for. Still, at least he is thinking in practical terms.

There is a silence in the kitchen. But it's a companionable one. Warm and a little fuzzy around the edges. And in the silence, I feel I might be able to tell my father about the other baby. The one I lost. And maybe about Red Butler. And the litany of disasters that have followed me like a litter of kittens since John left. I go so far as to imagine he might have some kind of solution. A fatherly solution that I can grip, like a lifebelt.

But then Declan turns on the gas hob to light a cigarette, bends towards the blue flame and sets fire to his fringe. Because it isn't the first time he has done this, I know exactly what to do. I smother his head in the throw that drapes across the back of the sofa in the corner of the kitchen and push him towards the sink, where I douse him with cold water, ignoring his strangled yelps and howls. Then I sit him in a chair and trim the charred bits of his hair off. In the end, I have to cut off most of his fringe. His forehead looks exposed and vulnerable without the protection of the fringe but, otherwise, he is fine.

The moment, however, is gone. As gone as Declan's fringe but, unlike Declan's hair, I doubt it will return. In fact, I wonder if it had ever been there at all.

'Go on,' I say. 'Have a quick dip. Dinner in fifteen minutes, OK?'

In fairness to Declan, he does have the wherewithal to look a little shame-faced. He holds the icepack I give him up to his forehead and backs slowly out of the kitchen. 'Where's your mother?'

'She's having a lie-down. Herself and Cyril have been practising for the past few hours and she's tired.' In fact, Maureen declares herself 'morbidly exhausted' and I have to help her up the stairs. It takes the pair of us ten minutes to remove all of her accessories, clear the layers of discarded clothes from her bed and find the eye-patches that Maureen insists on wearing when she is going for one of her daytime snoozes.

Declan does not reappear in the kitchen that evening and I assume he has forgotten about his dinner and gone to bed instead. It wouldn't be the first time. I dish up two bowls of lasagne — one for myself and one for Blue, who descends the stairs when he smells dinner. We sit on the couch in the den in a relatively companionable silence. Blue hasn't quite for-given me for the wardrobe incident but he is not one to cut off his nose to spite his face.

Besides, he loves my lasagne.

Even though there's no meat in it.

It's the roasted peppers that do it for him.

He loves roasted peppers.

16

I last two more days at my parents' house before I finally crack and flee to the relative sanctuary of my office.

'But you're supposed to be resting,' says Bryan the night before, when I tell him about my plans to return to work.

I switch my phone from one ear to the other and look around before speaking again. 'I'll get more fecking rest in the office than I will here,' I say.

'Speak up,' says Bryan. 'I can't hear you. What *is* that noise?'

I don't want to tell him that Declan and Maureen are in the sunken bath just off their bedroom. Declan is helping Maureen to learn her lines for *Romeo and Juliet: The Musical* and the scene they are practising involves lots of shouting and swearing and that, coupled with the drone of the Jacuzzi jets and the clinking of glasses — they are drinking champagne — merge to complete the cacophony of sound that is the upstairs of the house this evening. The situation is not helped by Blue, who sits outside the bathroom door, howling. He loves the heat generated by the Jacuzzi, seemingly oblivious to the effect the steam has on his fur, giving him a sort of a Three Degrees look.

'Oh, it's the television. I'll turn it down.' I stretch out a leg and close my bedroom door.

'Anyway, it's best if I keep busy,' I say, sitting back down on the bed. Here, all I have to do is organise Maureen and Declan and, even though it is a time-consuming task, it is not time-consuming *enough* and leaves plenty of room in my head to worry about everything else.'

'But you need to give yourself time,' insists Bryan. 'To come to terms with everything that's happened.'

'I am . . . I have . . . I . . . This is my way of coping, Bryan. You know that.'

'Yes,' he says. 'But how are you feeling? Physically, I mean?'

I consider the question. 'Apart from the nausea and the vomiting and the tiredness, pretty good, actually.'

The conversation is interrupted by Maureen. 'Scarlett, darling, we've run out of champagne and we're still working in the bath. Could you possibly . . . ?'

'I have to go, Bryan. Thanks for ringing.'

'I'll phone you tomorrow,' he says, before hanging up.

In the kitchen, I uncork a bottle of champagne, wash and slice some strawberries and spread Brie over most of a packet of crackers. For soakage.

'What time are we having dinner?' I ask, keeping my eyes averted as I set the tray on the bathroom floor. I'm interested to hear what they might say.

There is a shocked pause.

'Oh . . . well . . . I . . . ' Maureen is too taken aback to string a sentence together.

'Let's go out,' shouts Declan over the noise of the water in the bathroom. It is his staple answer to most things.

'You guys go ahead. I'll make myself a sandwich and have an early night,' I tell them. 'I'm going back to work tomorrow.'

'That's nice, dear,' says Maureen.

'Don't overdo it, will you?' says Declan, before returning to the script. 'Now, what do you think your character's motivation is here? In this scene?'

'Declan, I'm delighted you brought that up because I . . . ' and on and on and on and on they go, each more delighted than the other that they have a part they can play, a script they can read from, a director to tell them where to stand and when to sit and how to look. That is much easier than having a real life and they hug it to them like an old friend.

17

Going back to work feels like the first day of school all over again. I vomit this morning, just like I did all those years ago. Although I don't ask Phyllis and George to pretend to be my parents, like I did all those years ago. My parents were away — some film festival or other — and Phyllis and George both came to school with me that day.

I arrive even earlier than usual so not even the security guards have clocked on yet.

But I don't count on Elliot, who is also an insomniac and sometimes comes to the office when he has exhausted all other avenues, like counting hens (he says sheep just don't do it for him), reading the more obscure entries in *The Guinness Book of Records*, watching old episodes of *Little House on the Prairie* and drinking pint glasses full of cranberry juice with slices of lime.

He is in the kitchen, stirring chocolate powder into a mug of warm milk and humming 'You Raise Me Up' under his breath. When he sees me, he lets his spoon fall into the sink with a clatter. His hands fly to his mouth and his eyes widen. 'Scarlett, thank Christ you're OK.' Then he bears down on me and before I can say, 'Gerroffme,' he is hugging me so tightly that it hurts, on account of his skinny frame, all angles and bones. Also, he's so tall that my face is crushed against one of the buttons on his shirt and I know I'll have a red circular welt on my forehead for the rest of the morning. It's like being hugged by a stick insect. Still, Elliot hugs everybody. Even the male populace of the company, if they let him, which they mostly do.

Now Elliot pushes me away from him, holding me at arm's length. He scans my face with the anxiety of a parent checking a child for bumps and bruises after a heady fall from a pogo stick.

'Filly told us what happened.'

I kick myself for not providing Filly with a specific ailment instead of giving her carte blanche to make up anything she liked, forgetting — with the day that was in it — Filly's fertile imagination and her weakness for a good story.

'Well, I'm much better now, thanks,' I say, coaxing the healthiest smile I can manage on to my face.

'What do you mean, you're much better now?' Elliot's eyes are dinner plates of horror. 'Sit down, sit down. I'll make you a proper cup of tea. None of your flowery muck today.' He steers me into the least uncomfortable chair in the kitchen. I allow myself to be manoeuvred. It is easier that way. He throws two teabags into my cup and splashes boiling water on top of them. His hair, cut like Cian's from Westlife, is cocaine white. 'Drink that down, like a good girl,' he says, like I'm six. 'I've put four sugars into it and I don't want to hear a word about it. You need it, with the shock you've had, do you hear me?'

I nod. I need a lot more than sugary tea but I

suppose it's a start.

'Did the doctor give you the all-clear?'

'The all-clear . . . ?'

'Of course not. What am I talking about?' His face oozes sympathy.

My mind races.

Flu. Why didn't Filly tell them I had good old common-or-garden flu? Or measles. Or temporary blindness. A twenty-four-hour strain of it. Or acute dizziness brought on by a virulent ear infection. Something plausible. Something I could work with.

Elliot sets the cup on the table in front of me. He stirs it so vigorously the spoon rotates a further 360 degrees round the cup by itself before it settles — spent — against the lip.

'Thanks,' I say. I wrap my hands around the cup and wait for him to fill me in on what's the matter with me.

'It happened to a friend of mine. It took him six months to get the all-clear.' He shakes his head from side to side at the unfairness of it all.

'Yes, well, the initial prognosis is good so the doctor is very optimistic,' I say.

This seems to be appropriate because Elliot nods his head up and down several times. 'Yes, of course. I'm sure there's nothing to worry about. And you were so brave, defending yourself like that. Stupid of course. But brave too. Although, knowing you, you're probably a black belt.'

Jesus Christ, I'll kill Filly. And I'm *not* a black belt. I only made it to purple belt and that was a long time ago.

'Elliot, do you mind if we don't talk about it

145

just now?' I feel bad, not telling him. I will tell him. Just not now. Not yet.

Elliot, as sweet as the tea in my cup, apologises and changes the subject. 'I suppose you'll be wanting to talk about work then?'

I nod.

His sigh is resigned. 'So, where are we on Sofia Marzoni?' he asks.

'She's on board. She's coming in for a meeting next week.'

Elliot blesses himself. 'God help us all,' he says with his eyes closed.

'Look,' I say, leaning towards him and patting his knee. 'We've done four of them already, haven't we? I mean, how much worse can this one be, right?'

Elliot looks at me, worried. 'Christ,' he says, standing up.

'Maybe you got a bang on the head,' he says. 'During the . . . melee, I mean.'

The melee?

'I'm just trying to be optimistic,' I say, standing up.

Elliot shakes his head, more worried now. 'You see?' he says. 'That's not like you at all. Cautiously realistic, maybe. But *optimistic*? That's crazy talk.'

'I didn't say I was *actually* optimistic,' I remind him. 'I said, I'm *trying* to be optimistic. That's not the same thing at all.'

'I suppose not,' says Elliot, studying my face carefully like it's the menu at Kashmiri's Indian Food Emporium, which is his favourite restaurant in the world.

I smile at him. Not a huge smile. A discreet, barely there smile. I don't want to send him over the edge.

'Now,' I say, 'let's talk about the wedding-fair roadshow.'

'Oh, OK,' says Elliot, looking more bored than worried now. 'Where are we on the invitations?'

'Sent. Oh, and your mother has promised to bring Matt Henshaw of the *Independent* to the launch. She says he owes her one since she swung him an invite into Enya's castle. And he's promised to give it loads of coverage.' I take another gulp of tea and stand up, on surer ground now. 'And it's Simon's birthday tomorrow. I got you two bottles of his favourite wine. Don't wrap them or get him a card. Just give him the booze.'

'So it looks like I'm thoughtful but not lick-arsey?'

'Exactly.'

'What will I do without you?'

'Without me?'

'When you get the promotion. Or set up your own company. Or get poached by the Americans. *Damn* those Yankee Doodles.' Elliot hates America and Americans. He particularly hates the names they give their food. Like Twinkies. And Tatter Tots. And Hershey bars. He refuses to say the word Snickers, even though he loves those bars. He insists on calling them Marathons, despite the fact that the Polish twenty-something behind the shop counter on the corner has no idea what he means. He has to point.

'I'm not going anywhere,' I say. Not that

147

there haven't been offers. But I like where I work. I know how everything works and where everything is. I never have to ask questions. I like that.

'Promise?' Elliot inspects my fingers when I promise. To make sure that I'm not crossing them. If you cross them, it negates the promise, he tells me. I've never heard of that but he swears it's true. I hold my hands out with my fingers splayed. Before he even asks me, I ease my feet out of their shoes so he can see my uncrossed toes (the nulling and voiding of promises works equally well with crossed toes, apparently).

'Any word on when the interviews for the new position will be?' I ask.

'There's no need for you to worry about that. You'll get the job. You know you will.' Elliot sighs at the inevitability of it all. Except it's not inevitable.

'What about Gladys? She's still sleeping with Simon, isn't she?'

'Yes, of course. Sure, it's only early March. But Simon is very busy with that pan-European thing he's working on at the moment. I'd say the interviews won't happen until April and the affair will be long over by then. You know that.'

I nod slowly. In theory the affair should die of natural causes by the end of March, notwithstanding Gladys's attempts to resuscitate it, by fair means or foul. But I remember the look that passed between them at the meeting. Nothing about the look suggested that the affair was about to get the last rites or was even in ill health.

148

I drain the last of my tea. 'So, can I go back to work now?' I ask.

'What'll I do?' he asks.

'Well, you could work on the departmental budget forecast for the next quarter,' I say. 'Simon wants it in by the next board meeting.'

Elliot looks sorry that he asked the question now.

'The thought of it is much worse than actually doing it,' I say.

'You always say that,' he says.

'That's because it's true.'

'Can we not stay here and talk about Simon's sticky-out ears?' he asks in a last-ditch effort to avoid the budget forecasts, which he hates, although he is very good at them. Also, he loves talking about Simon's ears and, while I have to concede that you *could* hang a coat and umbrella off them, they're not a subject I've given much thought to.

'Can we talk about them tomorrow?' I say, backing out of the room.

'And what happened to you?' he asks.

'Yes,' I say.

'Do you promise to tell me everything?'

I nod at him.

'Even the bit about the police chase?'

The police chase?

I nod and smile and continue to back away. I can smile because I'm thinking about what I'm going to do to Filly when I see her. I've been watching *The Tudors* lately. Although lowering her into a vat of boiling oil seems messy and an awful lot of work.

18

Filly arrives with her usual 'Goodmorningsorry I'mlate', two skinny lattes, a bacon-and-egg McMuffin (for her) and a red-berry smoothie (for me).

I lean forward in my chair. 'What did you tell Elliot?'

'Tell Elliot? What? When?' She is buying time and we both know it. I do my stare. Filly does her best but folds quickly. Nobody can beat me in a staring contest.

'Oh, you mean . . . ' she eventually says.

'Yes, that.'

'Because you asked me to, remember?'

'I asked you to tell him I was *sick*,' I say. Blue stirs in his sleep and we both look at him till we are sure he has settled again. I lower my voice. 'Why didn't you tell them I had non-fatal cholera or a twenty-four-hour dose of malaria, like a normal person? And what's the story with the bloody *police chase*?' We both look again at Blue but this time he doesn't stir. In fact, he is snoring now.

'Well, I . . . '

'What the hell did you tell him?'

'Just that you were mugged and stuck with a syringe by a druggie and you had to go to hospital and get tested for HIV and hepatitis and, you know, other diseases.'

'Oh dear, sweet Jesus.'

'On the plus side, the police got the mugger,' Filly adds with a small smile that she thinks is helpful. It is not.

'Where did I get mugged?'

'Outside the flat. In Clontarf. On Friday morning.'

A daylight mugging by a drug-crazed spotty youth outside one of the most exclusive apartment developments in Clontarf? The Residents' Association will be up in arms.

Filly has the grace to look sheepish. 'Sorry, Scarlett. It was the best I could come up with under the circumstances.' Without her smile, Filly doesn't look as Australian as usual, even though she is wearing a T-shirt with a picture of two koala bears in a tree — I look closer — mating, I think. With her head bowed and her tiny hands wrapped around the coffee cup, she is *impossible* to be mad with.

'Who else knows about it?' I ask, holding my breath.

Filly fidgets before answering and my shoulders slump. 'Well, we had to tell Simon . . .'

'*Simon?*'

'Yes, he was looking for you. Something about the promotion . . .'

'*The promotion?*'

'Calm down. He says it'll wait till you come back, and he's not expecting you back till next week. That's what we told him.'

'Oh Christ,' I say, worrying at a loose thread on the hem of my skirt. 'So Gladys knows?'

'I'd say that's a fair assumption, yes,' says Filly.

'I suppose it could be worse,' I say in a vain

attempt to find relief where there is none. 'I suppose Eloise and Lucille could know. They'd spread it like a bush fire in the fecking outback.'

Filly doesn't nod and smile like she normally does whenever anyone mentions anything Australian. Instead, she chews the nail on her thumb and doesn't quite meet my eye.

'Filly . . . ?'

'Well . . . ' she begins, bending her face into the yawning rim of her coffee cup.

'There's no coffee in that cup,' I remind her.

She returns the cup to the desk. 'Eloise and Lucille know,' she whispers.

I think about the implications of this.

'I'm sorry, Scarlett, but they were looking for you. You haven't submitted your expenses for last month and you didn't respond to their emails and it's so unlike you they came looking for you.'

'You could have just told them I was on sick leave,' I say.

'I did. But they couldn't believe you were sick again so soon after . . . you know . . . the day after the Red Butler night . . . Anyway, they went to Elliot's office to ask after you and Gladys happened to be there and she told them.'

'They couldn't possibly believe that cock-and-bull story you concocted.'

'They do. They all do,' Filly assures me. 'They presumed you were a black belt in karate and I had to tell them you were only got to purple. Sorry about that.'

And they do believe it. Every time someone stops me to ask how I am, they cup my elbow with the palm of their hand and lean close to me

152

and all I can see is their concern and it's so real even I begin to believe it could be true. The bit they have trouble with is the capture of the mugger by the Garda Síochána.

'And the police *got* the guy who did it?' asks Terri from Marketing.

'You mean to say the guards actually *arrested* the mugger?' enquires Magda from Finance.

Even Hailey, the receptionist — has something to say. 'Welcome back, Scarlett,' she says when she rings me with the first of my calls. I'm too surprised to respond. Hailey *never* small-talks. In fact, apart from saying things like, 'Eamon MacLochlainn on line four,' she hardly speaks at all. She is originally from Hertfordshire but, apart from that, nobody knows the slightest thing about her, even though she's worked at the company for ten years.

'I can't believe they apprehended the perpetrator,' she continues. 'Will you have to identify him in a line-up?'

A line-up? Christ. I hadn't thought of that. 'Um, I . . . ' I begin.

'Forgive me, Scarlett, it's none of my business.'

'No, it's . . . '

'Eamon MacLochlainn on line four for you.' Hailey resumes her clipped tones and the conversation closes like a door.

But, in typical office gossip fashion, the subject has exhausted itself by lunchtime and my colleagues revert to normal conversations, like bargain-basement dentists in the north of Ireland, non-surgical facelifts, a free parking

153

space that someone has discovered behind Christchurch Cathedral, how many calories a segment of Terry's Chocolate Orange has and Duncan's lazy eye.

By the time Filly comes into my office at — I check my watch — 4.37 p.m., I have already been to two meetings, chaired a conference call, replied to 105 of my 197 emails, taken two phone calls from Hysterical Hilda — a WAG who is getting married in four months to a footballer ten years her junior and is *hysterical* about it — and rearranged the books on my shelf in alphabetical order by author, rather than by publication date, which is how I'd arranged them before.

Filly sets a packet of Fruit Pastilles on the desk. 'I've colour-coded them,' she says, 'just the way you like them.'

I peel the foil back from the tube of sweets. The yellows are at the top, followed by orange, red, green and then black, my favourites. I push the packet away.

'What am I going to do, Filly?' I say and my voice is a whisper, the words trapped between my fingers, which I hold against my face.

Elliot picks that moment to breeze into my office and perch on the edge of my desk. He always sits here, never on the chair or the couch. It's his way of keeping on his toes.

'Why are you panting?' Filly asks him.

'I ran all the way from my office,' he says, bending over with his hands on his knees, heaving like he's just finished a marathon. A proper man-marathon. It's exactly 12.25 metres from Elliot's office to mine. He is not a fan of physical exercise, preferring instead to watch yoga videos, ideally with a bottle of wine, which he has learned to balance on his head while sitting cross-legged in pinstripes on the deep, soft pile in his living room.

'Now,' he says when he catches his breath, 'I thought I might find you two in here so I've taken the opportunity to bring a bottle of wine and some Bombay mix so we can celebrate Scarlett's safe passage back to us.' He doles out paper cups, opens the bag of Bombay mix and fixes me with his toothy smile. When I don't smile back, he looks at his watch. 'Aw, Scarlett, it's practically five o'clock. Time to down tools, clock out, yeah?'

The smell of the Bombay mix is all over me, like smoke. It's in my hair and on my face and running down my clothes. My stomach rises like an elevator and there's nothing for it but to reach for the bin. The noise I make is guttural. I keep going even though it's the paper bin. The vomit is the colour of a red-berry smoothie.

'Jesus,' says Elliot when I finally finish.

Filly hands me a tissue, opens the window and puts the Bombay mix outside on the windowsill.

'Elliot, I . . . ' My tongue feels swollen and it's difficult to get the words out.

'Oh Christ, you're dying, aren't you?' he says, standing up, his body rigid. 'Oh Jesus, it's not bird flu, is it?'

'No, but I — '

'Because if you are, Scarlett, you can tell me. I can take it.'

155

'She's *not* dying,' says Filly, handing Elliot a tissue too, which he uses to dab delicately at the corner of his eyes, bright with tears. Filly looks at me, asking the question without saying anything and I nod. I'm too tired to do anything else. 'Scarlett is pregnant,' Filly says.

Elliot's eyes widen until they're like saucers in his face.

'And she doesn't know who the father is,' finishes Filly, who likes everything to be open and transparent.

'But . . . but . . . but . . . ' begins Elliot, and for a while it seems like he can't say anything else. 'But . . . you've only ever slept with three and a half men,' Elliot says. 'In your Entire Life.'

I nod at him. This is true. I count Jerry O'Rourke as a half because we stopped — abruptly — halfway through when his father — who was supposed to be in Dubai on a business trip — got an earlier flight home and decided to surprise his family. In fairness, it was Jerry who got the biggest surprise of all that day and my shame was one of Blue's farts after a box of After Eights: lingering and hard to forget. It was my first time and I was eighteen and three-quarters.

Elliot fills one of the paper cups with wine and drains it. Then he picks up the bin — the paper bin — with one hand, holding it as far from himself as he can, and places it in the corridor outside. He closes the door and leans against it, as if he might collapse at any moment.

'Start from the beginning and tell me everything,' he says.

I take a breath and begin. 'I was drunk,' I say.

Elliot's mouth gapes open and he turns to Filly, who nods. 'She was, Elliot. Proper drunk. Like Duncan-at-the-Christmas-party kind of drunk.'

'Jesus,' is all that Elliot can say. He allows himself a moment to digest this before he turns back to me. 'Go on,' he says warily, folding himself into the couch like a stepladder. It's the first time I've seen him sitting anywhere in my office other than on the edge of the desk and I watch as he stacks cushions between himself and Blue so the cat doesn't notice this invasion of what he regards as his territory. Of course, Blue *does* notice. But he pretends not to. He remains still, his ears cocked, as if he too wants an account of events. Some kind of explanation that will make everything clear.

'So,' I say, 'I was drunk.'

'You already said that,' Elliot points out.

I'm aware of this. But it is the only explanation I have. The only defence that makes any sense. Because the thing that happened never happens. Not to people like me. It was after John rang. When I'd stopped waiting for him to ring. We were in a club. A nightclub, I mean. I insisted we come and Filly didn't argue.

'Where are you? I thought you were coming home.' John sounded worried.

'I sought you were going to shtay with me for the resht of my life.' I regret lots of things about that night and that line is one of them.

'Come home,' John said, like he really wanted me to. 'We need to talk.' I remember the hope

157

that rose in me then like a mountain spring. I later learned that when you're that drunk, you're often unrealistically optimistic.

'What about? Have you changed your mind?'

'Well, no, but I'd still like to talk things through with you. Make you understand.'

'If you hadn't kissed me, none of this would have happened,' Filly says, bringing me back to the here and now.

'You *asked* me to,' I say.

'You *kissed* Filly,' says Elliot, leaning so far forward that I think he might topple off his perch on the couch.

'There were two men,' I say. 'Badgering Filly. And I knew she wanted rid of them. Her nose was twitching. You know the way it does when she's uncomfortable?' I look at Elliot and he nods. He knows about the twitching nose.

'They were talking about this threesome they'd had in Thailand,' says Filly, her nose twitching madly now with the memory.

'Why didn't you just tell them you weren't interested?' Elliot asked, even though he knows why.

'You *know* why,' Filly reminds him. 'I couldn't be rude to them. It's entirely at odds with my Australian nature. You know that.'

'So you kissed her?' Elliot asks me, anxious to get back to the main action.

'Yes.'

'Like . . . a proper kiss type of kiss?' Elliot asks.

'Well . . . I . . . '

'It was nearly as good as one of Brendan's kisses,' says Filly. 'I think I even closed my eyes.'

158

'Gosh,' says Elliot after a while. 'But what does that have to do with . . . you know . . . everything else?'

'The barman saw us,' I say.

'Red Butler,' supplies Filly like she can't help herself.

'But that's not his real name,' I add, as if this might help.

'What's his real name?'

'I don't know,' I have to admit, and Elliot looks at me like he has no idea who I am. 'Filly told him about the threesome conversation and we got talking and then he asked me for twenty-three euros sixty-five for the drinks and I had no money left and the laser card machine was down and he said I could dance with him instead.'

'You danced with a barman for *drinks*?' Elliot says, and the way he says it — out loud — makes it sound so much worse than it really was.

I turn to Filly. 'If you had just paid for the drinks . . . '

'I didn't have any money, remember?'

'You did. You had that twenty euros. You paid for the taxi to your house, remember?'

Filly pretends not to hear me.

'Anyway, we danced and then we kissed and then one thing led to another and — '

'Wait, wait. Hold up there,' says Elliot, pulling his hands up like he's reining in a difficult horse. 'Who kissed who?' Elliot always insists that the devil is in the detail.

'We just sort of . . . I don't really remember. Just one minute we were dancing and the next we were kissing each other. I was *drunk*, I keep telling you.'

But I do remember. And the memory is so clear it hurts to look at it. I think about the space between us. About a foot. Twelve inches. Maybe ten. I want it to be less. I think about his breath. I can feel it against my hair. He smells like coconut: hairy and sweet. The palms of my hands are clammy and I wonder if he can feel the heat of them through his T-shirt. I concentrate on the chandelier over his right shoulder. I count backwards, from ten, in Irish. I think about pension funds. I mentally rearrange my wardrobe in season order, subdivided by colour and fabric. But somewhere along the line of these thoughts, my resolve stumbles and I look up and the noise of the club falls away and the space between us measures about three inches. No. Exactly three inches. Or 7.6 centimetres. I close the gap and kiss him. I who have never made the first move in my life. I who have kissed *exactly* nine people. Well, ten if I include Filly. I kiss him and I remember every single detail. I remember my reflection in his eyes when he pulls away. I barely recognise myself. And when I grab his hand and walk off the dance floor, he follows me. I move without thinking. Without weighing up the pros and cons. Without registering that this is not in The Plan. And it feels outrageous and fantastic and terrible all at the same time.

A sense of abandon.

I've heard about it. And it feels so real. Like I've abandoned my former self. Even now, in my mind's eye, I can see her, standing alone on the

160

dance floor, looking at me with such bewilderment. Her arms are suspended in the air, in the shape of Red Butler, who has left her, in mid-dance. Her mouth forms the letter 'o' and she is wondering how to leave the dance floor without drawing attention to herself.

Abandon is a wonderful facility really and I wonder, as I trip along, dragging Red Butler behind me, gripping his hand, how I've gotten so far without it. I don't know where I'm going but abandon allows me not to care. We pass Filly but I don't even notice her sitting at the bar with her mouth hanging open. There is a door on the other side of the bar. A heavy black one. With a sign that reads, 'Staff only.' I head towards it. There is a part of me that knows once I step through that door, there is no turning back. Abandon sees off any uncertainty I might feel and I step through the door, sensing a room rather than seeing it. The lock slides back into place behind me and the music thumps like a fist on the other side of the door. Hands reach for me and we move deeper into the room until I feel a wall against my back. Except it isn't a wall. It is a stack of crates. Even the seediness of that isn't enough to stop me.

I remember a song, 'We Are the Angry Mob', the beat of it straining against the black door as if it is trying to get in. I remember the clink of the empty bottles in the crates, shuddering each time we move. I remember a plant on a table, its long, treacherous spikes slicing through the dark.

But mostly it is the abandon I remember. The taste of it — exotic and sharp, like limes. How

161

alien it feels. How exhilarating. The pulsing pleasure of it. I give myself up to it. I bite into it like an apple. I never close my eyes. I don't want to miss a thing.

Now, standing here in my office, even though I omit most of the detail and stick to the bald facts, it still registers as a pretty sordid story and Elliot lists dangerously to one side as if he is about to capsize.

When he finds his voice, he says, 'So you didn't get mugged?'

I shake my head.

'Or stuck with a needle?'

Another shake. Smaller this time.

'I don't know why I believed that cock-and-bull story in the first place,' Elliot says. 'I mean, once Filly used the word 'apprehended', I should have known it was a stack of lies.'

'I didn't say 'apprehended',' says Filly, stung. 'I'd never use a word like that.'

'You did,' Elliot insists. 'You said the guards 'apprehended' the mugger. I heard you saying it. You did.'

'Look,' I interrupt, standing up in an effort to get their attention, 'we're getting off the point. There was no mugger, apprehended or otherwise. Filly made that up because I was in hospital.'

Elliot leaps to his feet. 'I *knew* it,' he says. 'You *are* dying, aren't you? Oh Christ. But what about the baby? Will you be able to deliver it before you . . . ? Oh, Scarlett, I . . . '

'I. AM. NOT. DYING.' I shout that bit, loud enough for Duncan — struggling with a

162

pineapple in the kitchen at the top of the corridor — to crouch behind the fridge with pineapple juice dripping off his knife, which he holds like a dagger in his fist.

Elliot's face is a mix of relief and shock: I never shout. It's only when I sit back down I realise my legs are shaking. 'Elliot, I'm so sorry,' I say and my voice is hoarse, like I've been shouting all afternoon. 'It's just . . . I . . . I had . . . There were two of them. Two babies. I lost one.'

'Oh, Scarlett.' Elliot moves towards me.

'Don't,' I say, warding him off with my hands. 'Don't say anything kind.' I feel that feeling again. The squeezing feeling at the back of my throat.

Elliot returns to the couch and worries at the cuticle on his thumbnail. Filly drains her paper cup of wine and refills it. I pretend to hunt through my desk for something, even though I know where everything is. I do it until the squeezing at the back of my throat abates.

'So,' Elliot says at last. 'What's the plan?' He smiles at me; he knows this is a foolproof way of cheering me up. But this is the worst bit.

'I don't have one,' I whisper. I've heard about rock bottom. It feels even worse than it sounds.

'You don't have a plan yet,' says Filly.

'Sure it's early days,' chips in Elliot. 'Plenty of time to come up with one.' But his face, clouded in confusion, betrays him. He can't believe I don't have a plan. Neither can I. And despite Filly's optimistic use of the word 'yet', neither can she.

'The thing is . . . ' I begin, and Filly and Elliot's heads snap up like elastic.

'Yes?' says Filly, holding her breath.

'Go on,' says Elliot, removing his thumb from his mouth.

'Well, I want to have this baby.' This is the one thing I am sure of and I hold on to it like a cliff ledge. 'But I want her to have a proper family. You know what I mean. A mother. And a father. Who are there a lot of the time. And a proper home with the fire lit on a cold day and things to eat when she gets home from school. Ready to eat, I mean. Maybe soup. Something hot . . . '

'You could live in the suburbs,' Filly puts in. 'They have gardens in the suburbs. Children love gardens.'

'She can have all that,' says Elliot, standing up and assuming his thinking position, striding up and down the office with his hands held loosely behind his back.

'How?'

'All you have to do is tell John about the baby,' says Elliot, smiling now.

'He'll be back proposing marriage and looking at semi-Ds before you can say, '*Indiana Jones and the Temple of Doom.*''

Something about the way Elliot says it makes me strain with hope. He sounds so certain.

'How can you be so sure of that?' I ask.

'A couple of things,' says Elliot, on a roll now. 'First of all, there's his overinflated sense of duty.'

I nod slowly. This is true. His sense of duty is

swollen, like an overactive thyroid gland. At least, it used to be.

'Secondly,' Elliot goes on, getting into his stride now, 'there's the not-insignificant fact of the undoubted midlife crisis in which he is mired. He's forty-five; his mother died last year; he's worked for the same company for the last twenty years. He's a pristine example of a male midlife crisis. I can't believe you can't see it.'

I think about this for a moment. I've been so busy getting on with things that I haven't allowed myself to consider the question *why*. But maybe Elliot is right. Maybe John's leave-taking was more about him and less about me.

'John Smith is only *dying* for an opportunity to come back,' says Elliot, driving home his advantage. 'I'd bet Valentino Marzoni's fortune on it. I'd say he's weeping in his sandpit every night, thinking about you and his job and creamy pints of Guinness and Aer Lingus airhostesses with their big green smiles and their dark brown foundation.

'Then why hasn't he?' I ask.

'Why hasn't he what?'

'Come home.'

'Because, my dear Scarlett,' says Elliot, shaking his head at me indulgently, 'he doesn't want to admit — to himself or anyone else — that he's made a terrible mistake. Pride comes a close second to his ginormous sense of duty. You *know* all this. This is elementary stuff.'

I feel like I'm halfway over a hurdle. All I have to do is get my legs in position so I can hit the ground running. John would make a great father.

165

I know he would. He would be someone Ellen could rely on. In time, we could laugh at his short stint in Brazil. We could do some couples counselling to get over the hump. His face will stain with embarrassment when he explains to the counsellor about his mother and his job and his age. And I'll forgive him. Of course I will. And Ellen will have a mother. And a father. And a house in the suburbs. And a kitten. I'll get her her own kitten and Blue won't mind. Not at all . . .

'Eh, aren't we forgetting something?'

I look up from my planner, which I have opened on a blank page. I was just about to line the page with the ruler Filly bought me that says, 'There are no rules.'

Filly stands up and walks up to my desk. 'What about Red Butler?' she asks. I steady myself. For the first time in days, I feel hope. I grip it with both hands. I am not going to let it go.

'He was a mistake,' I say.

'But he could be Ellen's father.' Filly's persistence is usually something I admire.

'He's not,' I say, and suddenly I am convinced that I am right. 'I was careful' — I am almost ninety-six per cent certain of this — 'and everything was so . . . rushed and . . . it was just that one time.'

'But . . . ' begins Filly.

'John is Ellen's father,' I say, and my voice is so clear, so certain. I wonder how I could ever have doubted it.

'But . . . ' says Filly again.

'And I need to get him back,' I say, standing up now and facing her. 'For Ellen. Will you help me?' I look at her and I will her to be on my side. On our side, mine and Ellen's.

Filly opens her mouth to say something and closes it again. She shakes her head but then she looks at me and nods. A tiny nod but it is enough. I close my eyes and feel the relief flood through me until I am full with it. I am back on track. It's a slightly different track to the one I'm used to but it's a track all the same. All I need to do is keep running until I reach the finish line.

19

Even though I have a plan now, it feels precarious, like a china cup balanced on my head. One false move and it will fall and smash into a million pieces that no amount of superglue will fix. Tonight, I can't sleep. Not my usual brand of insomnia. This is an extra layer of sleeplessness that happens the night before one of my weddings or before one of Maureen's string of auditions at the local Amateur Dramatic Society. I have to wait till morning to ring John. He's better in the morning. I look at my watch. Another five hours until the alarm goes off. I reach for my planner and find an empty page. I flesh out possible dialogues, changing certain key words and phrases so I am prepared for all eventualities. I work out how long he's been gone — six weeks and three days — and drag an image of him into my mind. He is wearing a suit. I picture him digging. He is still wearing a suit, which I know is ridiculous but my mind won't put a pair of shorts and a T-shirt on him. I picture him with a baby sling strapped across his chest. The jacket of his suit crumples and creases under the straps.

I look at my watch. It's the middle of the night in Brazil too, although morning will come sooner there. John will have slept through the night as he always does. He attributes this to the fact that he only allows himself one cup of coffee per day, no tea or cola. He never really understood my insomnia. I admit that. He Googled it, of course. And presented me with myriad remedies, all of which I'd tried before. But I tried them again. For him. I think he might have taken it personally that none of them ever worked.

I turn to a new page and draw a line down the centre of it. 'Things I miss about John Smith,' I write at the top of one of the columns. I chew the top of my pen and count the intervals between Maureen's snores. Ten seconds. I cross out the word 'miss' and insert 'like' instead:

tidy
organised
loves cats
great sense of duty
sensible
brilliant at chess, Sudoku, Scrabble
early riser.

I put the top of my pen back in my mouth and worry at it with my teeth. I think about things I dislike about John Smith. But really, there is only one entry to be made in the right-hand column on the page: 'He left me.'

I remember the start of our last conversation. He said, 'Are you happy?' and I said, 'Yes.' I was happy. I definitely wasn't *un*happy.

'I'm not.' He spoke quietly but the words dug into me like a spade.

'Why not?'

'I'm forty-five.'

'I'm thirty-five. So what?'

169

'We don't have any kids.'

'We don't want kids.'

'We're not married.'

'That's because we don't believe in the institution of marriage. It's a sham that'll more than likely end in divorce and/or infidelity and/or excessive boredom directly leading to the loss of the will to live.' This was our mission statement. We both signed up to it.

'Yes, I know that but . . . ' John bent his head into his hands and sighed a sigh that would lift the leaves off a tree.

I moved towards him. His breath was warm with a hint of peppermint. He was close enough to kiss.

'What is it, John?'

'Everything seems so negative. We don't want to get married. We don't want to have children. I want to want something. I want to believe in something.'

Now, I close my notebook and try lying down. I turn the pillow over and press my cheek against the soft coolness of it. I look at my watch, the hands a luminous, alien green, John bought it for me for my thirty-third birthday. So you can see in the dark, he'd said.

Another four hours. I close my eyes and think about Ellen. I colour her in like a picture. Blue eyes, like John's. Blonde hair. Skin that is sallow and soft. The pink of her nails. The milk-white of her teeth, gappy when she smiles.

When I open my eyes again, it is morning-time and the alarm is ringing.

170

*   *   *

At the office, I close my door and pull the blinds. I pick up the phone, dial his number in Brazil. I know he will answer on the fourth ring. That's when he always answers. I don't know why but, in this current flux, it feels reassuring. Like something I can depend on. The phone answers after three rings and I nearly drop it.

'Jes?' someone says. Not a John Smith type of someone. A female someone. A woman.

'Eh . . .' I say.

'Jes?' she says again, and now I detect a note of impatience. A hot-blooded Latin-type impatience.

I clear my throat. 'Eh . . . is John there? John Smith?'

'Juan? Juan eh-Smith?' she says.

'This *is* his phone, isn't it?' I say, and now there is a note of impatience in my voice. A red-hot poker of impatience.

'Juan ees in shower. Zis ees Lolita. I will get him call-a you back? What ees name, please?'

'Eh . . . Scarlett. Scarlett O'Hara.' There is the traditional silence after I produce the response.

'Like moo-fees?' she says, and her voice is low and throaty and belongs to your basic nightmare. '*Go Wid-a zee Wind?*'

'Just tell him Scarlett rang,' I say, and I hang up without waiting for her to say anything else in her ridiculously sexy voice.

My phone rings immediately. 'Well?' says Filly.

'How did you . . . ?'

'I'm in the office,' she says, like it's nothing.

171

I check my watch. It's 8.07 a.m. The only time Filly has been in the office at this time was the all-nighter we pulled back in 2005, when Nanny McFee (real name Nancy but she had an unfortunate mole on the end of her nose) gave us a week's notice to organise her wedding. She'd finally found 'The One' after years in the desert and wanted to seal the deal before he could change his mind.

'A woman called Lolita answered his phone.'

A pause at Filly's end.

'Oh well, maybe he was down a hole or something. You know, digging or whatnot.'

'He was in the shower.'

'Oh.' When even Filly cannot think a positive spin to put on a situation, that's about as bad as things can get.

20

John rings me back and I am in a meeting. I ring him back and leave a message on his voicemail. He rings me back and I am cutting Elliot's hair in my office and don't make it to the phone on time. Elliot only ever wants millimetres trimmed off the ends of his hair and his hairdresser refuses to cut such minute strands so he gets me to do it for him. Unfortunately, I appear to have a flair for hair-cutting so I get to do it every six weeks. The word has spread and now Duncan gets me to give him a quick trim if he has to attend an event after work and hasn't booked his hairdresser (one of the best in the city with a waiting list as long as the summer solstice).

I ring John back and the phone rings out. I am *exhausted* with all the ringing and re-ringing. Eventually, I text him and wonder why I never thought of doing this before. Although John and I were never big texters. We preferred short, succinct phone calls in which everything is covered in under thirty seconds: no confusion, no smiley faces, no calloused thumbs.

So I text: 'I need to talk to you. Can you let me know when is a good time (GMT) to ring?'

And I wait.

It takes him less than a minute to respond.

'Will ring at 11 p.m. (GMT) tonight if that suits?'

The message startles me because there, right at the end of the message, is a smiley face. A proper one with the smile curling up towards the edges of the eyes. The eyes crinkle into slits with the intensity of the smile. That's how smiley the smiley face is.

I ring Bryan immediately.

'Well?' he says.

'John is ringing me tonight,' I say. 'At eleven o'clock Greenwich Mean Time.'

'That's good,' says Bryan.

'I suppose,' I say.

'There's more, isn't there?' says Bryan. 'What is it?'

'He texted me.'

'Only because you texted him first. Be fair.'

'He put a smiley face at the end of the message.'

'A smiley face?' Bryan's voice goes up an octave, which it does when he is taken by surprise.

'Yes.'

'Well, look,' begins Bryan, 'at least it's not a crying face, or one of those ones with the tongue sticking out, or a red, angry face, right?'

'I suppose,' I say again.

'Do you want me to come over tonight? Give you a bit of moral support?' he asks.

'I thought you were going out with Gráinne tonight?

'She dumped me.'

'I thought it was going well. You've been on three dates, haven't you?'

'Yes, but . . . '

'What happened?'

'I think it was my ringtone that drove her away.'

'Is it . . . ?'

'Yeah, still Phyllis singing the theme song from *Watership Down*.'

'What did she say?'

'She said it was *nice*.'

'Oh.'

'So I can come over, if you like.'

'Thanks, Bryan, but it's OK. I can manage. I was just a bit concerned, that's all. When I saw the smiley face. It's so unlike him.'

'Maybe he's changed,' suggests Bryan. 'For the better, I mean. Getting more in touch with his feelings and that.'

'Let's talk about something else,' I say.

'How are you feeling?' he asks.

'My symptoms this week include two nosebleeds, a gumbleed and heartburn after I eat Rancheros.'

'All perfectly normal,' Bryan says, and I can hear the pride in his voice. Like I'm his star pupil. 'Although I didn't think you liked Rancheros.'

'I didn't,' I say, opening my top drawer, where I keep my stash of them now. I take out a bag. 'And insomnia,' I add.

'But you always have that,' Bryan says.

'Yes, but now there's a proper reason for it,' I say. I like it when there's a reasonable explanation for things.

I promise to ring him in the morning with an account of my conversation with John. We say goodbye and hang up.

I check my watch. It's 2.32 p.m. (GMT). Eight hours and twenty-eight minutes to go before I speak to John and tell him about the baby. His baby. Maybe. Probably.

21

The phone rings at exactly 11 p.m. (GMT). I am sitting in the kitchen with my feet on the Aga, trying to coax Blue on to my lap to warm me and give me comfort. He resists my efforts and crouches instead outside a tiny hole in the skirting board where once — about fifteen years ago — a mouse appeared. Blue never caught that mouse and has never seen another one coming out of that hole since but that doesn't stop him lying in wait. He is hopeful. I love that about him.

I am alone in the kitchen. I have put my mother to bed with a hot-water bottle, a glass of wine, her eye-patches, slices of cucumber and the box set of *Dallas*. Or *Dynasty*. I can't remember which. Declan is attempting some DIY in the garage. At least, I think that's what he's doing. I can hear the bang of a hammer along with some agonised roars when the hammer hits his fingernail instead of the actual nail. George is tucked in the gate lodge as he always is, probably dreaming about Phyllis. He's been sweet on her since as long ago as I can remember but, being a shy and retiring individual, he's never worked up the nerve to tell her, and Phyllis — who has had her share of *suitors* over the years — has never seemed to guess at George's feelings for her.

I let the phone ring three times before

answering it. I don't want him to think that I'm sitting here waiting for his call. Even though that is exactly what I am doing.

I clear my throat.

I pick up the phone.

I take a deep breath.

And then I say, 'Hello?'

'Hello, Scarlett,' he says, and his voice is exactly the same as I remember it and that surprises me even though I know it shouldn't. For a moment, with the familiarity of his voice all around me, it's like the last few weeks haven't happened and he's just at the office, working late, ringing to let me know he'll be home in thirty minutes, asking me to switch on his side of the electric blanket.

'John,' I say. 'Thanks for calling.'

'Not at all,' he says, and now we are two strangers in a room having a random conversation at a party neither of us wants to be at. I grip the phone with both hands and wonder where I will start. He speaks first. 'I'm glad you rang,' he says.

'You are?' I hadn't considered that possibility.

'Yes. I . . . I thought about calling you myself but . . . I didn't know . . . I wasn't sure . . . '

'What's the weather like?' I ask, and then I pinch my upper arm. Hard. I don't care what the weather is like in Brazil. John, however, seems relieved at this break in the conversation. He talks about the weather. At length. The general gist is that it's hot.

Afterwards, there is silence, like the silence in a storm just before the thunder rumbles. Full of bristling electricity. It is John who puts an end to it. 'Why did you ring me?' he asks with his traditional abruptness. It's not that he's curt. He's just not good at conversations on the telephone.

'Something has happened,' I manage to say.

'Something bad?' he says in his matter-of-fact voice, and I can almost hear him bracing.

'Well . . . ' I seem to be faltering at every hurdle down the length of this conversation. I'm not quite sure how to categorise this. If you were to write down the bald facts of the matter and present them to him on a plain white page, it might *appear* bad. But Ellen doesn't feel like something bad. She feels like someone good. I consult the lines of dialogue in my planner. Nothing I wrote last night seems appropriate now.

I close the book with a snap.

'I'm pregnant.'

In the quietness of the kitchen, the words sound so distinct and clear. Even Blue looks up from the tiny hole in the skirting board and looks at me with his knowing eyes before resuming his watch.

John doesn't say anything. I feel the miles between us stretch and stretch, like a road through a desert.

Eventually he speaks. 'I wasn't expecting that,' he says.

'What were you expecting?' I am curious.

'I don't know. I thought maybe you wanted to arrange for Blue to visit Pythagoras and Newton.'

It's true that Blue did share an apartment with John's two cats for three and a half years. He mostly ignored them. When he had to acknowledge their existence, it was with a weary tolerance rather than any sort of affection. Perhaps absence has tainted John's memories of Blue.

'Where are they staying?' I can't believe I haven't given this any consideration until now.

'With my brother and his wife in Kildare. They live in a loft with two cows and a goat.' For a moment, I think he's talking about his brother and sister-in-law living in the loft with the cows and the goat.

'Oh,' I say.

'I don't understand how this happened,' says John after a while. 'We've always been so careful.'

'Well, it *has* happened,' I remind him, and the tension of the day appears in my voice, like cracks across a sheet of glass.

'Although,' he says, as if I haven't said anything at all, 'I do remember you had an upset stomach shortly before I . . . before my flight left.'

I remember now. I had a bad case of diarrhoea, although John is too polite to say so. Just as he is too polite to mention the fact that he left. Rather it was a flight that left. And he just happened to be on it.

'Diarrhoea,' I say, and I feel John's distaste down the phone and I am glad, even though there is nothing to be gained from it.

'An upset stomach,' he says again. 'That could have an impact on the effectiveness or otherwise of the contraceptive pill. I'll Google it.' Silence again.

'So,' I begin. 'How do you . . . you know . . . feel about it?' This is a new departure for us. We are not a couple who have conversations like this. At least, we weren't.

'I'll come home, of course,' is what he says.

'Will you?' I can't believe how easy it is. If John ever thought to ask *me* how I felt, I wouldn't know how to answer him.

'Of course,' he says again with the quiet certainty he has. 'But I have to stay here until the end of July. I told them I would and . . . '

'Of course you must stay,' I tell him. 'The baby's not due till October.' For some reason, I don't tell him her name. Not yet.

'I'm not expecting you and me to get back together or anything like that,' I say, my words falling over each other in their hurry. 'I just wanted you to know. I knew that you'd want to know.'

'I'm glad you told me,' he says.

'You are?'

'Yes.'

'There's more I need to tell you,' I say. I close my eyes when I say this and take a breath, not sure where to begin.

'I'm sorry, Scarlett, I'm going to have to go now. The battery on my phone is nearly dead and I have to get to work. I was supposed to be off duty tonight but Miguel and Lolita ate undercooked burritos this afternoon and the pair of them are ill . . . '

Lolita. That name again. I check myself to see

181

how I feel. Nothing. Not even delight that she has been struck down with undercooked-burrito poisoning. John is still talking.

' . . . so I have to fill in. My shift starts in five minutes. I don't want to be late.' John has never been late for anything in his life — except for his birth. He was nineteen days late for that.

'Well, there's just one other thing . . . '

'What is it?' I can hear him waiting for me to answer, twitching with impatience the way he does when he's in danger of being late. The curtain closes on what I had been trying to gather the courage to say. And I know there will be no encores. This is not a subject that can be rushed. It's probably a conversation that we should have face to face, I tell myself. *Coward*, my head whispers down to my heart.

'It doesn't matter,' I say. 'It'll keep.' I cross my fingers and toes when I say this. 'Take care, John.'

'Goodbye, Scarlett.' The line clicks and he is gone and I picture him, with his back ramrod straight and his face closed and unreadable, walking under a sky studded with a thousand stars with the heat of the day wrapped around him. He won't stop walking until he reaches his destination and then he'll pick up a chisel or a hammer or a spade or a knife and fork or whatever they use for whatever they're doing and he'll start work and he won't stop until he's supposed to.

22

I am late for work the next day on account of Maureen parking her car across the garage door so that I couldn't get mine out, which wouldn't have been much of a problem had she not lost her car keys. I found them eventually, behind the washing machine in the back kitchen, but the search took longer than it usually does.

So when I arrive, Filly and Elliot are already in my office. They stand up when I open the door.

'What did he say?' they both ask at the same time, like they've rehearsed it.

Blue gets a fright, squirms from my arms and makes a break for the door, disappearing down the corridor, probably heading to the canteen to make nice with the dinner ladies and score some leftover rashers.

'Did he ring?' asks Filly, reaching me in four of her tiny strides.

'Yes.'

'Did you tell him about Ellen?' asks Elliot, who looks like he got less sleep than usual, with his baggy eyes and his pale skin stretched across his face.

'Yes.'

'What did he say?'

'He says he'll come home,' and I have to stop there as Elliot and Filly do a triumphant dance about the room, yelling and cheering and clapping each other's backs. I can hear Elliot sing, 'I told you he would,' to the tune of 'You Raise Me Up' and punching the air with his fist.

Nobody says a word about Red Butler and, with the carnival atmosphere in the room, I don't bring it up. Besides, what is there to say?

'OK,' I say eventually, when it becomes clear that the singing and the dancing and the air-punching is going to run and run. Elliot and Filly sway a little before they are able to come to a full stop, like children who have spent too long turning and turning with arms outstretched on a patch of grass. They look at me.

'I need to get some work done now,' I tell them.

They look at each other. 'She's back,' they say.

I nod and smile at them as they gather themselves together and leave the office with promises to return at lunchtime.

For the first time in a long time, I am able to concentrate on work. I am expecting Sofia Marzoni in the morning and I need to sound as though I've given her impending nuptials the attention she expects.

I try not to think about the last time I saw her. It feels like something that happened long ago, to a different person.

I hunker down and bend my head to the work.

I am back.

It feels good to be back.

23

'Sofia Marzoni is downstairs in reception.' Filly's head curls round the door of the office.

My head snaps up from between my knees.

'She's early,' I manage to say, before removing a Tupperware container from my top drawer and vomiting neatly into it. The sickbags from Filly's airhostess friend have not yet materialised. I replace the lid and return the container to its place in the drawer, sliding it closed and wiping my mouth with a tissue.

'That's pretty vile, Letty,' says Filly.

'I know. But it happens so suddenly. It's not like ordinary vomiting. I'll never make it to the loo on time and, even if I do, everyone will know by lunchtime, what with Eloise and Lucille. They're always in the loos. Must be those figs they put in their porridge or something.'

'It's very distracting. Knowing there's a container of your vomit in the top drawer. You used to keep the paper-punch I gave you in there.'

'I still have it,' I say. 'I've just moved it to the second drawer.' I slide the drawer open to show her. The punch is in the shape of the Sydney Opera House and bears the colours of the Australian flag. I slot my head back between my knees. Filly recommends this position. Then again, she also recommends ginger and anti-nausea bands and Jacobs cream crackers and nettle soup, all of which have done nothing other than make me vomit all the more.

Filly has become used to speaking to the rounded dome of my upper back.

'Will I send them up?'

'Them?' I clench my stomach muscles and visualise myself not throwing up. I have tried this a couple of times over the last few days and find it as successful as the ginger and the wrist bands and the crackers and the nettle soup.

'Here,' says Filly, dipping the ends of my fingers into a glass of cold water. 'This will help.'

'All that does is make me want to pee.' I lift my fingers out of the glass and lick them, forgetting that water is one of the things I can't hold down. Water and everything else. Except — curiously — broccoli. 'Look, will I bring Sofia and himself up or what?'

'OK,' I say in a voice as weak as the tea you get in France.

'You're going to have to sit up,' says Filly. She is using her *determined* voice. She comes round to my side of the desk and I reach for the Tupperware container.

'I asked you not to use Persil any more,' I say. 'The smell of it makes me sick.'

'But the smell of everything makes you sick,' Filly says, not unreasonably.

'Yes, but Persil in particular. Please, Filly? It's just for the next few weeks. I should be fine after that.'

'OK, then,' Filly says. 'I'll check with Brendan. See what brand he's using.' Brendan has what I believe is a bit of a laundry fetish. He is always at

186

it, practically whipping the clothes off Filly's back as soon as she is in the door and feeding them into the machine, whether they need a wash or not.

'Thanks,' I manage before heaving over the container again. It is nearly full now. I look at Filly, using the same expression that Blue uses when he wants me to empty his litter tray, which George does now. According to Blue's vet and our family doctor, Ellen will be fine so long as I keep away from the litter tray.

'No way.' Filly backs away with both hands up as if I am pointing a gun at her, rather than a Tupperware container full of vomit.

'But you're her godmother,' I whimper.

'That's low,' says Filly.

'I know,' I agree.

Filly takes the container, wincing at the warmth of it against her fingers. 'Promise me you'll do the same for me when my time comes.'

I nod. Luckily, my stomach is finally empty and there is nothing but the terrible, hollow sound of dry retching, which makes even Filly blanch a little.

'I'll empty this and go and get them,' says Filly, heading for the door. She holds the container as far away from herself as she can without spilling it.

I lower my head towards my knees.

'For God's sake, go and brush your teeth and do something about this office. It smells like a rough ferry crossing in here,' Filly says before she leaves.

I lift my head, nod at Filly and then, when she is gone, I assume the position.

'And for the love of Christ, slap some make-up on your mug. You'd make a three-day corpse look healthy.' Filly returns briefly to issue this directive before disappearing again.

I barely make it to the ladies' before I throw up the water I'd licked from my fingers in the office one and a half minutes before. After that I feel a little better. Well enough to be able to examine my face in the mirror above the sink. Alert enough now to notice the vomit stain on the lapel of my jacket. I am too tired even to rub it away. My arms feel like heavy chains that I cannot lift. I know for a fact that if I lie down on the cold floor with its unforgiving ceramic tiles, I'd be asleep in seconds.

I fish a compact out of my bag, take a breath and open it. The smell is like dead slugs. Decomposing. On a hot day. Still, it is either that or someone will give me mouth-to-mouth resuscitation. I don't even look like death warmed up. More like congealed, cold death that has been left on a plate for three days.

The arrival of Gladys Montgomery into the ladies' is just one more thing to be miserable about.

'Scarlett, you look terrible. Are you still ill?' Gladys asks in a voice that suggests she hopes I *am* ill and that it is nothing too minor.

She locks herself into one of the cubicles before I have time to answer and begins to pee, long and loud. She is one of those people who can hold a conversation and pee at the same time.

'Sofia Marzoni's in your office waiting for you.'

'Is she?' I look at my watch. I can't believe I've been in here for nearly ten minutes.

'Yes. You should hurry up. The Marzonis don't like to be kept waiting, you know.' Gladys speaks loudly so that I can hear her over the torrent of urine. She pees like a donkey. Then she farts, a high-pitched squeaky fart followed by a little moan of satisfaction, as if there is nobody here but her.

I limp back up the corridor towards my office. I am limping because I stubbed my toe against the base of the toilet in my hurry to reach it and throw up earlier. I feel hot. My jacket is draped over my arm, the puke stain on the lapel carefully hidden from view. I can hear voices coming from my office. Sofia's voice, loud and guttural, Filly's voice, high and fast, and then a third voice. A man's voice. A gin-and-cigarettes voice. Some people might call it sexy. The soft slap of my shoes against the thick carpet in the corridor falters and then stops completely. I am ten feet from the door of the office.

'Ah, Scarlett, there you are.' Filly speaks in a jovial voice as she steps out into the corridor. Closing the door behind her, she adds, in a low hiss, 'What the fuck kept you? Get your vomit-ridden arse in here. Sofia is here with her fiancé — Daniel something or other — and she's getting antsy.'

'His voice . . . it sounds familiar. I . . . '

'We don't have time for chats Scarlett. *Come on.*'

I move towards the door.

Filly falls in behind me.

24

'Howaya, Scarlah? You look like a bucket of magnolia paint, so you do.' I am barely over the threshold of the office door when Sofia engulfs me in a panda bear of a hug. I surrender myself to the hug, mostly because there is nothing else to be done with it. Through the thicket of her dark hair, I see nothing.

'Jaysis, there's a smell of puke off you, Scarlah. Is it the mornin' sickness or wha?'

'Morning sickness?' says a voice.

Sofia releases me from her vice grip and turns round. 'I'd nearly forgotten you were there, so I did. Scarlah, this is Daniel Butler, me fiancé.' She moves aside so that I get the full force of him, like a blow to the head. Sofia's voice is a tank, rolling over me. 'Everyone calls him Red,' she says. 'Red, this is Scarlah O'Hara, the weddin' planner. Scarlah is expectin' a babby.' Sofia delivers the news in the same way a paperboy delivers his papers. She throws it, not looking. It soars in the air, rolling and twisting, and lands at Red Butler's feet. He doesn't pick it up. In fact, he doesn't do anything other than stand there with his mouth hanging open. I can do nothing but stare back at him.

'I *thought* you looked familiar,' says Filly.

'So your name really is Scarlett O'Hara?' says Red, and I can't believe it but he is smiling at me. Like nothing happened. Like his fiancée

191

isn't standing a foot away from him — I look closer — holding his traitorous hand.

Sofia looks from me to him and back again, like a tennis umpire at Wimbledon. 'You two know each other?'

'No,' I say.

'Yes,' says Red, at the same time.

'Well, I mean . . . what I mean is that we don't *know* each other as such,' I say in a rush. 'I . . . That is, we . . . myself and Filly . . . we met him in a . . . the place where he works . . . one night.'

'Oh, you mean the Love Shack?' supplies Sofia. 'Yeah, he works there sometimes. Just fillin' in, like. But he's really an actor. Did he tell you that?'

'Um, no. No, he didn't,' I manage.

'Very unassumin', so he is,' says Sofia, beaming at Red.

He smiles back at her. I study the smile. It is warm. Genuine. With not a trace of apprehension about it. Like he thinks — no, he *knows* — he has gotten away with it. I fight an urge to wrestle him to the ground and beat him to a pulp with one of Filly's stilettos. If Blue were here, he would help me scratch his eyes out. But Blue is in reception with Hailey, who has insisted on hand-knitting him a winter coat; it's his first fitting.

Sofia is speaking again and it takes everything I have to wrest myself away from these murderous thoughts and at least look like I'm listening to her.

'Jaysis, Scarlah, I hope you don't mind me

tellin' him,' she says, nodding towards Red with her trusting smile, 'but he's me fiancé — I tell him everything, so I do.'

I know I should say something but I can't think of a single thing.

It is Filly who rescues us in the end. 'Who would like a nice cup of tea and a chocolate Kimberley?' she asks. This is genius. This will give me the space I need to gather my wits about me. In my experience, no one has ever refused a chocolate Kimberley. I'm not sure it can be done. But the plan backfires.

'I'll come with you, so I will,' says Sofia, heading for the one place in the room I can't allow her to go: the door.

'No. Wait.' I make a grab for her. 'Eh, Filly can manage on her own, can't you, Filly?'

Filly nods but Sofia looks worried. 'I'm very peculiar about me tea, so I am. Two and two-thirds spoons of demerara sugar and the teabags have to be left in the cup until after the milk has been stirred in. And then there's the *crucial* bit.' She stops so we can ask her.

Filly obliges. 'What's the *crucial* bit?' she asks.

'You pour the water over the teabags *just before the kettle boils.*' She simulates the pouring of water into an imaginary mug to demonstrate. 'The only person who can do it right besides me is Red.'

I cast around, desperate not to be left alone in the room with him.

'Don't worry, Scarlah, I won't be long,' says Sofia. 'You can make nice with Red while we're gone. He's only lovely, so he is.' She ruffles his hair, smiles at him and is gone.

Filly pulls her face into an apology and sets off at a trot, after Sofia. The door clicks shut and we are alone. I can't get behind my desk quick enough and, once I'm safely installed, I peck furiously at the keyboard, opening a new file in the database.

'D-A-N-I-E-L B-U-T-L-E-R.' I spell the name out loud as I type the letters with two fingers. My contact with the keys is perhaps a little heavier than normal, my fingers perhaps a little more rigid. But nothing really noticeable. Nothing unprofessional.

'And your date of birth?' I say this without looking up, concentrating instead on the computer screen.

Red stands in front of me, his hands flat on the desk. I glance at them. I remember them.

'Scarlett,' he says, and waits.

I double-click on his name, delete it and begin to type the letters again.

'Yes?' I'm still typing. Random numbers now. Into the DOB field.

He moves to the window, blocking most of the light. 'Look, Scarlett,' he says, and then a pause and I hear him fiddling with the zip on his jacket. Pulling it up and then down again, the metal teeth jangling against my nerves. 'I know this is awkward for you and I'm really sorry. I just — '

I have to stop him there. The anger, simmering until now, suddenly comes to the boil. I stop typing and snap the lid of my laptop closed. 'Awkward for *me*?' I say. 'What about you? And your *fiancée*?' I spit the word out. I can't believe how angry I am. I am breathless with it.

'I'm sorry,' he says again. 'I didn't know you were going to be here.'

'How on earth did you not know I was going to be here? This is my bloody office.'

'Well, I know, it's just . . . '

'What? Sofia didn't tell you? She tells everyone everything. You should know that, being her *fiancé*.'

'No,' says Red. 'I mean yes. She did tell me. But I presumed . . . that night in the bar . . . I just thought . . . you know . . . ' He trails off. 'The thing is, I didn't think that Scarlett O'Hara was your real name.'

I look at him then. Everything is as I remember. The red hair, roaring and uncompromising, sticking up and out from the top of his head like a haystack. The St Patrick's Day green of his eyes. The general air of untidiness. Of carelessness.

'I know how this must look,' says Red, diving into the silence. 'But . . . ' He stops there and I can see him trying and failing to come up with some kind of explanation that will make the situation seem less . . . less . . .

'Squalid,' Sofia announces, flinging open the office door and marching inside. 'That's what it is, Filly. Four across. Squalid.'

The tea trolley rattles as Filly pushes it over the saddleboard with one hand, the other holding a folded newspaper in front of her face. 'Oh, yeah, you're right,' she says, peering at the paper.

'And then 'infidelity' will fit perfectly in seven down,' says Sofia, settling herself on the couch with an enormous mug of tea and three chocolate Kimberleys. She smiles at each of us in turn, the edges of her mouth almost reaching the corners of her eyes when she looks at Red. She unwraps two of her biscuits and hands them to him.

'Get them into you, pet,' she says. 'We need to fatten you up before this weddin', so we do.' She looks at me and Filly. 'I mean, look at the state of his hips.' She reaches over and pulls Red's T-shirt up to demonstrate. 'After all the macaroni I've fed him over the years, they still jut. It's just not right, is it?'

I shake my head with my mouth tightly closed. It's true. They *do* jut. I remember that.

It is Filly who grabs at the rudder of the conversation and steers it into safer waters. 'So,' she says in a parody of my most officious wedding-planner-type voice. 'Congratulations, first of all.' Sofia and Red look at each other and then at me and then at Filly. Like they have no idea what she's talking about. 'On your engagement,' she prompts them.

'Oh, yeah, that, right,' says Sofia, and she sort of sniggers into her cupped hand. Red doesn't say anything, mostly because he can't: his mouth is busy with chocolate Kimberleys.

'So,' I say, on surer ground now, 'we're thinking August wedding. Early autumnal theme and colours. Maybe gold and ochre.'

'Ochre?' says Sofia, frowning.

'A burnt orange,' Red explains before I get a chance.

'And some taupe,' I add.

'That's a light brown,' he tells Sofia before she needs to ask.

'I'm not sure about a colour that is *burnt*,' says Sofia slowly. 'It doesn't sound very appealing, does it?'

'It'll look great with your hair,' says Red, and suddenly his hands are in Sofia's hair, fluffing it and flaffing it this way and that, until he has it in an upstyle that makes Sofia look like a different person altogether: vulnerable and doe-eyed. Red looks around the office until he spots one of my manila folders that is the exact colour of ochre I am thinking about. He looks at me and I nod and pass it to him. He holds it below Sofia's face.

'Perfect,' he says. 'I wonder is there . . . ?'

I open the third drawer of my desk and take out a mirror. It is big enough to show Sofia's hair, face and the manila folder.

'See?' says Red, as I hold the mirror up.

'We-ell . . . ' says Sofia. For a moment I feel her wavering and I pick up the imaginary pen in my mind and hold it — poised — over the section entitled 'Wedding Colours', ready to put a tick by it.

'No,' Sofia says, and I put the pen back down, feeling foolish for entertaining the thought that any aspect of a Marzoni wedding could be decided so quickly.

Red returns the mirror and the folder to my desk and unwraps *another* biscuit. I concentrate on Sofia but I can see him out of the corner of my eye. Sprawled in one of *my* chairs in *my*

197

office. He scratches at the back of the manila envelope with a stubby, flaking pencil. I think he might be sketching Sofia's face. The *gall* of him.

'I want pink,' she says. 'Everything. The dresses, the cake, the castle, the flowers, the candles, the delf, everything. And I want that singer — whatshername . . . ?'

'Pink,' supplies Red, not looking up from his sketching.

'Yeah, that's the one. Pink. I want her to play a set in the evening. I don't know her songs but she's called Pink so I want her.' Sofia stops to take a breath. 'And the birds have to be pink.'

'The birds?'

'Don't worry,' she says. 'I'm not getting swans. Not after Carmella's wedding.' Sofia smiles at me, as though to reassure me that she isn't as crazy as Carmella. Maybe she isn't but it's close.

They were hired for the day, the swans, with a brief to float serenely round and round the water feature in the centre of the dining room. The male swan waited until the speeches began before hopping up on the back of the female swan, beating his great wings against the heaviness of the summer night as if to say, 'Would a ride be out of the question?' Apparently, a ride *was* out of the question because the female swan reacted savagely, making the most heinous of noises through her nose and beating the living daylights out of the male swan with her wings, trying to peck his eyes out with her beak and then standing on him and stamping her webbed feet against the snowy whiteness of his back.

198

'They mate for life, you know,' Carmella had whispered at me when she first mooted the idea of the two swans a-swimming.

'So, Sofia, what kind of . . . birds were you thinking of?' I ask now, as if this is a perfectly normal question.

'Pink ones,' she says. She looks at Red and he thinks about it.

'We could get flamingos,' he says.

'Well . . . ' says Sofia.

'They *are* pink,' says Red.

'I know,' she says. 'But are they pink *enough*?'

'Definitely,' he says. 'A salmon pink, I would say.'

Sofia smiles at him and shakes her head, as if she can't quite believe he's hers. He smiles back at her and I bend my head and type the word 'flamingos' into the database.

'Now,' Sofia pulls her face away from Red's and looks at me again. 'Where are we with the castle?'

'I've got one.'

'Great,' she says.

'But,' I say, and she leans closer, waiting. 'It's not pink,' I tell her.

'God, Scarlett, I know that,' she says, looking at me as if I am the lunatic and not her. 'But you can make it pink, can't you?'

I think about it. 'Well, I could give it a pinkish hue,' I finally say.

'A pinkish hue will do,' she says, smiling. 'Does it have a moat?'

'Yes.'

'And a drawbridge?'

'Of course,' I say. 'That's the only way in.'

She looks so happy and, for the first time in ages, I remember why I love my job. This bit at least. The delivery of the dream.

'And it's got turrets too,' I can't help adding, even though everyone knows that turrets are bog-standard when it comes to castles.

'Is there a tiny room at the top of a really tall tower?' Sofia holds her breath as she waits for the answer and I know she's thinking about the one where Sleeping Beauty pricked her finger on the spindle. This, I can provide.

'Yes,' I say, 'although it really is too small to be of any practical use to us.'

'It doesn't matter,' says Sofia, and she is far away, probably wandering up the spiral staircase to the smallest room in the tallest tower, in her pink wedding dress, which trails and sparkles along the ground behind her. Her pink Cinderella slippers make a delicious tinkling sound against the rough-hewn stone steps.

The meeting goes on and on and the challenges pile up and up (pink champagne I can do but a pink carriage drawn by four pink stallions?) and I do my best to ignore the baby in my belly whose father may or may not be in the room and I talk and talk and talk about the wedding until everything in the world looks a little pink and my head is full with things to do.

This is what I love about work. Somewhere along the long line of the morning, my anger and my shock fade to background noise and I find myself getting on with things. There is nothing else to be done with a Marzoni wedding.

I concede that Red Butler is unlike any other groom I have encountered. He doesn't slump into a stupefied silence. Or leaf importantly through the stack of newspapers on the table. Or frown at the ticking clock hanging on my wall. Or log on to whateverhappenedtosamanthafox.ie on his iPhone like Jeffrey Summers did back in 1998, however hard he denied it to Penelope Richardson, his then fiancée and now one of a pair of ex-wives. Instead, I have to admit that he *participates*. He has ideas. Ones that Sofia likes. Pink ones. He doesn't even blanch when Sofia discusses his wedding suit. Which is worrying, considering how much his outfit — and indeed the entire wedding — is going to clash with his hair.

* * *

'I *knew* you'd like him,' Sofia says, when Filly leaves the office with Red. After eating his way through the company's entire stock of biscuits, two bananas from Sofia's kitchen-sink handbag, a Coconut Snowball — donated by Filly — and a packet of flattened Chikatees he excavates from the back pocket of his jeans, he interrupts the meeting to declare himself 'peckish' and Filly has to show him where the canteen is so he can get some lunch. I check my watch. It is 11.07 a.m.

'I mean, I know he's not your type of fella but I just had a feelin' you two would hit it off. And I was right.'

My response sounds like a puppy being strangled and I have to clear my throat. 'You

201

certainly seem very . . . satisfied with him.'

Sofia throws her head back when she laughs. 'He's not a bleedin' suite of furniture, Scarlah,' she says.

'No,' I say, and smile, to show that I get the joke.

'But it's true,' she says. 'I *am* happy. Look.' She pulls up her blouse and points at her trousers where the waistband digs into the soft flesh of her belly.

For a terrible moment, I think she's going to tell me she's pregnant and I imagine Ellen with a Marzoni stepsister.

'See? I've put on weight, so I have,' she says, pushing the ends of the blouse back inside the trousers. 'I always put on an extra few pounds when I'm happy. You should have seen me after Italy won the World Cup last time round. *Huge* I was. And when Wham! split up? A stick insect would have looked like John Candy compared to me.' She beats her chest when she says this and bows her head. When I Google John Candy later, I realise that he's been dead since 1994 and I feel an unaccustomed sadness for this larger-than-life man, which I put down to pregnancy hormones.

Just when it seems as if they will never go, they get up to leave. Sofia suggests fortnightly meetings until about June, after which she recommends meeting once a week unless circumstances dictate that we meet more regularly.

I counter with a conference call once a month with progress reports emailed to her as and when necessary.

We compromise with the promise of a weekly

progress report punctuated by telephone calls, the frequency and duration of which is not discussed.

Sofia pulls my face into her cleavage and hugs me as she leaves. 'Tell me it's going to be better than Isabella's and Carmella's and Maria's and Lucia's,' she urges. With her arms wrapped round my ears, it is difficult to make out the exact words but I get the gist.

'Yes,' I say as best I can against the might of her chest.

She thrusts me away from her and eyeballs the living daylights out of me. 'I'm only gettin' married the once, Scarlah,' she says, and something about the way she says it makes me believe her utterly. She reaches her hand over to Red when she says this and he holds it tight and nods at her as if he too is planning on saying 'I do' only once, to her. In fact, he looks like he is ready to say it right now.

I swallow hard.

Red looks at the place on his wrist where a watch should be and says, 'I've just remembered. I'm supposed to be at the Irish Film Institute.'

'It's only round the corner,' says Filly. 'What time do you have to be there at?'

'Midday,' says Red, patting himself all over with his long hands, looking — I presume — for some class of a time-keeping device.

'You're thirteen minutes late,' I tell him, and this time even Sofia detects the icy patches in my tone and looks at me, confused.

'He's always late, so he is,' she says softly, as if this is something to commend him.

'You'd better run,' says Filly, nearly pushing him out of the office in much the same way as a fireman might push someone out of a burning building. Just before the rafters collapse.

Heads swivel as he lopes down the corridor and he acknowledges everyone with a wave and a smile, like a speeded-up version of the Queen: 'Goodbye, Marian. See ya, Carmel. Good luck, Michael. Thanks for the tip, Gladys.' It turns out that Gladys was the one who showed him where the last packet of Jammie Dodgers were (Duncan — partial to Jammie Dodgers — hides them behind the breadbin in the kitchen). He is still calling out as he disappears from view at the end of the corridor — 'Bye, Janine. Take care, Harriet . . . ' — and we stand there until we can't hear him any more.

'He's so friendly, isn't he?' says Sofia, gazing down the corridor as if he's still there. Her face is so open and honest I can hardly bear to look at her.

I excuse myself to go to the ladies'. I fill my palms with cold water and press them against the heat of my face. I hide myself in a cubicle that is not my usual one. I lower the lid of the toilet and crouch on it. I wait. For what, I'm not sure. I practise breathing. I look at my watch. It's 12.25 p.m. I work out the square root of 1,225. It's thirty-five, the same age as me.

★   ★   ★

Back in the office, Filly pulls on the face she calls her quintessential Australian face — optimistic

204

in spite of circumstances — and sticks in a smile (albeit a wry one) for good measure.

'Well, that didn't go too badly,' she says, 'considering.'

'Why didn't you warn me?' I ask. 'Why didn't you tell me that he was there?'

'I didn't recognise him,' she says. 'He looks different. In the daylight . . . '

'But his hair,' I remind her. 'You couldn't forget that. You couldn't mistake it for anyone else's.'

'I was *drunk*,' she reminds me and, because this is the only excuse I have as well, I can do nothing but nod.

I move behind my desk and sit down, flattening my hands against the wood, warming them. I see the paperweight in the shape of the *Starship Enterprise* — a birthday gift from Elliot — and I have to steel myself not to pick it up and hit myself over the head with it. Filly is worried enough about me.

Instead, I say, 'My plan is in flitters. Again.'

Filly — who may have guessed at my intentions regarding the paperweight — seems relieved. 'It just needs a little tweaking,' she says, petting me on the shoulder like you might an unpredictable pet.

She picks up the manila folder lying on my desk. 'That's a pretty good likeness,' she says, almost to herself.

'The *gall* of him,' I say, taking the folder out of Filly's hands and looking at it. 'I presumed he was sketching Sofia.' I stuff the folder into the bin and follow Filly to the canteen. She says I'll feel better after I eat something and, even though I know I won't, I have to admit that, for the first time in ages, I am suddenly starving for something other than nettle soup or crackers or ginger biscuits.

★ ★ ★

Later, when I take the folder out of the bin — to feed it into the shredder — I see that he has drawn me with my hair down around my face, despite the fact that it is pulled behind my head in a tight bun. In the picture, I am looking up, like I'm just about to give an answer to a question I have been asked.

I bend the folder in two and feed it to the shredder.

25

A car I don't recognise squats in the driveway at Tara. It is battered and bruised and looks like it has been dropped from a great height, rather than parked. It is a Mini. An ancient one. I think it might be a rust-red. More rust than red, though.

In the kitchen, Phyllis is back from Lourdes telling anyone who will listen about the miracle she witnessed.

'Blind as a badger, he was, Scarlett,' she says, flicking her feather duster at a cobweb that stretches from the fridge to the windowsill. 'Percy, I think his name was. Or it might have been James. Or Gordon. One of those trains anyway, from *Thomas the Tank Engine*,' she says. She raises her arms and dust motes fall through the air over her head. 'Anyway,' she continues, 'after the few auld prayers and whatnot, he says, 'Is it yourself, Mammy?' He came with his mammy,' Phyllis adds as an aside. ''You're looking well, so ye are. The blue rinse suits ye down to the ground, so it does.'' Phyllis glances at me to see if I'm paying enough attention. 'He hadn't seen his own mother since . . . ' she pauses to heighten the suspense, having a great flair for the dramatic, which is just as well, considering where she lives. ' . . . 1975. Could you credit it, Scarlett? Well? Could you?'

I have to stop myself hugging her. She will

know something is amiss if I do that. But it's lovely to see her again, with her familiar, gentle face and her bright blue eyes and her snow-white bun, as round as a Danish pastry.

So she talks and I listen but the day is catching up on me. I try not to think about it but the thoughts are like stray cats: they keep coming back.

'Scarlett, are you listening to me at all?'

'Of course I am,' I tell Phyllis. 'You were telling me about the young pup selling tap water — masquerading as holy water — for five euros in a Ballygowan bottle.'

'Anyway, I thought I'd give you a treat tonight. Make your favourite.' She stops, waiting for me to say it.

'Welsh rarebit?' I say, and put a smile across my face. Phyllis doesn't let anyone call it cheese-on-toast. I loved Welsh rarebit when I was five and Phyllis still makes it for me, insisting that it's my favourite. Also, it's the only vegetarian dish she is really comfortable making. She has no truck with tofu or lentils.

'Here, I'll do it,' I offer. I lift myself off the chair, using my arms as a lever. The day has mostly caught up with my legs, which feel as heavy as a pair of tree trunks.

Phyllis withers me with one of her looks. 'I'm not dead yet, Scarlett, girl,' she reminds me, although there is really no need.

'I know. I was just — '

'There's plenty of life in this old carcass, I'll have you know.'

'I know, I know. I was only — '

'I'm only in the late summer of my days. Mid-August, is all,' she recites. 'Now, run along there, like a good girl.' She dismisses me with a wave of her feather duster. 'Your father's got some writer fella in the den. Go and make nice with him.'

I smile at Phyllis. There is really nothing else to be done with her. She makes a swipe at me with the edge of a tea towel but, in spite of the tree-trunk heaviness of my legs, I sidestep her and do as I am bid.

There is silence in the den when I go in. The kind of silence that can be described as *studious*. Two heads pore over papers spread over the entire surface of the table, which has been extended to its maximum capacity. One of the heads is Declan's. I can still see the charred ends of his fringe, although it has grown a little since the incident with the cooker. The other head is covered in thick hair, raw and red. Orange, really. The colour of a bag of carrots. It's like a garish desk lamp, it's that bright. The penny is up in the air, twisting as it falls, but it doesn't drop until he speaks and I recognise the voice. Again. Gin and cigarettes. Some people might call it sexy. For a moment, I wonder if I can just back out of the room without anyone noticing. If it was just Declan in the room, I could. But Red Butler turns his head towards me the minute I take a step back.

'Scarlet O'Hara,' he says, like he's been expecting me. His smile is one of those gradual ones and spreads across his face like a pat of butter on a warm pan. He sits the wrong way round on the chair, his arms resting on the back with his chin tucked into the crease of his elbow. He makes the room look smaller than it is. Untidier. He looks like he has always lived here.

Before I have a chance to speak, a shriek rents the air and the intensity of it spins me round, toward the door. I see a streak of black that might be Blue tearing down the corridor pursued by a riot of fur that could be a wolf. Instinct takes over and I run. Down the hall, up the stairs, across the landing, their claws harsh against the yellowing wood of the floorboards. Blue is fast but the beast gains on him, finally cornering him in the bay window of my bedroom. Blue is rigid with rage, spitting and hissing and making his claws extend as far as they will go, which isn't as far as he'd like. Even I have to admit that his efforts to look intimidating appear rather feeble against the might of meat and fur that towers over him. I clench my hands into fists, remembering an article I read once about animals being able to smell fear through the sweat on your palms. My palms are slick with sweat. I move slowly towards them, forcing one foot in front of the other until I reach them. I bend slowly and pick up Blue and he lets me. That's how scared he is. We stand there, the pair of us, rattling. Blue buries his head in the crook of my arm.

'Al Pacino, heel, boy. I told you to play nice with Blue, didn't I?' Red Butler runs into my bedroom and he is immediately engulfed by the wolf, who stands on his hind legs with his front paws locked round Red's neck. There is a wet, sloppy sound as Red's neck and face and ears and head are licked like an ice cream. 'Are you all right?' Red asks as best he can, between licks.

I inch my head up, open my eyes, one at a time, and bring myself to look more closely at the animal. It is in fact a dog. Bigger than dogs have a right to be, but a dog nonetheless. With long, greying hair and a ribbon round his neck where a collar should be. Despite my fear of dogs — an incident with a collie playing the part of Lassie on a film set when I was seven — even I can acknowledge that this dog is not exactly ferocious. He sits now, in front of Red and thumps his tail like a hammer against the floor. When he opens his mouth, his tongue — long and pink — unfurls like a Slinky. Drool hangs from the corners of his mouth — great thick ropes of it — and gathers in a puddle on the floor. Red's hands pull gently at the dog's long ears and he bends and whispers soft reassurances into the space at the top of his head.

'What kind of a dog is that?' I ask. My voice sounds high-pitched and breathy, like I have reverted to my seven-year-old self with the fleshy part of my arm trapped between Lassie's jaws.

'He's a bit of a cross-section,' admits Red, straightening. 'Part wolfhound, part German shepherd and maybe part poodle.'

'Poodle?' I can't help saying. There's not a trace of poodle about this dog.

'I just say that because he's a little vain. He's fond of ribbons and he loves getting his hair shampooed and brushed. And looking at himself in mirrors. He's always at it.'

From the safety of my arms, Blue assumes his imperious bearing and peers down his nose at the monstrosity of hair and fangs that is Al Pacino.

Then a weird thing happens.

Blue struggles out of my arms and stands on the floor beside the dog. Even standing on the tips of his paws — which he does when he wants to appear masterful — he looks tiny. Al Pacino could be measured in hands, he's that big. With his tongue still lolling out of his mouth, he trots across the floor towards Blue. When he reaches him, he bends and licks the cat, all the way from his head to his tail. Not only does Blue let him, he settles himself in between Al Pacino's front paws and begins to purr, which is something he rarely does, even though he knows he's supposed to.

And then there is silence, apart from the slow, wet push of Al Pacino's tongue along the length of Blue's back. The silence stretches like a thin piece of elastic.

'Is this the guest room?' Red suddenly says, looking around. 'Maureen — your mother, I mean — said I could stay if I liked. Not that I will or anything. Of course not.'

'It's not a guest room,' I say. 'It's my bedroom.'

'Oh,' he says, and now his gaze shifts and I follow his line of vision to his shoes, which are trainers that used to be white and are held together with mismatching laces. 'It's very . . . tidy,' Red says after a while.

'Why are you here?'

'I ran after you. I thought you might be afraid of Al Pacino. Some people are. On account of his size. But he's a sweetheart really. All noise and no action, that's him.'

'No,' I interrupt him. 'I don't mean, why are you in my room. I mean, why are you *here*?' I wave my arms around the room to indicate the house. It's not much of a refuge but it's the only one I've got at the moment.

'Oh. That. Right,' says Red, his face breaking into a smile as he settles himself on my bed. He bounces a little, as if he's checking the springiness of the springs.

I fold my arms tightly across my chest and wait.

'I'm working with Declan, you see,' he says, and then stops, waiting to see if I might have something to say about this. I do not. 'I . . . I didn't realise he had a daughter,' he says. 'I mean . . . we don't know each other all that well. How would I know . . . ?'

I join the dots and the picture forms.

'Did you write that screenplay?' I cut in. 'The one without the 'r's?' My lips are pursed and my tone is clipped and I am glad for it. I feel able now to raise my eyes and look at him.

'Yes,' he says. 'The 'r' key won't move. It's stuck. But it's my lucky typewriter so I kept going with it.'

'You're a busy man, aren't you?' I say, and my voice is as sour as a lemon. 'Writing screenplays, getting engaged, working in the bar . . . ' I stop there.

'I know what you must think . . . ' he begins.

213

'You don't know anything about me,' I say, and my voice is contained but only just.

'Scarlett, what happened at the Love Shack. That was . . . '

'That was a mistake.' I bend to reclaim Blue but he resists me with a low hiss and a half-hearted flick of his left paw. Al Pacino waits until Blue settles again before resuming the tongue massage. I straighten and move towards the door. It suddenly feels like a long way off. I'm nearly there when he says it.

'The baby.' His voice is low, as if he doesn't want Ellen to hear him. 'Is there a chance . . . ? Could it be . . . ?'

'It's unlikely,' I say, but I stop walking.

'But a possibility,' he says.

'A remote one,' I concede, keeping my eyes locked on the door.

'Sofia told me what happened,' he says. And there it is. That feeling again. Churning. Like you've just stumbled off the fairground waltzer.

I look up. 'Sofia?' Even saying her name makes me clench. I see her open, eager face. Her huge smile. Her certainty that things will work out. The solidity of her trust in me. It's like a wall, it's that solid.

He doesn't even stop to think about it before he answers. 'Don't worry about Sofia. She'll understand.'

'She'll *understand*? She's your fiancée, for God's sake. She's my client. What bit of it is she going to understand? How?'

'Sofia is my friend. I've known her for years.'

'She's your *fiancée*, not your friend.'

214

'For a wedding planner, you sure have a funny idea of what constitutes a relationship.' For the first time, I can hear in Red's tone something that's not quite anger but perhaps a close relative. I am stung by it.

'What's that supposed to mean?'

'I just mean . . . I'm sorry . . . Just . . . just leave Sofia to me. She'll be fine.' Red steadies himself with a hand on the headboard of my bed. Al Pacino, sensing that something is amiss, comes to stand beside him and Red curls his fingers under the ribbon round his neck. 'Look, I know this doesn't look good but . . . well . . . there are things you don't know.'

'What things?'

'Scarrrrr-let.' Phyllis's voice climbs up the stairs like a song. 'Your Welsh rarebit is on the taaaa-ble.'

'Welsh rarebit?' Red asks.

'It's cheese-on-toast,' I say, clicking my tongue at Blue, who looks tiny, even without the might of Al Pacino towering over him.

'I should go,' says Red, uncurling a lead from his back pocket and hooking it on to the ribbon round the dog's neck.

'Yes,' I say. 'You should.' I leave the room but, instead of walking towards the stairs, I turn into the nearest room, which happens to be my parents' bedroom, close the door and move towards the bed, in its usual state of disarray. But tonight I can't bring myself to tidy Maureen's beads and scarves and hairpieces away. Instead, I push at them with both arms until there is a small vacancy just big enough to accommodate

215

me. I sit down. The room seems huge with just me in it. Even Blue has abandoned me. Pranced off with that ridiculous dog as if he's known him all his life.

I lie my hands across my belly and think about Ellen. She is alone too. The thought brings with it a surge of protectiveness. I make my promise. This child will have a *normal* father and a *normal* mother. There will be no complications. I won't allow any. She will have parents she can depend on. Me, for one. And John Smith. He was dependable before and I'm sure he could be dependable again.

She will have John Smith. I will get him for her. 'I will get John Smith for you,' I whisper down to her.

★ ★ ★

Down in the kitchen, Declan stands in everyone's way eating from a box of Rice Krispies tucked under his arm. Maureen makes a great display of putting out her cigarette, dashing it against the side of an ashtray and sending sparks everywhere. Phyllis dishes up great slabs of cheese-on-toast on to five plates and Red sits beside Maureen. He looks up when I come in and shrugs his shoulders in a helpless kind of gesture, his face creased in discomfort, and I know exactly what has happened. Maureen has *insisted* he stay and, while I know that her insistance is like the Russian Army in its doggedness, I still think he could have shown greater resistance to her advances. I look away and see his dog and my cat fast asleep in the corner, tucked around each other like brand-new lovers.

I sit down.

For a moment, we are an ordinary group of people, eating bread and cheese. Then Maureen starts to speak.

'So, Red, you were telling me about this film of yours earlier. Sorry I had to dash out. Cyril was having a crisis of confidence about his part. Have I told you about the play we're putting on?' She beams at him and runs her hand up his arm until it comes to rest on his shoulder. Red seems unperturbed by her familiarity but then again, isn't he used to the O'Hara women throwing themselves at him?

'Scarlett, are you all right?' enquires Phyllis. 'You've gone a peculiar shade of red.'

'She's just blushing,' says Maureen. 'She's always blushed, Red, from the time she was a baby, really.' Maureen turns to Declan, releasing Red from the grip of her eyes. 'Remember, Declan, the time you were on *The Late Late Show* and you told Gaybo that Scarlett was twelve and just starting secondary school when she was ten and going into fifth class? *Beetroot*, she was, when the camera panned to her.'

'That's because he also told Gay Byrne that I was in love with my teacher Mr Campbell. And I was eleven actually,' I say, but Maureen is already starting her next sentence and doesn't hear me.

'We still have the video of that show, Red,' she says, leaning in so her cleavage soars and sets, just over his plate, 'if you'd like to watch it.' She bends her head to her plate and spears a triangle of Welsh rarebit with a fork. There is no need for Red to answer. He'll be subjected to a viewing of that show, whether he likes it or not, if Maureen gets her way. She loves that particular show because she wore a dress that a Sunday newspaper later described as 'sensuous and elegant and deliciously full of the wonderful Mrs O'Hara'.

Red turns to me. 'And were you?' he asks.

'Was I what?'

'In love with Mr Campbell.'

'Of course not. I just thought he was a . . . a great teacher.'

'She was only ten,' Maureen reminds him.

'I was eleven,' I say through gritted teeth. I bend my face — hotter than a chilli pepper now — to my plate.

'Anyway, Mrs O'Hara, getting back to the play, yes, you did tell me about it,' says Red. Everyone's attention shifts from me back to Maureen and the normal order is restored.

I sip tea from Phyllis's special-occasion china cup, which is her way of letting me know that she missed me. I smile at her over the rim of it and she motions to me to eat up.

'Please, Red, call me Maureen, won't you?' The hand that was on his shoulder is now in his hair and she ruffles it between her fingers. I can't look.

'Anyone for tea?' Red stands up when he says this and she is forced to lower her hand.

'There's a bottle of wine in the fridge,' says

218

Maureen. 'I'll have a splash of that.'

'Me too,' shouts Declan, finally lifting his head from the script he has spread on the table.

'Me three,' says Phyllis, as she always does, admiring the piece of toast on her plate, which she has cut into about twenty tiny squares. She spends ages arranging her food on the plate before eating it.

'Anyway, Red, what was I saying?' continues Maureen. 'Oh, yes, poor Cyril. He was worried that perhaps he's a little old for the part. He's playing Romeo, you know.'

Cyril is not a little old for the part. He's way past being a little old for the part. He would be more suited for the part of Romeo's grandfather, if such a character existed, which it does not, as far as I remember.

'I'm sure you managed to assure him otherwise,' pipes up Phyllis, and is it my imagination or does she narrow her eyes at my mother in such a way that Maureen is at a loss of something to say, which is, at the very least, unusual.

'Red is getting married to Sofia Marzoni,' I blurt out in an attempt to drive the conversation away from the play. I can sense unrest from a long way off and arguments between Phyllis and Maureen can turn nasty. I've broken up my fair share of them over the years.

'There's more of those Marzoni girls?' Maureen is amazed at this. 'No wonder their mother ran away.'

There is the sound of a shin being kicked by the toe of a shoe under the table. 'Ouch,' shouts

Declan, who has a low pain threshold.

Phyllis apologises. 'I was aiming for Maureen,' she says.

'I was only saying . . . ' Maureen begins.

'It's OK,' says Red. 'Sofia often says the same thing, to be honest.'

We're not sure whether he is joking or in earnest. We concentrate on eating. Red Butler wolfs his food. He finishes long before everyone else. He likes tea, drinking three mugs of it sweetened with heaped spoons of sugar. His hands are long; he uses both of them to lift the mug and they overlap.

'So,' Maureen finally says after at least forty-five seconds of silence. She is not a fan of silence. She says it's too *quiet*. 'How did you meet Sofia Marzoni?'

Phyllis makes a 'tsk' sound under her breath and begins clearing the table.

'What?' says Maureen. 'I'm only asking him about his girlfriend. His fiancée.'

Phyllis tsks again and bends down towards the dishwasher. Every bone in her back creaks and moans as she bends and I get up to help her.

'It's nearly time for Vincent Browne,' I say. Phyllis loves Vincent Browne. She loves the way he speaks in monotone and never moves any of his facial features. She says it's relaxing. I stack the dishwasher, making more noise than I normally would so Red Butler knows I am not listening to him tell my mother about Sofia Marzoni.

'There's not much to tell, really,' he says. 'She's my best friend, I suppose. We've been friends for years.'

'And then,' says Maureen, taking up the reins of the story, 'one day, you look at her and it is like the first time you've ever seen her. The line of her neck, the way the light catches her hair, the soft dance of her eyes, and then . . . ' Here Maureen claps her hands with such ferocity that I drop a pot. She doesn't notice the clatter but sits there with her hands palm to palm now, as if in prayer. 'And then . . . ' she continues. Red Butler leans towards her, as if he wants to hear how the story ends. 'You realise that this woman . . . this friend . . . she's your soul mate. She's your dream of love.' Maureen's eyes close as she finishes her speech and, when they open, I know they will glisten with tears.

Red Butler doesn't laugh or look at my mother as if she is demented. Instead, he sets his mug on the table and holds his chin in his hand, his elbow on the table now that Phyllis is not here to flick it off. Eventually, he speaks. I turn on the hot tap at full tilt to let him know that I'm not listening.

'She invited me to her Christmas party. She'd just been dumped by my flatmate Patricia and . . . '

'Patricia?' I can't help asking.

For a moment Red looks confused. 'Did I say Patricia?' he asks, and he looks just like Filly does when she is playing for time.

'You did, Red. You said Patricia,' Maureen tells him.

'Sorry. I meant to say Patrick,' says Red. 'We call him Patricia on account of his nails. He keeps them long, you see. He's a guitar player.'

221

'So, anyway.' Maureen is anxious to gloss over the boring bits. 'You went to the party with her, she's heartbroken because of Patrick spurning her, and then?'

'Well, we . . . we got talking . . . you know, about relationships and the nature of love and . . . stuff like that, and . . . we, well . . . you know . . . '

'Fell in love?' Maureen says hopefully.

'Well . . . ' I hear the scratch of Red's neck against the collar of his shirt. He is looking around for someone to help him but there is no one. Phyllis is watching telly in the den and Declan is back in his study, crashing keys on the piano, which is the thing he does when he's trying to think. 'Well . . . I suppose so . . . I mean . . . yes. That's the general gist anyway.'

'Sounds like there's more to the story there,' insists Maureen, as persistent as a head louse.

Red reaches into his pocket. I hear the rattle of matches. 'Would you excuse me?' he says. 'I'm just going to go outside for a smoke.'

'A man who smokes,' Maureen says, clasping her hands against her chest. 'I just love a man who smokes.'

I close the door of the dishwasher too fast and it clatters against the dirty delf inside. Maureen turns towards me, looking a little surprised. I think she presumed I had gone to bed.

'Scarlett thinks smoking is bad for you,' she says, smiling wryly at Red and widening her eyes.

'She could have a point. I'm trying to quit at the moment,' he says, taking a cigarette from behind his ear. 'I light up, take two drags and put it out.'

'That's a terrible waste of a good cigarette,' says Maureen, shaking her head and clearly disapproving.

'Yes but, with this method, I reckon I've only smoked one full cigarette all day,' says Red. 'Which is a big improvement.'

'Brilliant,' says Maureen. 'Now wait till I grab mine and we'll head out.'

I am left in the kitchen on my own. I clear the table, finish stacking the dishwasher, sweep the floor and spray every available surface with Dettox, taking care not to breathe in when I am doing it. I see Red and Maureen out in the garden. She has him pinned against the garage wall and he can't get a word in edgeways. I know that because his mouth never moves. Instead, he nods and smiles. I know that because I see the white glint of his teeth at regular intervals.

I turn off the main light and switch on the lamp in the corner. I am tired but I don't want to go to bed. If I do, I will think about things and none of them will be good. I pick up one of my baby books (*What to Expect When You're Unexpectedly Expecting*) and sit on the sofa, under the soft yellow glow thrown by the lamp. I read. Ellen is growing arms. They are growing as I read. Right now. I wonder what that would feel like. To grow arms for the first time. Soon, she'll be able to suck her thumb — when she grows a thumb. I like thinking about her like this, floating, with her thumb secured in her mouth. She feels safe, deep inside me. She feels like someone I can take care of, when she is like this.

When I wake up, the kitchen is in darkness and someone has tucked a fleece blanket around me. I look at my watch. It's one o'clock in the morning. I pick Blue up from the end of the couch, where he has settled at my feet. I know by the way he lets me hold him that he is pretending to be asleep.

I move around the house in the darkness. The house is so familiar to me, even in the dark. Especially in the dark. Blue — used to my nocturnal wanderings — pushes his nose into the crease of my elbow and works up an authentic-sounding snore. Maureen and Declan are in bed but they're not asleep. Declan is reading the script — perhaps learning his lines — and Maureen is watching reruns of *Dynasty* or *Dallas*. I never know which is which.

'Thanks for covering me with the blanket,' I say. 'It's freezing tonight.'

Maureen looks up, confused. 'I thought you'd gone to bed.'

'Me too,' offers Declan, looking up briefly before returning his concentration to the script.

'No . . . I fell asleep on the couch in the kitchen. Must have been Phyllis.' I sit on the edge of an armchair.

'She never came back downstairs after dinner,' says Maureen, turning up the volume on the television. 'Says she's exhausted after Lourdes with all the late nights and the dancing and the drinking and the singing.'

'When did Red and Al Pacino leave?' I ask, looking away from them, towards the telly.

'About half an hour ago. We had to push him halfway down the drive to get the car started.'

'Does he have far to go?' My curiosity surprises me.

'He lives in a flat in Renelagh, I think,' says Maureen. 'Oh, I love this bit, where Sue-Ellen throws a whisky sour over JR's new suit. It's classic.'

Declan sets the script down and looks at me. 'It's tragic really,' he says with a deep sigh.

'It's only a whisky sour,' says Maureen. 'At least it's not a strawberry daiquiri. It's impossible to get strawberry stains out of a suit.'

'I'm not talking about *Dallas*,' says Declan. 'I'm talking about Red.'

I wait for Maureen to ask.

'The only thing tragic about Red Butler is that he's engaged,' she says, as if her husband of nearly forty years is not inches away from her in their bed.

'He's got no real family,' Declan says, while Maureen fans herself with a page of the script. 'His father left when his mother was pregnant with Red. She died a few years later.' 'She died of a broken heart,' Maureen says, her eyes glazing over at the *romance* of it all.

'Well, yes,' says Declan, 'no doubt. That and the breast cancer.'

'Who raised the boy?' asks Maureen, tearing her gaze away from the screen.

'I'm not sure,' admits Declan, retrieving the page from Maureen's fingers. 'Now, I have a lot of work to do,' and I can tell by the way he says it that he is delighted by this unexpected turn of

225

events. I haven't seen him like this in years. It makes him seem younger and more . . . competent somehow. 'Go to bed, Scarlett,' he says. 'You and Ellen need your sleep.'

'Goodnight, Scarlett O'Hara,' Maureen says, switching off the telly. She lies down and lays thin slices of cucumber over her eyes. It's what she always used to say, when I was little. She loved saying it almost as much as I hated hearing it. It makes me smile now. It seems like such a silly thing to get annoyed about. It seems like such a long time ago.

I leave the room but I don't go to bed. After sleeping on the couch, I know that there is no point. I wander the house instead with Blue in my arms. I make hot chocolate, read my baby book, replant and water the mostly dead Aloe Vera plant in the kitchen, check my emails and write my to-do list for the following day. When I can't think of anything else to do and sleep is still a long way off, I sing a lullaby to Ellen. I never sing. My voice sounds old and dusty, like it's been in a cupboard under the stairs for years. The only lullaby I know is 'Rock-a-Bye Baby' and I can't remember any of the words after the first line, which, helpfully, is the same as the song title. After that, I hum, my breath tickling my lips as I draw it out. When I get to the end, I begin again, my voice louder now, carrying down into the dark passageway. When I begin it for the third time, Blue looks up at me with his head to one side. He knows something is up. He just hasn't figured it out yet.

26

There's no time to formulate a new plan that will accommodate the emergence of Red Butler, who is suddenly all over my life like an itchy rash. So, for the first time, I move through the next few days without one, a rudderless boat shifting on water while storm clouds gather on the horizon.

'Just got off the phone with Simon.' Elliot runs into my office. 'He'll be back from London on Thursday,' he says when he gets his breath back.

I wait for him. I know there's more but Elliot does not like to be rushed.

'He says his top priority is the interviews for the new position.'

This is good news. It means I don't have to tell him about the baby before the interview.

Elliot frowns when he hears this. 'But, Scarlett, you have to tell him.'

'I won't get the job if I tell him. He hates working mothers. You know that.'

'And builders and non-nationals,' adds Elliot, almost to himself.

'But he hates working mothers more,' I say, even though I don't know if this is true. It just feels like it might be.

'But if you don't tell him and he gives you the job and then you tell him you're pregnant, he'll hold it against you for the rest of your

227

life,' says Elliot in his patient I'm-explaining-this-to-a-six-year-old voice.

'I know but at least I'll have the job, won't I?'

'Well, yes,' Elliot concedes, but he looks worried.

'What?' I ask. 'What do you know?'

'It's Gladys Montgomery,' he says, and he won't quite look at me.

'What about her?' I ask.

'My sources tell me that Simon's interest in her refuses to wane.'

'Shit.' I lift myself up from my chair and start pacing. 'But why?' I ask, even though I already know. 'Is she really that good in bed?'

Elliot can't answer. Instead, he nods his head slowly up and down. 'The best sex I ever had, God help me,' he adds, with his head hung in well-deserved shame.

'Christ,' I say, and sit on the couch beside Blue. 'I've no chance of getting the job now.'

'You're the best candidate for the position,' Elliot assures me.

I wither him with a look and he has the grace to look sheepish.

'I definitely can't tell him about the pregnancy, then.'

'But he'll find out eventually and then he'll have an actual reason to distrust you,' says Elliot. 'You'll never work as a wedding planner in this town again.' This is a little over the top but only a little.

'But if I tell him I'm pregnant, I won't get the job,' I argue.

'But at least you'll still have your old job,' says

Elliot. 'You're going to need it, with the baby and everything. I was looking at the prices of the nappies in my local M&S the other day. Shocking, it is.'

The phone rings and it's Hailey. Elliot takes his leave.

Oddly, Hailey is giggling and I think maybe it's Filly doing one of her impersonations so I ask a question only Hailey would know. 'What time did you put Sarah Johnson through to me yesterday?'

Without skipping a beat, she says, 'Ten forty-seven a.m.,' and I know then that it's her. Giggling. But her all the same. She composes herself. 'Sofia Marzoni on line four for you.'

I have to ask. I can't help it. 'What were you laughing at?' I ask.

'Oh, Sofia was just telling me something funny. She's quite the comedienne.' This is the longest conversation I've ever had with Hailey over the telephone.

I thank her and punch line four. 'Sofia,' I say, trying to inject some enthusiasm into my voice. This is her fourth call today. She tells me she needs to be in regular contact with me to create *synergy* between us.

'I hear you told John about the baby,' she says. She's also told me that she's my NBF (new best friend) on account of knowing intimate details of my life, which she does, although not intentionally. 'Filly told me. I think it's great, so I do. And he's comin' back. Brilliant. He sounds like the type of fella you could depend on. So long as he doesn't do another of his midnight flits of course.' A pause here, maybe to see if I am ready to laugh about it yet. When I don't, she rallies well. 'But Filly reckons that was just a one-off. She doesn't think he has another one of those in him. So you'll be able to concentrate on organisin' the weddin' with no more distractions.' Sofia stops to draw breath and I open my mouth to say something but I am too slow and she is off again. 'Now, I've been thinkin' about Pink,' she says. 'The singer,' she adds, as if remembering that everything about the wedding is pink, not just the singer, who, by the way, was incensed to be asked to perform a wedding gig. At least, her agent was. I haven't told Sofia this yet.

'Yes,' I say, and I wait.

'Well, I don't want her any more. Her music is a bit aggressive for a weddin', don't you think?'

This is good news. I hate telling my brides that they can't have something they want.

'I want Chris de Burgh instead. I want him to sing 'Lady in Red', only with the word 'pink' instead of 'red'. I want it for the first song.'

'I'll see what I can do,' I say. I'm a little more hopeful about Chris de Burgh doing the gig. He has an eager face, and it's possible that Elliot's mother knows Chris de Burgh or knows someone who knows him. She usually does.

'Tell him he's to get those eyebrows waxed before he makes an appearance at the weddin', right?'

'Eh . . . '

'I'm joking, Scarlah. Relax, will you? I should send Red over to you to do one of them back and neck massages. He's great at them, so he is. Got a grand set of hands on him, if you know what I mean.' Sofia is as subtle as a *Carry On* film and the fact that I know all about Red's grand set of hands makes it horrible.

'I'll ring you tonight. When I've more time to chat,' she says before hanging up.

I lie my head on the table and bang the telephone receiver against the desk a few times.

'What's all the noise in here?' My office is like Times Square on New Year's Eve. I'm mostly glad about that but I pretend — to myself — that I'm annoyed. I look up.

It's only Filly. She greets me with her usual 'Good-morningsorryI'mlate', two skinny lattes, a doughnut with pink icing and sprinkles (for her) and an apple and cinnamon Nutri-Grain (for me). It's not the morning. It's — I check my watch — seven minutes into the afternoon.

'How are you feeling?' she asks, like she asks every day.

'Fine,' I say, like I say every day.

'Any nausea?'

'Yes.'

'Good.' She always says this. 'Any vomiting?' she asks then.

'Yes, but only twice so far.'

'Good,' she says again. 'How are your gums?'

'Bleeding.'

'Excellent,' she tells me. 'You're so textbook, Scarlett,' she adds, and she is as proud as a mother hen with a fluffy yellow chick.

'Eh, thank you,' I say.

'*No problemo*, boss,' Filly says, tackling her

231

doughnut. It's finished in under ten seconds and I wonder — and not for the first time — where she puts it all. I look at her. Today, she is wearing the miniest of miniskirts and her long, thin legs are encased in yellow and brown tights, giving them a sort of newborn-giraffe look. She feels the cold of the Irish winters — and springs and summers and autumns — keenly and wears a variety of hats. This one is woollen with a bunny-tail bobble on the top and flaps that reach down over her ears, which are the only thing about her that are of average size. Because of this, they look *enormous*, like the ears of a pantomime elf, so Filly takes every opportunity to conceal them from the general public. The hat is a bright crimson and bears no relation to any other part of her outfit but, because it is Filly, it looks great on her.

'Simon's back on Thursday,' I tell her. 'He's interviewing for the position next week. Maybe early next week.'

'That's fantastic news,' says Filly, always optimistic in the face of impending doom. But her enthusiasm is the tiniest bit catching and I find myself straightening in my chair.

'Why . . . fantastic exactly?' I ask.

'This way, you won't have to tell him you're pregnant.'

'Elliot thinks I should tell him.'

'That's because he's a man,' says Filly in a tone that can be described as dismissive. Even though she has sourced her OTL (One True Love), as she puts it, she retains a healthy scepticism about our opposite numbers.

'So you think I shouldn't tell him,' I say, just to be clear.

'Not if you want the job,' she says, and I know it is as simple as that.

My phone rings again and I pick it up.

'Red Butler for you,' Hailey says.

My hand tightens around the phone.

'Scarlett . . . ?'

I gather myself together. 'What line is he on?' I say, like I normally would.

'He's here,' she says.

'You mean he's in the building?' This comes out louder than it should.

'Yes. In front of me. At reception,' she explains, slower now.

'Oh.'

'Shall I send him up? He says he knows the way.'

'I . . . '

'Scarlett?'

'Eh, thanks. I mean, yes. Yes, send him up. That would be — ' But Hailey has already hung up and I am left with the sound of the dial tone in my ear.

I shoo Filly out and wipe the sprinkles from her doughnut off my desk.

After that, there is nothing to do but wait.

27

'We don't have an appointment, do we?' I say, even though I know that we do not and I am aware of the tone of my voice, which could be described as pointed.

'No, we don't.'

I look at him to see if he is apologetic. He is not. He smiles at me and points to a chair and I steady myself by looking at my planner, which he takes for assent, even though I do not want Red Butler to be sitting in a chair in my office, with or without an appointment.

The word 'fraying' comes to mind. His clothes are threadbare. I see lines of white knee through the faded fabric of his jeans. His socks don't match. His shoes should be put out of their misery. Instead of a coat, he wears two jumpers over one vest, a shirt and a long, woollen scarf that he has wrapped several times round his neck like a brace, giving him an insurance-claim look.

'So,' I say in my thin, trying-to-be-polite voice, 'what can I do for you?'

'Well,' he says, crossing his legs, looking much more comfortable than a man with no appointment has a right to look, 'I've been thinking about what you told me the other night.' He waits in case I want to say something. After a pause, he continues. 'About the baby. Ellen. About Ellen.' He pulls at the lobe of his ear. His fingers seem much too long for his hands. 'I like the name, by the way.'

'Oh,' I say. I can't remember telling him about Ellen. About her name, I mean.

'Sofia told me,' he jumps in.

'Oh.'

'She also told me about John Smith.'

'What about him?' I pick up a pen and hold it with my two hands, just for something to do.

'Just that you rang him and he's coming back and he thinks he's Ellen's father.'

'He is Ellen's father,' I snap. 'Very probably,' I add in a lower voice.

'Yes, of course. I just wanted to . . .'

I look at my watch. 'Look, I have to . . .' I begin.

Red stands up and the room seems to shrink. 'I just wanted to say that I'm fine with the whole baby situation,' he blurts out. 'I mean, if she's mine. Which she probably isn't. You know, because . . . well . . . we only . . . you know . . . that one time and . . .' Red shakes his head as if there's water in his ears. 'I'm sorry, Scarlett, I'm making a dog's dinner of this. I just want you to know that I will be supportive if the baby . . . if Ellen . . . turns out to be mine.' The last of his breath rattles out of him and I realise that he is not as calm as he appears.

'And another thing,' he says, backing his way towards the door as if reassuring me that he is leaving. 'I'm not going to say anything to anybody. About you and me or about the baby.'

'There's nothing to say about you and me,' I point out.

'Exactly, exactly,' he says. 'Which is why I'll

never mention that night in the Love Shack to anyone or . . . '

'Why do you keep mentioning it, then?'

'Just to say that I won't mention it again, that's all.'

'Not even to Sofia?'

'Only if you want me to.'

'I don't want you to do anything. What you tell Sofia Marzoni is your business. You're the one who's marrying her.' The words point, like an arrow.

Red takes it well. 'Leave Sofia to me,' he says. 'You just concentrate on you and the baby and John Smith, if that's what you want.'

'It is what I want.'

'Good,' says Red. 'That's good.' And he smiles at me as if everything is grand. All sorted out and tied up in a neat bundle.

He moves towards the door and places a hand on the door handle before he stops and turns back to me. 'One other thing,' he says.

'Yes?' I'm not even trying to keep the impatience from my tone now.

'Just . . . if you need any help . . . someone to go with you to hospital appointments or . . . anything really . . . ' He trails off.

I stand up but I don't come out from behind the desk. If I do, he might see my legs, which shake like leaves in a brisk wind.

'That won't be necessary,' I manage to say. 'Now, if you'll excuse me . . . '

'Sure, I'm going. You don't have to see me out or anything. Or call security.' He laughs when he says it to make sure I know he is joking.

I can't even do a fake smile. It's the pity. I can't take it. It stains his face like a dye.

'Goodbye, Red,' I say because there is nothing else to be said.

'If you change your mind about the hospital appointments . . . '

'I won't.'

'OK . . . but if you do . . . '

'I won't. But . . . thanks.'

He stops talking then and, in the silence, I hear something. It sounds like the baying of a hound.

'Oh shit, it's Al Pacino. I'd better go,' says Red in an apologetic tone, as if he is sorry to have to leave.

When he has gone, I look out of the window. From the pavement outside the building, Al Pacino gathers a crowd as he strains at his lead, which is wrapped round a lamp-post, and throws his head back to howl a mournful and long-winded class of a howl. Then he stops and looks up and I swear he looks right at me and I shake myself and tell myself not to be so ridiculous, half hidden as I am behind the slats of the blinds. He stays like that for a moment, not blinking, not moving, just staring at me. Right at me. And then Red Butler appears and Al Pacino nearly beheads himself in his frenzy to get to him. And Red Butler kneels down in front of the dog and unwraps his lead like a Christmas present and, when he is free, Al Pacino launches himself at Red like a rocket and, for a moment, the pair of them are rolling around on the ground, in the street, like there is only the two of them and you can't tell which one loves the other more. I reach for the cord and pull the blinds until all the light has gone.

28

Somehow I make it to the end of the first trimester. I allow myself to relax. Just a little. What I feel is relief mostly. That Ellen is still there. I can feel her in so many different ways. She's in the red welts that my skirts leave across my thickening waist. She's in the apple drops that I buy by the half-pound in the corner shop in Roskerry. She's in the light of Filly and Bryan's eyes when they ask after her. She's in the hesitant tone of John's voice when he enquires about her. He rings every Friday night. Just as he said he would. At 8 p.m. Just as he said he would. These conversations are full of Ellen. If we didn't have Ellen to talk about, I wonder what we would say to each other. I haven't mentioned Red Butler yet. I'm still waiting for the right moment. He hasn't mentioned the flight that left which he just happened to be on. Perhaps he's waiting for the right moment too.

The second trimester of the pregnancy is both better and worse than the first. Better because of lots of things. The morning, noon and night sickness, for example, has slackened to just morning sickness and has become as much part of my early-morning toilet as flossing and writing my to-do list in my planner. My hair is another plus, shiny as a chestnut and even blacker than usual — a blue-black. It seems to grow faster now and I have to get it trimmed every four weeks instead of the usual six. The deadening tiredness lifts like a blanket of cloud from a mountaintop and, for the first time in weeks, I rediscover life after 10 p.m., instead of falling asleep after dinner and waking at one o'clock in the morning. Not that life after 10 p.m. is particularly interesting. It mostly involves sitting on the couch in the den, eating popcorn from a pudding bowl with Blue on his cushion beside me, watching reruns of *Inspector Morse* on the telly. But still, it is comforting to regain some degree of normalcy. While I am without a baby bump, my body lays down fat in other areas. I have hips now. Proper woman's hips. My face is rounder and, even though the skin there is still a death-rattle white, people tell me that I am looking well. They say it with their heads at an angle and with an air of bewilderment. As if they can't quite put their finger on it.

The best thing happens at the beginning of the second trimester. I'm supposed to be getting ready for a meeting when I feel something that makes me forget everything, just for a moment. It isn't quite a movement. More like a sensation. Tender. A discreet fluttering. Like a butterfly, fresh out of its cocoon, on its tentative first flight. It is neither pleasant nor unpleasant. I lift up my top and press my hands against my belly but the sensation or movement or whatever it is has gone and I wonder if I imagined it.

'Scarlett, would you get a move on.' Filly charges into my office and stops short when she sees me. 'What are you doing, standing there

240

with your top up around your tits?' And then 'Kerr-ist! Your tits are HUGE' in a grudgingly admiring voice.

'I . . . I think I felt the baby move,' I say. 'Just before you came in here.'

'What did it feel like?' Filly wants to know.

'Like . . . I don't know really . . . like a jelly, wobbling on a plate. A tiny one.'

'Well, it *is* week 13, quite early for movement but not unheard of'. Filly is currently reading *What to Expect when Your Boss is Expecting*.

'She's the size of a green bean now' Filly tells me.

'A green bean?' I imagine a green bean with two eyes, a nose and a mouth. And little hands and feet poking out. And maybe a tuft of hair sticking from the top.

'I love green beans' says Filly. 'My grandfather used to put them into salad. Green bean salad he called it.' I can't think of anything to say to that.

It's worse too, the second trimester. For a couple of different reasons. The job, for one. The promotion, I mean. Simon didn't come back on the Thursday he was supposed to. Instead, he was called to Spain, where the staff of a small company being taken over by Extraordinary Events International had barricaded their doors and barred their windows and were staging a sit-in to protest against the hostility of the takeover. Because it was a slow news week in Spain, the story made national headlines and the Spanish version of Joe Duffy (Juan Dufino) took it upon himself to spearhead the campaign against the nasty multinational, which Simon personified beautifully. It took Simon over a week to quell that particular fire, after which he had to 'recuperate' in a very expensive hotel overlooking Las Ramblas in Barcelona, which — coincidentally — coincided with Gladys Montgomery taking sick leave due to an unfortunate bout of Bell's palsy, which, happily, ended on the exact day that Simon flew from Barcelona to spend 'quality time' with his wife and children at their holiday home in the Seychelles. From there it was straight to a conference in Belfast, which kick-started a tour around Europe to copperfasten the pan-European partnership project we've been working on for years. He had to take some 'time out' after that, which — if my sources are to be believed, and they usually are — involves a chalet in the Swiss Alps, a young ski instructor called Sasha and all the Moët you can drink of an evening.

So, I haven't seen him. Or heard from him. And I don't know when he's coming back. And Gladys looks smugger and smugger every day. And the blip that was Ellen is now becoming a bump that is getting more and more difficult to conceal.

Worse too, this second trimester, because of Red Butler, who can often be found at Tara now. Sometimes with but mostly without Sofia. Rehearsing, he and Declan call it. This involves playing Connect-4 and sprawling along the larger-than-life couch that spans the breadth of the room, their heads at either end, their feet — with their shoes off, at Phyllis's insistence — brushing against each other. I keep a low

242

profile when he is at the house but, even from this vantage point, I can't help noticing the change in Declan when Red is around. More animated, funnier, sharper. Maureen tells him he's *showing off* and I know that she's right but it's a relief to know that he still can. And even better to see that he still wants to.

★   ★   ★

Today is the anniversary of Judge Judy. She died two years ago. I wonder if John will ring today to mark the occasion. Even though it is a Thursday and not a Friday. Even though it is 9.07 p.m. and not eight o'clock on the dot.

Judge Judy was our cat. Our joint cat. Some couples have joint bank accounts and mortgages and custody of children. We had a joint cat. I find the cat collar in the pocket of the trousers I wore the day I cleared my stuff out of John's flat. We got her from the local animal rescue centre. She was the only cat we owned together. We collected her on the evening of our three-year anniversary. To me, this was better than an engagement ring. This was commitment. But Judge kept running away and we would find her and bring her back. Until she eventually made it to the main road and got run over by a truck. A Kit-e-Kat truck.

I rub my finger across the plaque on the collar, where her name is engraved. John is not going to ring. He would deem it sentimental, an emotion he has no regard for.

I stuff the collar into the bin and I leave it

there for nearly seven minutes before I return.

'Do you need some help, Scarlett?'

I take my arm out of the bin and turn round. It is Red Butler, standing at the kitchen door. I hate John at that moment. He has turned me into someone who rummages in bins. There is a clatter of heels behind him and Sofia Marzoni appears. When they stand together, they are nearly the same height.

I stand up and peel the rubber gloves down my arms. 'What are you doing here?' It is difficult to ask this without appearing rude but I do my best.

'Declan invited us for dinner but then he forgot that he'd invited us so, when we arrived, he had to take us out instead,' says Sofia, jiggling herself out of her fake-fur jacket. I look closer. At least I hope it's fake.

'What were you looking for in the bin?' asks Red, taking the rubber gloves gently from my hands and donning them.

'Oh, it doesn't matter. It was . . . '

Already he is elbow deep in kitchen refuse. I hear the bell on Judge Judy's collar. Red hears it too and his head disappears into the bin, resurfacing moments later with the collar held aloft, like a trophy.

' 'Judge Judy,'' he reads from the plaque. 'Is she another of your cats?'

'She was,' I say, taking the collar from him and moving towards the sink to wash off the debris. 'She died,' I say in a loud cheerful voice. 'Two years ago today.' Despite my hearty tone, I am horrified to discover a lump in my throat. With my back to them, I squeeze my eyes tightly shut and conjugate the verb *manquer* in the subjunctive tense.

'I'm sorry for your loss, Scarlett,' Red says, and I look at him to see if he is laughing at me. There are some people who have no respect for grieving when it comes to domestic pets.

Somehow, Red finds a can of polish and a duster. 'Give it to me,' he says, nodding towards the collar. I hand it to him. He holds it between his fingers as if it is a fragile thing and wipes it carefully with the duster until it gleams like the day we bought it.

'It's important to have a keepsake,' Red says, handing the collar back to me. He does not ask why it was in the bin in the first place. I don't trust myself to speak so I nod my thanks at him.

Declan rolls into the kitchen, like he's on wheels. 'Ah, Scarlett, darling, I'm afraid I'm a little worse for wear,' he admits, sitting on the edge of a kitchen chair. It teeters before it topples, dumping him on the floor. Red and Sofia flank him on either side, grab an arm each and hoist him to his feet, lowering him then on to the sofa under the window. When he gets settled, he looks at me. 'Rather too much gin and not enough tonic this dinnertime,' he admits, a little pink around the ears, although this could be a nod to the gin rather than any shame he might feel.

'I'll make coffee,' I announce.

'Sterling idea, darling,' roars Declan before launching into a story involving Frank Sinatra, Marilyn Monroe and — I think — a Mafia boss called Carlito Corleone.

Sofia wanders down the hall in search of Declan's Oscar.

Maureen trips into the kitchen. '*There* you are, Red. I need some help with my lines. Olwyn — the poor lamb — is still holed up in that dreadful institution so it looks like yours truly will be treading the boards come July.'

'But, darling, I was *just* telling Red my story about Mari and Fran and Carlito.'

'But you told him that story last week,' she reminds him. 'And the week before, if I'm not much mistaken.'

Declan's ears bleed crimson now as he turns to Red. 'I haven't,' he says. 'Have I?' he adds in a whisper.

I pour the last of the coffee beans into the grinder, straining to hear what Red might say.

'You told me the story about Mari and Fran and *Antonio*,' he says. 'Carlito's brother. Remember?'

Declan slaps Red on the back and Maureen sighs and Red promises to go through her lines with her just as soon as Declan finishes the story and Maureen agrees and turns the full power of her smile on Red and he smiles back at her before turning his attention to Declan to hear the rest of the story that he's heard before.

I set the tray of coffee and cups and ginger cake on the table and turn to pick up the tray I have set for George and Phyllis, who are ensconced in George's gatehouse getting ready to watch *Dragons' Den*, followed by *Brothers and Sisters*.

'Goodnight, Scarlett,' Red calls after me.

'You're not going to bed already, are you?' says Maureen, aghast.

'We're going to play gin rummy in a bit,' says Declan, and the others look at him and I can see that this is news to them.

'I'm just going to the gatehouse to give George and Phyllis their supper. Then I'll probably go to bed. I'm a bit tired,' I say, edging towards the door.

'And you call yourself an insomniac,' Maureen says, shaking her head.

'I didn't know you had trouble sleeping,' Red says.

'Oh, yes,' says Maureen. 'She's like our resident ghost here at Tara, wandering the house at night with Blue in her arms. She's been doing it since she was a teenager.' She beams at Red as though this is something I have achieved rather than struggled with over the years.

I am spared from having to respond by Declan, who has fallen asleep on the couch, without even finishing his tale of Mari and Fran and Carlito. While Maureen goes in search of a tea towel to drape over his face and drown out the noise of his snoring, I slip from the room. But later, when I am wandering the corridors with Blue in my arms, I find a note in the kitchen. Propped against the kettle. Addressed to me. 'Dear Scarlett,' it reads, 'this might help.' A sachet of hot-chocolate powder is sellotaped to the page. 'And this.' A cinnamon stick, also sellotaped. 'Kind regards, Red.'

I pick up the note. The writing is childish, the

letters slanting this way and that. I move towards the bin, my foot on the pedal. Hot chocolate is for amateur insomniacs. Everyone knows that. Besides, the best-before date was three months ago, and the cinnamon stick is soggy at one end, as if it's been chewed. Visions of Al Pacino come to mind.

I hesitate. This is the first time ever that I have had company — other than Blue — on my night-time wanderings. Even if it's just a hand-scribbled note.

Useless, of course.

But kind.

I slip the note into the pocket of my cardigan and continue on my way.

29

It's at the semi-private clinic in Holles Street where I feel most alone. There are as many men as women in the waiting area. One man for every pregnant woman. I stick out like a throbbing, swollen, sore thumb. Filly offers to come with me but I shake my head. Someone has to man the office. Besides, two women together would stick out more than just me on my own.

Maureen is appalled by my decision not to go private but I have to buy a house, a pram, a car seat, a monitor, a cot, baby clothes, blankets, bottles and cream, and all these things add up. I put everything on a spreadsheet and cost each item and compare the total with the amount I have in my savings account. There is a significant shortfall. A longfall, really. Even though I opened that savings account when I was six, just after my first Holy Communion.

I don't confide these fears to Maureen. She will tell me that Declan will pay for everything. And so he would. If I let him.

So here I am in the semi-private clinic in Holles Street on a Friday morning. Officially, I am at a meeting with my florist to discuss the importation of flowers ('Any kind so long as they're pink,' Sofia says). The clinic is a hut in the car park at the side of the hospital. A woman who looks like she's possibly ten months pregnant struggles through the narrow entrance and sits heavily on a chair before bracing herself for the stairs that lead up to the consultation rooms. Everything about the place is narrow, including the woman who sits behind the desk. She purses her narrow lips, which lie in a narrow line under the shadow of her long, narrow nose and runs her long, narrow nail down a list of names, looking for mine.

'There's no O'Hara here,' she says, not looking up.

'Try under the 'H's,' I suggest.

She clicks her tongue and sighs and turns a page and finds me under the 'H's.

'That's a mistake,' she says. She does not say it is her mistake. She does not apologise. She looks at me then, although it is more a grimace than a look. I feel like apologising but I don't. I've made loads of mistakes but this is not one of them.

'Next,' she shouts.

I smile at her and say, 'Thank you,' which I know must nearly drive her over the edge. Politeness is to rude people as a burning match is to a witch tied at the stake. They *hate* it. Although I'm not sure if she's rude to everyone. It might just be me. We got off on the wrong foot, when I registered. I had to fill in a form that day. I signed the bottom of it and handed it to her.

'You forgot a bit,' she says, pointing at the box with the one question that I couldn't answer.

'No,' I say, 'I didn't forget.' I hope she might leave it at that. She does not.

'Why didn't you fill it in, then?' she asks, and

her narrow eyebrows arch in arrows on her forehead.

'I don't know the answer,' I say, in a low voice. We are behind a narrow partition but anyone on the other side of the partition can hear our conversation. Privacy — like everything else at the hospital apart from patients — is in short supply.

'You don't know who the father of your baby is?' She doesn't say it loudly but she says it loudly enough for anyone in the reception that afternoon to hear her.

'No,' I say, and the shame of it eats away at me like a virus.

When it becomes clear that I am not going to offer up my sordid little story, she shifts in her chair and says, 'I see.' I know what she sees. And it's not good. She looks at my form again. At the blank space where the answer to the question should be. She shakes her head and bends to the page and in big, block letters, she writes, 'Not known.'

'I have to write that in,' she explains to me, 'otherwise the form will get returned to me from every department I send it to because it's not completed.'

I sit on one of the narrow, hard seats that line the long, narrow corridor and wait for my turn. Nobody tells you what to do. You work it out for yourself by watching what other people do. First, you pee into a short plastic bottle with a yellow lid. Next, you stand in line with your bottle of urine hot in your hands. A nurse weighs you and shouts it out at the top of her voice. The third stage is tricky. You sit in the first empty chair along the corridor and *shuffle*, one chair at a time, until you reach the top of the queue, which could take anything from forty minutes to three hours. If you do not shuffle as soon as the chair to your right becomes empty, the person on your left will tap your shoulder and point out the empty chair to you. You have to be on the ball. You can't allow yourself to get distracted.

Now I need to go to the toilet. In spite of the fact that I gave the nurse a urine sample not thirty minutes ago. I could have filled the sample bottle to the brim if I'd wanted. Like I did that first time. Nobody tells you how much urine is necessary when supplying a sample. I think about the Sahara Desert and manage to hold on for two shuffles but there are still — I do a quick count — seventeen shuffles to go and I know I won't make it. I tell the people on either side of my chair that I will be back. I feel obliged to leave something of value on the chair as a guarantee of my intention to return. I ask them to shuffle my belongings along the queue in the unlikely event of a shuffle happening while I'm gone.

I'm only gone three minutes but when I return someone is sitting in my seat. Sprawling, really, his legs reaching all the way across the corridor. He leans towards the man on the chair beside him. They are both gazing at a grainy black-and-white scan photograph the man holds between his fingers.

'Amazing,' Red says, shaking his head.

The man nods and looks up. 'It's your first

time, isn't it?' he says. 'I can tell.'

I step in front of Red. 'What are you doing here?'

'Scarlett, hi.' He jumps up and smiles at me. 'How are you feeling?'

'How did you even know where I was sitting?'

He smiles at me and nods at the things I had left behind on the chair to secure my place in the queue. My key ring with the photograph of Phyllis and Blue, taken at Blue's last birthday party. Blue is sitting on Phyllis's knees, his front paws on the kitchen table as he leans towards a chocolate cake in the shape of a mackerel, which is his favourite fish.

'Also your jacket,' he says, nodding towards the chair.

'Oh,' I say.

'The way it's folded. It's so . . . neat.'

'Is there any other way to fold jackets?'

He laughs as if I've said something funny.

I pick up the keys and shove them into my handbag, then pick up my coat and sit down. 'But how did you . . . ?'

'It was written in the calendar on the kitchen door. I saw it when I was at Tara yesterday.'

I curse Phyllis, who writes everything in that calendar. 'Well,' I say, 'there was no need.'

'I know,' he says. 'And I hope you don't mind?' He looks at me with his head to one side and for once, there is no smile on his face, which for some reason makes me feel bad, as if this absence is my fault.

'Well, I . . . '

The man on the chair beside me makes a great

253

show of looking the other way, all the while waiting for me to answer. Just then the line shuffles up one place and suddenly there is a vacancy to my right. I sigh and indicate the chair with a curt nod of my head. The man beside me releases the breath he's been holding and Red's smile makes a reappearance as he slots into the chair beside me, like he's been sitting there all his life. I turn to face him but he gets in before me.

'Look, Scarlett, I know,' he says, training his eyes on the floor and speaking in a low voice. 'I know that I shouldn't be here. That you probably don't want me to be here. But when Filly said — '

'Filly?'

'I rang her this morning. There was no mention on the calendar of which hospital you were going to so I rang Filly.'

'Oh.'

'And she said you'd be here and I asked her if there was anyone with you and she said no, that you always go on your own and I just felt — '

'Don't say that you felt sorry for me.' I say it louder than I intend to and a few heads swivel our way.

'Christ, no. I wasn't going to say anything like that.' Red looks appalled at the notion. 'I was just going to say that I thought it might be nice to have someone to wait with. That's all. I even brought a pack of cards. Look.' He takes the cards out of his pocket. They are loose and dog-eared and it's highly unlikely that there are fifty-two of them.

'What card games do you know?' I ask, despite myself.

'I'm great at snap,' he says, beginning to deal the cards. 'Or beg-o'-my-neighbour. Now *there's* a game.'

'How about gin rummy?' I ask. He smiles apologetically and I smile back at him, without meaning to.

I teach him how to play blackjack. He calls clubs 'shamrocks'. I deal and we shuffle up the chairs. We play. I beat him in five straight games. Then I let him win one. This surprises me. I never let anyone win. The best part of an hour goes by. I'm surprised to find we're nearly at the top of the queue.

'I'd better go,' Red says, gathering the cards and shoving them back into his pocket. 'I left Al Pacino in the flat this morning. I wasn't sure what the hospital policy was on dogs.' He waves and says, 'Good luck with the doctor,' and then he is gone, leaving the scent of something warm and sweet in his wake, like melted chocolate.

'Sorry, Scarlett, I forgot to give you this.' Red is back again, holding out a battered brown-paper bag. Inside is a cheese sandwich, as flat as a pancake. 'I wasn't sure how long you'd have to wait.' He thrusts the bag into my hands and is gone again.

It is only really then that I think about Sofia Marzoni. My most important client. I'm wondering if she knows what a truly terrible card player she's marrying and, even though this is a flippant thought to think when you've just spent the best part of an hour with one of your most

255

important client's fiancés, the thought makes me smile. I shuffle along one more chair and then I'm at the head of the queue.

My doctor is not the chatty type. He bends his head towards my file and says, 'Eh . . . Scarlett O'Hara, is it?' He points to the examination table and I lie on it and pull my shirt up. He feels my belly. It is called palpating. He *palpates* my belly. His hands are freezing and the cold of them takes my breath away. He turns away and writes something in my file. He takes my blood pressure. He turns away and writes something in my file. He knows about the miscarriage. He never mentions it but I watch him, whenever he is palpating and taking my blood pressure and reading my file. I watch him like people watch airhostesses during a patch of turbulence. His face is impassive and I take comfort from it. Impassivity is good.

★ ★ ★

Outside on the street, my mobile phone rings. It's Filly.

'Simon is back,' she says. 'He was just looking for you.'

My pulse rate picks up. I can feel it.

'You didn't tell him where I was, did you?'

'Don't be a daft sow,' says Filly. She has a poor view of farm animals, especially pigs. 'I gave him the party line.'

'What did he say?'

'He looked suspicious.' This is not the end of the world. Simon always looks suspicious. 'He

256

said it's very early to be thinking about flowers for the wedding.'

'But he knows how organised I am,' I say, stung by the unfairness of it all, even though it is a pack of lies.

'He left a message for you.'

'A nice message?' I am clutching at straws here.

'It's about your interview.'

My hands tighten around the phone. 'Go on,' I say.

'It's on Monday,' Filly says. 'At three o'clock. He says he hopes that's not too short notice.'

It's about as short as notice can get.

'I'm on my way back,' I say, beginning to run down the road towards my car.

'Don't spare the horses,' says Filly, and hangs up.

30

The weekend feels longer than usual. For a start, John doesn't phone on Friday night at eight o'clock. When I ring his mobile, it's turned off. When I ring it again, it's still turned off. I can't even leave a message. I text him instead, inserting a smiley face at the end, then deleting the face just before I press the 'send' button.

I ring Bryan, who comes up with very logical reasons as to why John hasn't rung. A dead battery. Someone's nicked his recharger. He's down an underground tunnel digging and there's no reception. He's trapped under something heavy and his phone is out of reach.

'Let's talk about something else,' I say. I feel like I'm using stepping stones to cross a raging river, each one shifting under my feet.

'Declan rang me today,' Bryan says, obligingly.

'Really?' I say. Declan rarely uses the phone. He doesn't *trust* them, he says, since he played the part of that FBI agent in the movie *Phone Tap*.

'Yeah, he wants me to source a location for *The Jou ney*.'

'I thought they had that warehouse in Carlow?' I say.

'They did but the guy who owns it wants it back now. His wife has thrown him and all his belongings out of the house and he needs the warehouse back.'

258

'He's going to live in a warehouse?' This seems harsh.

'Yeah, but in fairness he deserves it. Apparently, he was having an affair with his au pair and the au pair's twin sister, who lives two doors up.'

I take a moment to digest this.

'Anyway, I've found the ideal location,' Bryan continues. 'It's a stone cottage by a lake in County Fermanagh. It's perfect. Remote and wild. Just like the father's character.'

'So you've read the screenplay?' I ask.

'Yeah, Declan snuck it over to me. I love it. So does Cora.' Cora is Bryan's boss.

'She wants to produce it but Red is resisting. He doesn't want to compromise but I think he's going to have to. His budget is threadbare. He says he'll sell his car if he has to but have you seen it?'

'Seen what?'

'His car.'

'Yes.'

'He'll have to let us produce it.'

'So you've met him?' I ask then.

'Red?'

'Yes.'

'I did.'

'And . . . ?'

'He reminded me a bit of Declan when he was younger. Very passionate about his art.'

'Well, that's not good news,' I say.

'Why not?' Bryan wants to know.

'Because Declan wasn't exactly ideal father material, as you know.'

'Well, yes, but he meant well, didn't he. His intentions were good.'

This is true but try telling that to a nine-year-old who waits outside the school gates for forty-five minutes on a cold, sodden Monday in February for a father who never arrives because not only does he forget to pick her up, he forgets to tell anyone else that he's forgotten to pick her up so they can go in his stead.

'Anyway,' I say, pushing my hair back from my eyes, 'statistically, Red is not the father. It's John, isn't it?'

Bryan sighs. We've had this conversation many times and I can hear him tire of it. 'We'll just have to wait and see, Scarlett. Let's just get this baby born, safe and sound, and then we'll worry about it, OK?'

I nod my head, which is foolish because Bryan can't see me doing it. Bryan makes me promise to ring him as soon as John Smith rings before hanging up.

But John Smith doesn't ring.

★   ★   ★

On Saturday, Filly and Elliot arrive at the house. Bryan can't come because he needs to prepare for a second date with a French woman he met at his yoga class. On Filly's advice, he has recorded 'Tom Traubert's Blues' as the ringtone on his phone. 'There is nothing nice about 'Tom Traubert's Blues',' she tells him.

As far as I can make out, the three of them are operating a rota and, at the weekend, one, two or sometimes all three of them can be found at Tara at various times of the night and day. They are kind and take me places. A circus at Custom House Quay. An aquarium that smells a bit like a jay-cloth that hasn't been wrung out in a while. The zoo.

We're talking about the interview. What else? 'It's not the end of the world,' Filly says. She settles herself on the couch in the den with her legs crisscrossed, making a pouch of her skirt between the triangle of her thighs and her calves for Blue to snooze in. He steps into it, as he always does, as dainty as a china teacup, and is asleep in seconds.

'You've got your presentation prepared, you know all the answers to any of his slimy questions, and you're the best wedding planner in the country. What else is there?' She looks at me, and with her hope and her faith, I almost think I can do it.

The door opens and Red Butler appears. 'Oh, sorry,' he says. 'I didn't realise you were here. I was looking for Declan.' He smiles around the room and the others smile back at him, like they can't help it. There's something a tiny bit infectious about Red Butler, I've noticed.

'He's at Hugo's house,' I say, not looking up.

Al Pacino bursts into the room, skidding to a halt when he reaches Blue, who is still curled in a ball on Filly's lap. When Blue sees him, he stands up, stretches and steps daintily on to the flat of Al's back. When he gets comfortable, the dog moves off, slowly now so that he does not

261

dislodge Blue. They disappear out through the door.

'That is one weird relationship,' says Elliot.

'Cats and dogs *can* become friends, you know,' says Filly, who always likes to see the best in people. And animals.

'Yes, normal cats,' says Elliot. 'But this is Blue we're talking about.'

Before I can roll up my newspaper to smack Elliot over the head with it, Red speaks up.

'Blue is a lovely cat. It just takes him a while to get used to people.'

'How long?' asks Elliot, looking at a day-old scratch that runs the length of his forearm.

I turn to Red. 'You can leave Al Pacino here, if you like. While you're at Hugo's, I mean. Hugo's a bit scared of him and I've got a bag of dog food in the back kitchen. I'll give him his dinner.'

'You bought dog food?'

'Well . . . yes. I picked it up when I was buying Blue's cat food. Just in case of emergencies.'

'Thank you,' he says. 'That's kind of you.'

'Not at all,' I say, even though I do not normally say things like 'not at all'.

He smiles again around the room and Elliot and Filly smile back at him, like they can't help it, and then he is gone and the room seems immediately tidier.

Elliot and Filly look at me. 'Not at all?' they both say, at the same time.

'Be quiet — he'll hear you,' I hiss at them.

'You're very . . . polite with each other,' Elliot says, frowning in confusion.

'Well, he's always bloody well here,' I tell him.

'It's impossible to maintain a consistent degree of hostility when the target is constantly around. It's exhausting.'

'He's cute, though, isn't he?' This unhelpful aside from Filly.

'He's a floozy,' I remind them.

'Oh, yeah,' says Filly, like she's just remembered. She shakes her head. 'He really doesn't seem the type, though, does he?'

I say nothing — just narrow my eyes at her — and she has the sense to drop the subject.

★   ★   ★

Later, Elliot treats us to lunch in Avoca. Filly gets a text from Brendan. 'He says to say hi and that he's doing a brisk business in lambs' livers,' she says, looking up from her phone.

'Did he really say the bit about the livers?' asks Elliot, shivering slightly. He's not been a big fan of liver since his biology teacher slapped a piece on the lab table and made the class watch while the liver curled itself round a bottle of milk.

'I'm afraid so,' says Filly, snapping her phone shut. 'Sorry, Elliot, you know the way he loves talking about meat.'

We nod. This is true.

Suddenly, I raise my glass towards them.

'I just want to say . . . ' I begin, and I have their attention now.

'Go on,' says Elliot, and Filly nods at me, waiting.

'Well . . . ' I say, feeling foolish now. 'I just wanted to say thank you. Both of you,' I say, a

263

little taken aback by myself.

'For what?' they say at the same time, looking confused, as if I have just asked them what time it is.

'Just ... you know ... for being so ... supportive and ... you know ... ' I trail off.

Filly and Elliot look at each other and say, 'Hormones,' at the same time. I want to disagree. I want to tell them I love them both. For lots of different reasons. I want to tell them how lucky I feel. That they are here. That they are my friends.

Of course, I don't tell them any of that but, when they look at me, I smile and somehow I think they know.

31

John does not return my calls or send me any more of his texts with the smiley faces. He arrives back instead. In person. On Monday morning. Unannounced and unexpected. Like a piece of lost luggage you've stopped waiting for.

Since I stopped throwing up in the morning, I enter the building through the front door again, rather than the fire-exit door at the back of the building.

It is 6.30 a.m. I have been up since 5 a.m., although I only got into bed at 2 a.m. for show. The insomnia worsens when something big is happening the next day. And today is the day of my interview. With Simon and the rest of the board. I hate that I need this job so much. That I want it. When I park the car, I take my pulse and I can hardly count it, it's that fast. My breathing sounds shallow and I can feel the frantic beat of my heart, like the wings of a bird trapped in my chest. I consider the symptoms and conclude that I am *nervous*.

I take Blue out of his cage and slip Filly's yellow ribbon through the loop of his collar. He only arches his back to halfmast and his hiss is quieter than usual. It is his way of being supportive.

'Thanks, Blue,' I whisper at him before stepping out of the car. I wait while Blue stretches himself across the width of the car — to illustrate the cramped conditions he is forced to endure, and I take my briefcase and handbag and laptop out of the boot. I hold the lead in one hand and everything else in the other.

I have a random thought. Sometimes, when sleep is scarcer than usual, I have random thoughts. They float into my head like a feather and skid along the ground before coming to a stop for a brief moment to allow me to think the thought. You have to be quick with random thoughts. The slightest distraction and they are gone, like the tail ends of dreams that you chase when you wake up. Today's random thought is this: Everything I own is right here. I look around me.

My car. My Aston Martin. My wonderful, impractical, racing-car-green Aston Martin. A 32-valve, 4.7-litre engine with a top speed of 288 kilometres per hour even though the fastest I've ever driven it is 120 kilometres per hour.

My cat. Blue St John O'Hara (Maureen insisted on giving him the middle name, which is the name she would have called me, had I been a boy).

My laptop with all my lists and my plans and my weddings — my life's work, really.

And even Ellen, sleeping now in my belly. Although I don't own her as such. But she is mine. That much I know.

I shift and the random thought disappears, like a bubble that bursts on a single blade of grass.

So, with everything I own, I walk to the front of the office. The rising sun pours itself like a drink all over the building, which is mostly glass, and I would shield my eyes from its glare, had I a spare hand. I walk up the steps like a child might, both feet on each of the steps, careful with my load. I don't see him until I am nearly at the top of the ten steps. And when I do see him, I can't believe it's him and I blink a few times like a person in the desert might when they come upon an oasis.

'John?' I stop on the ninth step and my voice sounds like somebody else's voice: high-pitched and breathy.

'Scarlett, I knew I'd catch you here,' he says, and he is smiling, pleased with himself. His smile is wider than I remember. His teeth whiter against the angry red of his face. The sunburn looks third degree. Mosquitoes have made a meal of John's face and have left him with a series of bites that weep and roar and settle on every available inch of his skin. I'd forgotten about the unrequited love that mosquitoes have for him.

'What are you doing here?' I ask, still standing on the ninth step.

'Here, let me take those bags for you.' He reaches me in two of his long strides and bends to pet Blue before taking the bags. To his credit, Blue turns his back on John and lifts his tail to reveal the red, mottled circle of his behind. John takes it well and turns to me and takes my handbag and my briefcase and my laptop. He isn't brave enough to take Blue's lead.

'You look well, Scarlett,' he says, and I see him snatching a look at my belly but Ellen is hidden beneath my suit.

'What are you doing here?' I repeat.

'Morning, Scarlett.' We turn to the voice and it is Elliot, leaping up the ten steps with two newspapers tucked under each arm, a coffee in one hand and a paper bag in the other, which I know contains an apple and cinnamon muffin. His umbrella swings from the crook of his left elbow. His gait slows as he realises who is with me. 'Oh. Good morning, John,' he says, slower now, glancing at me to see if I would like him to bash John over the head with the handle of his umbrella, which, in fairness, is a good, thick, mahogany one. I shake my head so slightly only Elliot can see it.

He stops when he reaches us, on the ninth step. 'What on earth happened to your face?'

John reaches his fingers to his face and lets them trail across one cheek. They bump across. The bites lie in various stages across his face and up and down his neck. Some — the newer ones — are angry and red and wet. The older ones — the veterans, Filly will call them later — have crusted over. I cannot decide which ones are the least painful to look at and then I realise that I am going to vomit, right there, on the ninth step in the front of my office building on the day of my interview with Simon. And the rest of the board. The time between realising you are going to vomit and actually vomiting is short. Less than a second. A tenth of a second. Not much time to decide where you will deposit your breakfast (a bowl of Phyllis's Coco Pops, only because I'd forgotten to buy porridge and Declan had eaten all of the Rice Krispies). I snatch my briefcase out of John's hand, open it and vomit inside. When I am finished, I lower the bag from my mouth and zip it up. I look at Elliot and John, who try to arrange their faces into something other than shock (Elliot, who thought I was over the morning sickness) and disquiet (John, who has never been good with bodily secretions. It's lucky, really, that he can't see his own face).

Elliot hands me one of his outsized linen handkerchiefs with his initials embroidered in the corner: EFCF. John takes a discreet step backwards.

I wipe the corners of my mouth and feel at a distinct disadvantage, standing there as I am with a briefcase of vomit hanging from my left hand. It's difficult to take control of a situation like that, even though I know both John and Elliot are waiting for me to do just that.

I hand Elliot the handkerchief. 'Eh, thanks, Elliot,' I say.

'No, no, you keep it,' says Elliot, not touching it.

'I'll give it back to you,' I say. 'After I've washed it, I mean.'

'Dry-clean only, I'm afraid,' says Elliot.

It is John who takes the situation in hand, once he realises that I am not going to. 'Scarlett, could I talk to you? In private, I mean?' He smiles at Elliot to indicate that no offence is meant and Elliot smiles back to show that none is taken.

'Certainly,' I say, seeing as we're all being so polite to each other. 'Elliot, could you . . . ?' I hold my briefcase out and, in fairness to Elliot, he hesitates for only a moment before taking it from me as if there is nothing untoward inside. He takes my handbag and laptop from John, calls Blue to heel like a dog and somehow manages to enter the building without spilling his coffee or dropping his muffin.

'Will we go to Rose's?' John asks.

I shake my head. Rose's is where we used to go, on the rare occasions when John came to the office to meet me. It's one of those cafés with chintz curtains at the windows and rose-patterned tablecloths and tea served in china cups on saucers and scones with clotted cream and homemade preserve. It's the type of place where you go to plan lovely things to do. Like planting a herb garden or doing a big clear-out of your attic space. I don't know what kind of conversation John and I are about to have but I don't want to have it at Rose's.

'Let's just walk,' I say, starting down the steps. I look at my watch. According to my daily planner, I'm supposed to be in the boardroom checking the connections for my laptop and making sure my PowerPoint presentation is flawless, even though I know it is. Instead, I am walking up Dame Street with my mosquito-and-sun-savaged ex-boyfriend, who may or may not be the father of my unborn baby and who is supposed to be wielding a trowel and turning the red clay of some remote village seventy-five kilometres from Sao Paulo. I decide not to say anything until John does. I concentrate on the world around me and am surprised to see that it is summertime. I have been measuring time in weeks for so long I forgot to notice the changing of the seasons. Dame Street is a carnival of bright flowers spilling from window boxes and hanging baskets. Swallows dart and dive, brave now in the soft focus of early-morning Dublin. We are nearly at Christchurch and neither of us has said anything. Somewhere a church bell rings and Ellen moves inside me, probably wondering what happened to her Coco Pops and all that lovely chocolate milk that now sits in a soggy sludge at the bottom of my briefcase.

'You don't happen to have a banana on you, do you?' I ask.

'As a matter of fact, I do,' he says, and produces one from an inside pocket of his jacket.

There is no one else in the world I could ask for a banana at — I look at my watch — 6.52 a.m. John has what I need. He always did. I loved that about him. I miss that. I sit on a bench in the grounds of the cathedral and John sits beside me. I peel the banana and eat it. Inside me, Ellen does a somersault. She loves bananas.

'Why are you here?' I finally ask, when the banana peel lies limp in my hands. 'I wasn't expecting you until the end of July. You said — '

'I know what I said,' he says, cutting me off. 'But I wanted to be here for the scan. It's next week, isn't it?'

'Thursday,' I say.

He takes out his diary and writes down the details.

'But why . . . ?' My mind feels sluggish. I can't take anything in.

'I wanted to be here,' he repeats. 'I've missed so much already. I don't want to miss any more.' There is a finality in his tone and I don't want to ask a question beginning with 'why' again. I go for 'how' instead. 'How long are you staying?'

'Staying?' John looks confused. 'I'm back for good.'

'Why?'

'You know why,' he says, and then he nods towards my belly. Towards Ellen. In this sitting position, she is evident in the strain of the buttons of my jacket. I undo them and the swell of my belly rushes up at me and I hear John's sharp intake of breath as reality bites him like a dog and, for a moment, we are nearly like a proper family with the smell of cut grass all around us, sweet like cake.

'I've come back to take care of you and the baby,' John says, and there is a hurt expression in his eyes, as if he can't believe I haven't worked this out by myself.

'There was no need for you to do that. I'm fine. We're fine.'

'It's my responsibility. You know that.'

'I thought I knew a lot of things but I didn't know that you were going to leave me.'

'I know . . . I . . . '

'What's different now?' I ask, even though I know the answer.

'We're going to have a baby,' he says, and the weird thing is, he smiles when he says it.

'You never wanted children,' I remind him.

'I never planned on having any,' he corrects me. 'But now that I'm going to . . . well . . . I've thought about it and . . . well . . . I'm OK about it.'

'You're *OK* about it?' I say and my tone is definitely scathing.

'I mean . . . I'm fine about it . . . In fact, I'm . . . ' Now John assumes a pained expression as he struggles to find the right word. 'I'm . . . happy about it. I'm happy.'

I look at him, trying to see him through the bites and the welts and the sunburn. And the thing is, he *does* look happy. Not in an ecstatic kind of a way, like the time he came second in the All-Ireland Amateur Chess Championship. No, it's more like contentment. He looks content.

An image of Red Butler buzzes into my head and I swat at it and squash it against the window in my head that looks out on to my brain. I lower my face into my hands and I think I must have groaned aloud because John's arms go around me and it's been so long since I've had any real physical contact I almost allow myself to lean against him and feel the familiar solidness of him and smell the familiar smell of him.

'John, there's something I have to tell you,' I say in a voice that is louder than necessary.

'Scarlett, look, I know we've loads to talk about and, don't get me wrong, I want to talk about it but I only allocated half an hour for this meeting and I need to speak to my old boss and get my old job back and I need to go to the flat and get it ready for you. For us. What about we meet after work?'

Something fizzes inside me and I stand up. I don't know where to start. 'First of all,' I say, holding up one finger to indicate that there is a list of items on my agenda, 'I am not moving back in with you.'

'No, of course not, I know that. Not right away,' he says, retreating a little. 'Obviously.'

'And secondly,' I continue, 'I did not allocate *any* time to you today, seeing as I thought you were rummaging around in some hole in Central bloody America.'

'South America, actually,' he says, and because it is John who says it, I know that he does not mean to sound so . . . so bloody . . . so *smug*.

'You *abandoned* me,' I remind him, and he recoils, like I've hit him.

'Come on, Scarlett, *abandoned* is a bit of a strong word, isn't it?'

'You *abandoned* me,' I say again, 'and now you waltz back here with — '

'I'm hardly waltzing, Scarlett. Be fair.' It's true. He doesn't know how to waltz. Or samba. Or can-can. Or jig. Or reel. Or any kind of dance.

'I have to go,' I say.

'I'll walk back with you,' he says.

'No,' I say. 'You won't.'

'Will you meet me after work?' he asks, and he looks like he really wants me to and a part of me wants me to. It would be so easy, to fall back into this relationship. To lie on it like a hammock and swing in the gentle breeze of it and wait for Ellen to come.

I shake myself. 'Not tonight, John. I have to think about things. There are things you need to know.'

He nods when I say this, as if he already knows the things he needs to know. In fairness to him, he usually does.

But not this time. How could he?

32

By the time I get back to the office, the day has begun without me and I am behind, where I remain until twenty minutes before the interview. I run to the boardroom to check the connection for my laptop and to go over my PowerPoint presentation one more time but Simon and the directors are already in there and a heated discussion is underway. I can tell by the hard creases of Simon's normally flaccid face. I creep away and bump into Gladys Montgomery, further down the corridor.

'Scarlett,' she says, and in her long-drawn-out drawl of a voice, it takes her several seconds to get the word out. 'You look a little nervous, so you do.' She smiles as if she's just told me that I have won a year's supply of cat food. 'Is that a *smock* you're wearing?'

It most definitely is *not* a smock. Merely a looser-fitting top than I normally wear, partial as I am to crisp, fitted blouses under my suits. My bump seems to have grown in the last few hours and I wonder at a child of mine having such a poor sense of timing. I hold the laptop against my belly.

'How did your interview go?' I manage to say.

'Fantastic,' says Gladys. 'Although Simon said it was more like an informal chat, considering our great working relationship. It was very relaxed, so it was.' She pops a Rennie into her mouth and arranges her face into a smirk.

Her breath smells of egg. She runs her tongue along her teeth to check for spinach. She must have eaten the vegetable quiche for lunch.

'I saw John walking down Dame Street this morning,' Gladys says. 'It doesn't look like Central America agrees with him, does it?'

'South America,' I say, but my tone is not as assured as I would like it to be. If Gladys knows John is back, then so does Simon and this is not a good thing for him to know, twenty minutes before my interview. He will put it down as a *distraction*.

'Whatever,' says Gladys, and moves off down the corridor. Her work here is done.

I return to my office and lower myself into a chair. I could lie down on the floor, I'm that tired. This is the problem with insomnia. When you feel like you actually *could* get some sleep, it's an unsuitable time of the day, like twenty minutes — no, fifteen now — before the most important interview you've ever done. The door bursts open and Filly stands there, panting.

'I just heard. Elliot told me. Are you OK?' She's been out of the office all morning with a vet. They went to a stud farm in Kildare to do a trial pink dye on one of the horses there. The tips of her fingers are pink.

'I didn't get time to test the connections in the boardroom,' I say.

'It doesn't matter. You tested them on Friday, didn't you?'

'Well, yes, but . . . '

'They're fine, Scarlett, don't worry.' She moves to my side of the desk and massages my temples with the tips of her fingers. I let her until I remember the pink dye. I leap up and rummage in my bag for a mirror. The skin on my temples is a delicate shade of pink, as if I've *deliberately* brushed some blusher there. I rub the skin but it makes no difference whatsoever.

'Aw, strewth, Letty . . . I forgot about the Jaysis dye,' says Filly. 'If it helps at all, you should see my coat. It's bloody ruined.'

'It doesn't help,' I say.

'The good news is,' Filly continues as if nothing has happened, 'the dye works a treat and it's the *exact* same colour as Sofia's dress and Red's shirt.'

'Delighted,' I say, rubbing at the skin of my temples now with a face wipe. I've rubbed it so hard that I can't tell if the dye has lifted or is merely skulking behind the skin, which is now the colour of a bunch of cherries.

'I'll redo your make-up,' offers Filly. 'I'll cover it up, you'll see. Nobody will notice.'

I don't know why I let her. I'd say it has something to do with the reappearance of John Smith into my life and the pear-shape of the day that I had planned so carefully. But I let her, forgetting that Filly can't do subtle daytime make-up. Her talent is for dramatic, night-time make-up that, in fairness, looks great in subdued lighting. She does not have a default button for the daytime. She throws everything she has at me: lipstick, lip gloss, blusher, powder, foundation, concealer, pencils, eye shadow, mascara. When she is finished with me, I look like I am going to interview for a job as a hostess in a lap-dancing club.

I look at my watch. Five minutes to go. I have run out of time. A certain degree of *resignation* settles on me. I don't recognise it at first; it is not a common visitor to these parts.

'Stand up and let's get a look at you,' commands Filly, and I do what I am told, which is part of this resignation that I am feeling. Filly frowns at my face. 'I *think* it's OK,' she says. 'I've gone for the barely there look. I mean, you're not going for an interview as a hostess in a lap-dancing club, after all. Although if Simon had his way . . . ' She sniggers.

'Wish me luck,' I say, picking up my laptop and my briefcase.

'Is that the briefcase you vommed into?' asks Filly.

'Yes.'

'Best not to bring it so. Mightn't create the right impression.'

Reluctantly, I set the briefcase down. I feel incomplete without it, like I'm walking down a crowded street with no knickers on under my skirt.

'And I'm not going to wish you luck,' says Filly. 'You won't need it.'

Suddenly, I'm superstitious. 'If you don't wish me luck, I won't get the job.' I don't know why I know this but I know it. I'm sure of it.

'You will.'

'I won't.'

'You will.'

'I won't.'

'You're going to be late.'

Filly knows how to distract me. I leave the office at a gallop.

33

The interview begins badly. First of all, there's the smell. Damn Calvin Klein for making it OK for men to wear perfume. And there's four different variations of it. The pregnancy has provided me with a sense of smell that would give a bloodhound a run for his money.

'You've gone very pale, Scarlett,' says Raymond, the finance director. He prides himself on his feminine side, which mostly manifests itself as an eagerness to purchase tampons for his wife every month. He loves this about himself. If he had his way, his out-of-office email reply would say, 'Raymond Darlington is out of the office, buying tampons and Panadol for his wife. He will respond to your message on his return.'

'I'm fine,' I say. 'Just a little hot in here. Could we open a window?'

But the windows are stuck fast, due to the hiring of a painting contractor last month. Except he wasn't a painting contractor. He turned out to be a Polish waiter, posing as a painting contractor, and he painted the windows shut with paint that you're not supposed to use anywhere near windows and they've remained thus ever since. Philip Webb explains this to me in tortuous detail, which, when you take his stutter into account, takes the best part of five minutes.

'OK, Philip, we get the picture,' says Simon. 'Shall we begin?'

They nod in unison, even Roger Everett, who is monosyllabic at best and rarely moves any part of himself, a fact not unrelated to his size. Filly calls him Mount Everett, even though I tell her not to.

'Here, have some water, Scarlett,' says Raymond, who probably thinks I'm *online*, which is the word he uses for periods. I would smile at the irony were I not concentrating so hard on not vomiting in the hot stench of the boardroom.

I accept the glass of water and drain it. In the silence of the room, every swallow is as distinct as a thunderclap. I set the empty glass on the table. Simon leans over and lifts the glass and rubs at the circle of water the glass deposits with a tissue and makes a great show of rummaging in every drawer until he finds what he is looking for, which is a coaster, and places it under the glass. The whole process takes no more than thirty seconds but it feels longer. Much longer.

'S-s-s-s-s-so, Scarlett,' says Philip, 'a-a-a-are you g-g-g-going to d-d-d-do a P-P-P-PowerPoint pr-pr-pr-presentation?' Philip *loves* PowerPoint.

'Yes,' I say, reaching for my laptop. 'I just need to set this up and . . . ' I plug the laptop in and turn it on and look around for the screen at the top of the boardroom, which was there on Friday when I came to check that everything was in place. It is not there. I blink and look again but it makes no difference. It is still not there. I turn to face the four men in their sombre suits behind

282

me. Eight eyes fasten on me, waiting.

'I . . . I thought the screen . . . It was here on Friday . . . '

'Oh, yes, Scarlett, I forgot to tell you,' says Simon, looking not the least bit sorry. 'Gladys took it away earlier. Said it needed to be repaired.'

'But . . . it was working fine last week.' I struggle to keep the note of panic out of my voice.

'You can just ad-lib, Scarlett,' Simon says, and he leans back in his chair with both hands behind his head and waits.

The other three — who always take their cue from Simon — do the same, apart from Roger, who can't reach his arms that far back.

Ad-libbing is not my strong point but there is nothing else for it. I have to do it. I'd prefer to do it standing up but Ellen is hidden under the table and I have to keep her there for the duration.

'I'll just . . . ' I begin, bending towards the keyboard of my laptop and pecking furiously at keys, trying to remember where I put the presentation. My mind is like an empty stage with the curtains tightly drawn. It's dark in there and, with eight eyes fastened on me, I try and try to remember what Plan B was. Surely I had one?

It's when I straighten from this position that it happens. The middle button on the jacket of my suit comes away with an audible 'pop' and skitters across the gleaming mahogany of the boardroom table, coming to rest in front of Simon, as if for inspection. Simon leans forward

283

and picks it up. He looks at me and I see what he sees. Through the gap between the top and bottom buttons of my jacket, Ellen rises, like a bun in an oven. I sit back too quickly on my chair, forgetting it is the chair we call 'the Windbreaker'. A sound like a high-pitched fart pings about the room and the directors shift in their seats and look everywhere except at my face, which is the colour of a punnet of strawberries.

I launch into the presentation suddenly and without warning. With a blank wall instead of a screen, the four men have nowhere to look but at me. Their glassy stares pin me to the chair, where I do my best to hide behind my laptop on the table in front of me. I trudge through my presentation, regurgitating it line by line and page by page. It's like wading through mud but I keep going, one heavy foot after another. The men let me, saying nothing. Except when I say 'scallions' instead of 'stallions'. Then Raymond stops me with an apologetic smile. 'She wants four pink *scallions*, you say?' Later, when I check the presentation for any errors I may have made, I have in fact typed the word 'scallions' instead of 'stallions'.

When I finish, Simon shoots a string of questions at me and I answer each one and I can hear myself and I sound like I know what I am talking about. Even when he starts on the most clichéd of interview questions, like 'What is your worst trait?' (perfectionism) and 'What is your best trait?' (perfectionism). I'm on the home stretch when he says, 'What is your greatest fear?' I go through the list in my head:

Something bad happening to Ellen.

Telling John about Red Butler.

Finding out who Ellen's father is.

Sofia finding out about Red and his possible relationship to Ellen.

There are so many fears that I have to cast around for one I can share with Simon.

'Not getting this job,' I say, and I can look him in the eye when I say that because it's true that it is one of my fears. But it's not my greatest fear and, oddly, this comforts me. Simon looks away; he is not good at eye contact.

'Well, I think we've heard enough,' he says instead, looking around at the other three directors, who nod, apart from Roger, who appears to have fallen asleep, although it's hard to tell with those tinted glasses he wears. Simon leans across the desk and hands me my button.

'Oh, thank you,' I say, taking it and hiding it in a pocket. 'I must sew it back on.'

'I think you may need a new jacket,' says Simon, and I look up at him but, with his hooded eyes and flaccid features, it is difficult to tell what he is thinking or if he is thinking anything at all. But still, there is an air of suspicion about him and I am *certain* that he knows. About Ellen. I stand up and shield her from him, with my laptop against my belly.

'We'll let you know, Scarlett,' says Raymond with his trademark girly grin. Then he looks at Simon to see if it's all right that he said that.

Simon nods and smiles his small, tight smile and I am dismissed. I walk away and stop at my

285

office, only to pick up Blue and my vomit-ridden briefcase. Elliot and Filly want a post-mortem but I am too tired. No. I'm way past tired. I'm weary. After months of not sleeping properly — years, really, but never this bad — all I can think of is lying down and closing my eyes. I don't even think I'll have to count any farm animals or recite the alphabet backwards or concentrate on anything pleasant (like rearranging my shoes in order of heel-height).

Sofia is in reception. She is draped across the reception desk, her dark head almost touching Hailey's greying bob. I think I hear Hailey laughing, although I can't be sure. I've never heard her laugh before. For a moment, I consider tiptoeing past them but I am too late and they sense me and leap apart like scalded cats.

'Jaysis, Scarlah, you shouldn't sneak up on people like that.' Sofia's words tumble out and land in a heap at my feet. If I didn't know her better, I'd say she was nervous. I look at Hailey, who pretends to take a call. Two bright red spots sit high on her cheeks, making me think of Annabelle, a doll I loved when I was six.

'I was just leaving,' I say, and even though it is only — I check my watch — four o'clock in the afternoon, neither of them comment on my early retirement from the office. 'We don't have an appointment, do we?'

'Eh, no . . . I was . . . in the neighbourhood . . . and I promised Hails here I'd show her my Wham! memorabilia collection the next time I was . . . passin' by.'

286

Hails? Wham! memorabilia collection? And Sofia's office is in Finglas. What the . . . ?

The phone rings and Hailey dives for it. I move closer to the desk and I can see the corner of a Wham! poster, which looks like it's been signed, and the top half of what looks like a pair of boxer shorts.

'Hailey's got Andrew Ridgeley's T-shirt from the Club Tropicana tour,' Sofia tells me, having fully recovered her composure. 'With the original sweat stains an' all.' She looks down at Hailey and smiles at her, and Hailey, who appears to have forgotten that I am there, looks up and smiles back at Sofia and the smile is the most tender thing I have ever seen. I wonder at a world where people connect with each other over something as innocuous as a pair of George Michael's underpants.

I clear my throat. 'Well, I'm going now. Goodbye.'

Hailey doesn't even ask me where I am going, in spite of the fact that I have not emailed her to tell her I am going out, as I'm supposed to do. She just says, 'Goodbye,' like everything is normal and I am in my office working as usual and she is not sitting at her desk with a Wham! sweatband wrapped round her wrist.

'See you, Scarlah,' says Sofia, who has not asked me any questions about the pink-dye trial or the Italian rosé risotto recipe I'm supposed to be sourcing for the wedding banquet, as Sofia likes to call it.

I drive to Wicklow on automatic pilot. Maureen is unsurprised to see me, even though it is only five o'clock in the afternoon.

'Darling, how are you? Phyllis was just going to make some mint tea. Would you like some?'

'I'm going to bed,' I say, already halfway up the stairs.

'Good idea, darling. Night-night.'

I stop walking. 'It's five o'clock in the day,' I remind her. 'Don't you want to know why I'm going to bed?'

Maureen looks confused. 'I presume you are tired,' she says.

There is nothing to do but nod my head and continue the long journey up the stairs. Maureen smiles, delighted that she got the answer right. I get into bed in my clothes and Blue — thrilled with this unexpected turn of events — gets in beside me and settles himself behind me, in the bend of my knees. I am asleep in seconds.

34

When I wake up, it's one o'clock in the morning and I get up, knowing that there is no more sleep to be had. I wish — and not for the first time — that I could sleep like a normal person but it seems I am destined to roam the house by night like the cat that Blue is not. I lift the rug from my bed and wrap it around my shoulders. In spite of the season, the house is cold at night, the thick stone walls resistant to the sun's rays. I pick up my phone. Seven missed calls, all from John Smith. Seven voicemail messages. Seven text messages. They all say the same thing: 'Call me.' I replace the phone in my bag and move towards the study with my laptop. I glide through the house, not turning on any lights. I like the world when it is like this: dark and quiet. The peace is like a lullaby, whispering through the dark and, even though it doesn't send me to sleep, it has a soothing effect, like a cat's purr.

I tell myself that I'll do some work but really I'm going to log on to the Womb Raider site and see if anyone else is up. It's a site for people who are unexpectedly expecting. I receive a weekly newsletter telling me what Ellen is up to. Today, I am twenty weeks pregnant. I click on the twenty-week icon and wait.

'You're twenty weeks already?'

The scream that roars from me is sharp, piercing. It shatters the quiet like a rock thrown

289

at a pane of glass. Upstairs I hear Blue howling. He hates waking up alone. He's afraid of the dark. I look all around the room but, after the glare of the laptop monitor, I see nothing.

'Jesus, sorry, Scarlett, I didn't mean to startle you. Are you OK?' The voice comes from the corner of the room. From the couch. I recognise it. A gin-and-cigarettes voice. Some people would call it sexy. I turn towards it and there he is, lost in a bundle of blankets on the couch, where — it seems — he has been sleeping.

'What the hell are you doing here?' I hiss at him. 'You scared me half to death.'

'Sorry,' he says again. 'Declan and I were working late and my bloody car wouldn't start and Al Pacino fecked off somewhere and I couldn't find him for ages. By then, it was after midnight and Maureen insisted I stay.'

'But why aren't you sleeping in one of the spare rooms?' I ask.

'Maureen couldn't remember where the clean sheets are kept and Phyllis had already gone to bed,' says Red. He struggles off the couch. 'I'll go and calm Blue down.'

Before I can say anything, he is gone. When he returns, Blue is in his arms, his head on Red's shoulders. Red runs his hand down Blue's back, like he is burping a baby.

'Did you find Al Pacino?' I ask. Blue would be devastated if Al Pacino went missing.

'He was in Sylvester's pen,' he says.

'Hugo's goat?'

'Yeah. He loves goats. And cats. He's not right in the head but sure' — here Red shrugs his shoulders — 'who is?'

There doesn't seem to be a lot to say to this so I turn towards my computer. But I can feel him behind me, looking at me, and I remember I am still wearing my suit, which doesn't go very well with my Bagpuss slippers, which are that oversized, cutesy variety of slipper but exceptionally comfortable. Phyllis bought them for me for my thirty-second birthday. I shove my feet under the desk and out of Red's line of vision and then, annoyed, I take them back out again and place them where he can clearly see them. What do I care if he knows I wear cutesy-girly cat slippers?

'I like your slippers,' he says, and I quickly stuff them back under the desk. 'Have you had your scan yet?' he asks.

'No.'

How does he know about the twenty-week scan?

'I've registered with the Fathers-to-Be-or-Not-to-Be site,' he explains without my asking him. 'Right about now,' he continues, 'Ellen is growing her very own set of toenails. How clever is that?' He sounds proud of her in a way that makes me feel proud of her. What a baby. Growing a set of toenails. All by herself.

'I'll come to the scan with you,' he says then. 'If you like, I mean.'

'That won't be necessary,' I say.

'But I'd *like* to come,' he says. 'I'd love to see her.'

I turn my chair round until I am facing him. The room is brighter now, lit by a shaft of moonlight that slides through the bay window. It fills the study with its own brand of light, a silvery light that catches on Red Butler's face, softening the dark stubble climbing up his face and across his jaw.

'Look . . . ' I begin.

'I know, I know,' he says. 'She mightn't be mine. But she *might*.' He speaks with an intensity that surprises me. He sounds like he has thought about this. 'And if she is, I want to be a father to her. A proper father, I mean. Fathers are important things for children to have. Like BMX bikes and Nike trainers and birthday cake.'

I remember what Declan said about Red's father.

'Please, Scarlett?' He shoves his hands under his legs as if to warm them but it is really because he has crossed all his fingers and doesn't want me to notice. I was about to say no before I saw him do that. There is something vulnerable about the gesture. I hear myself say, 'Yes,' instead, despite my best efforts.

'Yes?' he repeats and his look is one of surprise.

'It's next Thursday at nine thirty a.m. in Holles Street.'

He lays Blue gently on his warm spot on the couch and takes a battered notebook out of his shirt pocket. He rifles through it, looking for an empty space. Every page is filled with his slanted, loopy handwriting but he finds a spare line near the back and scribbles in the time and date.

'That's half nine in the morning,' I say.

'Yeah, I know.'

'You've written, 'Nine thirty p.m.''

'Oh.' He scribbles out the 'p' and prints a tiny 'a' in the margin.

'Ooh,' I suddenly say as Ellen kicks me with both feet.

'Are you all right?' asks Red, moving towards me.

'Yes. It's just . . . '

'Did she kick?'

'Eh . . . yes.'

'Can I feel her?'

I want to say no but instead I nod my head. The unaccustomed sleep seems to have dulled my natural responses. Red, sensing that I may change my mind at any moment, reaches me and stops, rubbing his hands together and blowing on them.

'What are you doing?' I ask.

'I'm just warming my hands.' He whispers the words, as if Ellen can hear him. And then he unbuttons the two remaining buttons on my jacket and spreads his fingers across my belly and I can feel the heat of his hands, through the thin fabric of my top, and I hold my breath and bite my lip and hope he hurries up, which he does not. He crouches beside me and waits. He has a capacity for stillness that is rare in a man of his size. I list the hotels around Ireland in alphabetical order to distract myself from the thudding of my heart, which, surely, he can hear. Abbeyvale House Hotel, Adare Manor, Adelaide Court Hotel, Ahern Country House. But it's no use. Now I am remembering the wide expanse of

293

his chest, smooth and pale as moonlight. The way it tapers into the narrowest of waists. The pulse that jumps from his neck when I kiss there. The weight of his belt buckle in my hands.

The blood pounds around my body like the beat of a drum and I silently beg Ellen to kick.

I close my eyes and wish for it.

And then she does. Not a hard one. One of her gentle ones, like she is playing footsie with my uterus.

Red straightens and his hands lift off my belly and I feel weak with relief. 'That was . . . ' He struggles to find the right word. 'Amazing' is the best he can come up with but his eyes glitter with their green light and I know how he feels. I know it because I feel it too.

For a moment, the pair of us stand there like eejits, smiling at each other; there is something infectious about his wonder. Then I cop on to myself and pull my jacket back around my belly and say, 'Well,' in a sigh, and look around the room as if I'm wondering what colour I should paint it.

'I'm going to go to sleep now,' he says. 'We're starting filming tomorrow.'

'Oh,' I say. 'OK, well, I'll just . . . ' But Red is already stretched out on the couch, covered with a blanket and what looks like two coats, fast asleep. I can't believe it. Surely he's just assuming the sleep position while he waits for sleep to claim him. But, no, I bend towards him and his breath is already that slow, long breath of deep sleep. I feel *put out*. Envious of his casual ability to sleep.

I tuck my laptop under my arm and move towards the kitchen. I think about returning one of John's phone calls but I doubt that he has *allocated* any time to me at — I check my watch — 2.03 a.m. I wonder how I feel about his return. It's what I wanted. Wasn't it?

I know how Maureen will feel. Ecstatic would not be overstating it. John can now attend *Romeo and Juliet: The Musical*, one more person in the audience who will clap a little harder when it is her turn to bow.

I quicken my pace. I am in Phyllis's telly room now and there is a copy of *The Jou ney* on the bookcase. I pull it out, careful not to make any noise. I settle myself in the armchair by the fire, where orange embers still burn. I tuck the fleece blanket around my legs and Blue — really asleep now — allows me to lie him on top of my feet to warm them. He is much nicer to me in the long hours of night, as if he senses my restlessness and wants to ease it. I begin reading. When I am finished, the first faint light of dawn traces lines across the horizon to the east. Declan is right. It is good. Very good. I feel like a trespasser, like I have read his diary. He is asleep down the hall and I know things about him now that I didn't before. The screenplay is about a father who leaves a family and a son who goes to look for him thirty years later, when he is waiting for his own son to be born. The father is dying when the son finds him and they spend the last days of his life together. Despite the subject matter, there isn't an ounce of

295

sentimentality in it. It is told with an honesty that is brutal and stark and unsettling.

I put the script back on the bookcase, exactly where I found it. It is five o'clock now. Too late to go to bed. Too early to go to work. Instead of sitting there worrying as I normally might, I take myself and Blue and Ellen to the kitchen and I make pancakes. With bananas and melted chocolate and honey. A stack of them. Blue can't believe his luck. Neither can Ellen. We sit there, the three of us, working our way through them until there is nothing left, not even crumbs.

We are methodical, the three of us. We don't stop until we're done.

35

Filly arrives in my office with her usual 'Goodmorningsorryl'mlate', two skinny lattes, a double chocolate-chip muffin (for her) and a tub of custard (for me). Before I say anything, I rip the foil lid off the tub and lick the underside clean. Then I throw the lid in the bin and make a start on the tub. I am finished in under fifty-five seconds. Filly hasn't even managed to take her muffin out of the bag. I would smile at this turnabout except my mouth is bulging with custard.

'So,' she says, 'where should we begin?'

'At the beginning?' I suggest, enjoying the last strands of custard as it slides down my throat. I've never liked custard before. In fact, I've never really had much of a passion for food. Now, I understand why people buy glossy cookery books just so they can look at all the lovely photographs.

'Have you spoken to John since yesterday morning?'

'Negative.'

'How do you think the interview went yesterday?'

'Really negative.'

'Oh.'

'The button of my jacket flew off and practically belted Simon in the face; I sat in the Windbreaker; Gladys stole the screen for my presentation.'

'Hold on, rewind,' says Filly, leaping to her feet. 'Gladys *stole* the screen from the boardroom?'

'Yes,' I say, concentrating on a line of custard stuck along the rim of the tub. I use the handle of the spoon to poke it out.

'I'll . . . I'll . . . I'll . . . '

While Filly is distracted, trying to think of something outrageous to do to Gladys, I take the opportunity to stick my tongue out as far as it will go and lick the last of the custard from the bottom of the tub. I can just about reach it.

'I'll . . . I'll . . . I'll . . . '

I toss the truly empty custard carton into the bin. Blue no longer rushes over to it, the way he used to. He knows that there is nothing left for him to lick. Instead, he throws me one of his collection of dirty looks and resumes his midmorning snooze with a haughty toss of his tail.

'I'll . . . I'll . . . I'll . . . ' Filly is still saying. 'I'll need some time to come up with a suitable revenge plan for Gladys but *don't worry, I'm on it.*'

I don't doubt her. Filly is *brilliant* at revenge plans. One of her better ones involved a car. The car of her ex-boyfriend Bruce, to be exact. He parked it on Level Two, Block B of the car park at Sydney Airport while he was away on business in Melbourne for a week. Filly — who had the spare keys and a *motive* (he called her a 'pygmy' when he broke up with her) — relocated his car on Level Four, Block A. Still at Sydney Airport but tricky to find all the same.

'So,' Filly says, 'do you want the bad news or

the weird news?' The fact that there is no good news comes as no surprise to either of us.

I think about it for a while. 'Give us the bad news,' I say. Because it's Filly, there's no way to tell if the weird news will be any better than the bad news.

'Simon's been called to the New York office for some Yankee-panky.' She waits for me to ask what Yankee-panky is.

'What is Yankee-panky?'

'Well, this one is a meeting about budgets but, really, it can be about anything at all so long as you're getting your bottom paddled somewhere in America, which apparently Simon is.' She pauses so we can both smile at the image, which we do. 'Anyway, the thing is, he won't be back till sometime next week at the earliest.' The bad news settles around me like a rain cloud. And it *is* bad. For lots of different reasons:

1. Simon hates having his bottom paddled by the huge cheeses in America so he's guaranteed to be in a bad mood on his return. Also jet-lagged, which will accelerate the mood from bad to rotten.
2. I doubt that there will be any news on the interview front until he returns. Maybe not for a week after he gets back, considering his i) bad mood after American bottom-paddling and ii) rotten mood when you take the jet lag into account.
3. My bump is even bigger today than it was yesterday and Filly says that it's just going to get bigger and bigger, which was fine when it

was true *in theory* but now that it's actually happening it's like that movie that Phyllis loves, *2 Fast 2 Furious*. By the time Simon returns, I will be the size of a medium-sized pre-fab.

'What's the weird news?'

Something is happening to me. It's been happening for a while now but I've been dodging it. Not facing it. I can't tell Filly or Bryan or Elliot because they just wouldn't believe me and I have only myself to blame for being the type of person this kind of thing would never happen to. But it's happening all the same.

I don't care. About Simon or the job. Well, I do. But not as much as I *normally would*. Not half as much as I should. The rise and rise of Ellen O'Hara, the button-missile episode, the Windbreaker, Gladys and her treacherous thievery. All that compared to the fact that Ellen has perfectly formed ears and can now recognise my voice just doesn't feature as prominently on my radar as it used to. I know this is a bad thing. But instead of worrying about this recent development, I find myself shrugging. Not in a visible, *actual* way. But in my head I'm shrugging. I'm *virtually* shrugging.

'Aren't you going to comment on the bad news before I deliver the weird news?' asks Filly, looking at me much too closely for my liking.

'Eh . . . Oh Jesus, that's terrible,' I say. 'About Simon and the Yankee-panky.'

'No, it's not terrible about the Yankee-panky,' Filly explains to me as though I'm a two-year-old. 'The bad bit is that, by the time he comes back, he'll definitely know you're expecting a joey.' A joey is a baby kangaroo. That's what Filly calls Ellen, even though I ask her not to.

'Yes, that's what I mean,' I say to Filly. 'That's the bad bit. Obviously.'

Filly shakes her head warily but decides to give me the benefit of the doubt and continues. 'Anyway, the weird news is . . . ' she pauses for dramatic effect ' . . . Hailey and Sofia went for drinks after work yesterday.'

This time, my reaction passes Filly's careful inspection. My jaw drops open in a Venus flytrap kind of way and I sit stock-still and just stare at her, rendered immobile and speechless by this revelation.

'I know, I know,' says Filly, rubbing her tiny hands together and stomping her tiny feet at the pure *weirdness* of it.

'But . . . but . . . but . . . ' I say, and I know just how George must have felt when he tried to explain the offside rule to Phyllis the other day; it took him the best part of thirty minutes and Phyllis was none the wiser afterwards.

'I *know*,' repeats Filly, still at the hand-rubbing and the feet-stomping.

'But Hailey never goes for a drink after work,' I finally manage.

'I *know*.'

'With anyone.'

'I *know*, I *know*.'

'Are you sure?'

'Elliot saw the pair of them over in Conlons.

301

In one of the booths. Thick as thieves, she said they were. Roaring, laughing and drinking like sailors.'

'That *cannot* be true,' I say.

'It is,' Filly insists. 'The really weird thing is that Elliot says they had Wham! memorabilia spread across the table. Loads of it. Pants and T-shirts and ticket stubs and signed posters and a lock of George Michael's chest hair, he thinks.

'There's more,' Filly says, and her voice is a whisper now as she leans towards me. When she is positive that she has my full attention, she says this: 'They stayed till closing time and, when they left, they swayed up the road together with their arms thrown about each other, singing 'Careless Whisper'.'

' 'Careless Whisper' is right,' I say, thinking about what Hailey would do if she heard about Elliot's careless whispers.

The pair of us sit in stunned silence, although Filly's is not as stunned as mine, being the informer rather than the informee.

The phone rings and Filly answers, 'Scarlett O'Hara's office, Filly speaking. How may I help you?' to the tune of 'I'm Walking in the Air', even though she denies this when I mention it. She covers the mouthpiece of the phone with the flat of her hand. 'It's John on line four,' she hisses at me. 'Will I put him through?'

One of my millions of mottos is never put off till tomorrow what you can do *immediately* so I nod in the resigned way I now have and reach for the phone.

36

I meet John in a public place. Safer, I'm thinking. Not that John Smith is the type of man who might hurl plates around a room or even raise his voice. But still. Better to err on the side of caution. Ellen wants tomatoes so I book a tiny little Italian restaurant — hey pesto! — on Crowe Street, which is one that I sometimes go to with Bryan (who has a thing about tomatoes), but never with John (who is noncommittal on the subject of tomatoes, and fruit in general).

I try to be late but I can't do it. In the end, I'm five minutes early. As is John so we end up arriving together. He holds the door open for me and I walk in and then I hold the door for him and he walks through. In this way, it is like he never left and the last few months never happened. We sit and look at each other for a moment and then pore over the menu, even though I know I will order what I always order, with a side dish of tomatoes.

'I presume you're not having any wine?' he says.

I wasn't going to. 'Yes, actually, I will. A glass of red. A Chianti, if they have one.'

John forces his facial features into neutral and stops a waiter to order the wine (for me) and a mineral water (for him).

Conversation is stilted, as I imagine conversations of this nature must be. It is hard to know where to begin. I don't feel angry, which is a disadvantage. Anger could mobilise my thoughts. Gather them like troops. Instead, my thoughts seem to have gone AWOL and my newfound resignation has me sitting in an armchair in my head instead of out searching for them.

'Your face looks better,' I say when the waiter leaves. 'I mean . . . the bites look better.'

'I got a prescription cream yesterday,' John says. 'Don't want you throwing up into your briefcase again.' He waits to see if I smile before he allows himself to, not knowing if this is a sensitive subject. I smile and he smiles back and, if anyone looks over at us, they will think we are a perfectly ordinary couple, having a perfectly ordinary dinner on a perfectly ordinary Tuesday night.

I stop smiling and take a huge slug of the wine the waiter sets in front of me. When would be the best time to tell John about Red Butler? Before starters? After the main course? Or over coffee? John doesn't eat dessert, which is a pity because maybe some good tiramisu would take the sting out of it. I procrastinate and before I know it we are halfway through dinner. We get to this point by talking about work. John tells me about the meeting with his old boss, who gave him his old job back. I tell him about the new position in work but, when he asks how the interview went, I just say, 'Grand.' All too soon, the dinner plates have been whipped away and the only thing between us is a wooden table with not even a napkin or a piece of cutlery to fiddle with and keep my hands from looking nervous.

'So . . .' John begins, and I recognise the tone from particular conversations in the past. Like when he asked me if he could kiss me that first time. And when he wondered if I would move in with him. And when he first told me he loved me. And when he suggested getting a joint cat. He began all those conversations like that. A big 'So' and then a pregnant pause and then the Conversation.

'I had sex with a man called Red Butler the night you told me you were leaving me and he could be Ellen's father.' I see the words registering in John's brain. He swallows them like they're a fillet of fish with bones hidden in the flesh. He gears up to say something.

'Did you say . . . Rhett Butler?'

'No.'

'You did. You said Rhett Butler.'

'No. I said *Red* Butler. Except that's not his actual name. It's Daniel. But everyone calls him Red on account of his hair, even though it's more orange than red, to be honest.'

'And who is Ellen?'

'The baby.'

'You know it's a girl?'

'Yes.'

'How can you be so sure? You haven't had your twenty-week scan yet.'

'We-ell, no, not yet but . . .'

'So how can you know the baby is a girl?'

'I just know, that's all.' I'd forgotten this about John. His ability to worry at something until he gets it. Already I am exhausted and it's only — I check my watch — 7.32 p.m.

The coffees arrive. Double espresso for John and a milky decaf for me. We concentrate on them. John watches me pouring two sachets of sugar into my cup but he doesn't comment. Now we are stirring and stirring, our heads bent to the task as if the welfare of the world depends on it. When my coffee splashes over the rim of the cup, I put the spoon down and wait for him to say something.

'So the baby mightn't be mine?' he says eventually. He is trying to keep his tone even but there is a catch in his voice that pulls at me.

I shake my head.

'But you're always so *careful*,' he says, almost to himself.

'I *was* careful,' I say. 'With . . . with both of you. I don't know how this happened. I mean, I know how it happened but . . . but I *was* careful. I *am* careful.'

'Christ, what a mess.' John pulls his hands slowly down his face and a part of me feels sorry for him. He reminds me of myself at the beginning.

'What are you going to do?' he asks me then, looking at me as if I might have an answer to that question. But there is nothing to do. Except wait. And see. I tell him this and disappointment settles on his face like drizzle.

'What about us?' he asks after a while.

'What about us?' I repeat. 'Did you think that you were going to come back here, get your old job back, get your old girlfriend back and get on with your life as if nothing had happened?' He hesitates for a moment before he denies the

306

accusation and in that hesitation I see that this is exactly what John Smith thought. Anger arrives then, like the cavalry and my thoughts, gathered around the sidelines of this conversation, send up a mutinous roar. I stand up.

'Wait, Scarlett,' says John. 'Please,' he adds, indicating the chair. 'Don't leave like this.'

And I don't leave like that. I've never executed a dramatic exit in my life and it seems like a poor time to begin that kind of behaviour. I sit down.

'I . . . I'm sorry, Scarlett,' John says, and I know he means it, with his hunched shoulders and his hands in tight fists on his knees.

'I'm sorry too,' I say.

'For what?' he asks.

'For how things ended up,' I say. 'This was not in my plan for us.'

He nods when I say this and I know he understands how much this upsets me, like a bottle of olive oil spilled on a brand-new carpet.

'Can I still come to the twenty-week scan?' he asks. 'I'd love to see the baby.'

'Of course,' I say. 'It's just that . . . '

'What?'

'Well, the thing is . . . Red Butler asked me if he could come too and — '

'Jesus, can we at least call him Daniel?' says John, and through the cracks in his even expression I glimpse the anger there.

'I've tried calling him Daniel but it's really difficult. You'll see what I mean when you meet him. It's his hair . . . It's really . . . '

'Yeah, orange. You already told me.' His tone is as taut as a tightrope. 'I thought he was a one-night-stand. How come you're in touch with him?'

'Well, yes, it's true, he was a . . . a one-night-stand . . . ' I try to smile when I say it to detract from the seediness of the expression but it does no good. John is still looking at me like he's never seen me before in his life. 'It's just that he's getting married to one of my clients and I'm planning the wedding.'

John's eyebrows disappear into his fringe. 'He's *married*?'

'No, no,' I say. 'He's *getting* married.' This sounds better but only marginally.

'So he was engaged when you . . . met him?'

'Yes, but I didn't know he was — '

'Who's the lucky woman?' He cuts me off.

'Sofia Marzoni.' John's mouth falls open and it takes him a moment to collect himself. 'You slept with one of the Marzoni girls' fiancés? Jesus, Scarlett. What were you thinking?'

'I wasn't thinking. My boyfriend of four years, six months, three weeks and two days had just left me. That day. To go and dig some hole in Central America.'

'It was South America,' John corrects me automatically, and it takes every bit of self-control I have not to lean over and grab his glasses, pitch them on the floor and stamp on them until they are mangled and useless. Instead, I sit on my hands and count to twenty.

John has the grace to look sheepish. 'I'm sorry, Scarlett, that wasn't helpful. It's just going to take me a while to . . . get used to the situation.'

I nod. I know.

308

'Plus, he's written a screenplay and Declan has a part in the film so he's been at Tara a lot recently,' I say.

'He's a writer?'

'And an actor,' I add, wanting to serve all the bad news in one portion.

'Jesus,' says John, and he looks at me as if he knows he has met me somewhere before but he just can't place me. He knows how I feel about actors. I mean, I enjoy them on the big screen but they are not always suitable for parts in real life.

'Look, John, I know this is not easy but . . . well . . . he asked me and he could be Ellen's father so I didn't want to say . . . '

'It's more likely that I am the father,' says John. 'The ratio is seventy-seven to twenty-three in my favour.'

'Did you just work that out in your head?' I ask, and he nods, not proud of himself.

'John,' I say, 'this is not one of your mathematical equations. We're talking about actual people here. You can't shuffle us around like numbers on a page.'

'It might sound a little clinical,' John concedes, 'but that doesn't stop it from being true.' His bottom lip sticks out, the way it does when he is not for turning.

He calls for the bill before I have a chance to say anything. He insists on paying and walking me to my car. We walk as we always do, in comfortable silence, never touching, always with a margin of at least twelve centimetres between us, which never bothered me before. When we

309

reach the Martin, he greets her like an old friend, running his hand along her bonnet. He puts his hand in his pocket afterwards and I know he is wiping it on the lining, although he does it discreetly so he thinks I don't notice. He does not try to kiss me or ask for a lift home. He does not ask me to move in with him or go out with him.

'I'll see you on Thursday,' is all he says. But I know that he has a plan. I know it in the calm set of his mouth and the slight angle of his head. He is a patient man. He is biding his time.

37

I drift through the next few days, like a cloud in a light breeze. Declan and Red are on location. Declan insists on calling it 'on location' even though it's only Fermanagh, which doesn't sound exotic enough to warrant the title. Maureen went too. 'To look after Declan of course,' she says, when I enquire after her motives. But really to get away from the drama of the Amateur Dramatic Society for a while and maybe to get a sneaky peak at Red in his underpants, if she's up early enough (doubtful) or late enough (more likely). Olwyn Burke remains indisposed and, as the summer ebbs, Maureen is feeling the pressure of responsibility and she's not all that keen on responsibility. If she had her way, it would be a four-letter word.

Bryan has gone with them, Red having finally agreed to allow the film company to produce it. Cora — unused to having to beg people for permission to produce their film — has taken against Red and, according to Bryan's daily emails, tensions on the set are as taut as Maureen's forehead after one of her Botox injections.

Simon's Yankee-panky is due to end on Friday and Gladys almost sprains her ankle and breaks her neck in her rush to reach my office and deliver the good news personally, in fastidious detail so I am in no doubt as to the extent of

311

their 'working relationship'. Instead of getting sweaty palms and a slight dose of palpitations, I find myself unable to summon up much ability to care. Instead, I throw Gladys completely by thanking her profusely and offering her a Malteser from the box that I now keep in my top drawer.

'Take a fistful,' I say, holding the box under her nose. Wrong-footed as she is, she cannot bring herself to accept, even though I know she wants to. I can tell by the slight flaring of her nostrils and the instant dilation of her pupils.

John rings. Every day. He drives these conversations and I sit in the passenger seat and look out of the window. He follows the signs that point the way back to our old relationship. There is comfort in the familiarity of the roads that lead back there.

Thursday arrives as it usually does, just after Wednesday and before Friday. But this Thursday is different and I realise I've been waiting for it for months.

In honour of the occasion, I wear an actual maternity top. I bought it online and it arrived this morning, like a sign, which I know is ridiculous but the thought persists, despite itself.

The top is varying shades of pink and reminds me of Sofia Marzoni's wedding. It has gathers at the front and I find my old basketball in the garage and experiment with it. It fits perfectly under the top and I view myself from all angles. So distracted am I by my outline, I don't notice

Phyllis coming in to get the hammer and nails to patch up the hole on the roof of the hen coop. Declan climbed up on it the other night for reasons known only to himself and put his foot through the roof. Phyllis — who prides herself on her DIY skills — keeps her toolbox in the garage.

'What in the name of all that's holy are you doing, Scarlett?' she asks me.

'I was just . . . ' I taper off.

'Are you *practising* having a bump?' Phyllis studies me as if she is making sure it is me and not some impostor.

'Well . . . not practising exactly . . . just . . . '

Phyllis takes pity on me, patting my arm. 'Don't worry, Scarlett, everyone does that.'

'Do they?' I ask, relieved.

'We-ell, maybe not everyone. But I remember your mother doing exactly the same thing when she was pregnant with you.' Since my whole life has been a careful plan to avoid being like my mother — and father — this piece of news does not bode well. I push the basketball out of my top and it dribbles towards Phyllis's feet.

She picks up her hammer and a packet of nails and moves towards the door, where she stops and looks back at me. 'It's today, isn't it?' she says. I nod and she smiles at me. 'I'll be thinking about you,' she says. 'And little Ellen in there,' nodding towards my real bump, which seems pathetic now, after the round splendour of the basketball.

Without thinking about it, I walk towards her and bend down and hug her. Her white, wiry

313

hair tickles my cheek and she smells like summer: earthen and bright.

'Get away out of that,' she says, but she tightens her arms round me before she lets me go.

38

I sit in the corridor outside the ultrasound department. I check my watch. Again. It's not half past nine. It's not even twenty-five past. Despite my best efforts, I arrived just before nine o'clock and, even though I've gone to the café and eaten a muffin and drunk a mug of hot chocolate, it's still only sixteen minutes past nine. I look up each time the door at the top of the corridor opens, its rusty hinge sending a creaky moan up and down the hall.

'Sorry, love, do you know what time it is?' The woman's bump rises like a sail in a gale before her and she walks with the curious gait of the heavily pregnant woman, leaning back, legs wide, one hand buried in the small of her back. Her pyjamas and dressing gown are brand barely-out-of-their-wrapping new, with sharp creases cutting the middle of each leg. She stops inches from me, gripping the edge of a windowsill, leaning on it like it's a stick. She fills her mouth with air so that her cheeks bulge and releases her breath slowly. It makes a hissing sound, like a punctured tyre.

'The exact time, if you have it,' she says. She's come to the right place.

'It's . . . ' I check my watch, just for show, 'nine twenty-one,' I say. 'And thirty-five seconds. Thirty-six seconds. Thirty-seven. Thirty-eight . . . '

'Eh, that's grand, love. The minutes will do.'

She smiles at me and then squeezes her eyes shut and the smile changes to a grimace and the grimace gives way to a facial contortion that has 'agony' written all over it. And then comes the sound. It is feral in its intensity and strangeness. Like something entirely separate from the woman herself. It is beyond a grunt or a moan, low and rumbling, like thunder.

I leap up and snap my head up and down the corridor. 'Eh . . . help!' I manage, but the corridor is deserted.

'What's the matter, love?' The woman straightens and looks at me. Her smile is back, like nothing happened.

'I . . . I thought . . .'

'Just a pre-labour contraction, love. Nothing to worry about.'

'You mean . . . you're not even in labour?'

'God, no. This is the ha'penny place compared to real labour, so it is.'

I sort of fall back into my chair. I can almost feel the blood draining from my face. I've thought a lot about Ellen over the last twenty weeks but I haven't given much consideration to her exit strategy. I mean, I can't even use large tampons. And a baby — even a dote like Ellen — is going to be a lot bigger than a large tampon.

The woman assumes a conversational tone. 'Are you having your scan today, love?'

'Eh . . . yes.'

'Ah. I remember my first scan. Ten years ago, it was.'

'You mean this is not your first baby?' I had

been comforting myself with the idea that the woman is a first-timer with a gaping hole where her pain threshold should be.

'God, no, this is number four. Now, number one, that was *really* painful.'

I try to swallow but it's like there's a lump of hardened concrete stuck in my throat.

'Hopefully, you have a high pain threshold, like me,' the woman continues, oblivious to my fear, which renders me rigid. 'See ya now,' she says, waving at me like nothing has happened. 'Good luck.' She doesn't add, 'You'll need it,' but that's what I hear all the same. She continues her torturous journey down the corridor, stopping once more to bend and keen, and finally disappears through the double doors at the end.

My phone vibrates and I reach for it, not even checking the screen to see who it is. After dwelling on the fact that I somehow have to squeeze Ellen out of an orifice that can't even accommodate a Super Tampax, never mind a Super Plus, I need a diversion.

'Hello?'

'Scarlett, just rang to see how you're doing. Wish you luck.' It's Bryan and I can hear the smile in his voice and I smile back at him, even though he can't see me.

'I'm fine. Just waiting outside the ultrasound room. I'm a little early.'

'There's a surprise,' Bryan says.

'How's it all going down there?' I ask, desperate to keep him talking so I can forget about the slowness of my watch and the

317

narrowness of my birth canal.

'Well ... ' he begins, like he doesn't really know where to start. 'Nobody is up yet, even though I bought this bell that I ring every morning, starting from eight.'

'Not even Red?' I can't help asking.

'He's the worst offender, which, considering he's the screen-writer, director, executive producer, not to mention lead actor, is pretty bloody offensive.'

'So ... he's ... he's still in bed, then?' I ask. Disappointment is not an emotion I feel often because I don't allow myself to expect too much from people but I feel it now and it feels light and empty, like the day has passed its best-before date and is beginning to curl and harden at the edges.

'Well, he hasn't put in an appearance yet,' says Bryan. 'But that's not the worst bit.'

'What's the worst bit?'

'Maureen and Hugo,' he says, and I hear him scratching his skin where the psoriasis has flaked and dried it.

'Stop scratching,' I tell him, as I always do. 'What have Maureen and Hugo been up to?'

'Well,' he says, 'at first it was grand because they were just at each other's throats all the time — vying for Declan's attention — but at least they were getting their angst out of their system.'

'What happened?' I ask.

'Well, after the incident involving a certain goat and a certain pair of dentures ... ' he pauses for dramatic effect, Declan and Maureen having rubbed off on him in their own peculiar

318

way ' . . . now they're ignoring each other and they keep saying things like, 'Bryan, could you ask your aunt to pass me the Worcestershire sauce?' and, 'Bryan, could you ask your uncle's agent to kindly stop making that horrendous noise with his tongue?' '

In fairness, Hugo does make a noise with his tongue to punctuate his sentences when he is tired. It's a bit like the noise a cricket makes with its back legs.

If the incident had involved anything else other than Maureen's dentures, Bryan might have been able to salvage it, but after five years of wearing them, Maureen continues to deny their existence like a creationist denies evolution.

'But that's not even the worst bit,' he says.

'That must be the worst bit,' I say, but I am *delighted* there's more. I calculate that at least two minutes and thirteen seconds have elapsed since Bryan rang.

'Well, you know the way Cora has taken against Red?'

'Yes.'

'Well, she keeps shouting, 'Cut!' and he keeps telling her that it's *his* job to shout, 'Cut!' and then she storms off and locks herself in the house where we're supposed to be filming and refuses to come out until Red apologises to her, which he won't, so *I* have to coax and cajole her out and then make sure that she and Red are never in the same room, which is pretty damn tricky seeing as they're filming the same film. I'm like a human bloody shield. The only people behaving themselves are Declan and me and Cáit.'

'Cáit?'

'Our landlady, the bean-an-tí.'

Bryan has a thing about bean-an-tís, since he was deflowered by one on his third trip to the Gaeltacht when he was sixteen years old. If you ask him what his best holiday was, he still says it was the two weeks in Galway in 1984, even though it rained every day and the schoolhouse had a hole in the roof directly over his desk and there was nothing except salty bacon and soggy cabbage to eat and the sea was as cold as November.

'Is she married?' I ask.

'What's that got to do with — '

'Aw, go on, Bryan. I'm trying to distract myself from the hospital smell.'

Bryan sighs but humours me. 'She's been separated for the last two years. Turns out her husband liked dressing up in her clothes even more than she did. They're still great friends, though. She's a very understanding type of person.'

'Is she pretty?' I ask.

Bryan sighs again. 'Yes, I suppose she is, in a Sandra Bullock kind of way.'

This is all good news. 'I see,' I say blithely, as if I'm not scribbling this all down in the notepad in my head. One final — yet vital — question. 'And does Cora like her?' Cora considers herself to be a great judge of character, which mostly involves her commenting on things she doesn't like about people.

'Christ, no, what with the bell-ringing and the starch in the sheets and the no Earl Grey tea. She *hates* her.'

'Good.'

'Did you say, 'Good'?'

'No.'

'You did. You said, 'Good.''

'OK, then. Yes. I said, 'Good.' If Cora hates her and she looks like Sandra Bullock, she must be lovely. And you deserve someone lovely.'

'Why?'

'Because . . . because you're my cousin and I love you.'

'Oh,' he says, and I am ashamed to realise that I may never have said that to him before. And I'm not talking about the cousin part. Obviously, he knows he's my cousin so it's not something I've ever had to spell out.

'Do you love me because I'm your cousin, or do you love me and I just happen to be your cousin?' Bryan becomes anxious on these issues.

'The second one,' I say, and I feel his smile coming down the line and it feels as good as homemade custard. No. It feels better than that.

The corridor is quiet when I hang up. I look at my watch. It's 9.27 a.m. The phone rings again and this time it's Sofia Marzoni.

'You never sent me my weekly update,' she begins.

'But it's only Thursday. It's not due until tomorrow,' I remind her.

'Yes, but you usually send it on Wednesday, or Thursday crack of dawn at the latest.' This is true and I curse my efficiency.

'Well . . . ' I begin.

'I just wanted to make sure that you're OK, is all,' she says.

'I'm fine. Just waiting for my scan.'

'The twenty-week one?' The twenty-week scan seems to be one of those things that people inherently know. Like knowing that a hissing cat is not a happy cat.

'Yes.'

'Aw, wave at little Ellen for me, won't you? Tell her her auntie Sofia was askin' after her.'

'Eh, I will,' I say, even though I have no intention of waving at Ellen. For a start, she won't be able to see me. And even if she could, I don't think I would do it. Well, maybe just a tiny, discreet one that no one notices apart from me and Ellen.

'And there's no rush on the weekly update,' she continues. 'I just thought there was something wrong when I didn't get it yesterday or this morning.'

'I'll send it through this afternoon,' I tell her.

'Whatever,' she says with a nonchalant air, as if this is not the second of her — on average — six daily phone calls to me to discuss the minutiae of the wedding day.

★ ★ ★

John arrives at exactly 9.30 a.m. I can tell that he has deliberated over his outfit because he is wearing a pair of cords that end in an enormous pair of trainers that would take the eyes out of your head, they're that white. There's not a mark

322

on them so he either bought them this morning or ages ago and never wore them. I suspect the latter. Under a jacket that might be classified as a blazer lies a shirt but no tie. John's hand keeps reaching up, as if to fiddle with the knot of his tie. He lowers it slowly when he remembers. He is a man who is uncomfortable in casual attire, preferring the anonymity of a navy suit and a white shirt buttoned to the neck and a wide-knotted tie with maybe a tiepin for special occasions.

He sits down beside me, then stands up and looks down at me. 'How are you feeling?'

'Fine,' I say. I don't tell him about my vagina-related fears and how I may have miscalculated the threshold of my pain tolerance, mistaking it for a high, level-with- the-sky kind of a one when it is in fact trailing along the ground, it's that low.

'Red Butler didn't show up after all,' he says, looking up and down the empty corridor.

'No,' I say in a bright voice, as if it doesn't matter.

★   ★   ★

The radiographer is the same one as before.

'Hello, Pete,' I say.

'Well, fiddle-dee-dee, if it ain't lil' ole Scarlett O'Hara.' Pete holds the back of his hand against his forehead when he says this, and assumes what he believes to be an authentic southern-belle accent but which, in fact, sounds more like a Kerry brogue.

John puts his hand on the small of my back. He knows I hate jokey references to the whole Scarlett O'Hara thing. But compared to squeezing a baby out of a hole the diameter of a euro coin — maybe a two-euro coin at a push — Pete's obtuse references to *Gone With the Wind* seem inconsequential at best.

It's 9.42 a.m. now and somewhere in Fermanagh Red Butler is asleep, oblivious to the insistent gonging of Bryan's bell. I climb up on the bed, hitch my top up over my belly and wait for Pete to get busy with the smearing of the gel. I worry about Ellen. About her having Red Butler for a father. If he can't be bothered to make it to her twenty-week scan, he's unlikely to remember any of her birthdays. He'll be late for her first Holy Communion, missing the vital bit where she manages to swallow the round wafer of bread without chewing it. He won't be there to carry her home from the park on his shoulders when she is tired after the swings and the roundabout and the monkey bars. He'll show up at the wrong church on her wedding day and Bryan will have to walk her up the aisle and give her away. He'll forget the name of her firstborn child and he'll have to text her every Christmas to ask her what her address is so he can send her a Christmas card. I am mired in these thoughts, hemmed in by them. They push at me like hands and I feel that maternal guilt that I have heard women talking about. Ellen deserves better than this.

There is the sound of shoes, beating a path up the corridor. Running. A loud knock at the door and then, before anyone says, 'Come in,' the suck of air as the door is yanked open and Red Butler stands there, huge and dishevelled, with sleep in his eyes and his hair in thick tufts, poking out of his head in all directions. I try to cover my smile with a mask of indifference but it is difficult. OK, so he's — I check my watch — fourteen minutes late, there's a chance that he hasn't brushed his teeth, a cornflake is caught up in the tangle of his hair, and there's no doubt that he's illegally parked somewhere. But he is *here*.

'So sorry I'm late,' he says, trying to sound like a normal person rather than someone in the throes of a severe asthma attack. 'Car . . . blacked out on me . . . Lansdowne . . . had to run . . . ' He trails off.

'Well, look, you're here now and we're only getting started so no harm done,' I say. I am so relieved on Ellen's behalf that I forget to feel awkward about being in the same room with my ex-boyfriend and my one and only one-night stand.

'We usually only allow one . . . eh . . . guest per pregnant woman,' says Pete, looking from John to Red and back again. 'Who's the father?' And now I do feel awkward. Like I'm wearing a fur coat at an animal-rights protest march.

'Well . . . ' John begins, mostly because he hates not being able to answer a question.

'The thing is . . . ' Red begins at the same time, pushing his fringe out of his eyes.

'Could they both stay?' I ask Pete, and in my question Pete has his answer and he nods quickly before turning to the equipment.

In the small room, there is only the sound of buttons being pressed and dials being turned and Pete humming 'Over the Rainbow' under his breath. Red and John stand on either side of me, their eyes fixed on the monitor.

'I'm sorry, I'm being rude,' I eventually say. 'John, this is Red Butler. Red, this is John Smith.'

I'm not sure there is an etiquette for this kind of situation. If there is, none of us is aware of it. John looks at Red and says nothing. It's his hair. It takes people a while to get past it. Then Red extends his hand across my swollen belly and John accepts the offer, allowing Red to pump his hand up and down with a vigour that is admirable, in the circumstances.

'OK,' says Pete, looking at the three of us as if we are a mathematical equation he is trying to work out. I can tell he is having difficulty adjusting his impression of me from school-marmish to good-time girl. I guess — correctly — that Pete prides himself on his perceptiveness. He stands beside me and squirts the gel in circles on my bump.

John and Red kill each other with politeness.

'Can you see the screen from there?'

'I'm not in your way, am I?'

'Yes, it's my first time too.'

Pete clears his throat in a 'Silence!' type of way rather than a beginnings-of-a-cough-and-cold situation. It's one of those 'Ah-hem, ah-*hem*' coughs. Silence descends and we concentrate on the monitor.

'Do you want to know the sex of the baby?' Pete enquires, moving the Doppler up and over my bump.

John and Red speak at the same time.

'Yes,' says John.

'Scarlett already knows,' says Red.

Pete looks at me and I nod. I *do* know but the professionals get uneasy if you know too much.

He glides the Doppler to the base of the bump and suddenly Ellen is there, on the screen, and when I look at her, I *recognise* her, as though I've seen her somewhere before. Before I know what I am doing, my fingertips are on the screen, trailing along the sweet curve of her head.

'Could you remove your fingers from the monitor, please?' Pete tries to sound professional but I can tell he wants to slap my hand away and maybe make me stand in the corner for a while. Think about what I've done. Again, I feel John's eyes on me, looking at me as if he has no idea who I am.

But here, in the quiet of this room, with Ellen lying on her back, like the curve of a moon inside me, I feel more myself than I've ever done before.

'It's a girl,' Pete finally says.

'Ellen,' we say in unison, like she's a poem we all know by heart.

39

'Did you get any photographs of Ellen?' Filly asks after her usual 'GoodmorningsorryI'mlate', two strawberry milks, a rasher buttie (for her) and a double-chocolate fudge sundae (for me).

'Yes,' I say, sliding the tiny black-and-white picture across the desk.

'Only one?'

'Well, he gave me three but John and Red were there so I gave them one each.'

'Kerr-ist,' says Filly. 'That's awkward. That's like Monica-Lewinsky-and-Hillary-Clinton-in-a-lift awkward.'

I think about it. 'Well, I suppose it was a little . . . stilted at first.'

'That's one word for it,' says Filly, wiping her strawberry-milk moustache with the tip of her tongue.

'But once we saw Ellen, everything changed,' I say, struggling to try to explain it.

'What do you mean?'

'Well, it was like we all forgot how we got into this situation and just concentrated on the situation itself. On Ellen.'

'Oh, this is interesting,' says Filly, studying the photograph.

'What?'

'She's got John's nose.'

'She hasn't. She has a baby nose. John's nose is long and narrow and pointy at the end.'

'Yeah, his nose definitely isn't his best feature,' says Filly.

'So you're saying Ellen has an ugly nose?' I can't believe Filly would say that.

'God, no, I'm not saying that. I'm her godmother. I'll be telling her she has a beautiful nose and taking her shopping for clothes. That's my job.'

Technically, clothes shopping and compliments are not the job of a godmother but Filly — whose religious education consists of watching *The Life of Brian* seven times — cannot be expected to know such things.

'You don't have to buy her clothes,' I say, panicky now. Today, Filly is wearing a canary-yellow jumpsuit and a pair of purple clogs. The clash of colour is like an insistent car alarm.

'She has very long fingers,' Filly says, peering at the picture. I had noticed this too, on the monitor, where she waved her hands like she was conducting an orchestra only she could see. In the photograph, her left hand is raised in a sort of a high-five and it's difficult not to notice her fingers. The slender length of them.

'She's got Red Butler's hands and John Smith's nose,' concludes Filly most inconclusively.

I take the photograph and put it into the section of my bag that I reserve for photos. Although the only other one in there is a battered shot of Blue as a kitten, asleep in the palm of my hand.

'So what about afterwards?' Filly asks. 'Did John and Red have a dance-off in Merrion Square?'

'Eh . . . no. Red's car broke down somewhere in Lansdowne so John gave him a lift to Heuston Station. To catch a train back to Fermanagh.'

Filly's face is a study in bewilderment. 'Jaysis,' she manages. 'If John were from where I'm from, he would have given Red a wedgie at the very least. But a *lift*?' She shakes her head at the senselessness of it all.

The knock on the door is so loud that I know who it is before the door is wrenched open.

'Surprise!' shouts Sofia, striding into the room at full pelt.

It's not a surprise. Sofia calls into the office, unannounced, anytime she happens to be passing by, which, recently, has been more often than not. She settles herself on the sofa, a safe distance from Blue, who is too busy licking his . . . *underbelly* . . . to notice.

'So,' she says, taking off her coat and rearranging her glossy black curls so they lie in waves down her back. 'Do you want the good news or the bad news?'

'The good news,' says Filly, who is a fan of instant gratification.

'The bad news,' I say. I like to have something I can look forward to.

'First of all, though,' says Sofia, 'I have to see the scan photograph.'

Her smile is so wide and her teeth are so white I try to persuade myself that the bad news can't be all that bad. Can it? I pass her the photograph and she concentrates on it for a moment.

'She has John's nose, the poor pet,' she says, almost to herself. 'Her fingers are very long,

330

aren't they? John doesn't have long fingers, does he?' She looks up and Filly and I shake our heads in tandem. 'Show me yours, Scarlah,' and, like an obedient child, I hold out my hands for inspection. There is nothing else to be done with Sofia Marzoni. She is like the moon, with her own gravitational pull.

'God, they're tiny, so they are. Like a doll I had when I was eight,' says Sofia, almost to herself.

'So,' I say, pulling my hands gently from her. 'What's the bad news?'

Sofia's face clouds over, like an Irish summer. 'We-ll . . . ' she begins, and I brace myself. 'I may have spoken out of turn.'

Nothing new there. But what did she say? And to whom?

'I told my father that you were expectin' a babby,' she says.

I think about this for a moment. It's true that Valentino Marzoni is a raging Roman Catholic who can say two decades of the Rosary in under five minutes and once considered going on *Mastermind* with his specialist subject 'Jesus Christ, 0000-0033'. But him knowing about Ellen (even though she was conceived out of wedlock, as he would say) is not the worst kind of bad news. In fact, it hardly registers on my bad-news radar.

But there's more. Of course there's more.

'That's not the bad part of the news, is it?' I ask, but it's a rhetorical question.

'We-ll . . . ' says Sofia and then sighs, a long, drawn-out Italian sigh that deflates her, like a week-old balloon. 'Papà may have mentioned it to Simon.'

'When?' I ask. 'Before or after the interview?' Not that it matters any more. I see my hopes for the job sailing away from me, like the *Titanic*, doomed before it ever reached the icebergs.

'I don't know, Scarlah. I only found out yesterday. I couldn't be sorrier, so I couldn't.' And she does look sorry. In fact, she looks so dejected that even Blue can't help patting her with one of his paws, albeit briefly.

The three of us sit in silence. After a while, we begin sneaking peeks at each other, the way people do when they are in a dentist's waiting room.

'Well, what's the good news, then?' Filly finally asks.

I sit up straighter in my chair. I'd forgotten about the good news, what with all the awful stuff.

'Oh, yeah,' says Sofia, brightening when she realises that Filly is still speaking to her. 'Well,' she says, beaming now and looking at me, 'you know the way you an' me were goin' to go and visit the castle where I'm havin' the reception?'

I nod.

'I've had a better idea,' says Sofia, standing up so Filly and I have to stretch our necks all the way back to see her face.

'I want us all to go. Me and Hailey, you and Filly, and Red and Brendan the butcher. It'll be like one of those American road-trip movies. I've looked at the budget and I reckon if I cancel the hot-air balloon trip from the church to the castle, I'll have enough to cover a weekend away for all of us.' She stops to take a breath and to look from Filly to me and back again to Filly.

Neither of us says a word. The silence is deafening.

'Well?' she asks. 'What do yiz tink? It's brilliant, isn't it?'

'Why is Hailey going?' asks Filly, which is the question I wanted to ask, once I got my coherent thoughts up and running again.

'Because,' she says as if this is obvious, 'I've asked Hailey to be the weddin' party's fortune-teller.'

I get an image of Hailey in a sagging tent with a scarf round her head and thick rings on each of her fingers, bending towards a crystal ball and telling me that I will come into money and travel across water, in a low, mysterious voice. I know that if I open my mouth to say anything, I will laugh and I have never done that and am not about to start now. The first rule on the top of the first page of the wedding planners' handbook is *never* to laugh at your clients' ideas for their weddings, no matter how . . . how . . . *peculiar* those ideas may be.

'She reads tarot cards, so she does,' continues Sofia, as if this is an ordinary conversation we are having about the weather and how inclement it's been. 'And tea leaves too,' she adds, swelling with pride.

It is Filly who rescues me from my speechless state. 'Do you think it's a good idea for the wedding party to have their fortunes read on the morning of the wedding? I mean, what if she tells them that they're going to die? Or their wife is going to run off with the man who works behind the counter in the local Credit Union? Or . . . or . . . ' Filly, running out of ideas, looks towards me for inspiration ' . . . or . . . their boyfriend is going to leave them to join an archaeological dig in Central America.'

'South America, actually,' I say, but nobody is listening.

'No, that's not goin' to happen,' explains Sofia to Filly, bending down to her with her hands on her knees, 'because Hailey will only tell nice, happy, lucky fortunes. If she's sees something in the cards — like death or destruction or pestilence or something — she'll just skim over it and tell them something lovely instead, like, you know, travellin' over water or comin' into money or fallin' in love.' She looks from one of us to the other until Filly and I nod mutely.

Filly leaves to make tea and get the chocolate Kimberleys without me having to ask her.

'Why do you want Brendan the . . . eh . . . butcher to come on the . . . eh . . . road trip?' I ask.

'Well, as the supplier of the meat for the weddin' banquet, it's only right that he should come on the road trip,' says Sofia, and because of the way she says it — with authority — it sounds like a compelling and reasonable explanation. In fact, I nearly wonder why I didn't think of it. It's true that I've asked Brendan to source meat that is pink. So far, all he's come up with is carpaccio of beef, which, while it's only one item, has the advantage of being not only pink but Italian. Sofia doesn't want salmon. She says it's too *obviously* pink.

'We'll go the weekend after next,' says Sofia, when Filly returns and doles out the tea and biscuits. 'Early on Saturday morning. I don't want to go on Friday evening. The traffic will be cat. Besides, Uncle Vinny can only lend me the bus on Saturday.'

'The bus?' Filly and I say.

'Well, it's only a minibus really,' she admits. 'But big enough for all of us. Scarlah, you can drive it. You have a PSV licence, wha?'

Filly and Sofia look at me expectantly and, for a moment, I consider denying it. It's Declan's fault. He insisted that I get a PSV licence the summer I turned twenty-one, just so I could drive him and a group of players and props up and down the country, stopping at every theatre and draughty hall along the way to stage the one and only play Declan ever wrote. 'One for the Road', he called it. It was a very long summer, as I recall.

'We could just drive down,' I say. 'You know, in our cars.'

'I can't drive,' says Sofia.

'And we don't have a car,' adds Filly. Not having a car is something Filly is very proud of, it being her contribution to the environment. It is also the main reason for her hazy relationship with punctuality.

'And Red's car has broken down,' says Sofia. 'Somewhere in Lansdowne, I think. Although God knows what he was doin' there when he's supposed to be filmin' in Offaly.'

'Fermanagh,' I say automatically.

'I knew it was somewhere with an 'f' in it,' says Sofia, pleased with herself. 'So you'll do it, Scarlah? You'll drive the bus?'

'We-ell . . . '

'Great. That's settled, then.' She stands up, stuffs two chocolate Kimberleys into her handbag — for later, she says — and drains her mug in one gulp. 'I have to go,' she says. 'One of our customers swears he saw an apparition of the Virgin Mary behind the counter of the chip shop in Clondalkin. After closing time, mind. The local parish priest has me demented, wantin' to bring the bishop down and everything. I said to him if the bishop wants a single of chips and a quarterpounder, grand. Otherwise, feck off.'

'Does Valentino know you told the parish priest to tell the bishop to feck off?' asks Filly.

'Kerr-ist, no. He doesn't even know about the apparition. If he did, he'd insist on closin' down the shop and buildin' the feckin' shrine with his own two hands. And where would my bottom line be, then, wha?' She smiles at us and waves with both hands before stepping into the corridor and closing the door behind her.

The office feels as big as a warehouse when she is gone, and as quiet as a crypt.

40

I spend the weekend at Tara with Ellen and Blue. The house is pathologically quiet. Phyllis and George have gone to some class of Lourdes reunion weekend. George only went because Phyllis was going, and Phyllis only went to see if Percy/James/ Gordon can still see and on the off-chance that there might be a bit of a singsong of an evening to go with her few glasses of sherry.

Maureen and Declan remain in Fermanagh, much to the vexation of Fermanagh County Council, I've no doubt. Without them, and Phyllis and George and even Red, whose presence at Tara I have become accustomed to, the house feels boarded up and empty.

Bryan keeps me up to speed on what is happening in Fermanagh. Declan has submerged himself so thoroughly in his character that he's refusing to answer to his Christian name and has taken to sleeping in an armchair in the cottage or 'on set', as he calls it. Maureen has taken such a dose of umbrage at this nocturnal abandonment, she has not only made up with Hugo but has begun flirting outrageously with him, even deigning to pet Sylvester and feed him the squares of Bourneville that he likes so much. Unfortunately, with Declan so focused on the film, he barely notices and this is like a red rag to the bullish Maureen. She takes it out on the bean-an-ti, who, given her sweet nature, has given them five chances. Because of Maureen's antics — which include indulging her passion for the *Mamma Mia* soundtrack at four o'clock in the morning, they are on chance number four.

'Has she stopped flirting with Red?' I ask when Bryan phones me on Saturday afternoon.

'Christ, no,' he says. 'Although I'm not sure Red notices really. He's all about the work. He talks about nothing else. Apart from Ellen.'

'Ellen? He hasn't said anything to Declan and Maureen, has he?' I haven't spoken to my parents about Red Butler's possible involvement with their granddaughter. It's on my to-do list of course. It just hasn't been ticked yet.

'No, no,' says Bryan, hurrying to reassure me. 'He just talks to me about her. He showed me the photograph. She's gorgeous.'

I can't decide how I feel about Red Butler with a black-and-white fuzzy photograph of Ellen in his wallet. I decide not to think about it.

'You don't think her nose is a bit funny, do you?' I ask instead.

'No, of course not. It's a cute button baby nose.'

'You don't think it looks like John's nose?'

'God, no. His nose is long and narrow and pointy at the end. Ellen's nose isn't a bit like that.'

'What about her fingers?'

Bryan pauses before answering. 'Well, they *are* long all right.' When I don't respond, he changes the subject. 'What are you up to?'

'I'm doing the seating plan for Sofia and Red's wedding.'

'How's it going?'

If it was a normal wedding, I would have finished the seating plan hours ago. Because it's Sofia's wedding, I'll be lucky to finish it by their golden wedding anniversary. For starters, Sofia has invited 214 of her closest family and friends, while Red has invited twenty-seven, one of whom is Al Pacino, who doesn't really count because he's a dog and will not be allowed in the dining room, although I haven't said as much to Red. Of Sofia's 214 guests, twenty-eight no longer speak to each other because of various family feuds, thirty-two are children under the age of eight, nineteen are ancient and ailing and can't sit near the speakers, or the windows, or the doors, or the children. Nor can they sit anywhere near at least two strands of the Marzoni family (on account of the feuds). Five are vegans, seven have nut allergies, seventy-four don't speak any English, and six are going through acrimonious divorce proceedings but have agreed to suspend hostilities for twelve hours so they can attend the wedding. Every time I think I've got it sorted, Sofia rings with updates: 'Don't put Uncle Lorenzo at the same table as Carmella. He's just cancelled his subscription to the swan sanctuary in Waterford and she's taken it very badly' or 'Just to let you know that Augusto and Alessandro have made up . . .'

'Your second cousins on your mother's side?'

'No, they're third cousins once removed on Papa's side, remember?'

'Oh, yes,' I say, scribbling the details in my

notebook, which is already full of such details.

'Anyway, they're friends again but Angelo — who took Alessandro's side during that feud — is now not speakin' to Alessandro or Augusto.'

'Was that the feud about the rigatoni?' I want Sofia to see that I'm on top of the brief.

'The fight wasn't *about* rigatoni, Scarlah. People don't not speak to each other for months over a particular type of pasta, you know,' Sofia tells me, and I can tell by her tone that she is sampling patience to see what it's like and it's not agreeing with her. 'It just happened while they were havin' dinner. Anyway, that was the fusilli feud, started by the Filipepi family, remember?'

'Oh, right,' I say, writing the words 'fusilli' and 'Filipepi' on the top of the next page, with four question marks after each word. I don't ask how families can have feuds called after various types of pasta (like the Macaroni Massacre of 1985 — nobody actually died but, as I understand it, faces were slapped, reputations were shattered and bolognese sauce dripped down the kitchen walls like blood).

'Anyway, we should be finished up by next weekend so I'll see you then, OK?' says Bryan now.

I tell him about the road trip and the minibus and Hailey and her tarot cards and tea leaves.

I don't tell him about Valentino's revealing conversation with Simon. Bryan is not just a worrywart. He's a cluster of worrywarts. Anyway, with the antics in Fermanagh, he has enough to deal with at the moment.

'What about John?' Bryan asks. 'Any word from him?'

Because it's Bryan, I tell him everything.

'He's coming down later. He says . . . ' I stop there, wondering how to put this.

'What? What does he say?'

'We-ll . . . he says he is going to . . . woo me.' There is a brief silence.

'Woo you? Did he actually use those words?'

'That's what he said.'

'But . . . but . . . it's not exactly a John Smith kind of word, is it?' It's a rhetorical question. We both know that 'woo' is not a word anyone would associate with John Smith. In fact, it is a measure of how shocked I was when he first mooted the idea that I did not even pick him up on it.

'First, he suggested couples counselling,' I say.

'That's probably a better idea,' says Bryan.

'Well, yes, but . . . '

'If you two are going to make a go of it, it's a good idea to talk about what happened.'

'I know . . . It's just . . . '

'This *is* what you want, isn't it, Scarlett? You and John and Ellen. A proper family. Isn't it?'

My mind crowds with things to say. I say nothing.

'Scarlett?'

'It's just that nothing is straightforward any more. I can't seem to concentrate on a plan. I don't even have a plan. Other than Ellen. She's my only plan.'

'Maybe after Ellen is born,' suggests Bryan.

341

'Maybe you could think about couples counselling then.'

'Maybe,' I say with not much conviction.

'Anyway,' says Bryan, 'let's get back to the wooing. What form will it take, do you think?'

'You're not taking him seriously,' I say. 'He was very serious about it on the phone.'

'I bet he has a book,' says Bryan. '*The A to Z of Wooing Women*. Or *You Too Can Woo*. Or *From Wooing to Wedding in Ten Easy Steps*. Or — '

'OK, OK,' I say, 'that's enough.'

But when John arrives, there are a stack of books in the back seat of his car, although I can't read any of the titles. He wears an outfit that I've never seen before. The collar of the shirt is tight and sharp and chafes red against the white skin under his jaw. It is a nondescript colour, like it's seen the inside of too many washing machines. I think about the shirts I bought him. Two new ones every season. Eight per year. Multiplied by four and a half years. Twenty-eight shirts. All a perfect fit. No nondescript colours. No forgotten plastic tags like the one I see poking out of the stiff neck of the shirt. Creases run down both legs of the jeans, as rigid and awkward as a three-legged race. The jacket has the kind of patches on the elbows that are not there to conceal a hole in the material. They are there for style. For show. For John Smith's version of style and show anyway. Bryan's voice cuts into my thoughts, 'Maybe it's his *wooing* outfit', and I have to turn my face away to hide the smile.

'What are you smiling at?' asks John, getting

342

out of his car. He smiles too. I can just about see it behind the huge fern and planter that struggle against the semicircle of his arms. 'This is for you,' he says, lowering the plant on to the front step, both legs bending, the way you're supposed to. He never gets me cut flowers. He says they're wasteful and I suppose he's right.

He disappears again into the car and I check but he doesn't refer to any of the books in the back seat before backing out of the car, this time with an abacus. 'It's for the baby,' he explains, when I don't say anything.

'It's . . . lovely,' I manage.

'Everyone has an aptitude for maths,' says John. 'You just have to catch them early enough.'

'Well, she's not even born yet so I think you're in with a shot,' I say, smiling at him.

He does not smile back. 'A lot of people underestimate the importance of maths,' he says, shaking his head, more with sadness than annoyance.

'It's OK, John. I'll make sure to give it to her as soon as she arrives. Now, are you coming in?'

John stops speaking and nods instead. We move inside the house.

'Oh, I forgot the shopping. I'll just be a minute.' When John returns to the kitchen, he has a Superquinn bag in each hand. Through the flimsy plastic, I see bunches of rocket, fresh pasta, a wedge of cheese that looks like it could be Brie, milk with added vitamins and minerals and folic acid and omega-3s, bread, decaffeinated coffee, sugar and a big bottle of Gaviscon.

'You didn't need to . . . ' I begin.

'I want to cook you dinner,' he says, unpacking the bags.

There are plump beef tomatoes and mushrooms with the clumps of earth still on them and a packet of cornflour and a bottle of white wine with the alcohol taken out. There is freshly squeezed orange juice and a carton of red-berry smoothie and two tuna fillets, straining purple against their wrapping.

'We do have cornflour, you know,' I say.

'I knew you would,' says John, who knows no such thing, remembering Maureen and Declan's unpredictable relationship with home-cooking. 'But because it's the lynchpin ingredient, I thought I'd get some,' he says. 'Just in case,' he adds. 'Now, you sit down there and relax.' He gets a glass down from the press and, even though he's got his back to me, I know that he is polishing the rim of it with his handkerchief, which he keeps in the pocket of his jacket and never blows his nose with. When the glass is John Smith clean, he pours a smoothie into it and sets it down on the table in front of me.

I've forgotten how this feels. Being taken care of. Having someone feed me a meal in a place that isn't a restaurant, where all the healthy food groups are accounted for. The room fills with sounds. Proper kitchen sounds. The splash of water against the sink. The hissing of the kettle, boiling. The soft rumble of the oven pre-heating. The clean slice of a knife along a shallot. The silence between us is a sound too. A low hum that you'd hardly notice.

'Is this you wooing me?' I direct the question

344

at John's back, which is ramrod straight and thinner than I remember.

He sets the peeler and the carrot on the counter and hesitates before turning round. His face has flushed a bright red, like one of the beef tomatoes.

'I shouldn't have said woo. I can't understand why I said woo,' he says, worrying at a button on his jacket.

'Why did you say woo?' I ask.

'I . . . I didn't want you thinking that I just wanted to pick up where we left off. Before . . . before I left.'

'Well, nobody's ever wooed me before,' I say, and I smile in an effort to alleviate John Smith's discomfort, 'but you never know, I might like it.'

John moves towards me. 'I want to take you away,' and I can tell he's been waiting for a suitable gap in the conversation to say this. 'Next weekend. Belfast, maybe? We could shop for a pram and a cot, maybe? They're much cheaper up the north.' He looks at me and I see his face fall as I shake my head.

'I can't,' I say. 'Not next weekend. I'm going away with Sofia and her wedding party to the castle. I told you already, didn't I?'

'No,' says John. 'You never mentioned it.'

'Well, it's all arranged,' I tell him. 'I have to go. It's work.'

'Is Red Butler going?'

I shrug my shoulders. 'Sofia wants him to,' I say. 'But I'm not sure if filming of *The Jou ney* will be over by then.'

John wheels round, returning to the worktop,

345

where he resumes peeling carrots with a little more force than before.

'Who writes a screenplay with no 'r's in it?' he says, almost to himself.

'I know,' I agree, 'but it's not bad, even without any 'r's.'

'You've read it?' While John does not turn round, he stops peeling, waiting for my response.

'Eh, yes,' I say.

'And?'

'It's . . . good.'

'Good?'

'Very good. I think you'd like it. A bit like an Irish, non-western version of *Unforgiven*.'

'I didn't like that film, remember?'

I had forgotten that. I decide to drop the subject. 'So I can't go away with you next weekend.'

'How about the weekend after?' John asks, persistent.

'Maybe we could go away sometime after Sofia and Red's wedding?' I say, without getting my diary out and picking a suitable date.

John lines four carrots, side by side, on a plate and begins cutting them into pieces with a vengeance. 'We can't have a conversation any more without ending up talking about Red bloody Butler,' he says, his words keeping time with the cutting of the carrots.

Organising Sofia's seating plan was easier than this and I find myself wishing that John had never come. I push the thought away.

'This is a Marzoni wedding, John,' I explain in a way that I never had to before. 'You remember

346

Marzoni weddings, don't you? Like Howth? You *do* remember that, don't you? With the sea lions? We had to call the Coast Guard in the end, to rescue Maria and Riccardo, after they swam all the way out to Ireland's Eye. Remember?'

I know John will remember this one. He picked strands of seaweed from my hair when I eventually returned home. I think the recollection will make him smile, take the sting out of this conversation.

But John does not smile. Instead, he sits down at the table opposite me and does that thing he does with his hands when he is concentrating hard on something: sort of massages one hand with the other, slowly, as if he's got arthritis. Then he switches and gives the other hand a turn. It's his version of smoking.

'The reason I wanted to take you away next weekend,' he finally says when both hands are red from all the rubbing, 'was because I was going to ask you . . . ' He stops and looks at me and suddenly I know what he is going to ask me and there is nothing I can do to stop him.

He reaches into the breast pocket of his shirt and now I see the square shape of a box through the fabric of his shirt. A small box. John has to push a bit of his hand into the pocket to allow his fingers to reach it. It opens with a click and he sets it on the table between us. Against the black velvet, the diamond is stark. And square. Set on a platinum band. It is simple. And beautiful. It's the ring I would have chosen and John knows this. I can feel it in the weight of his eyes on

347

me. I drag my eyes away from it.

'Why do you want to get married now?' I ask. 'You never did before.'

'You were never pregnant before,' he says.

I don't say anything. I close the lid of the box.

'I'm trying to be practical. I thought you'd appreciate that.' He opens the box again, pushes it closer to me.

'I . . . I don't know what to say,' I begin.

John shakes his head, impatient now. 'Don't say anything,' he says. 'Just listen. I've got it all worked out. I'm going to sell my flat and buy a house for you and me and the baby . . . Ellen. I've spoken to my boss about more flexible working hours and I . . . ' he pauses to glance at me before looking away again ' . . . I hope you don't mind but I've spoken to a crèche near the office and put Ellen's name down. Provisionally, of course. I know that you've probably organised childcare for her but . . . well, I was just passing and I thought . . . ' His voice trails off and now he is looking down at the table, wiping away crumbs that are not there. His fingernails are pink squares, the dirt of Brazil long gone.

'We could get married then, after the baby is born. In a registry office, if you'd like. A quiet wedding. No fuss,' continues John, who seems to be on a roll now.

This is the first time anybody has ever proposed to me. It should feel . . . different to this, I think. Better than this.

'And if you're not Ellen's father? What then? How practical do you think marriage will be?' I push the box back towards his side of the table.

'I could adopt her,' he says, and I can tell that he's thought about this. 'Red Butler doesn't seem like the kind of person who'll have time for fatherhood.' His fingers are on the box but he doesn't move it back this time.

'What do you mean? You don't even know him.'

'He's getting married. And he's an *actor*, for God's sake, Scarlett.'

'And a writer.' I struggle to be fair.

'Look, Scarlett, you know what I mean. You were brought up by actors and . . . ' He stops halfway through the sentence.

'And look how I turned out. Is that what you're trying to say?'

'No, I don't mean . . . '

'You left me,' I remind him.

'I know. I shouldn't have. I don't know what I was thinking. Or doing.' He pulls his hands through his hair. I wait for him to say something. He is waiting for something to say. Something plausible. Something that will make everything make sense. 'I came back,' he finally says.

'Only because of your overdeveloped sense of duty,' I remind him.

He looks away from me when I say this and I know that this is true. I thought it was true before. Now I know it is.

'It's not the worst place to start,' he says finally. 'Is it?'

'It's not exactly romantic.'

'Since when do you care about what's romantic?'

I look at him when he says this. He looks genuinely baffled.

'I . . . I don't care. Normally. But this is a proposal of marriage, isn't it? I mean . . . I know I've never been proposed to before but I *am* a wedding planner. I know how these things are supposed to go.'

'What are you talking about?'

'John, surely you know? You watch telly, don't you? There's supposed to be a bent knee and a waterfall or a lake or an ocean or some bloody body of water and . . . oh, I don't know, a bottle of champagne and not some horrendous wine with the good bit taken out . . . and . . . and . . . ' I'm floundering for some more clichés to throw into the mix.

'I could go and get some bubbly,' John says, trying to work out how long it will take him to drive to the nearest off-licence and back and how the timescale fits into dinner preparations.

'John, I don't *want* bubbly.'

'But you just said . . . '

'Yes, but . . . I . . . '

'Scarlett, I don't understand. I thought you'd be pleased. I thought you'd appreciate my preparations . . . my plans.'

And I know I should. It was my plan, not so long ago. But now there is a gaping hole in the roof of these plans. In the shape of Red Butler. His face swims up to the surface of my mind and he winks at me and smiles his wide and generous smile, warm as Sicily.

'Why didn't you ask me to go with you? To Brazil, I mean?'

'Because you would have said no. *And* you would have made me change my mind. You would have made me realise what a crazy idea it was. And I didn't want that. I wanted to go. I wanted to do something . . . unpredictable.'

I look down and see his feet under his chair. He's wearing his Saturday socks. The orange ones with the bear's head that say, 'Don't wake me till noon,' even though the latest he's ever slept in on a Saturday was nine o'clock and that was only because Blue stole his mobile phone (set to alarm at the usual eight thirty on Saturday morning) from his bedside table one Friday night — for reasons perhaps not unrelated to our recent acquisition of Judge Judy — and buried it in a flowerpot on the balcony. The rose bush in the pot kept vibrating every time we rang his phone in an effort to locate it, which is how we found it in the end. In perfect working order, I must say. Although the alarm-clock function never fully recovered.

'I thought I could depend on you,' I say. 'That's why I chose you.'

'You see?' he says. 'There's nothing romantic about that but I get it. It's why we should be together. We both want responsible people that we can depend on. There's nothing wrong with that.'

'Neither of us have been very responsible lately,' I remind him.

'We've made mistakes,' John concedes. 'We can draw a line under this . . . episode and soldier on.' I get a picture of the pair of us, trudging up a long, steep hill. Soldiering.

'You can depend on me now,' John says. 'More than you'll be able to depend on Red Butler.'

'Red hasn't let me down,' I say. The truth of the words take me by surprise.

'Give him time,' says John.

'Being catty is not going to solve anything,' I say, just as Blue comes into the kitchen. When he sees John, he arches his back and raises his tail and hisses louder than anyone would give him credit for. John barely registers the naked hatred on Blue's face and Blue — who does not like being ignored, especially when he is pulling out all the stops — leaves the room in a dignified manner, even though I know that he is heading to John's car, no doubt to spray at the windows, if he can reach.

John turns away from me and concentrates on something through the window. I just hope it is not his car.

'This isn't going the way I planned,' he says then, almost to himself.

'Things don't always go the way you plan them, John. I'm just getting the hang of that myself.' I touch my bump and Ellen kicks me and for the first time I can see her kick. Her kick is the shape of a foot. A tiny foot. I touch the place where the foot has been but it is gone now, although the skin is warm there, and I hold my hand against it.

'Are you all right?' John asks, frowning at my hand pressed against the bump.

'I'm . . . fine,' I say.

John clears his throat and sits up straighter in the chair even though he had been sitting fairly straight to begin with. I know he is gearing up to say something. I recognise the signs.

'I don't want you to give me an answer right away,' he says, 'but will you at least think about it?'

I close my mouth on the word I was about to say. A short word beginning with an 'n'. He is a clever man. It is one of the things I loved about him. His smarts. He knows me. He knows about my reasonableness. He knows that I will agree to think about it and not to answer right away because that is the reasonable thing to do. So I close my mouth on the word that I was about to say and I nod instead. A small nod but a nod just the same. John takes my nod and raises me a smile. He knows the nod is not quite a yes but it's not a no either. It could become acquiescence. He pockets the ring and I know he won't mention it again. Not today anyway. He has sown the seeds and he will water them every day and keep them in a sunny spot and feed them every week and wait for them to yield results.

After dinner, we sit on the couch in the den and the space in between us — about twelve centimetres — is the way it's always been. A comfortable space, devoid of tension, apart from when Blue jumps up and fills the space and reminds John of something he has to do in the kitchen. Blue is a bit like an elephant. He never forgets. He's also great at harbouring a grudge, although I don't know if elephants have a similar capacity for resentment.

We read. John's book is nothing at all to do with wooing. It is called *Baby on Board* and has a picture of a man in a suit sitting at what looks like a table in a boardroom with a baby in a sling plastered against the pinstripes of his navy suit.

I read the crèche brochure. My thoughts about the crèche are difficult to pin down; they don't seem to be one thing or another. They are an array of thoughts. A disarray, really. Like a lot of thoughts I've had over the last few months. There are some good thoughts. The crèche looks like someone's home, full of bright rooms with toys and books and children's paintings hanging crooked on the wall. Families feature prominently in these paintings, matchstick mothers and fathers with matchstick children gathered between them. Rectangular houses too with smoke curling from lopsided chimneypots and lots of yellow suns with smiley faces and, sometimes, sunglasses.

There is a garden with a swing and a sandpit and a turtle called Angelina. There is a kitchen with child locks on the presses and rosemary growing from a chipped teapot on the windowsill and a man with a belly that strains towards the camera. His name is Giulio and he comes from Sicily and he cooks breakfasts and lunches and dinners for the children. I wonder if he knows the Marzonis. He probably does. He's probably related to some branch of the family. There are three Giulios on the wedding guest list.

Then there are the thoughts that are not so good. Not sufficiently bad to rate as bad thoughts but not great all the same. I try not to think these thoughts and, in the past, this would have been enough. But now they seep in, like the damp on the gable wall of my parents' house in the wintertime. Ellen strapped into her car seat, one of a line of babies sitting in car seats in the baby room of the crèche at seven o'clock every morning, which is the time that the crèche opens. And Ellen strapped into her car seat, one of a line of babies sitting in car seats in the baby room of the crèche at six o'clock every evening, waiting for me to pick her up. Hoping that I don't confuse her with the babies to the left or the right of her, who are also hairless and gummy. I squeeze my eyes shut against these thoughts but they come at me like a train on a track. Ellen. She'll end up calling Giulio Dad. Or Papà. And me Auntie Scarlett. Or the nice lady who takes me home sometimes. And where will home be? And who will live there with me and Ellen and Blue?

'I've been thinking about a prenatal paternity test.' John's voice cuts across me and my disarray of thoughts disperse like smoke.

I've thought about this too.

'I'd prefer to wait until after Ellen arrives,' I say.

'I'd prefer to do it before the baby is born. That way, we all know where we stand and we can make our plans.'

In my old life, I would have wanted this too. To know where I stand and to make my plans. I stand up and move to the window. Outside, the heat drains from the day.

'It's a simple procedure,' John goes on. 'I've Googled it.'

I turn to face him. 'It's invasive, John. They

355

have to take a swab from the placenta with a needle. Something could go wrong.'

'Nothing will go wrong.'

This would be an appropriate time to tell him about losing the other baby. I press the palms of my hands against the swell of my belly and close my eyes. The thing is . . . I don't want to tempt fate. I want Ellen to be here and safe before I subject her to any tests. I don't know where to begin telling any of this to John.

John's phone rings. He answers on the fourth ring. 'Ah, Lolita, hello. How are you?' John nods at me before stepping out of the room and closing the door behind him. Blue stretches and rolls into the warm hollow left by John. I pick up the book Maureen is currently reading — *How to Put the 'Grand' into Grandmother* — and leaf through it.

Lolita. I realise that I haven't thought about her since that first phone call to John. The throaty huskiness of her voice. *Fuan ees in shower.* Women aren't supposed to forget about other women saying things like that about their boyfriends. Or ex-boyfriends. I put it down to Ellen, like I put everything that doesn't quite fit into the view I have of myself. I think about Red Butler. He's never mentioned a prenatal paternity test. Although he probably doesn't even know they exist. He doesn't seem to be much of a Googler.

I stop thinking about Red Butler. I'm supposed to be thinking about Lolita. As in, who the hell is Lolita? And why is she ringing John? At this hour of the night. Although it is only — I check my watch — half past eight, I concede. I try to talk myself into pacing up and down the room in an effort to become agitated but long rays of sunshine push through the window and pin me to the couch. I am heavy with warmth and food and Blue's head on my lap and the weight of Ellen inside me, quiet now with her secret smile playing about her mouth. Or at least that's how I imagine her.

The three of us are nearly asleep when John returns. Well, Blue and Ellen are asleep. My eyes are closed.

'Scarlett, I'm sorry about that. I know Lolita answered the phone to you that first time you rang. I know what you must be thinking. But I swear to you there's nothing going on between us. We're friends. That's all.' John expels this sentence from his mouth in a rush of anxious words. He sits on the couch beside me and looks at me. A worried look. I know this because he bites his bottom lip, revealing the line of his top teeth, forgetting about his braces.

He takes my hands in his and they are cold, despite the warmth of the room. 'You believe me, don't you, Scarlett?'

I nod. I don't know if I *do* believe him. But that's not the worrying thing. The worrying thing is, I'm not sure that I care as much as I should.

41

When I pass Hailey at reception the following Monday morning, she makes no reference to Sofia Marzoni, to the impending road trip or to her fortune-telling capabilities. Nor is there any mention of George Michael or Andrew Ridgeley. In fact, she looks as she always does, a quiet pocket of calm that belies the bedlam upstairs.

I pass her desk and nod at her, as I always do, and she nods back, as she always does. I am nearly at the stairs when I turn back towards her. She looks at me in her quiet, solemn way and waits for me to speak.

'Hailey, I just wanted to let you know that I'm pregnant.'

For a moment, I think she is not going to say anything. Then she smiles and it's like the sun coming out after a long, grey day. 'That's lovely news, Scarlett,' she says. 'Congratulations.'

For a moment, I think I might cry. It's the genuine warmth in Hailey's voice. And it's true. It *is* lovely news. Why didn't I tell everyone long before now?

I meet Eloise and Lucille walking along the corridor on the third floor. On their way to the ladies', no doubt.

'Good morning,' I say, stopping in front of them. They nearly walk into me, used to me breezing past them with a curt nod. 'I just wanted to let you know I'm expecting a baby.' In

358

the silence that follows this statement, I correct them on one thing that's been on my mind since that day in the ladies' when I took the pregnancy test. 'By the way,' I say, 'cats do *not* kill for pleasure. They are natural hunters. I just thought you should know that.'

The two women, with their dyed blonde hair and their French manicures and their fake tans, look like carbon copies of each other. Even their facial expressions are similar — a sort of a stunned bewilderment. They can't work out how they heard it from me and not from some other source, long before. They struggle to pick their jaws up off the floor and rally as best they can.

'Ohmigod,' squeaks one of them. Eloise, I think. 'That's, like . . . soooo amazing. Congratulations and all that.'

'Yes, Scarlett, congratulations,' the other one says, and I smile at them and continue up the corridor. It is the humane thing to do, releasing this pair back into their natural habitat so they can spread the news before they burst with it.

The next stop is Gladys Montgomery's office. She is on the phone to Tanya Forsythe.

'Yes, Tanya, that will be *no* problem whatsoever . . . Yes, Tanya . . . No, Tanya . . . Certainly, Tanya . . . Cheerio, Tanya. Take care . . . Goodbye, bye-bye, bye, bye, bye, bye, bye, bye.' Gladys hangs up and looks at me. 'That was Tanya Forsythe,' she says.

I cut to the chase. 'Gladys, I have some lovely news and I wanted you to be one of the first people in the company to know.'

Her face is set with shock and I realise that she

thinks I'm talking about the job. The promotion. And then I realise that I haven't given it too much thought since the interview last week.

'I'm pregnant.'

Gladys tries to respond. At least I think she does. I can see her mouth working but no words emerge. I pour her a glass of water and hand it to her.

'Twenty-one weeks,' I say, because I know that a part of Gladys is like a part of me and wants details and facts and figures and dates.

Delight pours into her face like water down a drain in a monsoon. While she appears to be looking at me, she is seeing something else entirely. Her future. Like the Yellow Brick Road where it curves and you see Oz for the first time and it glints like gold against the sun.

She stands up so suddenly her chair overturns and she doesn't even notice and she moves towards me and I smell the Rennies and she's so close now I see the gap between her two front teeth, the gum pink and fleshy and exposed.

'Congratulations, Scarlett,' she says, taking my hand and pumping it up and down. Her hand is warm and moist, like bread dough.

'Have you told Simon yet?' she asks. Behind her thick glasses, her eyes are doing the Haka.

'I'm just on my way to tell him now,' I say, and Gladys's eyes are almost black as the pupils dilate and dilate and threaten to burst their banks.

'His flight only got in this morning so he might not be in until tomorrow. He's exhausted, poor pet.' Gladys cannot do a poker face and, with the confidence of a royal flush in one hand and a full house in the other, she looks like she's about to climb up on top of the desk and burst into song. With the gap in her front teeth, there's every chance she might be a good singer but I don't wait to find out.

I'm only in the door of my office when Filly bursts in. She doesn't arrive with her usual 'GoodmorningsorryI'mlate', although she does have two full-fat cappuccinos, a Mars bar ice cream (for her) and a lime Solero (for me).

'Magda in Finance knows that you're up the spout,' she says, closing the office door with one leg and leaning against it as though she might fall down if she doesn't. 'She heard it from Harold, who was told by Terri, who heard it from Emily, who refuses to reveal her source.'

I check my watch. It's been twelve minutes since I told Eloise and Lucille. I can't help but admire their dedication and efficiency. If they were as good at their jobs as they are at . . . let's call it networking . . . there would be an outside chance of us getting our bonuses paid on time instead of the week-long delay that usually ensues every quarter.

The door bursts open and Filly is thrown to one side of the room while Elliot towers in the architrave. He doesn't say anything for a moment and bends instead, his hands on his knees, his face the colour of a brick (a red one), heaving with sharp breaths and general exertion.

'I . . . I . . . I . . . was talking . . . to . . . Marsha . . . ' Elliot struggles to push words out of his mouth in between pants.

361

Filly, who is a bit of kleptomaniac when it comes to other people's thunder, crawls out from behind the door and interrupts him. 'You were talking to Marsha in Promos and she told you that Magda told her that Harold told her that Terri told him that Emily told her that Scarlett is up the duff. Emily is refusing to reveal her source but just give me five minutes alone in a room with her and she'll be singing like a cockatoo.'

I'm pretty sure that cockatoos don't sing but I say nothing.

This bald statement depletes Elliot's remaining stock of oxygen and he collapses on to the couch, forgetting — what with the paltry oxygen stocks in his system — about Blue. Because of Blue's faster-than-the-speed-of-light reflexes, Elliot only manages to sit on his tail but Blue lets him have it anyway, with a cacophony of hissing and arching and looks that are way beyond dirty, they're that filthy.

I pour Elliot a glass of water and hand it to him. Then I pour Blue a saucer of milk (low fat) and set it on the floor as far away from Elliot as possible. Blue adopts an injured air but sidles towards the saucer all the same.

'I told Eloise and Lucille' — I check my watch — 'sixteen minutes ago. They've been keeping themselves pretty busy since then.'

'But . . . but . . . but . . . ' splutters Elliot, his breath returning to him but only in short spurts.

'Why?' Filly finishes for him.

I sit down at my desk. It's a good question and deserves due consideration before responding.

'In part,' I begin, 'it's an exercise in damage limitation. Simon already knows about Ellen because of Valentino. But he doesn't know that I know that he knows, if you know what I mean.' I look at Elliot and Filly to see if they are with me and they nod, indicating that they are. 'So,' I continue, 'I'm going to tell him before he tells me about the job so he won't be able to say I got the job under false pretences.'

'But you're not going to get the job now that he knows,' says Filly, her shoulders slumping in pre-emptive defeat.

'We don't know that,' says Elliot, but then he says, 'Not yet anyway,' and even his shoulders slump, although not as much as Filly's.

'Why else did you do it?' asks Filly then, in an effort to bat the mood up a few notches.

I stand up and walk to the window before answering. 'I want people to know,' I say. 'I want to wear smocks and leggings with elasticated waistbands and wide jeans with the stretchy panels. I want to talk about pelvic-floor exercises and epidurals and breathing techniques and perineal massage without people thinking I've lost the plot. And I want to walk like a proper pregnant woman' — I show them the walk, with my hand tucked into the small of my back, my bump thrust out and my legs wide — 'and stop pretending I'm not pregnant and that everything is ticking along as it normally does because it's not. Everything is different. Everything feels different. I feel different.' I am

363

a little breathless after this speech, short as it was, and I sit down again and wait for one or other of them to say something.

Eventually Elliot speaks. 'What's perineal massage?' he asks.

42

Simon's face bears traces of jet lag when he calls into my office the following morning. 'I believe congratulations are in order,' he says. I sent the email yesterday, when he didn't show up in the office.

'I wanted to tell you in person,' I say. 'Before you made a decision about the job.'

'It doesn't matter,' he says, swatting at my words like flies. 'I had already made up my mind. About the job, I mean. Before you told me.'

'Oh,' I say, and I feel it again, that blanket of resignation that doesn't feel one way or the other. It's just there.

Simon notices Blue lying on the couch and he moves to the window, which is as far away as he can get from the cat without opening it and climbing out on to the sill.

'I'm not going to beat about the bush, Scarlett,' he says, even though beating about bushes is one of his favourite pastimes and he's very good at it. I lean back in my chair and wait. He turns to me, an ill-fitting smile on his face. 'Congratulations, Scarlett,' he says.

'Eh, thank you, Simon. You already said that.' Perhaps the jet lag has dulled his memory.

'No, I mean, congratulations, you're the newest member of our management team. Welcome on board.' Simon's hand stretches across the desk and hangs there for a moment before I realise that I'm supposed to shake it.

'Aren't you pleased?' he asks, still pumping my hand up and down, albeit slower now.

'Well . . . yes . . . of course . . . It's just . . . with the baby and everything . . . ' My voice trails off.

'Your pregnancy doesn't feature in any company decisions. It can't. That would be against employment law, wouldn't it?'

This is true but it's never stopped him before. I think about Magda working part-time since the birth of her twins. Her career in a siding now, not even in spitting distance of the express track where it once was.

'Take a moment, Scarlett. You're over-whelmed. Delighted, so you are. But you deserve this promotion. You know that. You're one of our most dedicated members of staff and, once you get over the hump of having the baby and the first couple of months afterwards, you'll be back here like nothing happened. I *know* you.' Simon rocks back and forth on his heels, smiling properly now, sure of himself.

'I'm not going to lie to you, Scarlett, this promotion will mean long hours and hard work but you've never been afraid of that. And there are crèches that take children from dawn to dusk. Or you could get a nanny. A live-in one.' He pauses for a moment, probably imagining a nineteen-year-old Swedish nanny wandering down the landing towards the bathroom on the first storey of his house. Wearing a sheer nightdress that strains to cover her high, firm bottom.

Not so long ago, I would have agreed with Simon. That I would return to work after two, maybe three months. As if nothing had happened. Now, I barely recognise the woman who thought these thoughts. I hold my hands against my belly like a shield. Simon turns his head away from the gesture. So quickly I hear the crack of his neck as it swivels.

I stand up and pull my jacket tightly around my bump. 'Can I think about it?' I say. If Simon's face is anything to go by, he is as shocked as I am. 'Just for a few days,' I add.

'Well . . . I . . . ' Simon begins, and I am reminded of the time he applied for my gym. This feels nearly as embarrassing. Simon seems to remember this at the same time as I do. He collects himself, straightening his back and pretending to remove a piece of lint from the lapel of his jacket. 'I'll give you until Friday,' he says in a voice that does not brook negotiation.

'Could I have till Monday?' I ask, as if he hadn't used a voice that did not brook negotiation. 'It's just that I'm arranging the weekend trip to the castle with Sofia Marzoni and I won't have time to think about anything else until that's done.' Everything is already arranged but there's no need to tell Simon that.

'Fine,' he says, and the word is the bark of an angry dog. This dog is still on a lead but I know it's only a matter of time before the hounds are released.

43

Everyone converges on Tara at the same time, shoving peace and tranquillity down the steep flight of stairs in the basement and bringing with them bedlam and chaos. The noise feels like an old friend I haven't seen in ages.

Phyllis rushes through the house and straight out the back door to check on her hens. George trundles along behind her, laden down with suitcases and coats and two sticks of rock, one of which he gives to me.

'Who's the other one for?' I ask.

George reddens and looks at his feet. 'I got it for Ellen,' he says in his slow whisper of a voice. 'I know she can't eat it or anything . . . It's full of sugar and it's . . . it's terribly bad for you but . . . ' he catches my eye to make sure that I know that he knows all this ' . . . but I just didn't want to leave her out. It didn't feel right.'

'Thanks, George,' is all I can manage.

Lovely, quiet George, who attended all my school plays and even went to the parent-teacher meetings with Phyllis when Maureen and Declan couldn't. And he will do the same for Ellen if I ask him to. Except that I won't ask him to. Because I will go myself. I square my shoulders and make a promise to Ellen that I will go myself.

'Did you give the hens the sup of the pan like I told you to?' shouts Phyllis from the kitchen.

The sup of the pan is Phyllis's version of hen feed. It's grease. Lard. Fat. Whatever is left in the pan after Phyllis has finished frying the living day and night out of her dinner. And of course I didn't feed it to the hens. Mostly because the frying pan hasn't been out of the press since Phyllis left last week. And also because I worry about their cholesterol levels. So I give them grain and seeds and nuts. And while I have to admit that the eggs don't taste quite as good, the hens look a lot more sprightly.

There is a crash as the front door bangs against the hall table. Then thuds and clunks as Maureen and Declan scatter their belongings across the hall floor, where they will stay until someone — me — picks them up.

'Honey, we're home,' they sing in unison, and I am relieved because at least this means that they have suspended hostilities and I won't have to bounce like a ball between them for the next few days.

I hide the sticks of rock in the fruit bowl — if Maureen gets her hands on them, she'll use them as microphones whenever she sings in the kitchen — and step into the hall.

'Ohmigod,' shrieks Maureen. 'You've gotten so . . . so . . . pregnant.'

'Christ, you have,' says Declan, bending down towards my bulging belly and whispering hello to Ellen. 'You're *huge*, so you are.' He beams up at me, delighted.

'So the filming went well,' I say to his bent head.

Now he's humming the Beatles' 'Yellow

Submarine' in through the top of my bump. I feel Ellen move, like she's dancing.

'The shoot was a great success,' Maureen tells me, mixing a jug of wine spritzer with her coat still on. 'It's in the can, as they say.'

'I love it when you talk that fillum-talk,' says Declan, moving up behind Maureen and nibbling at her earlobe, like there's nobody else in the room.

Bryan struggles into the kitchen, laden down with bags and a biscuit tin and a selection of Maureen's feather boas and two lacrosse sticks that Declan insists on bringing everywhere even though a) he doesn't know how to play lacrosse and b) neither does anyone else he meets, although, apparently, it's big in Canada. It's just that Declan never seems to meet any Canadians.

He looks around him for somewhere to put everything and settles on the table, sort of shaking himself over it so everything falls into a pile.

'So . . . ' I say to him, picking up the bits and arranging them into two bundles: Maureen's stuff and Declan's stuff.

'He's in the garden, Scarlett. On the phone to the car mechanic,' Bryan says, and there is a smile around the edges of his face.

'I'd say he could do with some tea,' I say, backing out of the kitchen.

He sits on the gravel leaning against Al Pacino, who stands stoically, like a supporting wall. The mechanic is telling him something he doesn't want to hear. I can tell by the way Red drags his hand down his face. I hear the scratchy sound of stubble. His face is paler than usual, the freckles glaring like a picket line.

'So it's the engine, you say? . . . Well, that doesn't sound too serious, right? . . . Can you not just . . . I don't know . . . like, *weld* those pieces back together? . . . A new engine? How much is that going to cost? . . . But that can't be right. I bought the car for less than that . . . Now, there's no call for a comment like that. The car may be old but it's always been reliable. How many people can you say that about? . . . Yes, look, I'm sure your grandfather *is* reliable but that's not the point. I was just . . . OK, then, yes, I'll ring you in the morning.' Red hangs up and throws his phone into an overgrown hydrangea and then falls backwards as Al Pacino, thinking perhaps that this is a new game, with phones instead of sticks, pegs off to fetch it.

I stand in the shadows and count to twenty-four before I approach him. During those twenty-four seconds, Red moves not a single muscle. Not even when a fat-bodied bluebottle walks its twitchy walk down the length of his forearm.

'Red?' I whisper the word, thinking that perhaps he has fallen asleep.

His clothes have the look of clothes that have been washed too many times in the wrong wash cycle. There is an ancient grass stain on the sleeve of the used-to-be-white T-shirt. His jeans could pass muster as skinny jeans but the safe money is that they started out as baggy jeans that shrank in the wash. More than once. It is Al

Pacino who alerts Red to the fact that I am here. He bounds back to Red with the phone trapped between his jaws and stands up on his chest, jumping up and down until he is sure that he has Red's full attention.

'Scarlett O'Hara,' he says, smiling, despite the hundred pounds of dog flesh straddled across his chest. He struggles to get up but, in the end, it takes the pair of us — me pulling and him pushing — to persuade Al Pacino to come down off his perch. Afterwards, I am out of breath and Red arranges his denim jacket — creased and bleached from exposure to the elements — on the gravel so I can sit down, which I do. I hand him a cup of tea. He finishes it in two gulps.

'It should be me making tea for you,' he says, setting the empty cup on the ground. 'I bet your star sign is Aquarius, isn't it?'

'Yes,' I say. 'How did you . . . ?'

'They're nurturers,' he says. 'They take care of people. That's what you do, isn't it?' He looks at me when he says this and I squirm a little under his scrutiny. 'How are you feeling?' he asks.

'Fine,' I say.

'No lower-back pain?'

'No . . . Well, actually, yes. A little. How did you know?'

'Classic week-twenty-one symptom,' he says. 'Come here to me.' He gets up on his knees and shuffles behind me. Now, his hands are on the small of my back, his fingers kneading the flesh there like dough. The relief is sudden and exquisite, like a long-as-your-arm to-do list with all the items ticked. I think I might moan out load.

'Did you say something, Scarlett?'

'Eh . . . I was just going to ask you how the filming went.'

'I haven't decided yet,' he says in a voice that sounds like he's said something much more conclusive than that. And then, 'Could you get on all fours for me? I think I could get at you a bit better in that position.'

I can't believe I do it until I've done it. It's something to do with the way he asks. Like it would be rude not to.

'And if you can just sort of bend your knees back towards me. Yes, that's it. And widen your legs if you can. Just like that, yes. Now, come back some more and settle your bump in between your knees. Perfect. How does that feel?'

I feel the muscles in my back lengthen and loosen. His fingers curl around the place where my waist used to be and he rotates his hands round my back until I think I might bay like Al Pacino does when he sees a Guinness truck. With the pure pleasure of it all. I even go so far as to close my eyes and I don't even try to come up with something to say. Even when my back pain takes one last curtain call before packing its bags and slinging its hook, I say nothing.

And so it is in this uncompromising position that Maureen stumbles upon us, now dressed in one of her array of dresses that looks like a nightdress and floats around her like a ghost.

'Red? What on earth are you doing?'

373

'I'm giving Scarlett a massage,' he says, without stopping. 'Her lower back is giving her jip and I'd say her bottom is numb as well.' He bends his head towards me. 'Is it, Scarlett?'

'Eh, yes, now you mention it,' I say, wondering what he is going to do about it and hoping it might have something to do with the slow, circular motion of his hands.

'Classic week-twenty-one symptoms,' Red calls out to Maureen, who continues to stand there, her wine spritzer in one hand and a long, thin menthol cigarette in the other.

'Oh, yes,' says Maureen. 'I remember it well. Although I don't remember Declan massaging me . . . well, quite like that.'

'It's the best way,' Red explains, like he has massaged a vast number of pregnant women in their twenty-first week.

'I see,' is all Maureen says, and I can feel her eyes on me, full of questions to which I have no answers.

'Anyway,' she says, when it becomes clear that Red is not going to stop, 'I just came out to say that Phyllis has prepared frittatas. The fridge is full of nothing but eggs. You might have eaten some, Scarlett.'

'I did,' I manage. 'I had one every day. Blue won't eat them any more. Not since he saw *Chicken Run* in Hugo's house, remember?'

'Oh, yes,' says Maureen. 'Such a sensitive creature. A bit like myself, I suppose.' She swivels and marches towards the house. I smell Phyllis's rosewater, which she makes with petals and other bits and bobs from the garden in a mortar and pestle. Maureen sometimes sneaks it when she can't be bothered to go upstairs to get her Femme Fatale. 'Frittatas in five, darlings,' she says, throwing her voice back at us like Cyril Sweeney tells her to do whenever she is on the stage with actual lines to say, which is not as often as she'd like.

I struggle into a more conventional sitting position and look at Red. 'Thanks.'

'Anytime,' he says, taking a battered and frayed business card out of his back pocket. 'Call me.' He leans across the space between us holding out the card and I take it. 'If you need a massage, I mean. Or . . . just . . . you know . . . if you need anything at all.'

I look at the card. It is handwritten. The edges crooked like they've been cut with blunt scissors. The writing is small. Slanted. Although a great effort towards neatness has been made. His name is in the centre of the card, along with his telephone number. Underneath it, a list in a line of all the services he offers: *Actor, writer, director, producer, barman, masseur, weeder, dog-walker, handyman (shelves a speciality)*. The writing becomes smaller and smaller as it reaches the end of the line.

'Weeder?' I have to ask.

'I know,' he says. 'But that's actually one of the few services on my list that pays. I'd say if I did the maths' — he smiles at me then to demonstrate how unlikely this is — 'the money I've made from my writing has just about covered Al Pacino's food.' We both look at Al Pacino, who gazes at us with his huge brown eyes, which always seem hungry. Drool dribbles from both sides of his wide mouth and we can tell that he's thinking about Phyllis's frittata with beans and sausage on the side and maybe some mature Cheddar, grated and melting over the top.

'Although,' continues Red, 'to be fair, he does eat quite a bit . . . I'm going to need to do a lot of fecking weeding,' he says then, almost to himself, 'to get Julian back on the road.'

'Julian?'

'I inherited the name. The previous owner was a bit of a Famous Five fanatic, by all accounts.'

'Maybe it's time you got another one,' I suggest. 'I mean, one that's not quite so old.' I remember Red's car. I don't know how old it is but it could easily pass for eighteen. 'And you got paid for *The Jou ney*, didn't you?'

'Not yet,' he says. 'But I'm sure I will. Fairly soon.' He says this in the nonchalant voice of a man who does not have to pull dandelions out of the ground by their roots to pay the rent.

'So you'll be able to replace Julian,' I explain.

He winces. 'I know,' he says. 'But you know the way you get attached to something? Even though it doesn't make all that much sense?'

I surprise myself by nodding my head. I am even more surprised when I say, 'I do,' and smile at him, as if the setting sun is not making a circle round his head, giving it a blazing halo kind of look.

★ ★ ★

Around the table, the talk is full of *The Jou ney*. It's like old times, it seems to me, with everyone talking at the same time, at full tilt. I watch Red without appearing to. He manages three of Phyllis's frittatas even though she throws everything she has at them, including a sack of potatoes. He also demolishes half a sliced pan, two apples, three mugs of tea and three-quarters of a packet of custard creams. His appetite for food is the same as his appetite for everything else, I decide: voracious.

'Is Sofia not expecting you home tonight?' Maureen asks, her tone rather pointed.

'No,' says Red, 'she's gone to some horror film with Hailey. I'll see her at the weekend, when we go to the castle.' His eyes reach over the rim of his cup and fasten on mine. 'You're coming too, Scarlett, aren't you?'

I nod and begin clearing the table.

'You'll *both* be away this weekend?' Maureen says, looking from one of us to the other and back again. 'Who's going to help me with my lines?' she asks, pouting like a seven-year-old who didn't get a pony for Christmas.

'I can go over them with you tonight if you like,' I offer, stifling a yawn.

'You're tired, Scarlett.' Red stands up and turns to Maureen. 'Here, we can go into the den and practise now if you want.'

'You sure you don't mind?' Maureen says, already heading at a gallop towards the stairs.

I catch Red's eye. 'Thanks,' I say. 'That's . . . kind of you.'

'Not at all,' he says, and I know by the way he

377

says it that it is not something he normally says. He leaves the room at a trot, although there is no need, because Maureen does not reappear for half an hour and, when she does, her make-up has been re-applied and she is wearing another of her flowing nightdresses, this one a gentle duck-egg blue with a plunging neckline.

★   ★   ★

Later, Bryan drives Red home. Maureen heads towards the stairs, her hands full of her night-time routine: slices of cucumber, a cup of mint tea, her eye-patches, a copy of *Variety* and a pot of my night cream, which she hides between the pages. I can see the bulge of it.

'How's your back, Scarlett?' she asks me, pausing on the curve of the stairs.

'Eh, much better, thanks.'

'I'd say it is,' she says, still not moving. 'Quite the ladies' man, isn't he?'

'Is he?' I say, even though I know that it's true.

'Don't worry, Scarlett,' she says, tossing her hair like a horse. 'He's not your type of ladies' man. You're more of a John Smith girl, aren't you? I knew he'd come back.' She smiles at me and I know she thinks this is the right thing to say.

I nod at her and she continues up the stairs, jaunty now after scattering her pearls of wisdom. Somewhere in my head, a door bangs shut and I move through the house, locking the doors and checking the windows are tightly shut against the world.

44

I pull up outside Valentino Marzoni's house in Finglas at 8.30 a.m. I'm not supposed to be here until nine o'clock but the traffic was against me. The house is really in Glasnevin but Valentino insists on the Finglas address, in an effort to remain true to his humble beginnings.

There is nothing humble about the house. There is also no mistaking it, what with the grotto in the front garden and the life-size statue of the Virgin Mary sheltering in a brick surround, designed, built and lovingly maintained by Valentino himself.

There is a vehicle parked in the driveway. It is bright orange with yellowing net curtains parted along both sides. It is a minibus. An ancient one. A pair of gigantic furry dice dangle from the rear-view mirror. A peeling sticker on the back window says, 'Honk if you love Jesus.' I curse my twenty-twenty vision, which allows me to see the seat covers, a scalding kind of leopard print.

I concentrate on my pelvic-floor exercises, which I do in tandem with my breathing exercises to save time, although I still have — I check my watch — twenty-seven minutes to go.

At 8.38 a.m., I get a text. From Sofia. 'Come into the house, for God's sake.'

The bell on the front door plays a song when you press it. It's 'Ave Maria'. The door opens immediately and Sofia is there with her smile

379

and her hair that is big enough for two.

'Howeya, Scarlah.' She beams at me. 'Come in.' She beckons me inside the mausoleum of a hall, which is overseen by a massive painting of Jesus Christ with a red bulb burning in the centre of his chest. His eyes follow me about the hall, no matter where I stand.

'Hails will be down in a moment. She's just brushin' her teeth, so she is.'

'Hailey is *here*?'

'Yeah,' Sofia says, and do I imagine it or is her tone a little defensive? 'She lives in Skerries, so she does, so it made sense for her to stay here last night.' The fact that I live in Wicklow is not mentioned. 'We had a girls' night in, so we did,' Sofia continues. 'Gas, it was. Hails did me tea leaves. Apparently I'm going to marry a tall man with red hair who can do the tango as quick as look at you.'

'Red can tango?'

'He makes Fred Astaire look like he's dancin' on ice with his feet in two left shoes and the laces tied together.' Sofia smiles, basking in the reflected glory of Red's fleetness of foot.

Hailey looks different when she is not behind the reception desk at Extraordinary Events International. For a start, I can see all of her and not just her shoulders and head. She is longer than I imagined. Also she is smiling. And wearing make-up as far as I can see: there is a pinkness along her cheekbones. And her hair . . .

'Did you put colour in your hair?' I ask.

Hailey giggles into her cupped hand. This is new too, although I have heard her giggle before

— on the phone when she puts Sofia through — but not in the flesh. It suits her. She looks ten years younger.

'Sofia did it,' she says. 'Last night.'

'It really suits you,' I say, and it's true. The salt-and-pepper strands have been replaced with a vibrant brown — dark and glossy, like a chestnut.

The two of them are at it now, giggling. I feel like I've stumbled into a chapter of *Summer Term at Malory Towers* the morning after a midnight feast.

'Sorry I'm a little early,' I say. 'I . . . The traffic . . .'

'Don't worry about it, Scarlah. Hails said you'd be early so we're ready to go,' says Sofia, not noticing that Hailey has gone a peculiar shade of puce.

'I . . . I only meant . . .' Hailey begins.

'Don't worry about it, Hails. Everyone knows about Scarlah's pathological relationship with the clock,' says Sofia. 'Don't they, Scarlah?'

'Eh . . .'

'Wait 'n' ya see,' continues Sofia, on a roll now. 'When is Ellen due again?'

'Eh . . . the fifth of October.'

'Wait 'n' ya see,' Sofia says again, turning to Hailey. 'Ellen will arrive at a minute past midnight on the fifth. Am I right, Scarlah?'

There is a font in the shape of John the Baptist's head just inside the front door. The holy water collects in his open mouth. On our way out, Sofia dips her fingers in the water and presses them against our foreheads. 'For the safe journey,' she tells us when neither of us say anything. I bless myself. I'm going to need more than holy water and prayers to get us safely to the castle in the ancient bus but at least it's a start.

When the bus doesn't start immediately, Sofia explains that it's vintage. Very valuable, apparently. If vintage is another word for unreliable and clapped out, then vintage it definitely is.

When the bus fails to start on the second, third and fourth attempts, we get out of the bus and do that thing that people do when their vehicle won't start: stand round it, stare at it and shake your head, move to the other side of it and shake your head some more. After a bit of that, Sofia and Hailey turn to look at me, expectantly. I can do a couple of things with automobiles. One of the things is using jump leads so I get them from the boot of my car and do that. Already Sofia and Hailey look relieved.

The van's engine splutters, faint at first, then clears its throat and coughs into life. The gearstick is long and narrow and stiff. I use two hands to force it into first.

'Quick, get in,' I shout, anxious that we hit the road before the van changes its mind.

★ ★ ★

Our first stop is at Filly and Brendan's house. Although it's not a house as such. It's a couple of rooms over the butcher shop in Marino. They call one room the east wing and the other the west wing. They are as happy as sandboys in these rooms. They feel bigger than they really are, these rooms, stretching to accommodate the layers of love. It's everywhere. It's in the suitcase on the bed, where Filly's clothes have been carefully packed by Brendan, layers of tissue paper between each item even though these clothes will end up on the floor of whatever room Filly stays in. It's in the shelf of Matchbox cars that Brendan collects and that Filly spends hours searching for, when it's his birthday or Christmas or Friday or a rainy day (to cheer him up: he hates the rain, she tells me). It's in the chipped vase of lilies that drip their powdery pollen on the kitchen table. It's in the fact that Filly doesn't complain about this powdery pollen and how it gets on your clothes and your fingers and how hard it is to remove. But mostly, it's in the way they look at each other when they think no one else is watching. It is a look that makes me wish for more.

'Would you like tea or coffee with your breakfast?'

The house smells like a B&B in the morning. Brendan assumes everyone has the same carnivorous appetite as he has, even at — I check my watch — 9.03 a.m. I have seen his version of breakfast once before, his face barely visible over the mound of meat (rashers, sausages, puddings — both colours — liver, chops, kidneys and chicken wings). Quivering at the edge of all that flesh was one solitary slice of tomato, the only vegetable Brendan ever eats, and, even though tomato is, strictly speaking, a fruit, I don't correct him, not wanting to discourage even the most nominal vegetarian tendency.

'Eh, no, thanks, Brendan.' His face falls. 'I'll have a glass of water, though,' I add, to cheer him up.

'Just a glass of water with your fry?'

'No, I mean, just a glass of water. On its own. With nothing else. Thanks.'

'No fry?' Brendan believes there are two types of people in the world: those who eat meat and those who are dead. Vegetarianism is a dirty word in Brendan's world and I try never to mention it in front of him.

'No,' I say. 'But thanks.'

Brendan smiles at me, like I've just told him a secret he already knows. 'You'll have a rasher buttie at least?'

'No, thanks.'

'I'll spread some white pudding on a slice of toast for you. You'll take that, surely?'

'No, honestly, I couldn't . . . '

'What about a hot chicken roll?'

I shake my head.

'A grilled cheese and sausage sandwich?'

'No, Brendan, seriously, I — '

'OK, OK, I'll just do you one fried egg and two strips of bacon and we'll call it quits, yeah?' Brendan nods encouragement at me and turns back to the frying pan. He is a lovely man, apart from his military views on meat.

After breakfast — I get away with a fried egg, which I manage to eat in spite of the fact that it has been cooked in a puddle of pig fat — we pile on the bus. It groans under our weight but splutters to life and manages to edge down the road. The fact that the road slopes in a downward direction helps enormously.

We arrive outside Red Butler's flat in Renelagh. Despite my carefully compiled schedule, we are eight minutes late, due in no small part to the van, the pace of which can be described as 'leisurely' at best. Of Red there is no sign. The curtains on all three storeys of the redbrick period house are tightly shut.

'Sofia, can you go and call for him?' I ask.

'Wha?' she roars up at me.

I say it again, shouting this time to be heard over the raucous groan of the engine. 'I don't want to turn the engine off in case it won't start again,' I add.

'I'll ring him,' says Sofia, taking her mobile out of her bag.

Red doesn't answer his phone. Banging on the front door yields no results. In the end, Sofia throws stones up at a small window on the third floor. Her aim is good but she has to throw seven stones before we see the curtains twitch and Red's tousled just-out-of-bed head appear through the parting in the middle of the curtains. He sticks up two fingers, which could mean 'Fuck off' or 'I'll be down in two minutes.' Turns out to be the latter, although it's more like three and a half minutes. The top of his weekend bag hangs open and I can see boxer shorts and a dog-eared manuscript and a tin of dog food and an opened packet of cream crackers. A toothbrush sticks out of his mouth and Al Pacino strains against the lead in his hand. Under his arm is an ancient typewriter. His jumper is inside

385

out and back to front.

Blue, incarcerated in his cat cage, throws himself against the bars when he sees Al Pacino and I have to let him out, even though he is not scheduled to be let out until we reach the castle. The pair trot to the back of the bus, where they take up residence, Blue stepping daintily into the semicircle that Al Pacino makes with his front paws. They look out of the window like American tourists on a bus tour in Killarney.

'Morning, everyone. Sorry I'm late.' Red tacks the second sentence on in a manner that suggests he uses the phrase on a regular basis. 'Hi, Hailey,' he says. 'It's lovely to meet you properly. Sofia's told me loads about you.' Sofia and Hailey sit together in the third row, sharing a bag of Milky Moos.

'Hello, Red. I'm Brendan the butcher,' says Brendan, handing Red a foil-wrapped package that contains four sausages, two rounds of toast and a sachet of tomato ketchup. 'But not in *The Godfather* sense of the phrase,' he adds with his shy smile.

Red leans over the back of the front passenger seat and offers Brendan his hand, which Brendan accepts and they shake, firmly and briefly. I study the roadmap. Red feeds two of the sausages to Al Pacino and Blue, and wolfs the rest. When he looks at me, he smiles.

'So you think you can handle this baby?' he says, nodding at the dashboard.

'Yes, of course,' I say, struggling again with the gearstick, which tolerates second gear but is not so fond of first.

'Here, I've driven one of these before,' says Red, taking the gearstick from me. 'I'll change the gears. You just let me know when you're stepping on the clutch.'

And so we drive all the way to the castle in this way. Me yelling, '*Clutch!*' every time I want to change gears and Red wrestling with the gearstick and, even though it sounds like a most unsatisfactory way to drive, somehow it works.

45

We have the castle to ourselves for the weekend. Milly and Billy have gone to England for the launch of a book by the Duchess of York, who is one of Billy's millions of distant relatives.

'We'll leave Glynis with you for the weekend, Scarlett, darling,' Billy told me when I phoned to make the arrangements.

Glynis is their chef and the one in charge of the wedding banquet, as Sofia insists on calling it.

'We can come down another weekend, if you'd prefer to be there while we're around.'

'Gracious, no, Scarlett, darling,' said Billy. 'Milly and I trust you utterly.'

Although it's not me I'm worried about. I look at Filly through the rear-view mirror. She has already broken a door handle, spilled a can of coke and jammed the 'J' key on Red's typewriter. I make a mental note to tell Glynis not to serve any food on the good wedding dishes. The normal Monday-to-Friday dishes will do. Maybe even paper plates and plastic cups.

The van groans up to the top of a particularly steep hill and Red hauls the gearstick down into third gear as I stamp on the clutch pedal. For a moment I don't think we're going to make it. '*Clutch!*' I yell, and we're in second gear now, the van shuddering along.

'Can. She. Do. It?' Filly roars, and the others

take up the chant ('Yes. She. Can.') as the front wheels of the van gain purchase on the summit of the hill and the bus hauls itself, moaning and creaking, over the crest and everyone cheers and punches the air and high-fives everyone else and I catch myself smiling even though we are — I check my watch — forty-three minutes behind schedule and Al Pacino has weed on the back seat of the bus. Not only am I smiling but, when Filly confesses that she's broken the catch on Blue's cat cage, I yell out, 'Can. We. Fix. It?' and everyone shouts back, 'Yes. We. Can.'

I let the van freewheel down the hill to give Red a rest from wrestling with the gearstick. We are flying down the hill now, the passing countryside a glorious blur of wild flowers and hedgerows, and, while my foot hovers over the brake pedal, I don't press it, even though I know I should. My hair blows across my face in the howling wind of a draught that comes at me from the front window and the sun pours through every window, like melted butter. Sofia leads us through a tortuous version of 'The Wheels on the Bus' and I catch myself laughing out loud and I feel younger than I've ever felt before, even when I was young. I don't join in the singing but I *nearly* do.

'There's the castle,' Filly shouts, pointing out of the window. And there it is, the four turrets poking up like tufts of hair. The sunlight drapes across it, turning the grey stone walls to silver and, against the backdrop of lake and forest, the castle looks like a castle in a fairytale, where anything could happen.

The momentum of the hill lasts all the way over the moat and up the drive to the front door of the castle, the little wheels crunching like toast against the gravel.

Red and Brendan carry the bags inside, and Sofia and Hailey run from room to room, laughing and calling to each other, their voices bouncing like balls against the thick walls. Brendan hauls a crate of what turns out to be raw meat into the kitchen and, after a brief tussle with Glynis — who can be a little territorial about her kitchen — is allowed to load it into the fridge. He and Filly then repair to their bedroom to have a 'rest'.

Glynis shows the rest of us to our rooms. 'Sofia and Red, you're in here,' she says, opening the door to the largest bedroom, which looks out on to the immaculately manicured gardens at the front of the castle.

'Eh, excuse me, Glynis, but Red and I aren't married yet, you know,' Sofia points out.

'Oh,' says Glynis, who has gone a little pink around the edges. 'I'm . . . I'm sorry . . . I thought . . . I've only prepared three bedrooms . . . I assumed . . . ' If Glynis is waiting for Sofia to step in and change her mind, she's in for an Irish Rail type of a wait.

'Why don't you share the room with Hailey?' I suggest. 'I'm sure we could set up another bed in here. The room is big enough.' I look at Glynis, who nods and smiles at me.

'Sure we don't need an extra bed, do we?' says Sofia, looking at Hailey. 'That bed is huge, so it is. It's definitely a king-size. The whole lot of us could fit into it.'

I turn to Hailey to see how she is taking this turn of events but she is already picking up her bag and moving inside the room.

'The third room has twin beds so perhaps you and Red . . . ' Glynis looks at me, her voice trailing off.

'That sounds like a brilliant idea,' says Sofia, sitting on the side of the king-size bed and bouncing, making the springs creak in a way that suggests they are unused to such treatment.

Glynis takes this as a 'yes' from me and trots down the corridor, leaving me with nothing to do other than trail after her.

'I'll find a couch downstairs and sleep on that. Don't worry, Scarlett,' says Red, taking my bag from my hands and somehow finding a way to carry it along with his own bag, his typewriter and Blue's blanket while still managing to pull Al Pacino along on his lead behind him. Al Pacino has taken against a suit of armour at the top of the stairs and growls at it, his hackles as rigid and raised as his tail.

Glynis opens the door to the room and stands there, waiting for us. She is one of those women whose age is impossible to guess. She could be forty-one or she might be fifty-nine. Either way, she is a brilliant cook and has worked at the castle for so long she doesn't bat an eyelid at the thought of the wedding planner and the groom-to-be sharing a room. Even a twin room. Past Glynis I see the room, which is the size of about two average-sized twin rooms, the beds at opposite ends, a mini-marathon away from each other.

'No, it's OK, I'll . . . manage,' I say.

The words are barely out of my mouth before Red is over the threshold, flinging his stuff on every available surface and hoofing his shoes off — without untying the laces — shedding his jacket, which retains the shape of his body on the floor where he has dropped it, and stretching out on one of the beds. The place looks like it's been trashed and I pick my way carefully to the other side of the room, lifting my bag off the floor and Blue's blanket off a table and placing the bag under my bed, after hanging up all my clothes that need to be hung and folding the other bits into a chest of drawers. There is an en-suite bathroom and I place my toothbrush in the glass on a shelf above the sink beside my anti-stretch-mark oil, deodorant and make-up bag. This takes me two minutes, after which I sit on my bed and try to remember what I'm supposed to be doing next.

After a while I think of something to say to Red. Two things, actually: 1) the weather, and then, when we're finished talking about the warm loveliness of the day, we can move on to 2) the wedding vows, which is on my schedule, although not due for discussion until later this afternoon, at four o'clock.

Thus armed, I turn towards him. He's asleep, one arm dangling towards the floor. Al Pacino sits on the floor beside the bed, occasionally reaching down to lick Red's hand, like it's a vanilla ice cream. I look at Red's face, a lot of which is covered by his fringe, which could do with a good cut. The stubble is dark brown, as are his eyelashes, which stretch towards his cheekbones. He looks more or less the same asleep as awake: at peace with himself. Part of me is annoyed at his ability to sleep so carelessly.

I unthread Al Pacino's lead, which is wrapped round Red's fingers, and leave the room without making a sound. Al Pacino makes up for this by howling like the wind as I pull him from the room. Red Butler does not stir.

★   ★   ★

Glynis is in the kitchen, rearranging the fridge. She sighs when she sees me, shaking her head. 'Six packets of rashers, Scarlett. I mean, I thought you were only staying the one night.'

'It's Brendan,' I explain. 'He brings meat everywhere he goes. I don't think he can help it. He's a butcher, you see.'

Glynis makes a sound that is like the grunt of a disgruntled bear and heaves a vacuum-packed fillet of beef that could feed twenty people into one of the vegetable compartments at the bottom of the fridge.

'Have you seen Blue?' I ask. 'I'm going to take him and Al Pacino for a walk.'

This makes Glynis smile, as I suspected it would. Glynis is a cat and dog person but would veer more towards cats if she had to choose. She knows they do not kill for pleasure. She's never met Blue before today but has seen photographs of him and declared him to be 'a handsome devil', which is a fairly accurate description of him.

'No, I haven't, but I've spread some Philadelphia on crackers for him. My fellas love that.' Her *fellas* are George, William, Charles and Harold — big tomcats who have the run of the place.

I walk through to the drawing room, where Sofia and Hailey sit in a pocket of sunshine on a couch in the bay window. They have taken the Saturday paper apart and Sofia is reading her horoscope, while Hailey reads the editorial. They remind me of Saturdays past, in John's flat.

'Have either of you seen Blue?' I have to say it twice before they hear me. When they look at me, it's like they know me from someplace but can't quite place me.

'No,' they say, in perfect synchronicity.

I bang on Filly and Brendan's bedroom door. 'Sorry,' I shout through the door, although it's as thick as an oak tree and I don't know if they can hear me. I bang again and, after a while, the door opens a slit and Brendan's face appears round it.

'Yes?' he says, trying — and failing — to sound like he's delighted to see me.

'Sorry, Brendan, I didn't mean to disturb you and I wouldn't normally, you know that . . . '

'What is it, Scarlett?' Brendan senses the urgency in my voice and opens the door fully now, taking care that the bed sheet he has wrapped round himself is not revealing any of his . . . bits.

'Blue isn't in there with you, is he?'

'No,' shouts Filly from within the room before

her head appears under Brendan's arm. She is naked apart from the clips in her hair but stands there as if she is fully clothed. She attributes this lack of body consciousness to the fact that she is from Australia. 'Sure, everyone is practically naked in Australia,' she assures me. 'Because of the heat,' she adds.

I run down the passages. This is the trouble with castles. They're big. There are a lot of passages. All long and twisting and loud with the echo of my shoes against the stone floors. I've been in the castle before and know my way around but my brain seems to have forgotten this and I fight the panic that gathers in me.

When I start calling Blue's name — shouting it — I know that panic has gained the upper hand. Back in the kitchen, the crackers and cream cheese remain in Blue's bowl on the ground, untouched. Al Pacino has licked his bowl clean and, even though he looks longingly at Blue's bowl and licks his lips and drools all over the crackers, he doesn't eat any of them. Fear grips me like a fist and I find it hard to breathe. Blue loves cream cheese. If he were anywhere in the castle, he would smell it. His sense of smell is legendary, almost as good as mine since Ellen moved in.

In the hall, Blue's cat cage has never looked so empty. The door of it swings open, creaking a little in the draught from the front door, also open. I am running now. Into the gardens. Shouting his name. The moat is a hundred metres from the castle. Not as wide as it could be. But wide enough. I remember Billy telling me that the water is not deep. But it's deep enough. I think about Blue, four days old, in a bag that is tied at the top with string and weighed down by rocks. Fifteen of them. The memory stabs me like claws and I can't move. Something shifts inside me and, for a moment, I don't know what it is. I don't recognise it. I am unravelling, like a spool of thread. I don't realise I am crying. But I am. Great shuddering sobs that bang against the castle walls like a storm. I heave with the force of it, like my body is not used to such a deluge of tears. And it's not, given the time that has elapsed since the non-arrival of the Tooth Fairy when I was six and a half. My legs buckle under the strain of it and I am kneeling now, the sharp edges of the pebbles digging into my knees, and I am glad of it. Glad of this pain. Because I deserve it. I am a person who loses things. I have lost my family. My baby. Ellen's brother or sister. Gone. And now Blue. My Blue. The cat who buries his love like treasure. Like I do. Presuming that everyone will know it's there. Hidden. But there.

'Oh my God, Scarlett, what is it?' Filly races out of the castle, with Brendan, Sofia, Hailey and Glynis hard on her heels. They stop suddenly when they see my face.

'Are you . . . *crying*?' Filly asks.

This makes me cry harder, like all the unwept tears over the years are taking full advantage of the situation. They storm down my face, shedding like leaves in autumn.

'Of course she's cryin'. Would you look at the face on her.' This from Sofia, who hates people

396

asking questions when the answers are obvious. 'Oh my God,' she adds, her voice a whisper now and her hands making the sign of the cross up and down and across her body, 'is it the babby?'

'Should I call an ambulance?' offers Hailey, looking at me with a potent mix of fear and confusion.

It is Red Butler who pushes to the front and kneels down on the sharp stones and takes me in his arms and rocks me like I'm a baby, patting my back like he's burping me and shushing me.

'Stand back. Give her some air,' he tells them, as if I'm having a heart attack or something really serious.

'It's Blue,' I finally manage, pulling myself away from him. 'I can't find him.'

'For the lovin' honour of the Holy Divine Trinity,' Sofia says, lifting her hands to the heavens, as if beseeching the gods. 'I thought it was something *serious*.'

Red raises his head and mouths something at Filly.

She nods and addresses the others. 'Come on, everybody,' she says. 'We'll look inside the castle.'

With my face tucked into the soft skin of Red's neck, I cry and cry until his T-shirt is saturated with my tears.

'Please don't cry, Scarlett,' he says. 'I'll find Blue.'

'It's not just Blue,' I sob. 'It's everything.'

'Everything will work out. You'll see.'

'It won't. You don't understand. I've lost everything. It's all my fault.'

'You haven't. It isn't. Hush now. Take a breath.'

'I was going to have an abortion.'

'But you didn't.'

'And I lost the other baby. Ellen's brother. Or sister. Just like I've lost Blue.'

'But Ellen is still here. You haven't lost her.'

I hold on to these words and to the way he says them, so softly. I can feel the tears stemming. Shoring up. But I don't want to let go of Red. He feels like a bed I could lie on. Sleep on.

'I'll find Blue,' he says again, and I pull myself away from him and look up into his face. After my revelations, I am afraid of what I will see. But there is nothing except compassion on the face that has become so familiar to me.

'Do you promise?' I whisper.

'Yes.' He hands me a ball of toilet paper and I blow my nose and wipe the tears and snot and wet mascara off my face. Red stands up. 'Will you be OK?' he asks.

I nod and he turns in the direction of the moat. I can't look.

Somehow, I manage to get back inside the castle, where Glynis makes me her homemade herbal tea. It tastes vile but demands my full attention if I'm to get it down my throat and I am grateful for the distraction.

'It's four o'clock,' says Filly, in an effort to cheer me up. She knows how fond I am of keeping time. But I don't care that it's four o'clock, that Filly and I should be having a meeting with Sofia and Red about their wedding vows.

'How about a plate of rasher butties?' suggests Brendan.

Everyone shouts, 'Yes,' in carefully cheery voices.

'How about a nice game of Scrabble?' says Hailey, and again the chorus of 'Yes' as Hailey runs to get the game.

They play. 'You can watch, Scarlett,' Hailey tells me, when it becomes apparent that I am unable to raise even a modicum of excitement at the sight of the Scrabble board. Everyone is careful not to spell words like 'Blue' or 'cat' or 'lost' or 'moat' and, even though I see that Brendan could get bonus points with his letters ('feline'), he spells 'file' instead, for which he receives the minimum amount of points and ends up losing out to Hailey, who, it appears, is a Scrabble hardcore like me.

Ellen is quiet. I imagine her inside me, crouching and waiting for news of Blue. I feel like I've already let her down. Twice. I start crying again and, even though Sofia raises her eyes to heaven, she hands me a fistful of tissues and even suggests that Hailey search the tea leaves at the bottom of my cup to see if there is any sign of Blue.

When Red comes into the kitchen, he is alone. Even Al Pacino has abandoned him. Of Blue there is no sign. Before I get a chance to stand up and cup my hands over my mouth, he says, 'I found him,' and everyone slumps forward in their seats and the relief is as solid as a wall. 'In the hot-press,' Red continues. 'I tried to take him out but he spat at me and scratched my arm.' He holds up his arm where a long red welt traipses down the length of it. We nod our heads. He really has found Blue. There can be no mistaking him.

'There's a *hot-press* in the castle?' Brendan says, looking a little disappointed.

'Yes,' says Glynis, 'and an indoor swimming pool, a sauna and a Jacuzzi,' she adds, so he can be disappointed all in one go instead of in dribs and drabs as the weekend progresses.

My legs are shaky but they carry me to the kitchen door. I stop in front of Red. 'I . . . ' I begin and I can't say anything else, with the lump in my throat and my voice, hoarse after all the crying.

'I know,' he says, and he smiles at me and touches my arm before moving into the heart of the kitchen, towards the plate of rasher butties.

I walk as far as I can before breaking into a run. I reef the hot-press door open and there he is. With his blankie over his head like a bandana. Asleep. I place my hand against the warm fur of his head and, apart from a furious twitching of both ears, he lets me. Ellen's foot pushes against my side and I lie my other hand against the tiny bulge and I close my eyes and breathe in and out, like it's the first time.

★   ★   ★

After Blue's return, the world feels different. The air smells sweeter, the sun is warmer, the taste of

400

Glynis's spinach quiche like the first bite of a Cadbury's Creme Egg after a long and barren Lent. Even the smell of Brendan's half-cow roasting in the oven is benign. We are hopelessly behind schedule and, instead of fretting about it, I am in the walled garden, playing Frisbee with Red and Al Pacino and Blue. Although Blue is not playing as such. He is lying in a puddle of sunlight, licking the chocolate mousse that Glynis made him off his whiskers and snoozing.

Brendan and Filly have gone for a 'walk', although so far all they've managed to do is repair to their bedroom to change into suitable walking garb. That's what Brendan calls clothes. Garb. Apart from when they're dirty. Then he calls them laundry.

Afterwards, we lie in the long grasses at the edge of the herb garden. The air is heavy with the sweet scent of lavender and honeysuckle and jasmine. The lazy drone of honey bees is like the hum of a conversation between us. Red lies on his belly and makes a daisy chain as long as himself. His movements are languid. They flow like water. He is relaxing to look at. I look at him, in a way that seems like I'm not looking at him. Al Pacino sits as close as he can to him without actually getting on top of him. His tongue lolls, fleshy and pink, gently swinging to and fro like a pendulum.

'It's five o'clock,' says Red, even though he's not wearing a watch. 'Aren't we supposed to be discussing the readings?' he asks with a sly smile.

'How did you . . . ? Did you read my schedule?'

401

'Of course I did. It was open on the bed.'

'My bed.'

'In our room.'

I laugh. In the world that is slightly different since Blue's return, there is nothing else to do.

'Nobody seems all that bothered about discussing the wedding,' I say. 'Other than me, that is.'

'What's there to discuss?' Red says, propping himself up on an elbow and looking at me. 'You go to the church, say, 'I do,' and have a bit of a shindig afterwards.' He leans over and drapes the daisy chain round my neck. His fingers brush against my ear, sending a dart of electricity shooting around my body. 'Are you cold?' Red asks. Goosebumps — red and raised — sprout along my arms and I sit up and shovel them down the sleeves of my cardigan.

'A little,' I lie.

'Here.' He pulls his jumper over his head, his white T-shirt riding up to reveal the line of dark brown hair from his belly-button, pointing like an arrow into the narrow waist of his jeans. I pull my eyes away. It's like I'm back in the nightclub again. I think about quantum physics. I don't know very much about quantum physics but I think about it anyway.

'You know,' he says, as if he can't feel the static between us, 'if Ellen is mine, she'll probably have green eyes, like us,' he says, peering into my face, his eyes fixed on mine.

When I don't respond, Red looks away. 'I know that you are hoping she's John's,' he says slowly.

'How do you know what I hope?' I ask.

'Well, I know you don't approve of me.'

'You can't be all bad,' I say. 'You found Blue.'

'It's OK. I wouldn't approve of me either, if I were you.'

'Why?'

'You think I'm unreliable. Unfaithful to Sofia.'

'Well . . . ' I say. 'You were.'

'I suppose so,' he says after a while, 'but I want you to know . . . I want you to believe that I don't behave like that as a general rule.'

The thing is, I *want* to believe that. I mean, *I* don't behave like that as a general rule. And yet there were two of us that night. I shut my eyes against the image that screeches into my head, like a car crash.

'Look, it doesn't matter any more anyway,' I say. 'What happened happened and now we just have to deal with it.'

The conversation is leading us down a path that is getting narrower and narrower, towards a field with a swamp in it.

'Where is Sofia anyway?' I ask, not looking at him, making a song and dance about threading the yellow ribbon round Blue's collar.

'She and Hailey have gone into town to buy hats,' says Red.

Calling it a town is a bit like calling a huckster's shop a supermarket. As far as I remember, there's a pub in the village — Cassidy's I think — with a lean-to at the side that's an off-licence and a hardware shop. It also sells bread and teabags, Brussels sprouts and about twenty bottles of Anaïs Anaïs perfume.

Although I don't think there's much call for Anaïs Anaïs perfume in the locality because the bottles look like they've been there for many, many years.

As far as I know, there's no hat shop in the town.

Red settles back against the long grass, lying on his back now, tickling the lobe of Al Pacino's ear with the tip of a blade of grass.

If he were my fiancé, I wouldn't be somewhere with Hailey. I'd be here, lying in the long grass beside him, the pair of us baking in the sun like tomato and fennel bread.

These thoughts are like the worst kind of visitors, the ones that arrive unannounced and unexpected with a bag hanging on the end of each hand and enough clothes to see them through the guts of a week. I shake my head to make them scatter.

'You always look like you're thinking about something very serious, Scarlett O'Hara,' he says, with the smile that is never far away from the corners of his mouth.

'I was,' I say. 'I mean, I am.' There is an image in my head that has no bearing on weddings or hats or Brussels sprouts. It is an image of a kiss. Gentle. Salty and warm. With a hint of blackberries, subtle and sweet.

'What were you thinking about?'

'I was thinking about quantum physics, as a matter of fact,' I say with a sort of a strangled voice, as if there is a hand around my throat.

He laughs and I know he doesn't believe me. John would believe me. Although the flipside would be that John would want to know what aspect of quantum physics I am thinking about and I would flounder, although I could maybe mumble something about $E=MC^2$.

I stand up and brush myself down, even though there is not one single blade of grass on me.

'Don't go yet,' he says.

'Well . . . I should really . . . '

'There's loads of time. Stay.'

And even though I tell myself not to, I stay, as if it's as simple as that.

We lie on the grass for a long time, without speaking. The sky overhead is a silk sheet of baby blue with clouds like bubbles dawdling past as if time is nothing but a dirty rumour.

As if there is nothing but this day, this moment, here in the quiet warmth of the garden, with blades of grass tickling the bare skin of my legs and the weight of Blue's paw in my hand, which he has placed there as if by accident. We play the name-the-cloud-shape game. I've heard of this game but I've never played it before. John would not like it. I'm not good at it.

'It's a snowball,' I say.

Red is more imaginative. 'That one's a porcupine on a trampoline, look.'

'Oh, yeah,' I say, after squinting at it for a while. 'I can see the quills quivering every time he bounces.'

I try to get a little more adventurous. 'That's the grotto outside Valentino's house.'

'Oh, yeah, I see what you mean. But I don't think it's as big as the one in Valentino's garden.'

I have to agree. Although any grotto would be hard pressed to be as big as the one in Valentino's garden.

'A fire-breathing dragon.'

'A wishing well.'

'The number six.'

'No, that's a cat chasing his tail.'

'Blue.'

'Yeah, Blue.'

'Thanks for finding him, by the way.' I don't look at Red when I say that, remembering the things I told him, the way I lost control.

'Forget about it,' he says. 'I'd be the same if it was Al Pacino. They're family.' He doesn't mention the things I told him, the way I lost control. Instead, he concentrates on the clouds. 'That one looks like a country but I can't think which one.'

'Bulgaria,' I say, glancing at it.

'You're clever, aren't you, Scarlett?'

'I just have a good head for details is all,' I say. Usually, I like it when people compliment my brain. But not today. Today, I'd prefer him to say, 'You're beautiful, aren't you, Scarlett?'

No.

I'd prefer him to say, 'Can I kiss you, Scarlett?'

If he said that, I wouldn't say no, like I'm supposed to.

I'd say something completely different.

Here's what I would say: 'Yes. You. Can.'

46

We eat dinner outside. Around long trestle tables that Glynis covers with crisp, white linen tablecloths. She sets the table with the wedding delf, despite my paper-plate recommendation. She cooks us some of the pink wedding food: fillets of tuna, rosè risotto and a strawberry cheesecake. Brendan carves the beef at the table with what looks like a machete, making a great show of sharpening the knife against a length of flint, which he produces from his bag of knives. Everyone accepts a piece because Brendan takes it as a personal affront if they don't. Even me, although I hide the slice underneath some leafy rocket and move it to the edge of my plate so the blood that drains from it doesn't touch any of the food I'm actually going to eat.

The mood is a little holiday campish. Hailey and Sofia managed to buy hats this afternoon. One for everyone. They found them in a drawer in Cassidy's bar underneath the shelf with the fading bottles of Anaïs Anaïs. Although they are caps rather than hats. Peaked ones. With a picture of Cassidy's printed on the front in garish orange. They insist we put them on and everyone does — even me.

I notice things about Red Butler. He eats nearly as much meat as Brendan. Unlike Brendan, he eats vegetables too. He mops up the juices on his plate with slices of bread, which he folds and crams, whole, into his mouth. He spills things. He drops his fork and reaches down, picks it up and continues eating with it as if it's not ridden with bacteria. He speaks with his arms and his hands and his whole face. Not just with his mouth, like normal people.

He feeds Al Pacino the choicest cuts of beef from his plate. And even Brendan — who is neither a cat nor a dog person — can't bring himself to reprimand Red for what he would, under normal circumstances, call 'wanton waste'.

Sofia puts Hailey on her right-hand side and Red on her left. I try to picture Red and Sofia as a couple. Doing coupley things. Like buying pillowcases. Or arguing over whose turn it is to empty the dishwasher. Or even holding hands. But it is difficult.

Sofia spears a piece of fish with her fork and feeds it to Hailey, who smiles at her as she chews the tuna carefully, with her mouth closed. The gesture is so intimate I look away from it, feeling like I have trespassed on a private moment. I decide that it's easier to see Sofia and *Hailey* as a couple than Sofia and Red. But that's not logical. Not when Sofia and Red are getting married in — I do the sums in my head — six weeks and two days. I shake my head until the thought dislodges itself.

I mean, Sofia and Red certainly seem to *like* each other. But more as I imagine a brother and sister might like each other. Sofia gives him a dead arm when he teases her about the pink cassock she wants Padre Marco Marzoni

— Valentino's brother — to wear at the wedding ceremony. He takes an eyelash out of her eye when no one else can, using a corner of a tissue, which he rolls into a narrow line between his fingers. He sets her chin in the palm of his hand when he does it. She tells him to take his elbows off the table. He ignores her. She picks the strawberries out of his cheesecake and eats them, in a rather absentminded kind of way, and he lets her. He roots through her handbag and removes a lipstick from it, which he then smears across Brendan's mouth, when we decide that Brendan would make a lovely girl, on account of his long, curly eyelashes and his fantastically high cheekbones.

People like Red Butler. This is the conclusion I reach. They can't help themselves. He infects them. Like chickenpox. Except instead of getting sick and spotty, they come over all smiley and happy and hopeful. Although that could be the wine, I concede, as a third bottle is emptied and pitched upside down in the ice bucket.

Hailey sings a song (a George Michael song), surprising everyone with the high, sweet timbre of her voice. And the fact that she sings in front of us, like we're not here at all. Red joins in the chorus. He is as tone deaf as a wall but sings anyway, loudly and with his eyes closed, as if he thinks he's Luke Kelly. Or George Michael.

Brendan and Filly tell us they're going to the lake to 'fish', although maybe they really are going to fish. Brendan carries a long, serious-looking fishing rod in one hand and in the other is a jar of worms, seething and slipping around each other against the glass. Brendan doesn't eat fish, which he classifies as a 'vegetarian' food, but he likes to catch them. And gut them. He is a hunter-gatherer and this is one of the millions of things that Filly loves about him.

The moon rises, full and wide, throwing her silvery light against the forest of fir trees, like cobwebs. The breeze is soft and warm and strokes my skin like fingers. There's a feeling inside me spreading like jam across a scone. I can't put my finger on it. Then, when I look at my watch and remember that I'm supposed to be discussing wedding music with Red and Sofia, instead of here, with Ellen and the moon and the lake and the thousands of stars that push their bright lights through the black velvet of the night sky, I realise what it is. It is peace.

47

The second thing I do on my return from the castle is ring a relationship counsellor. I do this because of the first thing I do, which is to give myself a stern talking-to. Remind myself of my responsibilities. Put everyone back in their rightful place. Red with Sofia, for instance. Not anyplace else, like the walled garden of a castle, for example, playing silly games with clouds. Or asleep on the other side of the room we shared in the castle, his feet dangling off the end of the bed, the tangled mesh of his hair covering every inch of the pillow. Or kneeling on the driveway outside the castle with his compassion and his kindness.

So I give myself a stern talking-to. Remind myself of my responsibilities. And put Red Butler and Sofia Marzoni in their rightful place in my head.

Then I move on to me and Ellen. Our rightful place. I think it should be with John Smith. It makes sense. John is making a sincere effort. He has come home. He is facing up to his responsibilities, which is one of the things I loved about him. The least I can do now is to try and follow suit.

I still have the number of the counsellor I rang for Seamus and Sheila Doolally. Two days before their wedding. Seamus had been discovered standing at the kitchen sink with his pants round his ankles and the local librarian round his waist.

He thought Sheila was staying at her mother's that night.

She thought that he had allowed his membership of the local library to lapse, following a string of fines after late returns.

I find the number. The counsellor must be good because he managed to persuade Sheila to go through with the wedding and, as far as I know, the pair remain married, although all their reading material is now ordered online.

Dr Katastraf speaks excellent English, albeit with a thick Romanian accent. 'I haf vindow,' he says when I introduce myself.

'That's good,' I say, picking up my pen. 'When?'

'February,' he says.

'But that's seven months away.'

'I know,' he says. 'I am best in business. I am couples counsellor to the stars.'

'The stars?'

'Yes. You know Jimmy from *Fair City?*'

'No, sorry, I . . . I don't watch *Fair City*.'

'Pity,' he says. 'Is mar-fell-us show. Much underrated.' When he rolls his 'r's, it sounds like he's gargling.

'Eh, right . . . '

'If you come to me in February, you could be married before the summer solstice.'

'No, that's not it,' I say. 'You see, he's already asked me to marry him.'

'Then vat is problem?'

'It's . . . complicated,' I say eventually.

'Is no complicated,' he counters. 'You luf

412

heem, he luf you, you get married. Othervise, no.' There is an ominous silence when he finishes speaking and, to fill it, I make the appointment. I figure that I have until February to find a more . . . another one.

John is somewhere in the UK this week, working on a merger. I think it might be an industrial estate in Croydon. It's his boss's way of punishing him for his sojourn in Brazil, however brief. I email him and ask him to ring me when he gets back. I say there's something I want to talk to him about. I don't tell him what but I put a smiley face at the end of the mail to show him that it's nothing sinister. I'll tell him about Dr Katastraf when he gets back. I know he will see this as progress and I suppose it is. It is the right thing to do. For Ellen.

★ ★ ★

Filly arrives in with her usual 'Goodmorningsorry-I'mlate', two non-alcoholic mojitos, a breakfast roll (for her) and a hash-brown toasted sandwich with brown sauce (for me).

'I have tidings,' I say, in my Cyril Sweeney voice.

Filly, who has only met Cyril once but says that once is enough, laughs. 'What?' she asks, fishing her breakfast out of the bag.

'I've known since last week but I didn't want to say anything. To anybody. Until I had a chance to think about it myself.' It's suddenly vital that Filly understands this.

'Have you told anyone else?' she asks. I shake

my head. 'That's fine, then,' she says, waving away my concern with a flick of her wrist. 'Go ahead.' She pushes the breakfast roll into her mouth as far as it will go before biting down on it.

'I got the job.' I shouldn't really have said that. Not at that moment. Not when her mouth is full of food. Because she manages to say something that might be 'Ohmigod!' before she begins choking on what we later realise is a piece of bacon rind and turning the colour of a Spanish orange. Luckily, I am no stranger to the Heimlich manoeuvre, having grown up with people who love to talk, with or without food in their mouths. It's tricky to do with Ellen clamped between Filly's back and my front. I wrap both my arms round Filly's slight form, just below her ribs, and squeeze her as tight as she'll go without breaking her or squashing Ellen and the rind flies out of her mouth just as Elliot appears in the doorway. The rind lands in the middle of his forehead and stays there, stuck fast. Filly and I collapse around the office with the laughing. Elliot examines himself all over, patting himself down, checking himself for the source of our hysterics. It's not until the rind peels itself from his forehead and does a backflip on to the top of one of his shoes that he clocks it.

'Letty got the job,' says Filly, to distract him.

'I knew she would,' Elliot says, tapping his shoe against the bin until the rind slides off. 'That must be why Gladys isn't in today.' He straightens and smiles at me.

'Where is she?' I ask.

'She's taken to bed, which is now devoid of a certain Simon Kavanagh, according to Lucille and Eloise.'

'He dumped her?' This was always going to happen but the timing seems particularly cruel, even for Simon.

'Straight after he got back from the Yankee-panky, by all accounts.' Elliot takes a KitKat from his pocket, unwraps it and offers a finger of it to Blue in exchange for a seat on the couch, which Blue accepts. Elliot sits on the couch. 'The Yanks got wind of Simon's various . . . extramarital titillations and they don't like it.'

'How did they find out?' asks Filly, looking around the room as if there might be cameras as small as eyes embedded in the walls, and probably thinking about that time that Brendan picked her up from work, late one Monday evening, and they had that little 'set-to' in the boardroom.

'Wasn't Eloise over in the New York office for that finance conference a couple of weeks ago?' I ask.

'No, that was Lucille, I think,' says Elliot. 'But still . . . I see what you mean.'

'Anyway,' I say, 'I turned the job down.'

At first, neither of them says anything because they think they have misheard me.

'What did you say, Scarlett?' Filly's broad smile falters, then narrows before it falls off the edges of her face completely, like a man off a cliff.

'I told him I didn't want the job.' Elliot's

mouth hangs, and Filly's face is vacant without her smile.

'But . . . but . . . but . . . ' Filly begins without knowing quite where to start. 'What about our plans?'

'I know, Filly,' I say, 'and I'm sorry but my plans have changed. If I take this job, I'll only really see Ellen at the weekends and that's not even guaranteed.'

'Yes, but . . . '

'I didn't think I would feel this way.'

'Yes, but . . . '

'I mean, I've read about maternal instinct. It's in all the books. I just thought I didn't have it. I thought it was one of those things. Like being colour-blind. Something you're born with. Or without.'

Filly slumps in a chair, beaten.

'But it turns out that I do have it after all.'

Filly nods and tries to smile, like she's delighted about my recent acquisition of maternal instinct.

'But I also have a Plan B,' I say.

'What's Plan B?' Filly asks without much hope or enthusiasm. 'Set up a créche?'

'Christ, no. It's bad enough having maternal instinct.' I have a vision of me in a room with twenty babies, all with wet, red faces from weeping and wailing. All looking to me for succour. 'I'm thinking about setting up on my own. After Ellen is born. Maybe when she's six months. I've seen a house in Clontarf we can rent. With a big room in the attic that I could use as an office.'

'We?' Elliot hops in there.

'Me and Ellen,' I say. 'It's not far from John's flat so he could come and see her whenever he liked. Phyllis says she'll come and stay for a while after I go back to work, to mind Ellen.'

'So you're not going to marry John Smith?' Filly sounds relieved.

'I've made an appointment for us,' I tell them. 'With a couples counsellor.'

The pair take a moment to allow this to sink in. Then Elliot turns to Filly and shrugs. 'Well, if it worked for the Doolallys . . . ' he says, not finishing the sentence.

Filly nods slowly. 'So you might still marry John Smith?' she says.

'Well . . . ' I begin. 'I don't . . . It's probably a good idea. It's the right thing to do. With Ellen and everything. It's stability for her. Children like that.'

Elliot sighs. 'You're so sensible,' he says, with a melancholic air.

I pat his arm. 'You will be too,' I assure him. 'One day.'

He looks at me. 'Do you really think so?'

'Not really,' I admit. 'But anything is possible.'

'And what about Red Butler?' Filly asks, looking at me sideways.

I move some papers about my desk. 'He can see Ellen too. If . . . if that's the way things go and he wants to. Valentino bought Sofia a house in Drumcondra for her wedding. It's not far from there to Clontarf.'

'It sounds like you've got it all worked out,' says Filly, her shoulders still slumped like collapsed sand dunes.

'I'm going to need help. An assistant. A wedding planner. Someone to do the actual work while I drum up the business.'

Filly allows her head to lift a little so she can see my face. I'm smiling at her.

'Are you offering me a job?'

'Of course I am, you great Australian dingbat. What did you think I was going to do?'

'For God's sake, Scarlett, don't offer me a job,' says Elliot. 'We all know what a shirker I am.' This is true but still, I'm glad Elliot said it out loud. I'm glad he's OK with this.

'You're going to hug me now, aren't you?' I say, but instead of saying, 'Gerroffme,' as I normally would, I find myself reaching him first and I hug the living daylights out of him, which is not as easy as it sounds any more because of Ellen.

'Ooh,' he says, when I put him back down, 'what clients are you going to poach?' Elliot, who has a tendency to get a little camp around the edges when he's excited, rubs his hands together with a smile like a Cheshire cat across his face.

'Elliot, of course I am not going to poach any clients,' I say, appalled at the notion. 'But I can't help it if Chiara Marzoni has asked if I will organise her wedding next summer, now, can I?'

'Is that Sofia's cousin?'

'Second cousin once removed on her father's side,' I say. 'And she's got six sisters, all of marrying age, all in relationships of at least six months.'

'Ooh, you're going to poach the Marzonis?

What fun,' says Elliot, doing a little jig with his feet. He stops when Blue — who dislikes dancing and jigs in particular — drags his head two inches off the couch.

'That'll certainly get the cat fur flying,' says Filly, but her smile is back.

'I don't want any cat fur to fly,' I say. 'I've told Simon my intentions. I want everything to be above board. It's essential to maintain a good working relationship with Extraordinary Events International.'

'How did Simon take it?' Filly and Elliot ask at the same time.

'He's livid,' I have to admit. 'But you know Simon. He'll get over it. In time.'

They look at me with equal doses of bewilderment and pity. It's true that the pregnancy — Ellen — seems to have replaced my strict measure of realism with untold dollops of optimism.

'OK, a fair amount of time,' I concede, and their worried faces soften a little with this concession.

'Well, it's about time,' Elliot says at last. 'I don't know why you didn't set up on your own a long time ago.'

'I was afraid to,' I admit. 'Afraid to risk it.'

'And now?' Filly asks.

'Now?' I say, thinking about it. 'Now, I have a terrible hankering for green olives,' I suddenly realise.

'But you don't like olives.'

'I know. That's why it's a *terrible* hankering.'

'I know the perfect place for lunch,' shouts

Elliot, who is a walking encyclopaedia of eateries. 'The Olive Branch. It only opened last week so I haven't had much feedback on it yet. But . . . ' he pauses, making sure he has both of our undivided attention ' . . . they serve olives with everything. They even have olive-flavoured ice cream.'

My mouth waters when I hear this and I can already taste it on my tongue, even though I can't imagine what olive-flavoured ice cream might taste like.

'Don't worry, Filly, they have chocolate ice cream as well,' Elliot says, patting Filly's arm in an effort to remove the look of distaste from her face. 'Come on, it's my treat.'

'No, it's my treat,' I say. 'I'm the one with the hankering and the news.'

Elliot clatters out of the office to get his wallet anyway..

Filly waits until he is out of earshot. 'Are you sure about the counselling with John? And Red Butler? I thought . . . at the castle . . . I don't know . . . you and Red . . . after he found Blue . . . '

'I was a bit emotional,' I concede, reddening at the memory. 'But I'm fine now so it's time to focus on the job in hand, which is to get Sofia Marzoni and Red Butler down the aisle without any hiccups, OK?'

'Piece of cake,' says Filly in her usual positive way, but she is looking at me a little too closely for my liking and I shift uneasily and avoid her eyes. I have filed Red in a box in my head where I keep any *inappropriate* thoughts. This box rattles when you shake it. In fact, apart from Red, there's only one other inappropriate thought, which I had when I was fourteen and concerned a certain maths teacher with dimples and hair that was just long enough to be considered 'cool' but not so long as to warrant any repercussions from Sister Eithne (the head nun). I have sealed this box with masking tape and scored it with staples. Even so, I suspect that Filly knows all about it, the way she's looking at me now.

'So,' I say in a jaunty voice. I pick up a piece of paper from my desk and rustle it in my hands.

'They're a weird couple, though, aren't they?' Filly says, ignoring my jaunty 'So', which she knows is supposed to indicate a change of subject.

'We've married weirder,' I remind her, and she nods her head slowly.

'He's lovely, though, isn't he?' she says, almost to herself. She smiles and I know she is picturing his face in her mind.

An image rises, like the sun reaching past the horizon on a clear day. Red, in the castle kitchen, at two o'clock in the morning.

'Can't you sleep again?' he asks. I am sitting on a chair, reading the ISEQ index in an attempt to bore myself to sleep.

'No,' I say. 'I'm sorry. I didn't mean to wake you.'

'It wasn't you,' he says, grinning. 'It was Blue. He woke up howling after you left.'

'Sorry. He's afraid of the dark. I should have taken him with me.'

'I'm going to make you a Red Butler special,' he says, opening several cupboard doors at the same time. 'It's guaranteed to induce sleep in even the most hardened insomniac.'

'I've tried everything,' I warn him.

'Trust me,' he says, spilling milk into a cup and putting it into the microwave. He disappears through the kitchen door and I can hear him in Glynis's herb garden, and then the ripping sound of plants being pulled, possibly by their roots, out of the warm ground. Now he's back in the kitchen, chopping and rinsing and peeling and grating. Now he's bashing everything to a pulp in a mortar and pestle. He does this as if I'm not here at all, watching him intently. He moves around the kitchen as if he's lived here his whole life.

'Try it,' he says, eventually setting the cup of milk and . . . stuff . . . in front of me. I drink it. He watches me with his arms crossed across his chest. 'Try to get it all down you,' he says, and I'm six again with Phyllis coaxing me to take my cough medicine.

I do as I'm told and it's not too bad. There's a sweetness to it. Like honey. I drain the cup. He nods at me. A 'well-done' kind of nod. He takes my hand in his and leads me up the stairs. And tucks me into bed, so tightly I can barely move. And I feel my eyes dropping down, in spite of how close he is. And before I remember the state we have left the kitchen in — dirty cup on table, stalks and leaves and roots and muck on the cutting board on the counter, carton of milk, empty, on its side in the sink — I am lifted by warm hands down into a place that is dark and comforting and quiet. It could be the place where normal people sleep. I have imagined it many times. I move against it and it gathers its arms around me and I sleep like this until the night has passed. When I wake up, I smile when I see that the day has broken.

Now, I look at Filly and nod. 'Yes,' I say. 'He *is* lovely. Sofia is a lucky woman.' I stand up and shake the image off me like rainwater and force it back inside the box and sit on top of it so it can't get out again.

48

John's plane lands at exactly 5.55 p.m. on Friday, which is when it is scheduled to land. Thirteen minutes later, he marches through the sliding doors into the arrivals hall, pulling a bag on wheels behind him. This is the bag I call his airhostess bag. I can tell, just by looking at it, that it does not exceed the weight restriction. It never will.

John moves towards the exit, looking straight ahead. He walks straight past me, with the walk of a man who does not expect anyone to be waiting for him. And who can blame him? This is the first time I have ever come to the airport to meet him. This should not be the case but it is. I struggle to catch up with him.

'John.'

He slows, looking around him.

'John Smith.'

He stops and looks behind him and his eyes settle on me. 'Scarlett? What on earth are you doing here? Is everything all right?' He looks tired, his skin stretched taut over the fine bones of his face. The burns and bites are long gone. With his starched shirt and sober suit, he looks like he always used to.

I smile at him. 'Everything's fine, John,' I say. 'I thought I'd surprise you, that's all.'

In fairness, he *does* look surprised. Shocked, even. It makes me feel sad. It makes me wonder when we decided we would never pick each other up at the airport. What kind of couple does that? I don't remember ever having a conversation about it. We just fell into the habit, I suppose.

'Come on,' I tell him.

'Where to?' John always needs to know where he is going before he gets there.

'I'm going to take you out for dinner,' I tell him, even though I've already eaten dinner. I'm like a farmer now. I eat it in the middle of the day.

'Oh,' he says, and smiles. 'That would be lovely but . . . ' The smile clouds over. 'The thing is,' he says. 'You see, I've already eaten.' He pauses. 'On the plane, I mean.'

'You ate aeroplane food?'

He nods, mortified. 'I was distracted. Thinking about other things. And I just nodded when the airhostess asked me about the food. And she seemed so pleased and surprised when I nodded I didn't have the heart to tell her I didn't want anything.'

'What other things were you thinking about?' I ask, as if we are not in the middle of the arrivals hall in Dublin Airport on the busiest night of the week. As if there are no crowds roaring past us. As if there's just the two of us. Nobody else.

John frowns in concentration. 'Well, it was about us, of course.'

'Of course?'

'Of course,' he repeats, looking at me, confused now. 'What else would I be thinking

425

about? And Ellen, of course.' He adds, his face softening like butter in the sun.

'I've been thinking about things too,' I tell him.

'About Ellen?'

'And us. Ellen and us,' I tell him.

He looks at me carefully before he allows himself to smile. 'I'm glad,' he says.

I take a breath. 'I think it would be best for Ellen if we present ourselves as a . . . a unit.'

'Like a family unit?' John is anxious to be clear.

I nod my head.

'I agree,' he says.

I tell him about Dr Katastraf. Not about him being the couples counsellor to the stars but about him having a window, albeit not until next February. And about the Doolallys. The miracle of the Doolallys.

John lets go of the handle of his suitcase and reaches for me. His stubble scratches against my face. With Ellen between us, we don't fit like we used to. We pull away at the same time.

'So,' says John. Then there is the pregnant pause. Then the question. 'Why don't I make us something to eat?' he says. 'At the flat, I mean?'

I know exactly what he means. But I'm not ready to go back to the flat. Not yet. I'm afraid it will be exactly as I left it. Nothing changed, despite everything.

John rushes into the gap of my hesitation. 'No, you're right, we should go out. We should celebrate. I think I could manage a bowl of soup.

426

Or a green salad perhaps.'

He grips the handle of his suitcase and begins walking as if he had never stopped, me beside him now, our legs moving in perfect tandem, like first place in a three-legged race.

49

Back at Tara, Maureen has taken to the bed. It's the play, *Romeo and Juliet: The Musical*. It's been postponed, due in no small part to the remarkable recovery of one Olwyn Burke, who, on hearing that Maureen O'Hara was doing a not-bad-considering job of playing Juliet's nurse, got up, got dressed, demanded 1) her doctor, 2) a cup of Earl Grey tea, 3) a sachet of Sweet'N Low and 4) two digestive biscuits buttered and stuck together like a sandwich. Her recuperation was so rapid that one of the doctors — a junior one — is now using it as a basis for his thesis on which a bulk of the merit for his master's will be based.

Anyway, with Mrs Burke's rise from the not-quite-dead, Cyril has agreed to postpone the play to extend Olwyn's rehearsal time.

Maureen is *devastated*. She has driven Phyllis demented with her demands, like toast cut into triangles with the crusts chopped off and Cadbury's Creme Eggs with the eggy stuff scooped out of the middle. She doesn't like the eggy stuff. And in spite of the fact that it is the summertime and Cadbury's Creme Eggs are scarce on the ground at this time of year, Phyllis sources two and duly removes the filling from the chocolate casing, puts them in two eggcups and delivers them to Maureen's boudoir, as she likes us to call it.

I haven't told her yet that the new date for the play is the day of Sofia's wedding. I'm waiting for the right moment to tell her. That moment has not yet arisen.

The odd thing is, Maureen's angst is not having its usual effect on me. I mean, I'm doing everything that I normally would — pressing lavender into the pages of her self-help books, making her milky Baileys coffees at bedtime, rubbing make-up into the tired skin of her face before she allows Red or Declan to visit her — but, since my return from the castle, I feel more reconciled with the way things are. I stop fighting it. I relax into it. I think I might even be enjoying it.

Maureen's drama is like a snippet of life that slides past the lovely cocoon I have built for Ellen and me. Maureen seems to sense this and returns to us sooner than she normally would, still tear-stained but stoic. She declares her intention to knit a cardigan for Ellen. A pink one.

'If Olwyn bloody Burke can knit baby cardigans, then so bloody well can I,' she roars downstairs from her sickbed.

Olwyn Burke has three grandchildren but they're not allowed to call her granny. They have to call her Olwyn, which is a difficult word to pronounce when you're four, two and a half and six months respectively.

So far, Maureen has knitted two sleeves, one of which is longer than the other, but it's keeping her occupied so nobody comments on this irregularity.

'Are you going to get Ellen to call me granny?' she asks me.

'Only if you want her to,' I assure her.

'I'll . . . I'll . . . I'll be the poor mite's only granny,' she suddenly realises, which allows her to squeeze another few tears out of her eyes, which have nearly closed with all the weeping and wailing.

I think about it. It's true that Maureen will be Ellen's only granny, no matter who the father is. The poor mite, is right.

But even this thought is not enough to unsettle me. I am like a feather, floating on a light breeze while life rushes past. It's happening slowly. It's Ellen. I am consumed by her. Every thought I have leads to her. She's in the faint brown line that arrives on week twenty-six and runs down the centre of my bump. I'm delighted with it. It's so textbook. So me. She's in the ever-so-slight swelling of my ankles and wrists that the doctor proclaims 'normal', like he does with every other symptom I have. She's in the bottles of Gaviscon that I lower like water. She's in the way people notice my belly and smile at me now, for no particular reason other than Ellen. Ellen, whose eyes are as blue as the sky in this summer of sunshine, where the days roll into each other until I can't remember what day it is.

Red Butler is another snippet of life that rolls past. He has taken to dropping into the office with tiny gifts for Ellen. A babygro — pink — with teddy bears and bunny rabbits and lambs. A pair of bootees — white with pink dogs — impossibly small, tied at the top with a ribbon. A hat — pink with orange love hearts — that he can barely fit his fist inside.

'Look at this,' he says, taking some kind of a contraption out of a Mothercare bag. 'It's a sling.' He ties it round himself. 'You put the baby in here,' he says, pointing at the pouch on the front. 'I'll put this teddy bear in to demonstrate.' He takes a stuffed bear — yellow with pink-tipped ears and paws — out of the Mothercare bag and places it gently into the pouch, where it disappears through a leg hole. 'Oh,' he says, 'that's not supposed to happen.'

I speed-read the instructions. 'Here,' I say, 'this bit is supposed to go here and then this strap wraps round your waist, like this, and then that ties there and this clicks in here and . . . there, it's done.'

'How did you know that?' he asks, worried.

'I . . . eh . . . I just read the instructions.'

Red looks shamefaced. 'I never thought of doing that,' he says. 'Jesus, I already let her drop and she's not even born yet.' He picks the bear up off the ground and holds it aganist his chest, gently patting its back. 'At least I can do the winding thing. Look, I've been practising.'

I haven't even thought about how I'm going to hold her. 'Give me a go,' I say, and he passes the bear to me and I slot it into the crook of my left elbow and we peer at the bear and I forget to feel foolish because I'm doing it properly.

'Are you *practising* holding a baby?' John's head appears round the office door as it has been doing since I surprised him at the airport. I jump and drop the bear, which is the second time it's

431

been dropped in under five minutes, which is fine when you're a teddy bear but not so good if you're a real, live baby who is depending on you for everything.

'Hello, John,' says Red, turning round and smiling.

'I didn't realise you had company.' John's tone is sharp but even he has to smile when Red smiles at him. Like he can't help it.

'Come in,' I say. 'Red was just . . . '

'Leaving,' Red finishes the sentence for me. 'Bye, Scarlett. See you soon.' Then he lowers his head and speaks to my belly. 'Bye, baby Ellen. See you soon.'

John closes the door after him. 'I just came to bring you these,' he says, dropping a Mothercare bag on my desk.

'What is it?' I ask.

'It's a breast pump and breast pads and some cream that you rub on your nipples to stop them from cracking and bleeding.'

'Oh,' I say. 'Eh, thanks.'

*   *   *

I sit at the table and help Phyllis to shell peas.

'How's the Marzoni wedding coming along?' she asks me.

I press my fingers against a pod and four peas shoot into my mouth. 'Fine, I think,' I say, concentrating on the crunchy sweetness.

'You think?'

I nod.

There's a week to go. But no honeymoon

432

booked, pink or otherwise. Sofia says she's 'up to her tits' in work. Red is busy with Bryan and Cora, editing *The Jou ney*, which Bryan says is going to win prizes. They vaguely mention a week away after Christmas.

'Maybe Naples,' Sofia says when I ask her about it.

'Maybe Galway,' Red says, in a way that suggests they haven't discussed it. I can't work it out. In fact, I don't even try. It is just another snippet of life that flashes past.

'Scarlett, you're going to have all those peas eaten before I get a chance to cook them.' Phyllis interrupts my slow train of thought.

'Sorry.'

'How's Ellen?' she asks. 'The pet.'

'She's a bit . . . squirmy today,' I say. 'Like she can't get comfortable.'

'Why don't you go and sit on a deckchair in the garden? It's a lovely day.'

'And do what?'

'Nothing. Just sit there.'

'Nothing? Really?'

'Yeah. Try it. You never know, you might like it.'

'OK,' I say, getting up, slowly now, and standing with my legs slightly apart and my hand in the small of my back, like a bona fide pregnant woman. 'Phyllis,' I say, turning to her as I reach the back door.

'Hmm?' she says, unable to speak with the amount of peas she's got in her mouth.

'Do you think I'll be a good mother?'

Phyllis is not one of those people who tell you

things that you want to hear. I hold my breath and wait for her to answer. She is thinking about it, her head cocked to one side, chewing and chewing until the peas are gone. When she opens her mouth to speak, there is a greenish tinge about her tongue.

'You know, Scarlett,' she says, 'being a good mother is not something you are or you're not. It's something you work at. Every day. Not that I'd know really.' I've never thought about Phyllis being childless before. 'Do you think . . . ?' she tapers away, shaking her head.

'Go on,' I say. 'What were you going to say?'

'It doesn't matter.' Phyllis snaps a pod open and pops four peas into her mouth while I wait for her. 'I was just wondering if . . . ?'

'Yes?' I say, sitting down beside her again.

'Well, I was thinking . . . maybe Ellen could call me Granny Phil. I mean . . . if you don't mind . . . '

'I'd love that,' I say, taking one of Phyllis's pudgy pea-stained hands in mine and squeezing it quickly before letting it go. 'Maureen will be her only granny and I don't think she's all that keen on the whole *granny* title. It's nice to have someone you can call granny.'

'You never did,' Phyllis reminds me, although there is no need.

'I know. But I'd say it would be nice all the same.'

Phyllis nods and busies herself with her peas but I see two pink circles blooming on her cheeks, which is the thing that happens when she's pleased. 'Go on with you now, girl,' she says, shooing me with both hands. 'See how you get on in the garden doing nothing.'

I move towards the door.

'Scarlett?' I turn round. Phyllis has her back to me and is making a great show of clearing the table of empty pea pods. 'I think you'll be a great mother,' she says. 'I think Ellen is lucky to have you.' When she turns round, her eyes are suspiciously bright and I see the muscles in her face working furiously.

I've only ever seen Phyllis cry once and that was when Barry McGuigan won the World Featherweight title in 1985 against Eusebio Pedroza. She loves a bit of boxing. And Barry McGuigan. She calls him 'Bas'.

'Thanks, Phyllis,' I say, and I can feel my voice wobble, lurch and then fall over and my vision blurs around the edges as fat tears roll down my face.

'Come here to me, you silly slip of a girl.' Phyllis tries to regain her composure. But her hug is warm and soft and she smells of peas and hens and wild garlic and we stand like that for a long time, leaning against each other.

★   ★   ★

The deckchair creaks when I sit on it. The fabric is warm from the sun and I lie against it and rub my bump and sing Ellen a song that Phyllis used to sing for me, when I was a baby. It's called 'The Leg of a Duck' and it doesn't make much — any — sense and the lyrics are quite repetitive ('Oh, the leg of a duck and the leg of a duck and

435

the leg of a duck and the leg of a duck . . . ') but the tune is catchy and Phyllis calls it her 'Hallelujah Chorus' on account of its magical properties when it comes to soothing babies.

Even my voice sounds lazy. Lower, slower, than usual. I am in a stupor. I am waiting and, for the first time in my life, I am not trying to hurry the wait along. I am waiting and *liking it*.

50

It is Filly who drags me out of my lovely stupor. She senses my anchor skimming along the sea bed rather than holding fast against the strong current that is Sofia Marzoni.

She arrives into my office with her usual 'GoodmorningsorryI'mlate', two chocolate milks, a hot chicken and bacon sandwich with Vegemite (for her) and a Marmite sandwich (for me). The olive craving has been overridden by an oddly persistent yearning for Marmite.

'Right,' she says, after she inhales her sandwich — I check my watch — in less than three minutes, 'your time-out is over.'

'What time-out?' I am indignant.

She takes a different tack. 'OK,' she says. 'What have you done this week?'

I am surprised to find that I have to think about it. I look into the middle distance, which is where people often look when they are trying to remember something. No. Nothing there.

I open my BlackBerry. 'I had an appointment . . . '

'No. Something non-Ellen-related,' Filly says, wiping her hands on a sample of pink fabric from a flower-girl dress that Sofia left behind.

'I have been busy,' I say, blustering now. I move my mouse around its pad, trying to look officious.

437

'And you can turn off that bloody backgammon game,' says Filly, draining the last of her milk, which leaves a chocolately moustache across her top lip.

'How did you . . . ?' I can't help asking as I shut the game down. Just as I was about to beat the living daylights out of Dave from IT as well.

'Dave from IT told me that you and he have been playing all week and that he's just about to beat the living daylights out of you.'

'The *cheek* of him,' I say, outraged. And to think I had been going *easy* on him.

'Anyway,' says Filly, 'that's hardly the point, is it?'

I can't remember the point so I say nothing, hoping Filly will fill me in, which she does.

'The point is . . . ' She looks at me to make sure I am paying attention and have not relapsed into my lovely stupor, which I am sorry to say I have not. 'The point is, you haven't done a single thing since we got back from the castle.'

I open my mouth to contradict her. Then I close it again, not being able to come up with one solid argument in my favour. She is right.

'According to my book' — she's currently reading *What to Expect When You're Expecting a Goddaughter* — 'you're only supposed to get all dreamy and unfocused in the last few weeks of the pregnancy. You're way ahead of schedule, which I know is not unusual for you but, in this case, that's not a good thing.'

'OK, OK, fine, then. What do you want me to do?'

'I want *you* to tell *me* what to do. That's the

way it's supposed to be, isn't it? You are still my boss, aren't you?'

Technically, this is true but Filly has never mentioned it before. Things are serious if she is resorting to these tactics. I try to straighten in my seat but end up stretching instead. One of those lovely ones where you hear the bones in your back pull and click.

'Are you tired?' Filly asks in a voice that is still tetchy but edged with a modicum of concern now.

'Actually, no,' I say. 'Red's been making me this . . . this concoction every night and . . . '

'Every night?'

'Well, yes, I mean whenever he's at Tara, which is most evenings at the moment. He's working with Declan on a new project. 'Collaborating', Declan's calling it. You'd hardly recognise him these days.'

'Go on,' says Filly, looking at me now with eyes that are narrowed as if she's trying to work out how to spell 'manoeuvre'.

'Well, that's it really. I've been sleeping well. Well, not, well, exactly. But better. I've been sleeping better.'

'And what else does Red do? Apart from making you . . . concoctions.'

'Nothing. We just talk really.'

'What about?'

'Just . . . different things. Books and films and Ellen and . . . loads of different things really. It's been . . . nice.'

'Nice?'

'Yeah. Just . . . you know . . . nice.'

439

'I see,' says Filly as if she can see much more than she's letting on. She stands up and leaves the office, returning with the Marzoni-Butler wedding file, although it's more encyclopaedia than file and, with the weight of it, it could double as about five telephone books. Or a couple of cement blocks. 'We are going to go through everything and make sure we haven't forgotten anything, OK?'

A dose of reality crashes through the front door of my brain and says, 'Honey, I'm home,' at the top of its voice.

'You mean . . . you mean we haven't done that yet?'

'No. Not that I haven't reminded you about a billion times.'

'You're exaggerating,' I say.

'OK, I am a little,' she admits. 'I reminded you ten times.'

Ten times.

'You're still exaggerating.' She has to be.

'OK, I only mentioned it once yesterday afternoon but you just smiled at me and showed me a picture of the Moses basket you ordered.'

Oh, yes, I remember now. It's a darling one, with soft orange tulle arranged in folds around it, like a tepee.

'Letty? Letty? Are you listening to me?'

I climb out of the Moses basket and tune back into Filly, who looks like patience is a virtue she does not possess. I pull myself together, like the curtains I've picked for Ellen's bedroom.

'OK, then, let's do it,' I say in my most official wedding-planner voice.

An hour later, we are still going through the checklist and I am losing the will to live.

'Something old?' Filly asks.

'Valentino is giving her the diamond bracelet he bought for her mother two days before she ran away.'

'Oh,' says Filly, and I can see her trying to put her positive Australian spin on it. 'Diamond bracelets are . . . a good investment,' is the best she can manage.

'Something blue?'

'We-ell . . . ' Filly begins and I know I'm not going to like it ' . . . she wants Blue.'

'Yes, I know,' I say. 'Something blue. But what?'

'No, I mean, she wants Blue.' Filly nods towards my cat.

'She can't want my cat. Besides, he's not even Blue.'

'Well, he *is* a bluey-black, in fairness,' Filly says. 'She's bought a pink cat cage for him. And a pink dicky bow to go round his neck.'

Blue continues licking the tip of his left paw, as if impervious to the danger he's in.

'But . . . but . . . but . . . ' I say, trying to verbalise one of several reasons why Blue cannot go to Sofia Marzoni's wedding. 'He hates cat cages. He barely goes into his own.'

'We'll just give him a week's supply of After Eights. That'll keep him quiet during the ceremony.'

It's true that After Eights are Blue's current

441

confectionary of choice. There is one drawback.

'What about his . . . oh . . . flatulence?' Most people think that cats don't fart but this is not true. At least not for Blue. And especially after a feed of After Eights.

'It'll be grand,' Filly rushes in, sensing a weakening on my part and pressing home her advantage. 'No one will hear him over the string quartet and the organist and the banjo player.'

'Fine,' I say after a while. 'But you're putting the dicky bow on him, agreed?'

Filly blanches but nods her head and ticks something in her notebook.

Neither of us looks at Blue, who is now standing on his tippy-toes on the couch, staring at us, on full alert.

'OK,' I say, 'what's next? What about something borrowed?'

'Hailey's lending her a pen to sign the register with.'

'A pen?'

'It's a Wham! pen. The one George Michael used to sign Hailey's T-shirt back in 1984.'

There is silence while I digest this piece of information.

'OK,' I say, 'that's it, then. Everything else is brand new so we're all done.'

'Not quite,' says Filly, and something about how she says it makes my heart constrict in a way that threatens the circulation of blood around my body.

'It's Chris de Burgh,' she says.

'What about him? I thought he was a done deal.'

'He is,' Filly assures me with her brightest smile. 'It's just . . . '

'What?'

'He's refusing to change the words of the song.'

'To what? 'Lady in Pink'?'

'Yes.' Filly starts singing the song, or at least Sofia's version of the song. She has gone to great lengths to include words that rhyme with 'pink'. So there's a 'chink' of light and then there's being on the 'brink' of a new life and of course the 'clink' of the champagne flutes at the toast.

'OK,' I say eventually. 'Here's the compromise. We'll get Chris de Burgh to sing the original version of the song and then someone else can sing Sofia's version later. I'm sure Chris de Burgh would agree to that. He's been agreeable to everything else. He didn't even bat an eyelid when Sofia mentioned the pink tuxedo she wants him to wear.'

'The dote,' says Filly, and I nod. He *is* a dote. 'Hailey could sing Sofia's version,' suggests Filly. 'She has a gorgeous voice.'

'She does,' I agree. 'But would she do it?'

'I'd say she'd love to serenade Sofia,' says Filly, with the wicked version of her grin.

'OK, then, we'll run it past Chris and, if he's OK with it, we'll ask Hailey if she'll sing Sofia's version of the song later on in the night.'

'How much later?'

'Much, much later.'

'We-ll . . . ' Filly looks doubtful.

'It's either that or no Chris de Burgh. We'll never get a wedding singer that Sofia approves of at this short notice.'

'Baggsy you tell her,' Filly says quickly, before I have a chance to say it.

'No. I'm the boss. You said so yourself,' I say, delighted with myself. Filly looks mutinous, although there's not a lot she can say. 'And while you're at it, you can also tell her what the parish priest said when we asked him if we could paint the inside of the church pink.'

Filly gasps. 'That's low,' she says.

'I know,' I say, 'but you're the one who insisted I step out of my stupor.'

'Will I tell her what the priest *actually* said?' Filly asks.

'Christ, no. Just paraphrase. A lot.'

When Filly leaves the room, I lower myself back into my stupor and sit behind my desk and think about Ellen.

When I'm finished, I'll log back on to my backgammon game and beat the living lard out of Dave, I decide.

Maybe I'll go out at lunchtime and buy another jar of Marmite. Blue is partial to it smeared on a Ryvita.

51

When I allow myself to look back on Sofia Marzoni's wedding day, I do it through fingers that are clamped against my eyes. The images push and shove themselves in between the cracks, like lemmings headed for the perilous edge of a cliff. It is the worst day. And the best. When I take my hands away and look at it, I don't know how I didn't see it coming all along.

The day begins badly and goes downhill from there. I ignore it and keep moving from one thing to the next. Getting through it. Because, on a day like this, that's all you can do, isn't it?

The first pain comes at 5 a.m. I'm in bed but not asleep. It's a tight pain, like an accordion being squeezed between elbows. I see it travelling across my bump like a wave reaching for the shore. Ellen kicks against it and I lie both my hands on her and hum the tune of 'Twinkle, Twinkle, Little Star', making a mental note to Google the words of the nursery rhyme. But not today. Today is Sofia Marzoni and Red Butler's wedding day and every minute is accounted for, although — I check my watch — I have thirty minutes before the day officially begins. I waddle down to the study, where my laptop is, and log on to the Womb Raider site. I type in my symptoms.

The pain is a Braxton Hicks contraction. I let go of the breath I've been holding. I scan the page. My uterus is practising being in labour. I love that. It's so organised. Twelve weeks to go and Ellen and the team are having a delivery drill. Such foresight. I make myself a cup of camomile tea and take it into the garden, where the day has already begun. Thick-bodied bees disappear inside the folds of flowers, which reach for the sun like hands. Phyllis's hens peck and strut inside the run that George built for them years before. The breeze is slight and the sky lightens as the sun gains. It feels like the beginning of time, in this gentle half-light of morning. Away to the east, I hear a distant rumbling sound, like the low growl of a dog. It sounds like thunder but a storm seems unlikely, in the fresh grandeur of the day. I look at my watch. Four minutes thirty-two seconds before I'm supposed to be up. Seven hours, four minutes and thirty-two seconds before Red Butler gets married. I drain my cup and move back inside the house.

★ ★ ★

Two hours later, I'm in the Martin. Even with the windscreen wipers at full tilt, I struggle to see out of the front window with the rain that lashes against it like whips. Blue — who is afraid of thunder and lightning and rain and windscreen wipers — sits in his cat cage with his front paws covering his eyes, howling. Not even when I start singing his favourite song — 'Don't Cha' by the Pussycat Dolls — does he relinquish his position. I am shouting rather than singing

446

('Don'tchawishyourgirlfriendwashotlikeme?'), to be heard over the hurl of the rain against the car and the smack of the thunderclaps. My phone rings. It's Sofia Marzoni. Again.

'How far away are you now?'

'About five minutes further than the last time you rang,' I shout toward the mobile, my hands tightening on the steering wheel. This does not bode well. I'm not supposed to be this stressed at this hour of the day. Even on a Marzoni wedding day.

'Scarlah, I *need* you. Everything's goin' pear-shaped. It's rainin' Blues and Al Pacinos over here.'

There's nothing I can do about the weather but something about the way Sofia says that makes me worry that she thinks there is. 'I'll be there in an hour,' I say. 'We can talk more then, OK?'

'The seatin' plan needs a tiny bit of tweakin',' she says, and I can tell she's decided that this is the best time to tell me, when she's out of reach.

The traffic lights are red so I lower my head to the steering wheel and wait.

'It's Isabella and Paul,' she explains. 'They got back together last night and now she wants Paul to come to the weddin' so you'll have to do a bit of a reshuffle with the seatin' arrangements.'

'Last *night*?' I can't believe this. If Sofia is to be believed, their divorce was so acrimonious that even their two legal teams couldn't be in the same room with each other without a brawl ensuing.

'Yeah, at the dinner last night.' Valentino

447

rented out the entire Merrion Hotel for the Italian guests and treated everyone to dinner there last night. I think he hoped his runaway wife would turn up, as he has hoped at all the celebrations he's hosted over the years. 'Anyway, Paul was at the hotel doin' a bit of business.'

I've never quite understood what it is that Paul actually does. Whenever the Marzonis tell stories involving Paul, he always appears somewhere 'doing a bit of business'.

'What happened?' I don't really want to know but Sofia has stopped hyperventilating for the moment and I want to keep it that way.

'Oh, the usual,' Sofia says, with a bored air. 'A big fight at first.'

'You mean like a shouting match?' I say, just to be clear.

'God, no,' says Sofia, like she can't believe how naïve I am. 'Isabella clattered him about the foyer with her handbag.'

'That must have hurt.' Isabella is one of those women who could fill a shopping trolley with the stuff she puts in her handbag.

'A minor concussion is all,' says Sofia, and I can see her in my mind's eye, waving the injury away with one of her long hands capped by her long nails that by now — I check my watch — should be painted an embellished shade of fuchsia.

'Don't worry, Sofia. I'll find somewhere to put him.' I say this in my best *can do* voice, which, I have to admit, does not sound as convincing as it should. The seating plan is on its eleventh edition. If I had to compile a seating plan at a

Palestinian-Israeli convention, it could not be more difficult.

'I knew you would,' says Sofia, and I can hear a smile crack on to her face like an egg. 'Just don't put him anywhere near Florentina Bonivento. Or Carlo Bonivento.' There is a pause and I wait, sensing more. 'In fact, just don't put him near any of the Boniventos,' she adds.

I try to swallow but my throat is dry. There are about seventeen Boniventos on the wedding guest list and, due to various incidents over the years, I have scattered them like confetti around the banquet hall where dinner will be served, in an effort to keep them at arm's length from several members of the extended Marzoni clan.

I knock at the door in my head where I keep all my solutions but, other than a vague suggestion about putting Paul at the children's table, there is a silence that does not fill me with any confidence.

'OK, Sofia, I'll bear that in mind,' I say, and even I am impressed with my voice, which sounds like the voice of someone who has everything under control.

Because of the rain, the traffic is heavier than usual, which is not as bad as it might be, giving me time to edit the seating plan. It's within my reach when Sofia rings back.

'One other thing,' she says like she never hung up. 'Whatever you do, don't put Paul beside Angelo, Alessandro or Augusto. In fact, just don't put him beside anyone beginning with an 'A'. That'll make it easier for you to remember.'

I take a moment to allow this to sink in, and to

449

remove Paul from his newly acquired seat between Isabella and Angelo. Or Alessandro. I can't remember.

'What about your father and your sisters? Could he sit beside any of them?' I am clutching at straws.

'Jaysis, Scarlah, I didn't think I'd have to tell you not to put him anywhere *near* them. Isabella may have forgiven him but the rest of us have a way to go, wha?'

'No, of course not,' I backtrack. 'I was just . . . making sure.'

'You had me worried there, so you did,' laughs Sofia although it is more of a nervous laugh than it should be.

'And how's . . . eh . . . Red holding up?' I put as much *nonchalance* into my tone as I can.

'Red? I'm sure he's grand. He's gettin' ready at his flat and then goin' straight to the church, as far as I know.'

'He's not . . . on his own, is he?'

'Yeah, his best man has three kids and he has to bring one of them to a football match this morning. But it's an important one, I think. A semi-final or something.'

Red's best man is one of a string of foster fathers Red had from the age of three to eighteen. I learned this from Filly, who is very good at pumping people for information that they may not particularly want to share with you. I think about Red in his flat by himself. On his wedding day. Struggling with his tie, no doubt. I've never seen him wearing a tie.

The line of traffic inches forward and I put the

450

car in first and concentrate on getting through the day ahead.

By the time I arrive at Valentino's house, I have come up with a plan that involves Paul and Isabella sitting at the table with Fintan — Red's botany-student friend, and Bryan — whom Red now calls Kofi Annan since the diplomatic hellhole that was the period in Fermanagh — as well as Cáit, the Sandra Bullock-lookalike bean-an-tí, whom Red has dubbed Mary Robinson on account of her fantastic defence of basic human rights (mostly Bryan's) during that same period. Red invited Declan and Maureen as well, but what with *Romeo and Juliet: The Musical* opening tonight, Maureen is unable to attend and Declan is not allowed to because Maureen needs him to straighten her hair, another of the tasks he classifies as DIY and is surprisingly good at.

The front garden of Valentino's house is dominated now by a lifesize statue of the Infant Jesus of Prague, as it has been on four previous occasions, for the weddings of Isabella, Maria, Lucia and Carmella. Only this time the statue is barely visible through the deluge of rain that pours like a shroud around it. The garden is a sea of mud and four — pink — flamingos do their best to wade through it while the rain beats their heads like batons.

'Eh, the flamingos . . . ' I begin as one of the five Marzoni sisters answers the door. I think it is Carmella, although they look so alike she could be any one of them.

'They're grand, so they are. Even if they

451

wanted to, they couldn't fly away, their feathers are that saturated with the rain and the mud halfway up their legs. The dotes.'

It is Carmella. I detect the slightest hint of a Waterford accent, which is where she works now. In the swan sanctuary.

'Aren't they supposed to be delivered directly to the castle? By the flamingo specialist?' I ask.

'Ron from Flamingos Rock Ltd rang me last night. There was a bit of a problem . . . '

'A problem?' I jump on the word.

'Yes, well, it's a sensitive problem. Not something that Ron would want us talking about, if you see what I mean.'

I don't but something tells me not to ask Carmella to elaborate.

'Anyway, Ron and I have known each other for years. He knows I'm experienced. I told him I'd bring them down myself and get them settled.'

'But I thought you worked with swans?' I ask.

'Swans, flamingos, whatever,' Carmella says, giving the dismissive flick of her hands that is characteristic of all the Marzoni women. 'Jesus, are you all right, Scarlah?' The pain takes me by surprise and bends me in two so my face is down around my shins.

'I'm just checking my shoes,' I shout up at Carmella. 'Don't want to walk mud all over the . . . eh . . . carpet. Is it new?'

'Yes,' says Carmella. 'Papà ordered it in specially for the wedding. Are you sure you're all right?'

The pain reaches the edge of my bump and slides away, like it was never there. I rise slowly, blinking against the white spots that blot the perimeter of my vision. 'So,' I say in a jovial voice that distracts her further still, 'where is the blushing bride?'

'You'd better come into the kitchen,' says Carmella, turning away from me so I can't see her face.

I follow her, almost afraid to walk on the carpet, which appears to be a replica of the fresco of the Last Judgement on the altar wall of the Sistine Chapel. I tiptoe across it but it's impossible not to stand on at least one of the faces. I close my eyes and make it to the kitchen from memory.

The kitchen is like a pub on St Stephen's Day. A really popular pub. After a particularly long and dreary Christmas Day. Carmella takes my hand and hauls me through the — mostly Italian — crowd. I do a quick headcount and am amazed to discover there are only sixteen people in the room. They look like they're all arguing with each other but I have enough Marzoni experience now to know that they are not. The conversation throws itself around the room like punches and I am grateful when Carmella pulls me out of the room. My gratitude is short-lived, however, when I realise that we are now in the room they call the Magnet. I never knew why it was thus christened but what I do know about it makes my blood run cold in my veins. It is the room where confessions are made. Secrets told. Accusations thrown. It is where Valentino gathered his little girls the day he told them their mother was gone and wasn't coming back. It is where Isabella told Valentino that she was going to divorce Paul, even though he'd had an inkling already, after Maria's wedding. It is where Sofia took Carmella to tell her that her Gucci bag — a real one loaned to Sofia after weeks of lobbying — had fallen into a deep-fat fryer in the chip shop in Whitehall and smelled like a quarter-pounder with cheese and looked like a battered sausage.

It is not a room you want to be in when you are waiting for someone to tell you something. Because it's never something good.

'Tell me what's wrong,' I say to Carmella as soon as she closes the door. She looks deflated, as Marzonis often do when they are denied the opportunity to dramatise and embellish a story.

'It's Sofia,' she tells me, and then pauses, waiting for my reaction.

I nod at her. 'Yes?' I say, and my voice is a whisper as a film reel runs through my head in a trailer of possibilities, all disastrous.

'Well' — Carmella draws herself up to her full height (an inch over six feet, I estimate, given the perilous incline of her shoes) — 'she's taken to the bathroom and is refusing to come out.'

'Why?'

'I don't know but Maria looked through the keyhole and says that she's sitting on the edge of the bath eating Rancheros.'

I think briefly about a Ranchero smothered in Marmite. My mouth waters.

'Is anyone in there with her?'

'Just Hailey.'

'*Hailey?*'

'Yes.' Carmella looks surprised by my question. 'She told us our fortunes this morning. I am going to travel across water and meet a tall, dark, handsome stranger who will sweep me off my feet.'

'But . . . you're married,' I remind her.

'I know,' she says, smiling. 'Exciting, isn't it?'

'Right,' I say, picking up Blue, who has been cowering in his cat cage ever since he saw the flamingos on the lawn. Turns out I can add flamingos to the list of the things he's afraid of. 'I'll go up to her.'

'Good luck,' says Carmella, squeezing my shoulder briefly with her long hand.

If the downstairs of the house is like Grand Central Station at Thanksgiving, the upstairs resembles Heathrow Airport on Christmas Eve. Valentino — a great fan of Pavarotti — practises his party piece, an emotional rendition of 'O Sole Mio', on the landing, oblivious to the throngs of people who struggle to get past his outstretched hands and trembling voice.

Sofia is in the en-suite bathroom off her bedroom. I put Blue on the bed and slide some After Eights through the bars of the cat cage. I knock on the door.

'Sofia? It's Scarlett. Can I come in?' From inside the door, I hear the muffled whispers of two people. Hailey's whisper is the muted one. Sofia's lends itself more to the stage-whisper variety and is perfectly audible.

'I can't let her in. She'll persuade me to go through with it. You know what she's like.'

Some muted, normal whispering from Hailey

455

that I can't hear. And then, 'But everything is different now. Isn't it?' A silence, although that could be Hailey whispering back. I can't be sure. 'I know it's only six months. But six months seems too long to wait. Doesn't it?' More silence. I lower my legs until my eye is flush with the keyhole. It seems that Sofia has become wise to this little window since Maria's peeping-Tom session and has stuffed it with toilet paper.

'Sofia,' I say again, 'please open the door. It's' — I check my watch — 'a quarter past nine. You're supposed to be at the hairdresser's in fifteen minutes, remember?' Sofia is having pink daisies threaded through her hair and, because she has a lot of hair, this could take some time.

There is a click and the bathroom door opens a chink and Hailey's head appears round the edge of it. She looks like she's been attacked by Sofia's make-up bag, although her lipstick — roaring red — is smudged and strands of her hair are standing on end, as if it's been rubbed with a balloon.

'Hailey,' I say, getting up from the bed, where I had temporarily taken refuge. My legs are a bit shaky. I feel hot too. Although Valentino insists on having the heating as high as it will go — despite the season. He says it reminds him of Sicily. 'What is going on?'

Hailey slips through the chink in the door and closes it, standing with her back against it in case I might try to storm it.

'It's Sofia,' she says in her impeccable voice.

'What's wrong with her?'

'She's . . . ' Hailey begins, and then she stops

456

and looks at me in her careful way. 'Are you all right, Scarlett?'

'Yes,' I say. 'I'm fine.'

'You're very pale, if you don't mind me saying so. Paler than usual, I mean.' If Hailey is saying this, I must be white as a shock of ghosts.

'I think I just need to go to the . . . ' I don't make it to the end of the sentence before running towards the en suite, where I do end up storming the door and I reach the toilet just in time and fill the bowl with my breakfast (toasted bagel with Marmite and lemon curd) and the mint Aero I ate on the drive up, against my better judgement. I back up to the edge of the bath and sit down, forgetting about Sofia, who says, 'Eh, excuse me,' in my ear and I jerk out of her lap like a cat on a bed of pine needles.

'Jesus, I'm sorry Sofia. I . . . I forgot you were there.' I have to sit somewhere so I close the lid of the toilet and sit on it. Without even wiping it with one of the antiseptic wipes in my pocket. I wipe my mouth with some toilet paper and look at Sofia for the first time. I barely recognise her. For starters, she's not wearing any make-up and her face is bald without it. Like someone else's face. I keep a stash of lotions and potions in my bag for wedding days where tears flow as fast as champagne. But I'm not sure any of them are up to the challenge of Sofia's face. It's ruined with tearstains.

'Hailey,' I shout from my perch on the toilet seat. She appears in the doorway immediately, like she's been waiting there all along. She has wiped the smudged lipstick off the edges of her mouth and her face is pale now, as if worry has worn the worst of the make-up away.

'Yes?' she says.

'Can you go to the kitchen and slice some cucumbers and bring them up here? And some teabags if you can find any.'

'OK.'

Sofia looks at me, confused. 'What are you going to do with the teabags and the cucumbers?' she asks. Her voice is a hoarse whisper and she looks terrified, like I'm going to do something horrendous with the cucumbers, like make her eat them (Sofia is not a great fan of most vegetables and green ones in particular).

'I'm going to fix your face,' I tell her, rummaging in my bag for the highest-strength potion I have.

'Aren't you going to ask me what's wrong?' she asks, pouring the crumbs at the bottom of a packet of Rancheros into her mouth.

'I'm going to fix your face first. Then we can talk.' When you're dealing with pre-wedding jitters, it's best to lead the bride up the aisle one baby step at a time so that she arrives safely at the altar without really noticing.

'Let's sit you on the bed,' I say, taking Sofia's huge, cold hand in mine. Sofia shakes her head but stands up and allows me to lead her out of the bathroom, which may be one small step for me but is one giant step for Sofia.

'I can't feel me arse any more,' she says, looking at me.

I will do many things for my brides but I draw the line at massaging their numb bottoms. Sofia,

458

realising this, slides her hands down her back and massages the cheeks of her bottom with both hands.

By the time Hailey comes back, Sofia is lying on her bed with a cold compress over her eyes to reduce the swelling. I arrange the slices of cucumber around her face like a garden salad and put two wet teabags under the compress and she lets me, as malleable as a ragdoll. Hailey sits on the other side of the bed, holding Sofia's hand, her face full of quiet concern, as if death itself has Sofia in its sights.

'Now,' I say in an intensely cheerful voice, when I have finished with Sofia's face. Already I can see the patches of red skin cooling and receding. I get up from the bed, feeling optimistic, which later I will berate myself for. It is such a rookie mistake.

The bed creaks as I move off it and, in that instant, Sofia rises like Lazarus from the pillows, my careful concoctions falling from her face and landing in a soggy puddle in her lap.

'What the fuck is wrong with me, Scarlah?' she says, and I can see all my good work coming undone as tears spring again to her eyes and begin their determined trek down her face.

'Nothing,' I say, sitting down beside her once more. 'You've just got pre-wedding jitters, that's all. It's completely normal.' I can't look at her when I say this, even though it's only a bit of a lie. I *have* seen wedding jitters. Of course I have. Just not in this league before. But then again, this is a Marzoni wedding. Everything is larger than life. Why not the jitters?

'I can't get married,' she says then. 'Not today.'

'But it's your wedding day. If you're going to get married at all, it's the best day to do it,' I say, and the smile on my face hurts me, it's that forced. I am refusing to take her seriously, a tactic that worked very well on the morning of Freda Penworth's wedding. The fact that Freda's marriage didn't make it as far as the first-year anniversary is neither here nor there. I got her up to the altar in an off-white off-the-shoulder wedding dress and a tiara that lit up when she said, 'I do,' which is what she paid me to do.

'You've been planning this for months,' I remind her.

'No, *you've* been plannin' it for months.'

'Only because you asked me to. You *paid* me to, remember?' I am stung by Sofia's words, which sound like an accusation.

'That's just money,' she says with the ease of someone who has deep-fat fryers full of the stuff.

'What about Red?' I ask her.

'He's a dote, so he is,' she says. 'He won't mind.'

He won't mind?

'Anyway, you're not well, Scarlah. We should postpone it to another day maybe.' She looks at me hopefully.

'I'm . . . grand now. Just shouldn't have had the mint Aero so soon after the lemon curd and the Marmite. That was a mistake.'

There is a rap of knuckles on the bedroom door, loud and long enough to make the three of us jump and stare at it as if Attila the Hun himself is standing on the other side of it with blood dripping from the stump of the wooden club he holds in his hand.

'Sofia? Come-a out-a and let your papà feast-a hees eyes on your-a beea-you-tee-ful face-a.'

Hailey and I look over at Sofia, whose face is red and puffy and swollen and barely recognisable as her own.

'Sofia,' Valentino says again, louder now, 'what ees a-going on in zere?' There is a peevish edge to his voice. Valentino has less patience than Sofia, whose ration is meagre at best.

'Oh shit,' squeaks Sofia, with her hands over her face. 'It's Papà. He'll *kill* me. He says he could have opened those two chip shops in Belfast he's been talkin' about, for the cost of this weddin'.'

I count to five — there's no time to count to ten — and get off the bed, push Sofia back into a lying position, shove the cucumber and teabags back on her face and, before she has time to tell me not to, throw an eiderdown over her and hiss, 'Stay there,' before dashing into the bathroom, turning the shower on, dashing back out and closing the bathroom door behind me.

'Pretend to be doing something,' I tell Hailey.

'Like what?' She has the look of a chicken in a coop with a fox.

'Here,' I say, pushing Blue's cat cage towards her. 'Pretend to be grooming him. Or something.'

I open the bedroom door a crack and have to look up and up before I encounter Valentino's face, which is as red as a redbrick wall and, even

461

though I know it's because of his tendency to overexert himself when he sings, it still makes me catch my breath a little.

'Valentino,' I say in a suspiciously jovial voice, 'it's lovely to see you again.' This lie is as bald as Valentino's head, given that the only time I ever see him is at a Marzoni wedding.

'Sofia ees necessitated downstairs for-a zee photographing.' Despite the years that Valentino has spent in Dublin, he insists on speaking in the same broken English that he arrived with. Although he understands *everything*.

'She's . . . she's in the shower. She'll be down in five minutes. Maybe ten,' I say.

'She had-a zee shower already.'

'She's having another one. I . . . eh . . . I spilled some . . . coke on her and she's all sticky so she's . . . eh . . . having another shower.'

Valentino leans forward and looks at me with his hooded black eyes. He flicks his eyes over my head then and into the bedroom, where they fasten on the long, lumpy shape of Sofia Marzoni under the eiderdown. He snaps his eyes on me again.

'But-a you don't-a drink-a zee Cokey-Cola, Scarletta. Ees no good for you, you say.' I'd forgotten about Valentino's elephantine memory.

'Yes, well, you're right, Valentino,' I say, nodding and trying to come up with something plausible. 'But I've become a bit addicted to it since' — I nod down towards Ellen — 'the baby.'

Valentino loves babies. They are his Achilles heel. If he were allowed, he'd talk about his five babies to strangers in the street and drag them back to his house, if they agreed — and maybe even if they didn't — and show them the reels and reels of footage he has of them, learning how to walk and how to talk and one particularly unsettling one of Sofia taking a bite out of Maria's leg and even this one makes Valentino clap and smile and nod indulgently at Sofia. 'Teething' is his explanation for this display of wanton aggression, even though Sofia is about six years old at the time.

There is a high-pitched squeak behind me and Valentino — who was just about to leave — stiffens and peers into the room again, sniffing like a dog on the trail of a rabbit.

Hailey arrives behind me. 'Sorry,' she says. 'Blue gave me a fright.'

Valentino examines Hailey carefully before nodding and moving away. I close the door and lean against it, the shake back in my legs.

'That was close,' says Sofia, pushing the eiderdown off her and getting up.

'What was that squeak about?' asks Hailey. 'It was so loud.'

'Oh, yeah, sorry about that,' says Sofia, putting her hand on Hailey's shoulder and squeezing gently. 'One of the tea-bags burst and I got wet tea leaves all over my face. Up my nose and everything.' It's true that Sofia's face is speckled with wet tea leaves. On the plus side, the cucumbers and tea have weaved their brand of magic and, with some concealer and a bucket of foundation, there's a chance we can rebuild her.

I look at my watch. 'Right,' I say, using my no-nonsense voice, which I reserve for brides on the brink of a nervous meltdown — and for Maureen when she can't decide what to wear to the village shop — 'let's get you dressed and out to the hairdresser's. What are you wearing?'

Sofia nods towards a pink tracksuit hanging on the door of the wardrobe. It looks brand new and I guess — correctly — that it is her wedding-day tracksuit.

'Hailey can drive me to the hairdresser's,' says Sofia, smiling in Hailey's direction.

I look at Hailey, who smiles back at Sofia, and it is like I'm not in the room. My wedding-planner antenna is suddenly up and about, twitching madly, and I know then, for a fact, that in order to get Sofia up the aisle in one piece, I have to separate these two women. 'You can go with your sisters. They're all getting their hair done as well. I . . . I need Hailey to stay here with me and . . . and help.'

Sofia opens her mouth to argue and it is Hailey who steps in with her quiet dignity. 'Go on, Sofia,' she says. 'I'll be here when you get back,' and Sofia closes her mouth and nods and begins to dress herself like an obedient child.

When we have bundled Sofia safely out of the house, I beckon Hailey into the Magnet and close the door against the cacophony of sound that is the kitchen. 'Listen, Hailey,' I begin.

'I agree,' Hailey says, before I have a chance to get started.

'With what?'

'I'll think of some excuse to be gone before Sofia gets back. That's what you were going to ask me to do, wasn't it?'

464

I nod my head slowly. Hailey avoids my gaze.

'I'll take Blue to the church and get him ready for the wedding, OK?'

I open my mouth to say something but she is gone in her soundless way and I am standing on my own in the room they call the Magnet for reasons I can't remember right now. I put my hand on my forehead, which feels hot and clammy. Although, since I deposited my breakfast in Sofia's en suite, the pain in my belly has evaporated like a puddle of water on a hot day. Also, the delivery drill in my uterus has abated and, in the cool shadows of the Magnet, I take a moment to adjust my calm exterior — which had slipped off my shoulders back there — and take a couple of deep breaths and pinch my cheeks to encourage some colour to stain them. I press my hands against my belly and am rewarded with Ellen's hand, which pokes out like hope, and I touch it and set my shoulders in their rigid line and close my eyes and brace myself before moving out into the day.

52

I step from the calm crypt of the Magnet into the raucous roar of a Marzoni wedding day in full swing. The pink champagne flows, which has the effect of raising the volume on the already loud conversation that fills the room like a football stadium on a Saturday afternoon. The photographer snaps his way through the house and Valentino insists that everyone repair to the flooded plain that is his garden for photographs, as if there is no rain and no mud. The sound that a high heel makes as it sinks into thick mud is a sickening sound. A sucking sound. Still, the guests do it because Valentino asks them to and the air is filled with the sickening, sucking sound of sinking heels. They gather around the grotto and smile. They pull their heels out of the mud and move to the lifesize statue of the Infant Jesus of Prague, where they gather and smile. They pull their heels up again and stagger to the horses and carriage, which have just arrived, and smile. I smile too. There is something a little uplifting about seeing a group of people in their finery and muddy heels traipsing around the soggy mud bath that is Valentino's front garden, in the relentless rain of an Irish summer's day.

I stop smiling pretty quickly when I see the horses. Four of them. With the pink dye running down their faces and their manes and their legs like rivers. I grab two umbrellas and reach them in four — squelchy — strides and reach my arms up and out and hold the umbrellas over them, which is about as useful as putting a colander on your head in a monsoon.

'What are you doing?' asks the man in charge of the horses. His name is Ed.

'I'm trying to shelter the horses.' Even as I say this, I see the water draining from the horses. It is as pink as candyfloss. 'I thought the dye was waterproof?' I shout to Ed over the backs of the four horses.

'So did I,' he says, smiling and shrugging his shoulders in an indifferent kind of way that makes me want to reach over and pull his hair.

'What are you going to do about it?' I ask him, my mouth in a thin line to prevent any words escaping that I might later regret.

He shrugs again. And smiles again. 'Ah, sure,' he says, 'nobody'll even notice in this rain, will they?' He's probably right but, with Sofia in such a volatile state — even more volatile than usual, I mean — I feel a heightened sense of responsibility to make sure everything else is perfect.

I reach for my phone and punch in John's number. He answers on the fourth ring.

'John, I need help.'

'What is it? Is it the baby?' There is a sound of a plate crashing and I realise that John was sitting on his couch eating toast from a plate on his knees. The same plate that broke when he stood up in a panic. I curse my thoughtlessness. 'No, John, sorry. The baby is fine. It's Sofia's fecking stallions that are the problem.'

'The pink ones?'

'Yes.'

'The dye is running in the rain and you're wondering if it's OK to use pink food colouring to patch them up?'

'Pink food colouring? John, you're brilliant!'

'Oh,' he says, and I can see his small smile edging around the corners of his mouth. 'Thank you. I'm surprised you didn't think of it yourself.'

I worry at my lower lip with my teeth and wonder why I didn't think of it myself.

'Do you suppose it's OK to use pink food colouring on horsehair?' I ask.

'I'll check with Dermot.' Dermot is John's brother and a vet.

I hang up and wait, my arms aching from holding the brollies over the horses. Despite the pain, I refuse to lower them. I equate that with giving up, which I have never done and am not about to start now.

One minute and forty-three seconds later, John rings back.

'Yes, it's fine. Do you have any pink food colouring?'

'I'm going to check in the presses in the kitchen. I'm sure there's some there. You know the way the Marzoni girls love fairy buns with pink icing.'

'Ring me if you need anything else,' John says. 'I'm here.'

Suddenly, there is a lump in my throat. He is here. And he will be here for Ellen. I know he will. He is as dependable as a dolmen. I smile down the phone at him and hang up.

'Are you crying?' asks Ed, the horse handler.

'Yes,' I say, giving him the benefit of my biggest smile, which Filly calls 'toothy'.

'Oh,' he says, disarmed by my honesty.

'Right,' I say, trying on my no-nonsense voice again for size. It seems to work and Ed straightens his shoulders and looks at me. 'Can you help me to unhitch the horses from the carriage and take them round the back? There's a big shed where they can shelter.' Ed shrugs and smiles but does as he is told.

I find three bottles of pink food colouring in the Marzoni kitchen and pour them into a bucket of water. It takes a while but, when I have finished, only the closest inspection would pick up on the fact that the horses are now two different shades of pink and smell like the sugar lumps they love to crunch. I stand back to look at them.

'That's not bad,' says Ed.

I smile at him and head into the house to wash the pink dye off my hands.

Sofia is back now and there are the requisite oohs and ahs at her hairdo — an up-style with masses of tiny pink daisies, like a meadow in summertime. Her make-up is done too and there is no trace of this morning's *incident* on her face at all. I check my watch. All that's left to do is get her into her dress, which, while it is heavy and complicated and festooned with all manner of zips and clasps and buttons and hooks and eyes, should only take about ten minutes to pour her into. Fifteen, tops. I breathe out. Despite

469

everything, we are on schedule.

'Scarlah, come here ta me,' Sofia shouts from the curve of the wide staircase, which sweeps to the first floor of the house, where she is posing for photographs. I approach her slowly. My plan is to keep her busy until it is time to go to the church. Give her no time to dwell on whatever was bothering her this morning. Keeping busy is a great distraction from life. I've been doing it for years.

When I reach Sofia, she leans into me and stage-whispers into my ear, tickling me and making me want to giggle, which I do not. 'I need to talk to you. In the Magnet.'

Immediately I decide that, whatever happens today, I will not enter the Magnet with Sofia. I grip the banister for support. The walk up the stairs has winded me — while the staircase is a long one, it's not *that* long — and there is a pain down low in my back that wasn't there before. 'Just let me make a couple of phone calls and I'll be right with you, OK?'

'Promise?'

'I promise,' I say, putting my hands behind my back and crossing every single one of my fingers and toes.

Now, it's a game of cat and mouse with Sofia. I immerse myself in busyness even though there's not a lot left to do. I insist on having the readers practise their readings in the front room. Two of the readings are in Italian and I allow the soft curves of the language to pour over me, like warm water.

Now, I am at the hob in the kitchen, stirring a

pot full of scrambled eggs to feed Ed and Uncle Lorenzo, who have found each other over a common love of horses and a love-hate relationship with swans.

Then there is the disappearance of one of the four flamingos and the subsequent search for him, which takes the guts of half an hour. I eventually find him in the shed perched on the back of one of the horses — Clive, his name is — picking fleas off Clive's back with his long beak, which infuriates Ed, who claims that none of his horses have fleas, even though the evidence is as plain as the tiny flea struggling between the pointed end of the flamingo's beak.

I send Carmella, Isabella, Maria and Lucia upstairs to wrestle Sofia into her wedding dress. 'If you have any problems, just ring me, OK?' I tell Carmella.

'Why don't you come and help?' Carmella asks. This is a reasonable question, as I have always fastened the Marzoni women, who have a leaning towards the painfully tight brand of wedding dress, into their various gowns.

'It's Clive. He's in a terrible state after the flamingo incident,' I tell Carmella, again with my hands behind my back and my fingers and toes crossed tightly. 'Ed needs my help. Just . . . just call me if you need me, OK?'

With Federico Bonivento's help (turns out he lives on a nature reserve fifty kilometres from Sicily and knows a thing or two about wildlife), I gather the four flamingos into their four cages and secure them in the back of Uncle Vinny's vintage van, where they make a tremendous

471

splash of colour against the leopard-print seats.

'You're sure you'll be OK driving the birds to the castle?' I ask Federico again.

'Well, Uncle Vinny is driving but I'll go with him. It'll be fine.' He smiles at me and thumps Uncle Vinny in the arm in what I presume is a comradely gesture.

Vinny says nothing. He is a huge man in a black suit with a black tie and a black shirt. Even his cufflinks are black. He grunts and folds himself into the front seat of the van, his head bent at an awkward angle against the roof.

All that is left to do is help Valentino with his tie; he tells me at every wedding that I'm the only woman he knows, apart from his wife, who can knot a tie properly. He still calls her his wife. Even after all these years.

Ed hooks the horses back up to the carriage and I shovel four enormous steaming pats of horse dung up off the driveway before waving the wedding party out of the house, where they spill on to the muddy pond that is the front garden in their bright colours, like soggy confetti.

Even now, in her pink wedding dress with her pink wedding bag and her pink wedding tiara and her pink eye shadow, Sofia makes eyes at me and I am about to give up and go to her when my mobile phone chooses that moment to ring and it's Filly and I fall on it.

'GoodmorningsorryI'mlate,' Filly begins, and I have to stop her there.

'What do you mean, you're late? Where are you?'

472

There is a pause and I can hear the rustle of Filly's shirt or jacket as she checks the time. 'I'm at the church. And no, I'm not late.' She sounds surprised. 'Sorry, Scarlett, what I meant to say was — '

'Is Red there?'

'Yes.'

This produces a feeling that is new to me. It is a mixture of relief and regret, with a dose of inevitability. I mean, I've been planning this for months. I *knew* this was going to happen, didn't I?

'Great,' I say.

'How's Sofia?' Filly asks.

'Bearing up,' I say, chancing a glance over to the wedding party, where Sofia is busy biting her false nails.

'Has Hailey arrived yet?' I ask.

'Yes. She's got Blue all lovely, so she does. And he seems really at home in his new cat cage.'

'Did he let her put the pink dicky bow on him?'

'He licked her afterwards and even smiled a bit.'

It's true. Blue *does* smile. Just not very often.

'Is Al Pacino there too?'

'Yes. In his matching pink dicky bow. They're adorable, the pair of them.'

'OK, well, the wedding party are leaving now so I'll see you shortly, OK?'

'Wait,' says Filly, 'I rang to see how you were feeling.'

'I'll tell you later.'

'No. Tell me now.'

There is no sidestepping Filly when she is like this so I tell her. About the Braxton Hicks. And the shaky legs. And the vomiting. And the clamminess. And the pain in my lower back. It takes ages to tell her. It's not a list of symptoms, it's a bloody catalogue. Filly does not interrupt.

'Scarlett, those symptoms . . . I'm not sure if . . . '

'Look, Filly, they're mostly gone now, apart from the back pain and the clamminess. It's probably just Marzoni-wedding nerves. It's nothing. I shouldn't have told you. I'm sorry that I did.'

'Well, I'm not,' says Filly, and I can hear her gearing up for one of her lectures, in which she will insist I go to the hospital for a check-up when I know there is no need. I am twenty-eight weeks pregnant and I'm having a bad day, brought on by the kind of stress that comes with a Marzoni wedding. That's all.

'Filly, I have to go. It looks like Clive is going to do his business in the driveway again.'

'Clive?'

'One of Ed's four stallions, remember?'

'Oh, *Clive*.'

Just as I hang up, Clive lifts his tail and deposits another load on to the ground. I sigh and go round the back to retrieve the shovel, which Ed takes and gives to Uncle Lorenzo.

By the time Lorenzo has cleaned it up, the wedding party are in the carriage and are being waved off by the remaining wedding guests and the neighbours, who line the streets now, the men waving their handkerchiefs in the air, the

474

women using theirs to mop up the tears that spill and roll down their faces. After all, this is the last Marzoni wedding. Or at least the last of the first Marzoni weddings. If Carmella is to be believed, it sounds like Isabella and Paul are planning on tying the knot. Again. With me as the wedding planner. Again. I know I'll need every job I can get my hands on once I set up on my own. But still. I decide not to think about it today. I'll think about it tomorrow.

53

Back in the Martin, the quiet is like a lullaby and I know that, if I put my head across the steering wheel, I'll be asleep in seconds. So I don't put my head anywhere near the steering wheel. I eat two of the Marmite cracker sandwiches I've stashed in the glove compartment and drink some of the peppermint tea that Phyllis poured into a thermos for me this morning. Then I put the key into the ignition and turn it. Nothing happens. I turn it again. And again. Still nothing. I get out of the car and lift the bonnet. Smoke pours out and I slam it closed. There's a burning smell. Before I can think about a solution, I have to vomit. Again. I do it in Valentino Marzoni's front garden, a respectful distance from the grotto, into a rhododendron bush. Some of the neighbours are still out on the street and look at me with a curious mixture of pity and disgust. I take my phone out and redial John's number. He answers on the fourth ring.

'John, I need help.'

'Again?' He's not being smart. He just can't believe I need help again so soon.

'My car won't start.'

'Are you at Sofia's house?'

'Yes.'

'I'll be there in five minutes.'

He hangs up before I can thank him. I close my eyes tight to stop the tears that threaten. I am thinking about Ellen when she's eighteen and in town at Christmas with no taxis available. About her ringing John at two o'clock in the morning. About John, who will get out of his warm bed on a cold December night, who will pull his trousers up over his pyjama bottoms and his Arran jumper over his pyjama top and pour warm water over the frozen windscreen of his car and belt himself in against the cold seat and drive into town to pick her up from wherever she is. He will always be there for her. This much I know.

I stand on the footpath and wait. There is a vomit stain at the bottom of my skirt and I rub at it with a tissue. I check my watch. It's 12.36 p.m. Twenty-four minutes before the wedding.

John's car appears at the top of the road and he beeps his horn. I try to run but I have to stop and lean on the garden wall to catch my breath as another Braxton Hicks contraction bears down on me.

'Scarlett, are you all right?' It's John. He stops his car in the middle of the road and gets out of it. He runs towards me without even closing the car door. By the time he reaches me the pain is gone and I manage to straighten and smile weakly at him.

'What is it, Scarlett? Is it the baby?' Colour has drained from his cheeks and his face looks thinner as a result.

'No, no,' I say. 'Well, yes, in a way. It's a Braxton Hicks contraction.'

'I've been reading up on those,' says John in a way that surprises me not in the least.

We both turn as a car scorches down the road, beeping its horn. The driver leans out of his window holding his two fingers aloft before swerving round the obstruction that is John's car.

'I suppose we should go,' John says when the noise of the screeching tyres has abated. He holds his arm out and I grip it, glad of the support. While the pain has gone, it has left me a little breathless.

We get into the car and, despite the driving rain and John's sedentary method of driving, we arrive at the church in twelve minutes and twenty-two seconds. I look at my watch and estimate that I have maybe five minutes to spare before Sofia arrives.

I turn to John. 'Thank you,' I say.

'You'd do the same for me,' he says, and it is a statement with not a trace of doubt in it.

I nod. I would.

I lift my handbag from the seatwell. 'I have to . . .'

'Go,' he says. 'I know.' He leans across me and opens the car door. I smell peppermint and mothballs. 'I'll wait here,' he says. 'Just for a little while. Just in case you need . . . a lift or anything.'

'Thanks,' I say again.

'Go on,' he says. 'You don't want to be late.'

I run as best I can inside the church to make sure that everything is as it should be. It is a sea of pink. I smile when I see it. A pink carpet rolls like Al Pacino's tongue up the central aisle, bordered by a riot of flowers and ribbons and balloons — all pink — like a birthday party when you're six.

The altar is lit up with candles — pink ones — that dance and flicker and make everything seem possible. The string quartet and the organist and the banjo player are dressed in varying shades of pink, which looks grand on the women but a little unfortunate on the only male member of the ensemble, the banjo player, who appears to be wearing a pair of curtains — albeit pink ones — in a tight band about his person.

Every pew is occupied with wedding guests and their collective whispering roars around the church. Of Red, Filly and Hailey there is no sign. I dart up the side aisle.

'Where's Red?' I ask Filly, when I find her scoffing Blue's After Eights in the little room off the altar. Today, she is wearing a pink and white candy-striped double-breasted suit with tiny pink pumps and her hair — dyed pink — with extensions in a plait wound round her head like a crown. She looks like something you could eat. She looks adorable.

'He's gone outside with Al Pacino,' she says, trying to swallow the evidence without my noticing.

'I didn't see him.'

'He's gone round the back. Al Pacino needed to do his business.'

'How's Blue?'

'As windy as Chicago. And the smell of them. Like he had fourteen pints of porter and a doner kebab last night.'

'Dammit. I *knew* we shouldn't have given him those After Eights.'

'I know. That's why I'm eating the rest of them,' Filly says brightly, like she's just thought of that excuse.

'Good of you,' I say, using the voice that Filly calls 'dry'.

There is a clatter of heels and Hailey arrives into the room. It's immediately obvious that she is new to heels. She walks like a child in a pair of her mother's shoes. She concentrates on it. She looks down. She tries not to fall over.

'Scarlett,' she says when she sees me. She carefully sits herself down on a chair before she continues. 'How is Sofia?'

'On her way,' is the best I can come up with.

'Good,' says Hailey. 'Blue is fine apart from an . . . unfortunate bout of flatulence.' She doesn't look at me when she says this, perhaps sensing that I might be a little embarrassed by my farty cat. 'It's not all that unusual, mind,' she continues. 'I had a cat once with a similar . . . condition.' She allows herself to look up at us now before lifting herself out of the chair and taking a moment to stabilise herself on her heels. 'I'd better get into my place. It takes me a while to get anywhere in these.' She smiles an apologetic smile at us and teeters away, although it takes her some time to vacate the room.

'I'm going to get Red,' I say. 'Make sure he's in place before Sofia arrives.'

'Maybe I should go and get him,' says Filly, raising her eyebrows at me in a way that I don't like.

'I think I can manage it,' I tell her.

'OK, then, I'll go and help Padre Marco into his pink cassock. He's not that happy about it so a little flattery and persuasion might be needed. Maybe a rasher sandwich. Brendan gave me a stack of them this morning for emergencies.'

'OK, see you in a bit.'

The rain has stopped when I step outside, although the sky remains leaden, as if it is only taking a brief break.

'Scarlett O'Hara.' I turn round and there he is. In a purple velvet suit and a pale pink shirt and a purple tie with tiny little pink love hearts scattered across it. Al Pacino pulls the hand off him as he strains at the lead. I smile at him. At the pair of them. There is nothing else to be done with them.

'Here, let me just fix . . . ' His tie is askew and I reach up and unknot it. My knuckles brush against the warm, scratchy skin of his neck and I feel the fizz of electricity vibrating around my body. I pull my hands away but it is too late.

'Your fingers are frozen,' he says, cupping my hands in his and blowing softly on them. Now he is rubbing them between his fingers, lost in the task, as if I am not even here. I look straight ahead and concentrate on the past participle of *descendre*.

'There,' he says, and his voice is like a smack of thunder in the middle of the night and makes me jump. 'All done. Now you can do my tie. If you don't mind.'

It takes me longer than usual to knot the tie. My fingers feel like somebody else's fingers.

481

Although I have to admit they *are* warmer than before.

'Thanks,' he says, when I eventually manage to get it done. 'You're good with ties, aren't you.'

'Yes,' I say. 'I'm good with all manner of knots, in fact.'

He smiles at me and in my head I give myself a good kicking. *I'm good with all manner of knots?* I wait until the electricity that fizzes around my body burns itself out. It takes longer than I want it to.

'Have you noticed anything different about me?' asks Red, in an oddly shy way.

I look him up and down. Still the same head of hair, thick as thatch. Still the infectious way he has of smiling, with his whole body. Still the awkward way he has of wearing clothes, as if nothing fits.

'No,' I say.

He holds out his wrist for inspection. There's a watch strapped to it. It chafes red against the white of his skin. It's ten minutes late and has a Mickey Mouse face. But still. It's a watch. I look up and smile at him.

'You didn't have to do that,' I say. 'I have enough timekeeping devices for all of us.'

'I thought I'd share the load,' he says, peering at the watch like he's trying to remember how to tell the time.

'OK,' I say, dragging my no-nonsense voice out again, even though it says it's exhausted after all its earlier efforts, 'I just came out to get you and put you where you're supposed to be.' There is a lump in my throat as I say the words.

'Oh, yes,' he says, 'and where is that?'

'What?'

'You said you were going to put me where I'm supposed to be.' Red leans towards me, the beginnings of concern seeping into his face.

I shake myself and tell myself to get on with it. 'Oh, yes, sorry, I got a bit distracted there,' I tell him, pretending to rummage in my bag for something.

'I didn't think you got distracted, Scarlett O'Hara,' he says, and he is smiling now.

'Sorry,' I say, gathering myself together. 'You're supposed to be standing at the front pew, remember? Beside the best man. Just like at the wedding rehearsal.'

'I meant to ask you, how is Sofia?' His face is a map of concern as he waits for me to answer.

'She's . . . ' I begin, wondering what to say.

'Oh, no,' Red says, banging his spare hand against his forehead. 'I *knew* this would happen.'

'No, no, she's fine,' I tell him quickly. 'She's on her way.'

'She wasn't crying, was she?' he asks, brushing away my assurances.

'Well, a little, but . . . '

'Was Hailey with her?'

'I separated them. Hailey is here now.'

'I should have been with her this morning. I told her that. But she wouldn't hear of it.'

'Well, it *is* bad luck,' I say, even though I don't believe in that kind of superstition.

'Shit,' Red says, pulling his free hand through his hair and ruining all the good work that Filly had done earlier with the bottle of gel I gave her.

483

'Look, don't worry, Red,' I say, taking a step closer to him. Now I can see dark smudges under his eyes, which I recognise as the lack-of-sleep variety. His eyes are still as vivid a green as any I've seen. It is like looking at the sun and I have to look away. 'Sofia just had some pre-wedding jitters, that's all. She's fine now. I got her into the carriage and she's with her sisters and her father and she's . . . she's fine.' It's only a small lie. I mean, she is much better than she was, which is a not-too-distant relative of fine, isn't it? And I've dragged us all this far. Falling at the last hurdle is not something I intend doing.

Red looks at me before he answers. As if he's wondering what to say. Or if should say anything at all.

'Did you ever start something,' he says, 'something that seemed like a good idea at the time? It made perfect sense at first but something happens along the way? And it doesn't make sense any more?' He stops there, floundering for a way to make sense of what he's trying to say. But it does make sense. It makes perfect sense. The clouds in my head shift and clear and it's like the sun coming out and suddenly I know what I have to do.

'I have to go,' I say, already turning away as I say it. Nearly running.

'What?' says Red. 'Wait. Where are you going?'

'I'll be back,' I say, not turning round.

I only stop running when I reach the car. I stand behind it and look at the back of his head. He sees me through the rear-view mirror. We

484

look at each other for what seems like the longest time. Then he reaches over and opens the passenger door and I get in.

'Is everything OK?' he asks. From a distance I can hear the clop-clop-clop of horses' hooves against the tarmac of the road.

'Everything is in place,' I tell him. 'Sofia should be here any second. I can hear the carriage.' I pull the car door closed and the sound is gone.

'That's good,' he says. 'I'm glad.' But his voice is guarded now as he waits for me to say what I came to say.

'John,' I begin, shaking my head. 'I'm sorry.'

There is a pause. 'You're not going to marry me, are you?' he says after a while. There is no trace of bitterness in his voice. There is resignation.

'No,' I say, and my voice is a whisper. 'I should have said something earlier. I was afraid to. I was afraid to have Ellen without you. You were my link with stability and normality and reality. I didn't want to break that.'

Another pause and, for a moment, I think he's going to tell me to get out and drive away. Instead, he leans back and closes his eyes.

'I shouldn't have left you like that,' he says then. 'I've ruined everything. I should have stayed. Or taken you with me. Or . . . or something.'

'I let you go,' I say. 'I never even asked you to stay. Or take me with you. Or anything.'

'The worst part is, I don't even know why I left,' he says. 'I've asked myself a thousand times and I still don't know.' His voice is shaking now and I reach over and take his hand in mine.

'You wanted more,' I said simply. 'So did I, if I'm honest. I was just afraid to admit it. Afraid to change anything in case it turned out to be not as I planned it.' I can hear the hooves again, louder now, getting closer.

'But what about Ellen?' he says after a while. 'What will we do about Ellen? And she might not even be mine. Christ, it's such a mess.'

I take a moment to think about this, even though I have thought about little else over the last few months. But now, in the new space in my head that feels decluttered, like my office after its spring, summer, autumn and winter clear-outs, the mess just doesn't seem that messy any more.

'John, look at me,' I say, and with my two hands I turn his face towards mine, savouring the familiarity of it. 'Ellen is going to be born surrounded by people who love her. Me and you and Red and Filly and Bryan and Phyllis and Declan and George and Maureen. There's nothing messy about that, is there?'

For a while, there is silence but it's not an angry silence or a sad silence. It's a thoughtful silence and I know that John is giving the question due consideration before answering, which is something I've always loved about him. I wait for him.

'We-ell . . . ' he says after a while. 'It's not ideal . . . '

'No,' I agree. 'It's not. But Ellen will be ideal. Won't she?'

'I can't wait to see her,' he says, and I can see the glimmer of a smile dawning on his face.

'Me too,' I say.

'I was just trying to do the right thing,' he says.

'I know,' I say. 'So was I.'

'But you're right. About us, I mean.' The words are as final as the thump of clay on the lid of a coffin before it's lowered into the earth. 'It's the right thing to do. For both of us.'

And at that moment, as I sit in John's car with fresh rain zigzagging its way down the windows like tears, my hair slung along my face like pieces of soggy seaweed, everything is clear. I let myself look at it and, even though it was there all along, I can see it now. That he is right. That I am right. That this is the right thing to do.

'Can we still be friends?' I ask through my tears. 'I mean, not just because of Ellen but because of us.'

'Of course we can,' says John. 'Who else will listen to me when I want to talk about the evolution of taxation law in the last century and its impact on trends in the pork-belly market?'

'That will be me,' I say.

'Because you're my friend,' he says.

'And you're mine.'

We lean across the handbrake and hug each other, crying now, weeping like a pair of old maids at the funeral of the last eligible bachelor in town.

'*Scarlett!*' From behind the car, I hear the crunch of high heels. I turn round. Through the back window, I see Filly and Hailey running towards us. Well, Hailey does her best to run. It's more of a fast walk, her face screwed up in concentration as she tries not to teeter off her heels. Filly jogs in front, pulling Hailey along by the hand. Red brings up the rear, dragging Al Pacino behind him.

'I'd better go,' I tell John, opening the car door.

He nods. 'I know,' he says.

I step out.

'Good luck,' says John, and I know from the faces of Red, Filly and Hailey that I'm going to need it. I close the door and John pulls away. He doesn't look back.

'What's wrong?' I ask as the four of them skid to a stop in front of me.

They answer at the same time, their words falling over themselves like drunks at closing time.

'Wait,' I say. 'I can't make out anything you're saying.' Now none of them speaks and I am none the wiser. I point to Filly. 'Right,' I say, 'you first.'

'Well . . . ' she begins and I can see she is wondering where to start. 'It's Sofia,' she finally says.

I curse myself for not speaking to Sofia in the Magnet earlier. 'Where is she?'

'She's in the carriage,' Red says, already pulling at the knot of his tie like it's strangling him. He nods to the left and I see the four pink horses and the gilt-edged carriage, parked on a double-yellow line outside the church grounds.

I release my breath. At least she is here.

'Go on,' I say.

'She is refusing to get out,' Filly responds.

This piece of news is greeted with silence by myself, Red and Hailey. Filly looks at me, expecting me to say something.

'Let's go,' I say, with as much authority as I can muster.

The four of us march towards the carriage, where the pink stallions stand with their heads bowed, as if they're ashamed of themselves. I push through the crowd gathered around the carriage — Sofia's sisters and a thunderous-looking Valentino — and climb into the carriage. Sitting all alone, with her huge eyes and her huge hair and her huge wedding dress, Sofia Marzoni looks like she's just escaped from the only Walt Disney animated film that has a sad ending. I sit beside her.

'I'm so sorry, Scarlah,' she says, looking at me. 'I thought I could but I can't. I just can't do it.'

My original intention when I climbed into the carriage was just to fix this situation. Put a plaster on it. Give it a pair of crutches. Let it hobble up the aisle. Instead, I take Sofia's cold hand in my newly warmed one and squeeze it tightly.

'I'm sorry too,' I whisper to her.

'Why?'

'I should have talked to you back at the house. I was afraid this might happen. I was trying to avoid it.'

'I've been tryin' to avoid everything too,' Sofia says. 'I thought I could do it. But everything's different now. I just can't . . .'

The carriage lurches to the side and Red Butler appears in the arch of the door and

489

struggles inside. He takes one look at Sofia and bends down to her and holds her so tenderly, like she is a piece of crystal that might crack.

'It's OK, Sofia. It was a stupid idea in the first place. I shouldn't have encouraged you.'

Another lurch — deeper this time — and now Valentino fights his way inside, a dogged look on his face but his tie still perfectly straight.

'What-a ees going on?' He addresses this question at me and I know I should know the answer, considering my position as wedding planner, but I don't. There is, however, one thing I *do* know.

'Sofia is not getting married today,' I tell him.

Sofia, Red and I all sit back as far as we can go after I deliver this bit of news. Valentino breathes in and in until he looks like he is fit to burst. He opens his mouth to say something but Sofia gets there first. 'I'm sorry, Papà,' she says. 'I'm in love.'

'I-a know you are een-a love,' Valentino manages. 'That's-a why I haf spent such a fortune on zees wedding day, remember?'

'No, Papà' Sofia says. 'Not with Red. I'm in love with . . . with Hailey.'

I've heard of the word apoplectic but I've never seen it in action until now. The buttons on Valentino's shirt strain to retain him. His eyes widen and bulge. His hands bunch into fists. His face looks like I've been at him with the pink food colouring.

In a spectacular show of bad timing, Hailey chooses that moment to scramble inside the

490

carriage. Valentino is so apoplectic he doesn't even notice.

'I . . . I've known for ages,' continues Sofia. 'Not about Hailey. About myself, I mean. Since I was a teenager really. But . . . but I know how you feel about . . . about people like me and I know you wanted me to get married, like all my sisters and I was afraid not to and afraid to tell you and just . . . afraid.'

You could hear a pin drop in the cab. Nobody moves. Nobody even breathes. Eventually Valentino turns to Red. 'And you?' he hisses at him.

Red clears his throat. 'Sofia is my friend. She asked me for my help. I . . . I was just trying to help.'

'But marriage ees an *institution*,' roars Valentino into Red's face. 'A *Holy Sacrament*,' he adds, his voice rising. 'You cannot seemply use eet to hide.' He turns to look at Sofia's sodden face. 'Or-a to help a friend.' He glowers at Red. 'Ees-a much too important.'

'It's not Red's fault,' says Sofia, looking at Red. Despite everything, she smiles at him. In fairness, it is difficult not to. 'I asked Red to marry me. He only agreed after I begged him. He thought he was doing me a favour. We were going to stay together for six months and then Red would pretend to have an affair, I'd find out about it, divorce him and go and live in a quiet place somewhere, where you would understand my decision never to get married again and I could just get on with livin' my life. And it would have worked out fine too. But then I met Hails.'

Valentino glowers down at Hailey, who bravely

stands her ground. Even though Valentino's face is not as pink as before, he still manages to look pretty intimidating. Colour drains from Hailey's face as Valentino towers over her.

'And-a what haf you got to-a say-a for yourself?' he asks her.

For a moment, I think Hailey might be too petrified to speak but then she opens her mouth. 'I . . . I'm in love with Sofia,' is all she can manage but it is enough.

Now it is Filly's turn to climb into the cab. There is no room for her but, because she's so tiny, she manages to squeeze in. 'Did I miss anything?' she asks in a mastery of understatement.

'I'm in love with Hailey, so I am,' Sofia says, and this time she is smiling.

'I *knew* it,' says Filly, slapping her hand against her thigh. 'And Hailey's in love with you, isn't she?' Filly asks, wanting to ensure that Sofia's love is not an unrequited one, not being a great fan of unrequited love.

'I am,' Hailey calls out in her voice that is like a song. A celebration.

'Oh, that's lovely,' says Filly, who loves happy endings.

'And I might be Ellen's father,' Red suddenly says, and all heads swivel towards him and wait to hear what he has to say next.

'Who zee hell ees Ellen?' Valentino asks with a kind of world-weariness.

'Scarlett's baby,' recite Red, Sofia and Hailey, like a class of junior infants singing their times tables.

492

'Jaysis, you pick your moments, Red, so you do,' says Sofia. 'This *is* supposed to be my weddin' day, remember?'

'I know,' says Red, 'and I *am* sorry. It's just that, I know I should have told you before now but everything just got so . . . complicated . . . '

The fight seems to go out of Valentino then, like air out of the cancelled hot-air balloon. For a moment, there is a perfect kind of silence in the carriage as we shuffle like strangers in a lift that is stuck somewhere between the basement and the ground floor.

Valentino turns to me and I shrink back from his glare. 'And-a you, Scarletta O'Hara?' he says and everyone seems to hold their breath. 'Have you anything to-a say for yourself?'

Before I can think of a single thing to say to Valentino, the pain comes again. This time, it grabs me from behind, digging into my back like a spade. I make some kind of sound and get to my feet and stand there like I'm waiting for something but I don't know what. The pain moves round to the front of me and bends me in two and then there is a gush of something warm and wet down my legs. It gathers in a puddle on the floor.

'Jaysis, Scarlah, did you wet your pants?' It is Sofia, delighted with the diversion.

The pain flows through me and ebbs away and now I'm just a woman standing in a pink carriage drawn by four pink stallions with a puddle of water between her legs.

'No, I . . . '

'Is it your waters?' asks Red, looking from my

face to the puddle and back again. 'Jesus, it's your waters. They're not supposed to break until . . . '

'Until the baby is coming,' Hailey finishes the sentence for him in her careful, quiet way.

'The baby can't be coming,' says Filly. 'You're only twenty-eight weeks.'

'Sofia was-a born at thirty-one weeks,' offers Valentino, who tries to move but cannot, braced as he is between Hailey and Red.

It is difficult to double over in the carriage, given the crowd of people in here, but I do it anyway. The pain is the same as before, a squeezing, grinding pain that makes me close my eyes as if I might see it otherwise. My hand fumbles around in front of me until I find someone's hair and I pull it. Hard. I keep pulling on it until the pain stops and then I coax my eyes open. 'Sorry about that,' I say to Red, my breath coming in gasps. 'I had to grab something.'

'At least there's loads of it to grab on to,' says Red, but he's not smiling any more. He looks worried.

'You're in labour, Letty,' says Filly, consulting her *Birthing Partner Handbook*, which she has taken out of her bag. 'There's a section in the book on page one hundred and forty-five about how to deliver a baby but I haven't read it yet. I'm only on bloody page twenty-three. Jaysis.'

'I can't be in labour. I'm only twenty-eight weeks pregnant,' I say, and then I can't say anything any more as another pain reaches for me and knocks me sideways like a wave roaring towards the shore. 'I don't even know how to do the breathing stuff,' I pant, as the contraction wanes. 'I haven't started my antenatal classes.'

'Just breathe,' says Red.

'What do you mean?'

'I mean, like, in and out. Like a normal person. But concentrate on it. As if you were in a yoga class. You *have* done yoga, haven't you?'

'Eh, yes.' Right now, I can't remember if I've ever done a yoga class but I'd say I have. It seems like the kind of thing I would do.

'Right,' says Red. 'Everybody out.'

'But . . . ' everybody begins at the same time.

'OUT!' shouts Red, and this time, they do as they are bid. Red clears a long bench at the back of the carriage. 'Here, Sofia, give me your wrap. Scarlett can lie on it.'

'But it's *silk*,' she tells him. 'It cost me four hundred and thirty-five euros. And that was in a bloody *sale*.'

'Eet cost-a how much?' roars Valentino as Sofia hands the wrap to Red and watches him spread it along the bench before manoeuvring me on to it.

'I know, I know,' says Sofia, 'but it was in a *sale*. I couldn't just leave it there, could I?'

'I'm sorry, Sofia,' I manage to say. 'I'll try not to — ' Another gush of water rushes from me, darkening the impossibly delicate pink of Sofia's wrap.

'Oh, Jaysis, call an ambulance,' says Sofia, not even commenting on her ruined wrap.

Filly squeezes herself out of the carriage. I can hear her on her mobile. ' . . . need an ambulance double smart. We have a woman in labour here.

495

She's only twenty-eight weeks pregnant.' A pause then before Filly speaks again. 'Yes, of course she's in real, proper labour. I just told you. I grew up on a farm in Australia, you know. I've seen enough sheep in labour. I know what it bloody well looks like.' Another pause. 'I *know* she's not a bloody sheep but — '

Red sticks his head out of the carriage window. 'Filly, this is an emergency. Stop talking about bloody sheep and ask them when they'll be here.'

'When can you get an ambulance here?' asks Filly obediently.

'*Twenty minutes?* The baby will be born by then at the rate she's going,' says Filly, and although she can be prone to exaggeration, this time I am afraid that it could be true. I bend myself in two as another pain stampedes down my belly.

Red kneels on the floor in front of me and wipes the beads of sweat off my face with a large, clean-ish handkerchief. 'Can you move?' he asks me. 'I'll drive you to the hospital. It'll be quicker than waiting for the ambulance, OK?'

I open my eyes and nod at him before the pain comes again. I kneel on the floor and rock myself back and forth. It is the only position where the pain is tolerable.

'The pains are coming too fast,' I shout at him. 'We have to go now.'

Red looks at me, looks at his Mickey Mouse watch and seems to come to a decision. He pokes his head out of the carriage. 'Holles

Street,' he yells to the driver. 'Don't spare the horses.'

'I'm not covered for this kind of carry-on,' says the driver.

'JUST GO!' Red roars at him, and there is a lurch as the carriage begins to move.

'I can't go to the hospital in a horse-drawn carriage,' I manage to say before I realise that I just don't care any more. About anything. Not even about Ellen, who is coming much too early. Dangerously early. All I can think about is the pain. It's everywhere. Inside me and around me. It's like something tangible that you could reach for and hold on to. I reach for it and hold on to it. My head fills with it until it feels like I'm not even here any more. I don't know how much time goes by.

Red holds my hand and uses the other hand to press his mobile against his ear. He is on the phone to the hospital.

'I don't know,' I can hear him saying. 'The pains are coming one after the other. There doesn't seem to be any pause between them . . . How painful are they? I have no bloody idea. They look pretty painful. What kind of question is that? . . . OK, OK, no, I haven't checked. What am I supposed to be checking for? . . . Oh, OK, hold on, I'll look.'

Red sets his phone on the floor and puts his hands on my shoulders. I feel the warmth of them through my shirt. There is a dip in the pain and I concentrate on breathing in and out. 'OK, Scarlett, I need to check you,' says Red very quickly, without quite meeting my eyes.

'OK,' I say.

'OK?' This is not the answer Red Butler was expecting but, in spite of this, I do my best to sit up and hitch my skirt up over my knees.

I lean back on my elbows. 'Just do it quickly,' I tell him. 'Before the next one.'

Red wipes his hands on his trousers, rolls up his sleeves, kneels in between my legs and begins to ease my knickers down my thighs.

'Just reef them,' I shout at his bent head. I can almost see the next contraction rolling towards me like a tank. This time, Red yanks at the flimsy material and I hear a ripping sound and his head bends closer.

'Oh Jesus,' he says. He reaches for the phone on the ground beside him.

'What is it?' I shout through the gap between my knees. 'What can you see?'

Red presses the phone to his ear and looks at me and says, 'I think I can see the top of the head.'

I roll myself over until I am on all fours again. The urge to push comes from a place deep inside me where I have never been before. It is primal in its simplicity and I bear down on it without making a sound.

'Stop pushing,' shouts Red. 'You're supposed to pant. That's what they said on the phone. Don't push. We're nearly there.'

I try to do what I'm told. I try to pant. But the need to push rages across my body like a hurricane and leaves me and all my good intentions in its wake. It clenches every muscle I have. It leans against me. It grips me like hands.

It bowls me over. I push with my whole body.

The carriage jerks and shudders to a halt. Red kneels beside me, holding the phone between his shoulder and his ear. He sticks his head out the window of the carriage. 'I don't know where we are,' he says. 'We're in a traffic jam. We can't go any faster . . . No. There's no bus lane . . . Where's the ambulance?' Snippets of this conversation reach me. I think I hear car horns, blaring, the neighing of the horses, people shouting.

'OK,' Red keeps saying. 'OK.' I don't know if he's saying it to me or the person on the phone or even to himself. He struggles out of his jacket and his shirt, pulling at it until the buttons fly off like popcorn kernels in hot oil. I don't ask him why. I can't. All I can do is push. The pain is hot now. It burns like a fire. It hurts to push but it's all I can do.

Red somehow manages to flip me on to my back and his head disappears again between my legs. 'The head is coming,' he shouts down the phone. 'Yes, I think so. I think she's facing down . . . Yes, I've got my hands underneath.' A pause and then he looks up at me and roars, 'Push, Scarlett!'

'I can't,' I say. 'I can't any more.' My voice sounds like it's coming from far away. From a place I've never been before.

'Just one more push,' Red says, reaching one hand to my face and brushing my hair out of my eyes. He smiles at me. 'You can do it,' he whispers.

'I can't.' I have never been more sure of

anything in my life. There is nothing left inside me to push with.

'You can. You can do anything, Scarlett O'Hara.' And, as if I have opened a drawer inside me where I keep a reserve of energy for emergencies only, I prop myself up on my elbows, take a breath and push again. This push is different. Slower. Gentler. I feel something against my skin. It feels like the contours of Ellen's face moving against me. Moving through me, past me.

'I have her head in my hands,' Red shouts, and in his voice I hear the thing that I feel. It is a sense of wonder and I push through it and now there is a warm, rushing, slippery sensation and the pain is gone and I know that Ellen is here. She has arrived.

54

I don't notice the sound immediately. My blood pounds in my ears and my breathing is laboured and loud. Then I hear it. It is the worst sound I have ever heard. It is the sound of nothing at all. The silence is suffocating and thick, like smoke. I pull myself up through it. I see Red. He wraps Ellen in his pink shirt. It goes round her too many times. Her body makes no impression under the fabric of the shirt. In the silence, all I can hear is the rustle of the fabric in Red's hands. The silence pours into the carriage like nightfall until it is full to the brim with it. It makes it difficult to speak. I lean down instead, my arm outstretched. I put my hand on Ellen. She makes no sound. Her eyes are closed. Her skin feels like liquid against my fingers. She is blue.

Now there are people everywhere. Some in white coats. Some in blue ones. Some in green ones. Now there is noise. Everyone talks at the same time. All I can hear is the silence, louder now.

'Why isn't she crying?' I shout, but it is like shouting in a dream where no one can hear you. I see the cord, pulsing between me and Ellen. A woman in a white uniform worries at it with scissors. 'Don't cut it,' I shout, louder this time so that she looks at me with a curious look as if she has noticed me for the first time and is wondering what I am doing here.

'I have to,' she tells me. 'We need to work on the baby. We need to get her inside.'

'Ellen,' I say. 'Her name is Ellen.' It seems suddenly vital that the nurse — and all these people — know her name. 'Ellen O'Hara,' I say, and I lean forward and squeeze the nurse's hand and she smiles at me and nods. 'Will she be all right?' I ask and my voice is a whisper now. Smaller than Ellen. There is no answer.

The nurse's head is bent and now the cord is cut and Ellen is lifted up and away from me. Hands reach for her but they are not my hands. I feel like I am standing with my face pressed up against the window of my life. There is nothing I can do but watch.

The nurse turns to me before she leaves. 'We'll get a gurney to bring you in,' she says.

'I'll come with Ellen. I don't need a gurney.' I struggle to get up.

'No,' she says. She turns to Red. 'She hasn't delivered the placenta yet, has she?'

'I . . . I don't know . . . I don't think so . . . ' he says in the voice of a man who wouldn't know a placenta if it was served to him on a plate with a side salad. His face is way past pale. His teeth chatter as if he is cold.

Once Ellen is gone, the carriage is quiet again and I know, with the most brutal clarity, that she won't make it. I try not to know this but I see it. I see it in the kindness on the nurse's face. I see it in the way that Red holds my hand, tight, in a way that should hurt but does not. I close my eyes against it but I see it anyway. I don't cry. Or

502

shout. I let them load me on to a gurney. I say nothing as they wheel me into the hospital and down corridors that all look the same and into a lift and we move up into the body of the building. I push when they tell me to and I hear a midwife saying, 'The placenta is delivered,' in a cheerful voice as if there is some point to it.

The stitches don't hurt. I want them to but they don't.

'How long is this going to take?' I ask the nurse.

'Not long,' she says.

'I need to see Ellen.'

'The doctors are working on her,' the nurse says, not lifting her head from between my legs.

'Can I see her?'

'Yes, of course. Just as soon as you've finished here, OK?' She looks up then, reaches across the place where Ellen used to be and squeezes my hand, the one Red is not holding.

They don't let me walk. I'm too weak, they say. I don't feel weak. I feel empty. And cold. I allow myself to be lowered into the wheelchair. A nurse wheels me. Red walks beside me, still holding my hand. We say nothing to each other. There is nothing to say.

We are on the fourth floor now. It is quieter here and the building seems to huddle around me. Another corridor, the same as all the others. The nurse talks, a monologue of words that stretch behind me like the tail of a kite. I don't hear what she is saying. Her voice bangs against the walls and her words rise and disappear into the ceiling, which is yellowing, as if stained by all these words that have been said before, to people like me: To mothers like me.

★ ★ ★

The ward is still, the silence here deeper. Thicker. Red tightens his grip on my hand and we move into the room. A nurse stands at a window, worrying the top of a pen with her mouth. I can hear her teeth scraping against the plastic. She stops and ticks something on the clipboard she holds with one hand. She says something to a doctor who stands beside her in a white coat with a stethoscope draped round his neck. He points at something on the clipboard and she nods and ticks again. They look up together, like puppets being pulled by the same string.

'Ah, you must be Ellen's mother,' the doctor says, smiling at me and bending a little at the waist as if he's speaking to a young child.

I nod. I am Ellen's mother. No matter what happens. No matter what he's going to say now. I am Ellen's mother.

'She's over here,' says the nurse, pointing to one of a line of incubators. I feel along her line of words, trying to read her like Braille. She smiles at me and nods over at the incubator. I decide that she sounds encouraging and I allow myself to look now. In the direction of her nod and her point. The incubator is covered with a soft fabric. I think it might be yellow. There are machines beside it. With numbers and letters and blinking lights, some red and some green. Wires snake from these machines and slither like snakes into the incubator, where they disappear from view.

'What . . . ?' I begin. My voice is rough and dry, like sandpaper.

'We're giving Ellen oxygen through a nasal cannula,' the doctor explains.

'She needs a little help with her breathing,' the nurse adds, crouching down so that her eyes are level with mine. She has kind eyes, warm and brown. They turn down at the edges and, if she were not smiling, she would look sad. 'It's common enough for babies like Ellen to need some assistance with breathing for the first few days.'

'Can we see her?' It's Red, although I don't recognise his voice. It is as tight as his grip on my hand.

'Of course,' says the nurse, and I look at her name badge — Andrea — and repeat her name in my head over and over like a mantra, although I don't know why. She wheels me closer to the incubator. My eyes are level with the little circular window on the side of it, like a porthole. She leans across me and lifts the cover.

For a moment, it seems like it's empty. There's nothing there. Then, like eyes adjusting to the dark, Ellen swims into my view and steadies herself there. I let my breath out slowly. A plastic tube is tucked behind her ears and tracks across the narrow width of her face. I lie the palms of my hands on the glass wall of the incubator. It is warm. I look at her. I drink her in like camomile tea. Tiny seems too big a word for her. I could fit her into the palm of one hand. Hairs, as fine and downy as the gossamer threads of a spider's web, cover her face. Her chest rises and falls in a way that seems much too fast for her tiny frame. I see her eyes darting behind lids that are closed, as if she is looking for me, wondering where I am.

'I'm here, Ellen,' I whisper in at her. 'I'm here.' I turn to the nurse. 'Can I . . . ?'

'Of course you can,' says Andrea, smiling her warm chocolate smile at me. She shows me where to wash my hands and how to smear them afterwards with the alcohol rub. And then she opens the porthole, carefully, slowly, like she is opening a safe that is crammed with gold, and she nods at me and I slot my hand inside and lower it until it hovers over Ellen and I touch her, with the tips of my fingers, and it is like dipping them into warm milk, she is so soft. Her skin lies in folds around her as if there is too much of it, giving her a wizened look and making her look as old as the world. She is not as blue as before but not as pink as the photographs of the babies in my baby books. Through the skin of my fingertips, I feel her heart hammering in her chest.

I close my eyes and concentrate on Ellen. On her chest, rising and falling. On her heart, hammering. I touch her tiny hands, which are bunched into tiny fists, and I tell her — I promise her — that everything will be fine. I think if I concentrate hard enough, I can make it true.

'Hello, Ellen,' Red whispers beside me, his hand still in mine. I smile at him before I lift my fingers up and away from Ellen and ask Andrea to show me how to close the porthole properly. I ask her about the machines and she tells me what each one does, what every line and light means, the number that the display is not supposed to go under or over. I concentrate on every word she tells me, committing it to memory. The more I know — the names of the doctors and nurses, the mechanism of the beeping, blinking machines — the better chance Ellen will have. This makes no sense. Of course, in some part of me, I know that. But it feels like something I can do for Ellen. It feels right.

Outside in the corridor, I hear voices.

'. . . can't go in there, sir . . . only two visitors per baby . . .'

A second voice, raised and sharp. ' . . . the baby's father . . . have to see them.'

It is only when he starts calling my name that I know who it is.

'SCARLETT O'HARA!'

I lift myself out of the wheelchair and shuffle as fast as I can towards the door. 'John.'

He is out of breath, like he's run a long way. 'Scarlett. Thank God. I just heard. I got here as quickly as I could. This man wouldn't let me in.'

The security guards fixes me with a glare. 'Do you know this fella?' he asks me, jerking his head in John's direction.

John bends over, leaning his hands on his knees, trying to regain his breath.

'I do,' I say. 'He's the father.' I cross my fingers behind my back, even though it might not be a lie at all.

'I thought that was the father in there.' He

points towards the door of the ICU.

'It is. I mean, he is. That is, he *could* be as well. We're just not a hundred per cent certain . . . yet . . . ' I trail off.

'What's *he* doing in there?' asks John, noticing Red for the first time.

'Red delivered Ellen. In the carriage. Just outside the hospital.'

'So *you're* the one responsible for those fecking pink horses?' says the security guard, looking at me.

'Are they still there?' I ask, remembering them for the first time.

'Well, they've crapped all over the car park and won't let any cars in or out but, other than that, they're grand, so they are.' When I can't think of anything to say to that, he throws his arms in the air. 'I'll leave yiz to it. Sounds like you've enough to be gettin' on with.' He turns and leaves, shaking his head and mumbling under his breath.

I shuffle towards John and he pulls me against him without looking at me. For a moment, we say nothing. Just hold each other, leaning into each other. I take such comfort from the solid familiarity of him.

He looks right at me when he pulls away. His eyes sweep around me, anxious. 'Are you OK?' he says. 'When Filly rang, I thought . . . '

'I'm fine,' I rush in.

'And Ellen?' he says, setting his features in a rigid line, bracing himself.

'She's OK, John,' I tell him. 'She's got a tube up her nose to help her breathe and she's in an incubator and she's tiny. She could fit into your hand, she's so small. But . . . but she's here. And she's so beautiful. I've never seen anything so beautiful.' I stop there, my voice wobbling.

John steadies me with a hand on my arm. 'Can I see her?' he asks.

'Wait here,' I tell him. I tiptoe back into the ICU and explain the situation to Andrea in as few words as I can manage. She doesn't say a word until I have finished.

'It's two visitors per baby in this ward,' she reminds me, even though I know this already.

'Couldn't you make an exception?' I ask her.

She frowns. 'There wouldn't be any . . . ' she pauses, searching for the appropriate word ' . . . trouble?' she finally says.

'God, no, nothing like that,' I assure her.

'We-ell,' she says, worrying at her bottom lip with her teeth. Then she looks out of the window towards the corridor and her eyes fasten on John Smith. She smiles and her face lights up like dawn. I follow her line of vision. John Smith stands in the corridor outside, looking in. Smiling back. For a moment, no one says anything. Then Andrea collects herself and drags her gaze back to me. 'I suppose we could make an exception,' she says.

I shuffle out of the room to tell John before she changes her mind.

55

Red perches on the edge of an unforgiving plastic chair on one side of Ellen's incubator. I sit on the other side of it, still in the wheelchair, only because it is, hands down, the most comfortable chair in the room and my vagina remains in flitters. John stands at the head of the incubator, his eyes fixed on Ellen, as if she might disappear if he looks away. She is still asleep, still breathing her frantic, erratic breaths with the plastic tube still tracking across her tiny face and up her tiny nose. He hasn't touched her yet. He says he is afraid he might hurt her.

He looks at me when I reach my hand into her. 'What does she feel like?' he whispers.

I think about it for a moment before answering. 'Home,' I whisper back. 'She feels like home.'

Red nods and smiles. He has touched Ellen. He knows that this is true.

The doctor tells us that Ellen can't maintain her own body temperature.

'Yet,' Andrea adds, patting me on the shoulder in her gorgeous gentle way.

I don't want Ellen to get cold so I limit myself to opening the porthole and putting my hand on her once every hour. There is a second hand on the big clock on the wall and it does its best to haul the hands round the face but, after fifty-two minutes, I can wait no longer and I reach for her again.

'Scarlett?' Andrea appears beside me, as silent as a ghost.

John whips his head round and smiles when he sees who it is.

'Is there something wrong?' I stand up, forgetting about the pain between my legs. 'No, no, don't worry. Everything is OK,' Andrea says, steadying me with her hand round my arm. 'Your family is here,' she says.

'My family?'

'Yes. Declan and Maureen and Filly and Bryan. They're outside in the corridor. They are your family, aren't they?' She looks at me carefully now, perhaps wondering if the pain between my legs has perhaps affected some part of my brain. The part that knows who my family are.

'Maureen?' John says then. 'She's here? But what about the show? It's tonight, isn't it?'

'I know,' I say, swallowing hard.

'Oh, yes, Maureen told us all about it,' says Andrea, nodding. 'Romeo and Juliet: The Musical, isn't it?'

I nod.

'She said, 'Stuff the show,'' Andrea tells us.

We stare at her with our mouths hanging open.

It is John who finds his voice first. 'Maureen said that? She actually said that?'

'Yes,' says Andrea.

'Oh Jesus.' John looks at me and the pair of us smile nervously at each other.

'I didn't realise Declan O'Hara was your father, Scarlett,' says Andrea. 'I loved him in that film . . . What was it called again? The one where he plays the gay head chef? Remember? And married to that awful woman who . . . ' a pause as Andrea tries to think of a delicate way of putting it ' . . . puts herself about quite a bit.'

'*Fairy Buns and Tarts*,' I tell her.

'Oh, yes, that's the one.' She smiles her soft marshmallow smile and moves away.

★　★　★

Outside in the corridor, Maureen is weeping and wailing like an extra in *Angela's Ashes*.

'Oh, Scarlett, darling,' she says when she sees me and launches herself at me, like a rocket. When she reaches me, she stops and lowers her head and rummages for something in her handbag. 'Here,' she says, handing me something warm and damp. 'I've made you this.' It is a cold compress, I think, although it's more like a lukewarm compress now, after the journey to the hospital in Maureen's tiny little clutch bag. 'And Daddy brought you the pillow from your bed.' She waves her hand at Declan, who produces the pillow from behind his back. Maureen punches it enthusiastically. 'That makes it more comfortable,' she explains, pushing the pillow behind my back. The pillow is as comfortable as it's always been but now there are two fist-shaped indentations in it and for these, and the lukewarm compress, and the fact that she is here — albeit in a very tight and low-cut habit — I am enormously grateful. Her face, a wild splash of rouge and powder, peers like a moon from the tight confines of her wimple.

'But what about the show? You're going to miss it,' I say, looking at my wrist where a watch is supposed to be. I had to take it off to touch Ellen. I don't remember where it is and I can't even make a stab at the time. In fact, I couldn't say if it's the day or the night.

'Darling,' says Maureen, putting on her *appalled* face, 'I couldn't possibly go on tonight knowing that . . . that my granddaughter . . . is . . . is . . . struggling for her every breath.'

'She's doing well, Mrs O'Hara,' pipes up Andrea, reading the situation like a picture book. 'She's getting a little bit of help with her breathing but she's pinking up nicely.'

'Yes, but . . . ' Maureen says, feeling her grip on the drama loosen ' . . . she's in *intensive care*, isn't she? I simply *had* to be here.'

'Well,' I say, 'I'm glad you're here.'

'You are?' Maureen asks, the curtain going down on her *appalled* face and lifting again to show a genuinely puzzled face.

'I am so very glad,' I say, standing up and moving towards her. I have to reach up to hug her, forgetting how tall she is. For a moment, Maureen lets me hug her, her arms dangling uselessly at her sides. And then, like someone getting back up on a bicycle again after twenty years, she remembers herself. And me. And hugs me back. With both arms. Tight. And I smell the smell of her. Theatre curtains and Rescue

Remedy. And I squeeze my eyes shut and breathe her in.

'You can go and see her if you promise to be quiet,' I whisper into her hair.

'Is she tiny?'

'Like the My Little Pony I had when I was seven.'

'Polly?'

'No,' I say. 'Molly. Polly was my Care Bear, remember?'

'How much does she weigh, Scarlett?' Declan asks. Hugo had asked him this question earlier when the news broke about Ellen's arrival and had been aghast when Declan confessed that he did not know.

'Just under two pounds,' I say, and I bite my lip, remembering the two pounds of sugar in my recipe for break-up pavlova. It doesn't seem like an awful lot of sugar.

'How much under two pounds?' asks Declan, also biting his lip. He might be thinking about the two pounds of sugar that goes into the making of a batch of strawberry daiquiri.

'Not much,' I tell him. 'Come on. It's this way.'

The pair of them melt into the room, walking on tiptoes.

The lift pings and Filly and Bryan step out into the corridor. They take turns to hug us all and then Filly presses a carton of chocolate milk and a KitKat into my hands. 'Thought you might be peckish after everything,' she says, smiling.

'How is she?' they ask at the same time, and I

tell them what I know.

'I'm so sorry but you won't be allowed in to see her,' I say. 'It's parents and grandparents only.'

When Maureen and Declan re-enter the corridor, Maureen is weeping and wailing again, this time like one of the main characters in *Angela's Ashes*.

'She's sooooo . . . sooooo . . . sooooo . . . tiny,' she wails at the top of her voice, making it difficult to understand what she is saying. It's because of her hands that I can make it out. She holds them, palm to palm, about five inches apart. Filly asks John for a tissue and approaches Maureen with it. She wipes her tears and gets her to blow her nose and gradually the weeping and wailing is reduced to heavy breathing and hiccups. Which is when Maureen notices Red Butler.

'Red? Is that you? What on earth . . . ? Aren't you supposed to be . . . ? Isn't this your wedding day?'

As always, Red smiles before he begins to speak and I look around at everyone in the corridor and notice that they smile back at him. Like they can't help themselves.

'Well — ' he begins before Filly interrupts him.

'Sofia called the wedding off,' she tells Maureen, whose eyes are like dinner plates in her head.

'Oh dear Lord,' says Maureen. 'Whatever for?' And she looks at Red with such naked admiration that even he shrinks a little from her gaze.

'Sofia's in love with Hailey, you see,' pipes up Bryan, who has been filled in on the day's events by Filly.

'Hailey? Who's he?' Maureen asks, although she might not if she knew about the lines that appear on her forehead when she is really puzzled.

'She's the receptionist at Extraordinary Events International,' I supply, not wanting to appear to know nothing at all, seeing that I'm supposed to be Red and Sofia's wedding planner.

'Hailey's a *girl*?' This from Declan. 'How can Sofia be in love with a *girl*?' It's not that my father is homophobic, it's just . . . well . . . he can be a little slow on the uptake.

My mother sets him straight. 'Declan, she must be a what-doyacallit? A *homosexual*.' She turns to Filly. 'Sofia and Hailey are *homosexuals*, is that right?'

Filly nods at her, her mouth in a tight line, which is what she does when she is trying not to laugh out loud.

Maureen advances on Red. 'My poor, dear boy,' she tells him, holding out her arms.

'It's OK, Maureen,' says Filly. 'Red knows. He's known all along, haven't you, Red?'

'Eh, yes . . . '

Maureen stops inches from his face and lowers her arms. 'My poor, dear boy,' she says again, looking at him with her head tilted in compassion. 'You must have really loved her if you still wanted to marry her and her a *homosexual*.'

'Shouldn't you be in propping up a bar

516

somewhere, my good fellow?' says Declan, who hates to see a genuine opportunity to drown your sorrows wasted.

'Red delivered the baby,' says John.

'And he might be Ellen's father,' I finish, deciding that there's never going to be a good time to let this particular cat out of the bag.

Maureen's mouth works furiously to form words. 'But, John . . . ' she manages after a while ' . . . aren't you angry? Aren't you going to clock him?'

'I've known for a while now, Maureen.' John shifts uneasily from one foot to the other.

'Well?' she says. 'Did you clock him when you first found out?'

'Eh, no.'

'Oh.' Maureen seems disappointed by the lack of drama.

'Let's go and get a nice cup of tea, shall we?' says Filly, steering Maureen away carefully, like a shopping trolley with a gammy wheel. Bryan falls in behind them with Declan bringing up the rear. They trail down the corridor like a rabbit-proof fence.

Red smiles at me. 'There's never a dull moment with Maureen around, is there?'

'There never was,' I agree, moving towards the door into the ICU. I am twitchy now with the need to see Ellen. I move using a run that looks like a walk and John and Red struggle to keep pace with me.

I stop at the door. Suddenly, so that Red bumps into the back of me.

'Sorry,' he says. 'What's wrong?' And then he sees them too.

Three people. In a huddle around Ellen's incubator. A green shirt, a blue shirt and a white shirt. One of them is Andrea and my eyes fasten on her. She scans a machine with her lower lip trapped under her top teeth. The machine beeps and spits, jangling against my nerves like fingernails down a blackboard. A doctor slips his stethoscope through the porthole that Andrea holds open for him. He listens to Ellen with his whole body, his head cocked and his knees bent. He closes his eyes and shakes his head.

It is only when Red nudges me gently from behind that I realise I have not moved. It is four steps to the edge of the incubator but it feels like a journey in a dream, where you move but make no headway. The doctor straightens when we arrive and Andrea closes the porthole. I look at Ellen. With so many people around her, she seems smaller than before, the delicate pattern of blood vessels clear beneath her paper-thin skin. My throat constricts and I open my mouth to ask the question but no sound comes out.

'Sit down, Scarlett,' says the doctor in a quiet voice.

I shake my head and reach for Andrea's hand, who takes it. Her hand is soft and I concentrate on the warmth of it. Red takes my other hand and squeezes it.

'Scarlett, the baby's breathing has become a little more unstable,' says the doctor.

I hold my breath. I decide that if I don't

breathe at all while he is talking, Ellen will be OK.

'We're going to need to intubate her.' He stops, waiting for me to say something.

I look at him, my breath held tight inside my chest.

'Do you mean put her on a ventilator?' asks John when it becomes clear that I am not going to say anything.

'Yes,' the doctor confirms.

'Why?' asks John. 'What's wrong?'

'We're not sure yet,' says the doctor, looking at his clipboard. 'There could be a problem with her lungs. Maybe an infection. We're going to run some tests.'

Nobody speaks until Andrea steps into the void. 'The ventilator will help Ellen breathe much more easily. That could be all she needs. Just a little help. Just for a little while.' She turns to me. 'This is not uncommon, you know,' she adds, smiling down at Ellen before she looks back at me.

My lungs scream at me with the need to take a breath.

'If it is an infection, what will you do?' John asks in his dogged way.

'Well,' says the doctor, 'we'll put her on the machine and we'll run some tests and then we'll have a better idea of what we're dealing with, OK?'

I squeeze Andrea's hand but still I don't breathe.

She pushes me gently into a chair. 'Scarlett, love, you're going to have to breathe now.'

Gently she guides my head between my legs and circles her hand on my back, the way Phyllis used to whenever I was sick. I release the breath I've been holding in a long, noisy gasp. For a moment, I think I might pass out, or vomit, before I tell myself not to do either and gradually my breathing returns to normal and my heart stops banging against my chest like a squash ball.

Everything happens quickly after that. They take X-rays. They take blood. They sedate her. They intubate her.

I follow Ellen around, the palm of my hand always flat against her incubator as if, if I break this tenuous connection between us, she'll get away from me. I'll lose her.

Her nappy goes all the way up to her armpits. She sucks the fleshy skin at the base of her thumb. She seems untroubled. As though she trusts me completely. I have never felt less trustworthy. I feel like I have done nothing but let her down.

'Scarlett?' The doctor stands in front of me, his head tilted at an angle. John and Red are on either side of me. John has spent the last thirty minutes Googling the uses of a ventilator with premature babies. He says things like 'endotracheal tubes' and 'positive-pressure' ventilators. Or 'oscillatory' ones. And 'high-frequency' ones. He tells me about each of them: what they do; how they work. He quotes statistics, time-frames, possible outcomes. This is his way of coping. I nod but don't listen to any of it. I keep my hand flat against the side of Ellen's incubator, careful not to let go. Red sits beside Ellen. He says

520

nothing but his presence is solid, like something you could lean on.

'Scarlett?' the doctor says again, with an edge of impatience in his voice.

I glance up.

'Well,' he says, 'the good news is that all the tests we've done so far have come back fine.'

'What's the bad news?' I ask, and I can't look at his face now. I look back down at Ellen and close my eyes and wait for him to answer.

'It's not bad news as such,' he says, and I can hear his feet shuffling. I bite my lip. 'We'll keep her on the ventilator for the time being.'

'So she still can't breathe by herself,' I say. 'Is that what you mean?'

He nods.

'Not yet,' says Andrea, catching my eye and smiling her warm, lovely smile at me.

'How long will you keep her on the machine?' I ask.

Red puts his hand on my shoulder. I can feel the tremble of it. Nobody makes a sound as we wait for the answer.

'It's very difficult to say,' says the doctor. 'We just need to wait and see.'

'Wait and see?' This seems much too hard. I shake my head and look at him. 'There must be something else we can do, surely?' I ask. 'As well as the waiting and seeing, I mean.'

'This is the best we can do for the moment,' says the doctor as he prepares to leave.

'Some babies just need a short period on the machine,' says Andrea. 'As little as twenty-four hours.'

521

'Some need a lot longer than that.' The doctor jumps in with a warning frown in Andrea's direction. I know he is just doing his job. Managing my expectations. But I grab Andrea's words and hold them tight. Twenty-four hours. That sounds better than *waiting and seeing*. We can do twenty-four hours. We gather round, three hands now, flat against the warm glass of the incubator.

Andrea checks the machinery around the incubator and I watch her carefully, taking comfort from her nods and her smiles and the gentleness of her. She smiles at the three of us before she moves away in her soundless way. We listen to the low hum of the monitors. We concentrate on the lights and the lines. We don't fight sleep because there is no sleep to be fought. Twenty-four hours. We settle in. We wait.

56

You can discover a lot about a person if you watch them long enough. And twenty-four hours is long enough. The seconds bleed into minutes and the minutes stretch into hours. We move like snails through this new space and I can't remember anything before this block of time and I can't imagine anything after it. I look at Ellen. She sleeps. Sometimes she splays her legs and arms and fingers and toes, all at the same time. She seems to smile when she does this, like she's enjoying it. This is something I do as well, after the night has passed, regardless of whether sleep has come for me or not.

She likes to put her hand on her face. Sometimes trying to suck parts of it. Mostly laying it flat across her cheek. Or her ear. Andrea says this is her way of comforting herself. This is a good sign, she says.

I see her pulse beating in her wrist and the top of her foot.

I look at the clock face on the wall — six hours now. I try not to think about this. Instead, I make a list of all the places I will take Ellen. The zoo. The pantomime. Disneyland. Maud's icecream parlour in Howth. Dollymount Strand. St Anne's Park. There is room in the garden in Clontarf for swings. Maybe a seesaw. And a sandpit.

I pray too, although I'm a bit rusty. It's

wishing really, not praying. But I begin these wishes with a 'Please, God' and this is what turns the wishes into prayers, I think.

Occasionally one of us leaves. To go to the bathroom. To walk out a leg cramp. To make sure Al Pacino and Blue — who are being minded by Sofia and Hailey — are behaving themselves. I'm sure we eat something but I can't remember what. Doctors and nurses come and go, reaching in to Ellen, examining her, checking the machines, smiling at us and shaking their heads when we ask if there is any change.

But mostly we sit there. And watch Ellen. And sometimes reach our fingers in to touch her. Skim her, really. She likes when you rub her belly with the tips of your fingers. Gently, so she doesn't bruise.

It is a vigil, this wait. We offer up these hours. In return for Ellen's safe delivery from any harm. I know it's a lot to ask. We don't complain about tiredness or stiffness or the blood that has stopped circulating in various limbs. We offer up the pain and discomfort. It is all we have to bargain with.

We don't really speak to each other during these hours. We are too busy hoping. John reads his sheaf of papers on premature babies that he asked his secretary to courier to the hospital for him earlier. He reads them until I know he could recite them off by heart.

Red tells her stories of long-ago heroes with flowing hair and ruddy faces and great battles that are fought and won with endings that are always happy.

I sing her lullabies. When I don't remember the words, I make them up. Her favourite one is 'Rock-a-Bye, Baby', which is funny because Phyllis says that was my favourite one when I was a baby.

And then, somehow, it's the next day. Twenty-four hours have passed.

57

Someone shakes me and it's only when I open my eyes that I realise I've been asleep. I jerk forward in my chair and peer at Ellen, who is asleep. I scan the machines and the wires, ignoring the muscles in my body that scream at me, as if I've just gone ten rounds in the Welterweight World Boxing Championships. John and Red are also asleep in their chairs, their necks hanging at awkward angles in a way that will hurt when they wake up. I look around for Andrea, who is at the incubator beside Ellen's, checking the temperature of the tiny baby inside. According to his chart, he was born three weeks ago at thirty-one weeks and was four pounds. Now he is a hearty five pounds three ounces. This baby is a good-news story she can tell her family about when they ask how her day was.

She looks up and smiles at me. 'The doctor will be here in fifteen minutes,' she tells me in her gentle way. 'He'll examine Ellen then, OK?'

I nod and try to smile back. I've waited twenty-four hours. Another fifteen minutes won't kill me. Although it nearly does. I fill in the time by telling Ellen all about Blue. How he might be a little jealous of her at first. Just because he's been an only cat for so long. How he'll get used to her. How he'll love her. How he doesn't play any games but is fond of looking at the pictures in my bridal magazines and pointing with his left paw at the dresses he particularly likes. He has a great eye for style, so he does, I tell her, and do I imagine it or does Ellen seem to be listening? Could it be wishful thinking or is she pinker than before? I don't share any of these thoughts with Ellen. I don't want to raise her hopes. I continue talking to her. Now I'm telling her about Al Pacino and how he turned out to be Blue's best friend and how Blue never really had any friends before he met Al Pacino. I discount his love-hate relationship with Sylvester, mostly because it's more hate than love at the best of times. I tell her about Phyllis's hens and the fluffy yellow chicks that will appear next spring like tiny bundles of sunshine scattered about the chicken run.

I'm still talking when the doctor arrives. He nods at me without saying anything and moves towards Ellen. He opens the porthole and reaches his hand inside. I check his nails. Square and clean and short. So far so good. He touches Ellen's chest with the flat circle of the stethoscope and I flinch, imagining the coldness of it against the postage stamp of her chest. He takes her blood pressure. Her temperature. He examines every inch of her and it takes so long, or at least that's how it seems to me. John and Red — awake now — remain in their chairs and I can tell they are concentrating on not moving, not speaking, not breathing, just waiting, like me. Waiting for Ellen.

The doctor nods and straightens, guiding his hand out of the porthole without touching the edges. He wraps the stethoscope round his neck and scribbles something on his clipboard. I wait for him to finish. I examine his face. There is a ghost of a smile about it. He writes fluidly, which I take as another positive sign. He dots an 'i' and puts a full stop at the end of whatever words he writes.

He turns to me. 'The baby's vital signs are good,' he says.

'Good enough to take her off the machine?' I ask, and my voice is hoarse.

He pauses before answering and I can see him selecting the words he is about to use. 'I think we could try extubating her,' he says. 'But we won't really know how she'll react until we do. We might have to put her back on the machine. Or we might not. We just have to try it and see, OK?' He looks at me to make sure I understand, even though I don't understand. It all seems so vague and unpredictable. But this is the system and there is nothing to do but try it and see.

John, Red and I huddle in a knot at one side of the incubator while the doctor reaches his hands in towards Ellen. I close my eyes and wait. I can't look. Red takes my hand and squeezes it tight. On the other side of me, I hear John trying to control his breathing. I hear the doctor talking in hushed tones as if he doesn't want to disturb Ellen. 'That's it,' I hear him saying. 'Gently now . . . A little more . . . We're nearly there . . . '

And then I hear it. Tiny it is, like the mew of a day-old kitten. I open my eyes. Andrea has heard it too because she is smiling and nodding and looking down at Ellen like she has just performed a miracle. And she has. She has cried her first cry.

'Is she . . . ?' I begin.

Andrea steps towards me and nods. 'She is breathing by herself, Scarlett,' she says, and I see my face reflected in her eyes and it is the face of a woman who got everything she ever wished for. It is my face. I barely recognise it.

There are lots of questions I know I should ask but I don't do that. Instead, I take Andrea in my arms and hug her tight. She resists at first, perhaps a little startled by my wanton display of affection. But then I feel her responding, hugging me back, and I am laughing and I can hear John and Red laughing too, a low ICU type of a laugh but a laugh all the same and, when I let Andrea go, it's like I have stepped into another world and this one is bright and clear and brand new and I breathe it in and draw it around me like Sofia's gorgeous silken wrap.

'There's a way to go yet,' warns the doctor, his face puckering with concern. He takes a step back from me, perhaps anxious at the prospect of me hugging him next. 'Her breathing is still a little laboured and I'm going to give her some extra oxygen with the nasal cannula for a while. But' — he releases a cautious smile on to his face — 'she's off the ventilator and that really can be seen as a marked improvement.'

A marked improvement. I feel a rush of emotions, charging towards me like a victory march. One of them is pride. I swell with it. Ellen is making a *marked* improvement. She's not even supposed to be born yet and already this tiny dot in the incubator beside me has made such a vivid impression on me. On all of us. It's like she's always been here and I can't remember the world before she arrived.

58

'I have a present for you,' says Declan, marching into the ward, doing his best to ignore the adoring stares of the nurses and the patients and even some of the doctors. I never get used to people looking at my father like this. To me, he is just Declan. Always in need of a haircut. Always looking around him like he's lost something. An old soak. Faded and worn, like a favourite pair of jeans that you can't part with. Although there is something different about him now. He seems sharper somehow, the blurred edges of him in focus. Filly calls it the Red Butler syndrome.

'What is it?' I ask, a little warily. Over the years, Declan has brought me all kinds of presents from various film locations around the world. Often clothes that were too big or too small for me or books in languages I didn't understand. Once, a frog that he smuggled in an inside pocket of his coat all the way from Florida. I called him Hoppy and he lasted for two days before succumbing to the crippling cold of an Irish November.

'It's that house you were going to rent. The one in Clontarf. With the office space and the garden.' He presses a sheaf of papers into my hands. 'Aren't you going to say something?' he prompts me.

The ward is filled with the studious sound of

people pretending not to listen to this conversation.

I lean towards him. 'You can't buy me a *house*,' I finally say.

'Why not? It's what you need, isn't it? Now that Ellen is here.' He beams, delighted with himself.

'But . . . but . . . that's just crazy. It must have cost you a fortune. It's the worst possible time to buy property. That's why I was going to rent it.'

Declan sighs and sits on the edge of the bed. 'It's just money, Scarlett,' he says. 'Anyway, I got paid last month for a film I did back in the eighties. They forgot to pay me and I never noticed until they called me a few weeks ago.'

'What film?'

'What's this it's called again?' Declan frowns and pushes a clump of hair behind his ear. 'The one where I play the barber . . . '

'*Cutting Edge*,' I tell him.

'That's the one.' He slaps his knee and looks delighted with himself. 'Anyway, apparently it did really well and they've paid me a fortune for it and what am I going to do with all that money? Haven't I got everything I need?' He smiles at me and looks about him. 'How's Ellen, by the way?'

'Brilliant,' I say, and now my smile is wider than his. 'They're taking her off the oxygen completely today.'

'What a trooper, eh?' says Declan, and I nod, agreeing with him completely.

'But, Dad, look, I can't accept this,' I say, nodding at the paperwork in my hands. 'This is not a present. It's a house. You can't just *give* someone a house.'

'I can. I can do whatever I bloody well like,' says Declan, setting his face into the expression that Maureen calls bullish. 'Besides, it's not a house. It's a home. And it's not just for you. It's for Ellen too. And I got it for a song, if you must know. My negotiating skills are legendary. You know that.'

The only reason his negotiating skills are legendary is because of how desperate they are. How awful. We're talking about the man who bid against himself in an auction for a horrendous painting of a nude because he wanted to make sure he got it. Declan said it reminded him of Maureen, a remark that caused her to ignore him throughout an entire, bleak winter. It could have been a lot of things: the downward ski slope of the nude's breasts, or perhaps her sagging dimpled bottom, or the drooping spare tyre of mottled flesh that spilled down either side of the model's belly. Declan said it was her eyes that attracted him, and in fairness they *were* her best feature. It was just difficult to notice them, with all the other stuff going on. The painting has long since been consigned to the attic. It's still there, in a black plastic bin liner, shrouded in cobwebs, as if even the spiders can't bring themselves to look at it.

'Anyway,' says Declan, taking the papers from me and pushing them deep into the bag I am packing, 'it's done now and that's an end to it.'

'But why?' I ask. 'Why have you bought me a house?' I am not someone who gets a house for free. It seems irresponsible. Feckless.

Declan begins to pack my toiletries away and I let him, even though I know I will unpack and repack them after he leaves. 'You've always been so independent,' he says, not looking at me. 'You've never asked for anything.'

'That's because I had everything,' I remind him. 'There was nothing to ask for.'

'Well . . . ' He shrugs his shoulders and I think he might be thinking about the time he was hauled up to the headmistress's office at my primary school to discuss arts and crafts payments, which were in arrears by years and ran into a tidy four-figure sum. He doesn't speak for a while. Then he says, 'Look, Scarlett,' and he puts his hands on my shoulders and the weight of them is warm and reassuring, like beans on toast.

'This is something I can do for you. And Ellen. Something practical.' He says the word like he's been practising it. 'Let me do this thing for you both. This one thing. After that, I'll never do anything again. I promise.'

'You could have just bought Ellen a rattle,' I say, struggling against the temptation of a house with an office space and a garden.

'Oh, I did,' he says, reaching for an enormous plastic bag that looks like it could line a skip. 'I nearly forgot.'

Inside the bag are at least twenty rattles, about ten soft-cloth books, four teddy bears and two cot mobiles.

'One of the mobiles is for the cot I bought. I got George to set it up in your room. At Tara.

For when the pair of you come to visit us.'

I keep my head down, keep staring into the bag where the primary colours of the toys meld together into a lump of viscous Plasticine.

'Jesus, Scarlet, you're not crying, are you? Maureen will kill me if she hears I made you cry.'

I shake my head, still not trusting myself to speak.

'Don't worry, Declan, she's supposed to cry today — it's day three and her hormones are up in arms.'

I look up and smile through my tears. It's Filly, an open book in one hand (*Your Premature Goddaughter*) and a plastic bag in the other with sausage rolls (for her) and a jar of Marmite and lemon curd (for me).

'I brought poppy-seed rolls too,' she says, shaking the bag at me. 'I'll make you a Marmite and lemon-curd sandwich, OK?'

I nod, even though I can't think of anything more disgusting. Marmite and lemon curd? What was I thinking?

She settles herself as best she can on the edge of the bed. It is difficult for her, on account of the net tulle she wears beneath her skirt. It matches her hair, which is now a bright tangerine. With her emerald-green top and her white legs, she looks like a tiny Irish flag.

'I got you some disposable knickers too,' she says, throwing a sack of them on the bed.

'Eh, thanks, Filly,' I say, shovelling the sack under the bed.

'Your vagina *is* in tatters, isn't it?'

'Well . . . yes, I suppose you could say that.'

'So you can just throw these ones away after you're finished with them. Handy, aren't they?'

I think about this for a moment. 'Wait till Brendan hears about knickers that you throw away.'

'I haven't told him about them,' Filly says darkly. 'Obviously.'

'You've dyed your hair,' I say. I want to talk about something other than flittered vaginas and disposable knickers. 'It's lovely.'

'I only had it pink for the wedding,' she explains, offering Declan one of the five sausage rolls in the bag. 'It didn't seem right to keep it that colour after everything that happened.'

For the first time, I think about the disaster that was Sofia Marzoni's wedding day. I smile at the image in my head. And then I start to laugh.

Filly looks at Declan. 'It's the hormones,' she explains. 'It can go either way.'

Declan nods and reefs himself off the chair. He's not a keen conversationalist when it comes to what he terms 'women's bits and bobs'.

'I'll go and get coffees,' he says, backing away. 'To go with your . . . eh . . . sausage rolls and the . . . Marmite and curd. OK?' And he leaves before either of us can say anything.

'So,' I say, 'what's been going on?'

'Loads,' says Filly, starting on her third sausage roll, although she is slowing now and I can tell she's having second thoughts about the fourth. 'After Sofia and Hailey *came out* . . . ' she pauses to heighten the drama of it all

' . . . there was this big tête-a-tête with Valentino in the sacristy.'

'Was there shouting?'

'Not so much. But there was a crash at one stage.'

'Did Valentino throw something?'

'No, but Hailey thought he might so she picked up the decanter of altar wine, just to get it out of harm's way, and she dropped it on the floor.'

'That was the crash?'

'Yes,' Filly admits, 'but we didn't know that at the time. So then Angelo, Alessandro and Augusto sort of *stormed* the sacristy. You know how those boys love a good fisticuffs.' Filly looks at me and I nod quickly so she'll get back to the story. 'And they're all in there for about twenty minutes and I can't hear a lot, just muffled voices and occasional roars and a chair breaking.'

'Someone broke a chair?'

'It was Angelo, actually,' says Filly, looking into the bag and deciding against the last sausage roll. 'You know how big that fella is. And the chair had a loose leg anyway. So the whole thing sort of collapsed underneath him and he ended up on the floor. But the funny thing was,' says Filly, who can always be relied on to find the funny thing in any scenario, 'he was still in the seat part of the chair. Stuck. It took the lot of them to pull him out of it.'

This could be true. Angelo has one of those bottoms that could accommodate two people, it's that wide.

'Anyway, with the collapsing chair and the

stuck bottom,' Filly goes on, 'everyone just starts laughing. I can hear them through the door. Not that I'm eavesdropping, mind.' She looks at me in a way that suggests that not only was she eavesdropping but she was probably doing it with a glass chalice pressed up against the door of the sacristy. 'So anyway, they're laughing and then talking in Italian, all of them together, even Hailey, I think, and then I hear the sound of weeping and, by this stage, I can't bear it any longer so I push the door open and there they are in a big group hug, all weeping and wailing and talking Italian and laughing, with the broken glass and the spilled wine and the bits of chair lying around them. It was a mess, Scarlett. You would have hated it, so you would.'

'Who was crying?' I ask, leaning forward.

'They were all at it,' says Filly, surprised I even had to ask the question. 'All the Marzonis, I mean. Not Hailey, obviously. She was trying to find a brush and pan to sweep up the worst of the glass.'

I nod and smile. 'What happened then?' I ask, lying back against the pillows, suddenly tired with all the drama.

'Not a lot, actually,' Filly admits, disappointed. 'Valentino made an announcement from the altar but it was in Italian so I haven't got a clue what that was about. Then there was a lot of hugging and crying and some wailing from Isabella. You know how she can wail.'

I nod my head, remembering the wailing of Isabella Marzoni.

'And then they all went to the castle and had a

party and lived happily ever after,' finishes Filly, reaching for the bag again and deciding to put the last sausage roll out of its misery.

'What?'

'Well, you know the way Valentino hates anything to go to waste.'

This is true. We're talking about the man who has had the same holy water in the font in the hallway of his house for so long there are bits of moss in it. And possibly frogspawn.

'And what about Sofia?' I ask. 'And Hailey? And the whole homosexual thing?'

'The Marzonis seem ok with it. Even Valentino. Hailey and Sofia make such a lovely couple. I always thought that. Even before I knew.' I nod. So did I.

Filly crumples the bag into a ball in her hand and lobs it towards the bin. It misses and lands on the floor. She looks at me when I say nothing.

'Are you tired?'

'No.'

'Have you been getting any sleep?'

'No less than usual.'

'Do you need help packing?'

'No, thanks. I just need to repack my toiletry bag and I'm ready to go.'

I don't want to leave the hospital. Not without Ellen. But these are the rules. The nurses press two packets of industrial-strength Ponstin into my hand (for the flittered vagina) and smile at me and tell me there's no room at the inn. They do it in their lovely, gentle way but it doesn't change the fact that I have to go home without Ellen. They show me how to use the breast pump; they thank me for the chocolates and wine; they wave goodbye and I walk with my head down, not able to bear the pitying looks of the other mothers, who sit on chairs at their bedsides with their babies cradled in the crooks of their arms, like extensions of themselves.

Filly walks beside me, carrying Sofia's silken wrap, which is now a paler shade of pink than before and stiff with starch after a vigorous seeing-to in the hospital laundry. I stop off at Ellen's room on the way.

'I'll see you soon,' I whisper in at her. This sounds better than goodbye. 'I'll be back in the morning. First thing,' I promise her, and she opens her eyes and smiles at me.

'Probably a bit of wind,' says a student nurse whose job seems to be to escort me off the premises.

I nod and turn away but I keep the memory of the smile tucked carefully inside me and I take it out many times over the course of that first night and the many nights after that until it is creased and worn, like an old photograph that you fold inside a wallet.

59

Ellen is due in five weeks. She is seven weeks old. She weighs four pounds three ounces. She is a genius. She can do so many amazing things. Like maintain her own body temperature. Like breathe on her own, without any assistance. She can suck now. My milk spills down her chin. I hear the gulp of it down her throat. She likes to hold on to the little finger of my right hand when she's feeding. She is as pink as Sofia's wedding day. She loves it when I blow gently on her toes. She spreads them like fingers when I do it. This is her way of saying, 'Do it again.' She likes being held against the warm skin of my chest with my shirt buttoned up around her. This is called kangaroo care, the nurses tell me. I like the idea of this. Ellen in my pouch. She likes Winnie the Pooh stories and her favourite character so far is Eyeore, despite his pessimistic disposition.

Andrea still comes to visit her but Ellen is no longer a resident on her ward. I notice that her visits are longer when John is there. They have discovered a shared interest in ancient coins and have taken to bringing in some of their rarer specimens to show each other.

'I found this one when I was on that archaeological dig I was telling you about.' He passes her the dull bronze coin. It's nearly as big as a saucer.

Andrea holds the coin in her hands and gazes

at it. 'They let you *keep* it?' she whispers.

John nods. 'They said it was worthless.'

They shake their heads slowly in tandem at the cruelty of the word.

'It's beautiful, John,' says Andrea, her eyes shining.

'I know,' says John, looking at Andrea.

When I come in, Andrea concentrates on her clipboard and John returns to his notes. I take them out of his hands.

'What are you doing?'

'Just turning them the right way round,' I tell him. 'You were reading them upside down.'

John opens his mouth to say something. He and Andrea turn matching shades of crimson. He closes his mouth and I smile at him.

Ellen is still on the fourth floor but in a ward they call a 'step-down' area, where there are less machines. A kind of ICU *Lite*.

I develop a routine of sorts. My days are spent in ICU Lite with Ellen. At night, I alternate between houses, like a nomad with an overnight bag instead of a herd. Tara is too far away from the hospital. Too far away from Ellen.

Sometimes I stay with Filly and Brendan, where Brendan tempts me with all manner of meats and feeds my clothes into the washing machine. Even the clean ones.

Sometimes I stay with Bryan. Sometimes Cáit is there. She *does* look a little like Sandra Bullock.

I don't stay at John's flat. But I see him a lot. At the hospital mostly. We talk to each other, over the top of Ellen's incubator. We smile at each other, like we've just met and we know we're going to get along.

On Thursdays, I stay at Sofia's new house, which Valentino bought her as a wedding gift. With the recent downturn in the housing market, he will make a loss on it if he sells it now. At least, that's what he tells Sofia. Hailey is always there when I go over. She hasn't moved in but there is a shelf in the bathroom where she keeps her toothbrush and flannel. She is the only woman I know who has a flannel.

Red lives there too. Just for a little while. Because he gave up his flat two days before the irreparable breakdown of the original plan — the one where he and Sofia live together as man and wife for six months until Sofia finds him in bed with some gamine young blonde — he has had to throw himself at the mercy of one Sofia Marzoni, who, harbouring the softest of soft spots for him, provides him with the comfort of one of her two spare rooms while he flat-hunts. They rub along well together, this unlikely trio. Red is in charge of the laundry — turns out he has somewhat of a gift for getting red wine out of white jeans and ironing the complicated, fussy blouses favoured by Hailey. Sofia cooks. Pasta mostly. She can make a tomato sauce in two minutes and thirty-five seconds. She asked me to time her and I did, being an obedient kind of houseguest. Hailey is in charge of cleaning, although I have noticed that she doesn't hoover under the beds or move the army of china ornaments Sofia collects from the top of the sideboard when she dusts. She tidies more than cleans. She is a great fan of the humble spider plant and every time I go there she has snuck another one in. Somewhere unobtrusive so they go unnoticed until one day you look around and they're everywhere: on top of the toilet cisterns; lining the kitchen windowsill; spilling from the bookcase; sprawled on bedside lockers; and one hanging precariously from a bracket — put up by Red — in the hall. Red is not as good at DIY as he is at laundry.

The strange thing is that I don't feel like I have nowhere to call home. I feel like I have lots of places to call home. The place that is in fact home is ready for me but I don't want to move in yet. Not without Ellen.

I pretend not to notice the growing excitement I feel on Thursdays. The feeling that used to start on Thursday afternoons, then Thursday mornings, but now I find the feeling inside me as early as Wednesday evenings. It is like butterflies taking flight, this feeling. It is like Ellen kicking me in the early days. Letting me know she was there.

It feels wrong to feel this feeling when your daughter is in the ICU, even if it is the ICU Lite. Even when she is exceeding everybody's expectations. Even when the sternest of the doctors smiles at her. Like he's trying not to smile.

On Thursday nights, I find myself ducking into the bathroom on the ground floor of the hospital, where there is a well-lit mirror, to clean my face and apply a small amount of make-up.

Small enough so it looks like it's left over from this morning.

I dab perfume behind my ears. I brush my teeth and my gums and my tongue. Then I floss. I look in the mirror and smile. A wry smile. A charming smile. A warm smile. A friendly smile. I stop when I realise I am practising my smiles.

I tell myself that this is freshening up. Maureen would call it dolling yourself up. Filly would call it getting yourself ready for Red Butler.

★ ★ ★

This Thursday night is different from all the other nights. Because of tomorrow really. Tomorrow, the three of us will meet at the hospital to get the results of the DNA paternity test we took on Monday. I had to take the test too even though, with her black hair and green eyes and worried face, she is like a piece that is cut out of me. Swabs from the inside of each of our cheeks. Even Ellen's, although it took ages on account of the fact that she pursed her lips together like she was zipping them shut. Like she doesn't want to know.

Tomorrow is different for another reason too. Tomorrow, when I leave the hospital, I won't be on my own. Ellen will be with me. We are moving into our own home. There is nothing in the house apart from a double bed — donated by John from his spare room — and the Moses basket that I ordered months ago. The darling one with the soft orange tulle arranged in folds around it, like a tepee. And a steriliser. Two of them actually. Declan got a *consignment* of them from his friend Harry for 'half nothing', he says, but he won't disclose the price, which means that he paid at least twice as much as he should for them.

So tomorrow is not going to be your common-or-garden Friday. Maureen is calling it Freedom Friday but I've grown used to this nomadic way of life and the not knowing. I've felt like a part of something, like everybody has wrapped themselves around me and Ellen. Especially Red. Tomorrow will change all that.

It's only when I grow cold that I realise I'm standing outside Sofia's garden gate, not moving. I check the house to see if anyone has noticed me but the curtains are drawn. I take a deep breath, set my shoulders, replace my worried look with a half-smile, which is the best I can do in the circumstances, and move into the garden towards the front door.

★ ★ ★

We start off by pretending that this is just another Thursday night. The sixth in the series. But already it's different as soon as I walk in the door. For a start, I smell burning.

'Is it that time already?' Red shouts from the kitchen. 'I'm trying to make dinner but . . . I got a bit behind.'

Every inch of every counter is taken up with bowls and cutlery and plates and saucepans and baking trays. There is a recipe book open on the counter, a puddle of milk spilled on it from a carton that lies on its side with no lid. Red's hands are covered in flour and there is some caked on the left cheek of his face. There is also some in his hair, as if he has run his hands through it. Steam rises from a sauce that is bubbling furiously on the hob. According to the recipe, this sauce is supposed to be *simmering*. I can tell, without having to stir it, that a lot of it is stuck to the bottom of the saucepan. There is salad in a bag. And pasta, pulpy and cold, in a colander in the sink.

'I don't know what time it is,' I tell him, hardly aware of a note of pride in my voice.

He stops what he is doing — worrying at the sauce with a wooden spoon — and looks at me. 'You don't know what time it is?'

'No,' I say, smiling now. 'I took my watch off when Ellen was born and I haven't been able to find it since.'

'And you haven't bought a new one?'

I shake my head.

'Jesus,' is all he has time to say. He's at the oven now, opening the door. Black smoke rushes from it. This is the source of the burning smell. He lifts out a cake of what might once have been tomato and fennel bread, although it is difficult to make it out through the charred and blackened crust.

'Did you bake bread?' I ask.

'I don't think it's deserving of that title any more, do you?' says Red, picking up the hard lump of burnt dough. He drops it again immediately, blowing on his hand. I can tell that he would curse out loud and maybe kick a kitchen appliance if I were not here.

I move towards him and take his hand and lead him to the sink. 'I'm just going to run it under the cold tap,' I say, trying to ignore the electrical current that throbs around my body.

The cold water helps. I douse both our hands as if we are on fire. He is inches away from me. I examine his fingers. 'Just seeing if you've any blisters,' I manage. His fingers are long and slender. There are no blisters.

'Eh, I think they're fine,' Red says finally, and he has to pull his hand out of my grasp. 'Christ, I'm so sorry about dinner. It's a bloody disaster.'

I can't believe he's thinking about dinner. Right now. When all I can think about is the soft curve of his mouth and the hollow at the base of his throat that I kissed what feels like a hundred years ago. I want to do it again. He's still talking about dinner. 'I mean, it's fecking macaroni and cheese, for God's sake. The recipe says it's foolproof. And look at the state of the sauce. It's lumpier than the semolina I made for dessert, and that semolina is *really* lumpy. And I've overcooked the pasta. I mean, who does that?'

Forlorn. That's the word for him. It makes me smile, this overgrown man with the flour and the smoke and the disappointment. I take off my coat and roll up my sleeves.

'Right,' I say in my best wedding-planner voice, although the kitchen is such a mess it's difficult to know where to begin. 'Is it the four of us for dinner?'

'Yes,' he says, waving a hand towards the

548

kitchen table, where he has set the table. Properly set it, I mean, with linen napkins and crystal wine glasses and long, narrow candles, already lit.

'Sofia and Hailey are upstairs,' he says. 'Practising being lesbians, according to Sofia.' We take a moment to digest this piece of information. 'They said they'd be down for dinner at half seven.'

'Right,' I say, lifting Red's Mickey Mouse watch off the counter and shaking flour off it. 'We have twenty minutes.' I take the batteries out of the smoke alarm and open the kitchen window to allow the smoke to disperse.

The first thing I rescue is the sauce. I pour it into another saucepan through a sieve, which catches all the lumps and the burnt bits, leaving us with a gorgeously creamy cheese sauce, which I show to Red. 'You see?' I ask him. 'It's actually perfect. Just needed a bit of editing.'

'What about the bread?' he asks, and when he looks at me, I almost believe I can rescue the smoking, blackened remains of the loaf.

'We-ell . . . ' I begin, hating to disappoint him when he's gone to so much trouble. I take to it with a knife and, when I'm finished with it, it's the size of a scone. I cut it in two and hand the bigger half to him. The pieces are small enough to be eaten in one go. We chew in silence. We chew for a long time. It's chewy. Very chewy. Especially the middle bit, which may still be dough.

'What do you think?' he asks. He looks like Ellen when he is worried. I take an enormous drink of water, to try and wash the dough down.

'It's delicious,' I tell him, when I am finally able to prise my teeth apart.

'Well, it's nicer than the first loaf anyway,' he admits, nodding to the brown bin, where I see the remains of his original efforts. Somehow, I manage to keep my face straight.

'OK,' I say, 'you put on some more pasta and I'll do the salad.'

We work in silence that could be called companionable.

★   ★   ★

After dinner, Red and I watch *Brothers and Sisters*, which I pretend to hate. We take photographs of Blue and Al Pacino, who sit on an armchair that we call 'their' armchair. We sit in our usual positions: me on the couch with my legs curled underneath me; Red cross-legged on the floor with his back against the couch. Close enough to touch. We don't touch. We are careful with each other. We talk about our favourite bits of Ellen. Her eyes, Red says, and we don't talk about the fact that they are green. Like his. Like mine.

Her nose, I say, which is a cute button nose with not an ounce of John's nose about it.

'I don't think Kitty should marry Robert right in the middle of the presidential campaign. He's way too distracted,' says Red, nodding at the telly.

'Sorry?' I say, turning my head away from the window, where I had been watching leaves loosen their grip on the boughs of a tree in the front garden and begin to fall away. In spite of the Indian summer we have enjoyed, the season is finally packing up. Getting ready to leave.

'Are you thinking about tomorrow?' Red asks.

'Yes,' I admit.

'It's OK,' he says, turning off the telly. 'So was I.'

'What about Kitty and Robert? And the campaign?'

'Distraction,' he says, and I nod.

Without the telly on, the room seems unnaturally quiet.

Finally, Red opens his mouth to speak. 'You know,' he says, 'I really hope Ellen is mine.'

I nod. I know this. I see it in the way he holds her, carefully, like she's the chalice John found during his brief dig in Brazil that turned out to be a priceless bit of history that archaeologists have been digging for forever.

It's in the tiny beanbags he makes for her and arranges about her body when she is asleep. 'I read about it in a book,' he explains when I ask him about it. 'It's supposed to simulate the comfort of the womb. It'll make her feel more at home.' The nurses nod and smile at him. So does John, though he tries hard not to. There's just nothing else to be done with him.

'You know,' I say, leaning forward, 'it's more likely that John is the father.' I explain about the mathematical equation that John has formulated to work out the odds.

Red nods slowly. 'I suppose a father should be good at maths. Otherwise, you've no one to ask

551

for help with, like, fractions and . . . and
. . . what's that one with the sine and the cosine
and all that?'

'Trigonometry,' I say.

'Yeah, I'd say John knows all about trigonometry.'

'He does,' I say, 'but, to be honest, Red,
stuff like that doesn't really matter. I mean,
look at me — my dad wouldn't know a maths
theorem from a hole in the ground and it
never bothered me.'

'Yeah, but you were probably great at maths,
weren't you?'

Now doesn't seem like the right time to tell
Red about the A I got in honours maths in the
Leaving Cert. I shake my head. I don't know
why we're talking about maths.

I say goodnight and head for the door, pausing
when I get there, my hand stopped in mid-reach
for the handle. I turn back to him. 'Red?' I
begin.

He is stretched out on the floor with Al Pacino
beside him, occasionally reaching up to lick his
face or his hand. Red's hair could do with a cut.
Even a good brush. There are dog hairs all over
his jumper. And cheese sauce. There are dark
circles under his eyes. And he could do with a
shave. The room smells like dog. I take it all in. I
don't want to forget any of it. This easy
companionship that we have shared. This
sprawling on the floor in Sofia's front room on a
Thursday night. Because from tomorrow, everything will change. From tomorrow, nothing will
ever be the same again.

He looks up at me and smiles his long, lazy smile. 'Yes?'

'I just wanted to say thank you. I never said thank you.'

'For what?' he asks, gently pushing Al Pacino's legs off his chest and sitting up.

'For Ellen. For delivering Ellen.'

'You did all the work,' he tells me.

'You were so calm,' I tell him.

'I didn't feel calm.'

'You were, though.'

'When I think about it, it feels like the best and worst moment of my life.'

I nod. I know exactly what he means.

'When she finally came out and I held her in my two hands, even though she would have fitted into one. I was terrified. That I would drop her. Or hurt her.'

'You didn't,' I remind him.

'She was so small. And still. For a moment, I thought . . . '

'I know,' I say, not wanting him to finish the sentence.

'And I could see the pulse of the cord between you and her. It was so strong. I've never seen anything like it. It made me think of my own mother. I was nearly three when she died and I don't remember anything about her. Not a single thing.' He looks up at me, smiling to take the melancholy out of the words.

'I'm sure she loved you very much,' I tell him. And I *am* sure about this. He is an easy man to love.

'My father left her, you know,' he tells me, not

quite looking at me. 'When she was pregnant with me.' There is an edge to his voice now and he concentrates on petting Al Pacino.

'Did you ever try to find him?' I ask, still standing at the door, not sure whether to come back into the room and sit down.

'No.' he says, and I know there are other things he could say but he closes his mouth tightly against the words.

'Do you think you ever will?'

'No.' He stands up then, shaking his jumper in an attempt to rid it of Al Pacino's pelt. 'I'm afraid to,' he says then. It sounds like a confession, the way he says it.

'What do you mean?'

'I mean, I'm afraid that I'll find out I'm just like him. I don't want to be like a man like that. A man who can abandon his family when they need him the most.'

'But you're nothing like that,' I tell him, moving back inside the room. I am stung by this fear of his. It is so unfounded.

'How do you know?'

'You're still here, aren't you?' I say, taking a step towards him. 'After everything that's happened. You're still here.'

I feel like I'm balancing on the edge of a brave new world. I take a breath and step out and into it.

I don't decide to kiss him. I don't ask him if I can. I just do it. Without thinking about it. Without asking permission.

I smell sweet fruit. Maybe berries. When I kiss him, I remember his mouth and the way it fits on mine, like the click of a key in a lock. He is like a song that I thought I'd forgotten but, now that I'm singing it, I'm surprised to find I know all the words. The kiss feels like our first one. It is different from before. This one is warm and salty and gentle. It is like a lullaby. You could fall asleep to a kiss like this. I pull away.

'You're not my type at all,' I tell him like we're in the middle of an argument.

'And you're not mine,' he says and we're kissing again, harder now, moving about the room, glancing off various pieces of furniture. He hitches me onto his hips and I wrap my legs about his waist and hold on tight. His hands are in my hair and his breath is hot against my ear.

'I love you.' The words are up and out before I can do anything about them. I bury my face in his neck and bite him, hoping that maybe he didn't hear me.

But he lifts his head and looks at me. He props me on top of the sideboard. One of Sofia's china dogs teeters at the edge before it falls and shatters against the floorboards. Neither of us notice.

'Did you say you love me?' he asks. He never takes his eyes off mine.

'Eh, yes, as a matter of fact I did,' I say, trying to catch my breath and regain some composure.

'Oh,' he says and I can't tell what he's thinking and I feel a hot burn of embarrassment travelling up my face and I'm trying to work out a way to get back to where we were before I had to go and ruin everything.

'I'm glad.'

'You're glad?'

'I am,' he says and now he's smiling at me in that gorgeous way he has, with his whole body. The whole lot of him is smiling.

'I think I've loved you for ages,' he tells me, lifting me off the sideboard and kissing me again. The soft scratch of his stubble against my face is almost more than I can bear. He steps over the broken pieces of the china dog and lowers me onto the couch. Now he's unbuttoning my shirt, taking his time, concentrating on each button. I have to tuck my hands underneath my back and force myself not to help.

'Why didn't you say anything?' I ask. He stops unbuttoning and looks up at me. I curse my curiosity.

'I . . . I just thought it seemed a bit frivolous, what with Ellen and the . . . the whole situation.'

'It's not because you've seen my vagina in flitters, is it?' I've worried about this, even though I know it seems like a trivial thing to worry about when there are other, more important things to focus on. Still. I worried about it anyway.

I feel Red shaking under my hands. He is laughing. Or trying not to laugh. I love the way he laughs. He laughs with his whole body.

'Is it?' I ask again. I have to know.

'Christ, no,' he says. 'And to be honest, I wasn't thinking about your vagina and whether it was in flitters or not. I was just trying to make sure that you were OK. That Ellen was OK.'

'Let's go to bed,' I say, as if this is something I've said a hundred times before.

'Are you sure?' Red asks. 'What about your . . . eh . . . vagina? Is it . . . ?'

'Still in flitters?' I finish for him.

'Well . . . ' he says, hesitating. 'Yes. I suppose that's something I should know about.'

'No.'

'No, it's not in flitters or no, it's not something I should know about?'

'No,' I say again. 'It's not in flitters.'

'OK, then,' he says. 'Good.'

He takes my hand and leads me up the stairs to his room. I step over the newspapers that lie on the floor around the bed. Bits of newspapers, not in any order. And not even that day's newspapers. I step over a week's worth of clothes that lie where they have been dropped. I step over the loose change that has slipped from pockets and lies in precarious patterns all around the floor.

'Kiss me again,' I say, pulling him down to me by his ears, the tips of which poke out ever so slightly from the thicket of his hair.

'Bossy, aren't you?' he says.

'You have no idea,' I tell him.

Afterwards, we lie tucked around each other, like crescent moons. There are so many reasons why I shouldn't be able to go to sleep. The brightness, for one. A shaft of moonlight falls through the window where we have forgotten to pull the curtains.

Blue and Al Pacino, for another. They insist on sleeping at the bottom of the bed, even though they have perfectly comfortable baskets down-stairs in the kitchen, beside the radiator. I'm used to Blue being in my bed. But a dog? I am not the type of person who sleeps in the same room as a dog, never mind the same bed. Except it seems I am. Now.

The noise of the television, blaring downstairs. Sofia and Hailey are big horror-film fans and through the walls and the doors and the floor come the muffled shrieks and screams of unsuspecting teenagers whose cars and jeeps and vans and mopeds break down in various, isolated, stretches of countryside.

And of course tomorrow. The result. And what that will mean. For all of us.

But since it's this Thursday and not any other Thursday and this Thursday is different from all the other Thursdays for so many different reasons, something strange happens. I fall asleep, with Red holding one hand, Al Pacino occasionally reaching up to lick the other and Blue draped in his long-legged way across my legs. I sleep like a normal person. Unconsciously. Peacefully. Without having to count sheep or any other farm animal. I don't wake up at four o'clock in the morning. I sleep all the way through. All the way through till morning.

60

A Year Later

'GoodmorningsorryI'mlate,' says Filly, setting her apology on my desk: two banana milkshakes, a packet of cheese and onion Hunky Dorys (for her), and a flapjack (for me).

I look at my watch. 'You're not late,' I say.

'I am,' she says. 'Four minutes and thirty-four seconds late, actually.'

'You're becoming me,' I tell her.

'I know,' she says, making a face. 'I'm even thinking about getting a Filofax.'

'Jesus.'

'I know.'

She looks dejected at the prospect and I decide to rescue her. 'Have you started making colour-coded to-do lists and then ticking off each item as you complete them?' I ask her.

'Christ, no,' says Filly, affronted by the idea.

'Well, you're grand, then. You've a way to go yet.'

Filly sits down and opens her crisps in relief. 'We're all set for this afternoon, aren't we?'

'Yes,' I say, opening a file on my laptop. 'Cake, flowers, decorations, music, seating plan, gifts, guests, outfits . . . ' I think that's everything.

'I can't believe it's been a year,' says Filly, and, without saying anything, we both get up from our chairs and move to the window, pressing our noses against it, as we always do.

Down in the garden she is crawling through the flowerbed, stopping every so often to pick the petals from the rosebush, which is nearly bare now. There is muck under her tiny pink fingernails. There are leaves in her dark hair. She has lost a shoe. Blue and Al Pacino flag her on both sides. Her sentries. She uses the long hair on Al Pacino's strong body to pull herself into a standing position. She lets go and falls down, landing on her nappy bum and narrowly missing Blue's head. Blue doesn't hiss at her. He doesn't even show her the points of his claws. Instead, he pushes his head under her pudgy hand so she can pet him, which she does.

'What time is the party?' Filly asks.

'Four o'clock,' I tell her.

'I suppose we should do a bit of work on the Chiara Marzoni wedding, then?' sighs Filly.

I nod my head. Slowly. 'I suppose we should.'

'Scarlett?' Red's voice travels up the stairs.

'Yes?'

'You haven't seen Ellen's other shoe, have you? The pink one with the grey elephants?'

'It might be under our bed. In your trainer. She was rooting there this morning.'

He takes the stairs two at a time and for a moment I consider making some excuse so I can poke my head out of the office and drink him in like a tonic. But I don't need to. His head appears round the door.

'Got it,' he says to me. 'Thanks.' He stands there, looking at me, and I drink him in like a tonic.

His hair could do with a cut. And his face could do with a shave. There is a hole in his brown jumper, which has a reindeer's face on it, despite the fact that it is only August. His socks don't match and look like they should have been binned two years ago. Then he smiles and it's like the sun has come out after a long, dark winter and Filly and I sit there, grinning foolishly back at him. We know we look like a pair of eejits but we just can't help ourselves. It's official. Red Butler has infected us.

'We're going to the park. See you later,' he says, turning and moving away.

'OK,' I say. 'Just remember the party's at four.'

'Don't worry, I've remembered to put my watch on and I've totally got the hang of the o'clocks and the half pasts, haven't I, Filly?'

'Oh, he has indeed, Scarlett,' Filly says, nodding her head. 'Next week, we're starting on the quarter tos and pasts, and after that he'll be able to get a job with the Talking Clock, he'll be such a pro.

'How come you're minding Ellen today anyway?' asks Filly. 'I thought John took her on Thursdays.'

'He does but he had to go to a meeting today so he asked me to swap my Tuesday for his Thursday.'

I look at my rota, admiring it. We all have a day. Mine is Monday, Red on Tuesday, Phyllis and George on Wednesday, John on Thursday and Declan and Maureen (with some assistance from Bryan when he can) on Fridays. We all get a go of her.

For the rest of the morning we concentrate on Chiara Marzoni. She's not quite as demanding as Sofia but the difference is so slight it's barely there. Her wedding animal of choice is the humble llama. Two of them. A pair. The problem is Alfonso. The male. He's a bit, well . . . frisky. Insists on riding the night and daylights out of Imelda (the female) and, because she's such a docile old thing, she just stands there and lets him at it. And it's not even llama mating season. I Googled it. And there's nothing more off-putting at a wedding — especially a Marzoni wedding — than a pair of llamas mounting each other in a carefully constructed pen in the centre of an elaborate boutique hotel foyer. Filly and I bite our pens down to the nibs in an effort to come up with a solution that won't involve neutering, which was Filly's original suggestion.

The phone rings. 'How's my favourite goddaughter, Scarlah?' Ellen is Sofia's only goddaughter but she still insists on calling her her favourite. Ellen has three godmothers and two godfathers. We got away with it because Padre Marco christened her and, even though he said he wouldn't do it for just anybody, he did it for Ellen. Sofia, Hailey and Filly, they're the godmothers.

'She's fine. Gone to the park with Red.'

'We're pickin' up the cake and the candles on our way over, OK?'

'She's only one. She only needs one candle,' I remind her.

'Oh,' says Sofia, disappointed.

'But it doesn't matter,' I rush in. 'Sure, she's only one, she's not going to know about the candle-age ratio just yet.' Although privately I think she might.

'Well, we got fifty of them,' says Sofia, 'but they're edible ones — marzipan, I think — so we could just light one and eat the rest, wha?' Her voice has the gravitas of someone who is discussing the benefits of antioxidants.

I smile down the phone at her. 'That's great. We'll see you and Hailey soon.'

I put the phone down and turn to Filly, who is not thinking about oversexed llamas, as she is supposed to be. She is thinking about balloons, as it turns out.

'I think we should start blowing up the balloons,' she says. 'I got a hundred of them. It'll take us ages.'

The doorbell rings and it's John and Andrea.

'I got the meeting postponed,' John explains before I ask.

'Just because it's Ellen's birthday?'

'Of course,' he says, looking at me like I'm crazy.

I smile and wave them inside. They are looking for chores to do, so I put them on balloon detail. When I go into the kitchen to check their progress, their faces are pure puce, their cheeks puffed out like bullfrogs, but they sit close together, smiling at each other over the swelling pink of the balloons, holding hands while they blow and then reluctantly pulling their hands away when it's time to tie the balloon closed.

563

John Smith has become a displayer of public affection. It suits him. He is into yoga now. And Pilates. He talks about things being *zen*. He and Andrea go on meditation weekends whenever Andrea is not on duty at the hospital. Once, when I called into his flat unexpectedly, he was wearing a kimono. Andrea was there too. In a kimono as well. A matching one. The flat has a familiar feel, like someplace I've visited before. Not like someplace I've ever really *lived* in.

Maureen and Declan arrive at half one and declare themselves to be 'perished with the hunger'. Well, Maureen does anyway. Today, she is full of the joys of spring and summer because her play (*Who's Your Daddy?*) has been picked by the Amateur Dramatic Society for their winter production. 'It's all-singing, all-dancing,' she says in an effort to take the sting out of the fact that it is about me and Ellen and John and Red. It is melodramatic, sensationalised and blown out of all proportion. Maureen calls it 'magnificent'.

By three thirty, everything is in place. Because everyone is already here, I decide to start the party now, even though the invitations said 4 p.m. *sharp*. We crowd into the garden, where I have set up trestle tables covered in pink crêpe paper, pink glitter and pink confetti. All different shades of pink so everything can be seen. The wine glasses are pink plastic goblets, and the plates are pink and bear the smiling face of Barbie. Scientist Barbie, who looks the same as all the other Barbies except she has her hair in a bun and wears thick-rimmed glasses. John and

Andrea have done a wonderful job with the balloons, although their faces look like they could use an icepack, each as brick-red as the other. The balloons — all pink — bob on long, pink ribbons, which are tied on to chairs, tables, the stems of the pink plastic glasses and the collars of the guests-of-honour, Al Pacino and Blue, groomed and glistening and waiting patiently for the birthday cake to be cut. Ellen sits like a pudding in her brand-new sandpit in the shape of Eyeore. Her thumb is covered in sand but she sucks it anyway.

Declan has brought his latest toy with him. A monstrosity of a camera that comes with a tripod. 'It says it should only take five minutes to assemble,' he says to me after he's been fiddling with it for half an hour. So far, he has managed to put two of the three tripod legs together and tear page two of the instructions, which he is holding, upside down, on his knee.

'Here, let me,' I say.

And it's true. It *does* take five minutes to set it up. Less, in fact. Four minutes and thirty-two seconds.

I pour everyone a glass of pink champagne and tell them to gather round the sandpit, where Ellen is making what Phyllis calls a pud-pie, a careful mix of water and sand.

The photograph hangs in the front room, over the fireplace. I look at it much more often than people are supposed to look at their family photographs. It makes me smile, this photograph. A little pink around the edges where the dipping sun has melted into the world.

'I can't see Ellen through the viewfinder,' roars Declan from underneath the great black cloth behind the camera. 'John, can you get into the sandpit with her and put her on your lap? He sets the timer for thirty seconds and gallops towards us, tripping up on Angelina Ballerina, who sprawls on the grass.

And so, when the camera's shutter opens and closes on the scene, Declan is on the ground, with his champagne flute held high in the air, not a drop spilled. Maureen reaches for him with her arms outstretched and a great smile on her face that may actually be a shriek because, for a moment, it looks like Declan is going to land right in the sandpit, beside — or on top of — Ellen and her father. Everyone sits on the grass, smiling. There's Phyllis, tucking in a corner of George's shirt that has escaped from the waistband of his corduroys. There's Sofia, pushing a rosebud behind Hailey's ear, while Hailey smiles her small, careful smile.

Al Pacino and Blue are in their usual position: Al standing with his head high and his shoulders back, and Blue sitting in the shelter of his friend's front paws, manicuring his claws on a piece of flint. Filly sits beside them, her polka-dot dress fanned out on the grass around her, like a game of Twister.

Red sits cross-legged on the grass in bare feet beside the sandpit. Ellen leans over to rub her nose with his, which is the thing they do. In the photograph, they haven't quite reached each other. They are on their way.

In the sandpit, Ellen stands on her father's

knees and plants a big wet kiss on his nose. John kisses her back, his hands wrapped round her waist. Loosely enough so she thinks she's standing on her own. Tightly enough so she'll never fall. His nose glistens with drool where Ellen has kissed him. But he doesn't wipe it off. I don't think he even notices. Instead, he wears the face he wore the time he came second in the All-Ireland Amateur Chess Championships.

Bryan and Elliot stretch out on the warm grass, smiling the smile of men whose mouths are crammed with chocolate Rice Krispie buns.

I stand behind this circle of people and I think about later.

Later, John, Red and I will put Ellen to bed. We all get a job: John baths her, I put her pyjamas on, and Red reads her one of the hundreds of stories he writes and illustrates just for her. The three of us will stand beside her cot and sing a version of Thin Lizzy's 'Sarah' to her until her eyelids flicker and fall, her thumb slips from her mouth and she begins to snore her tiny baby snores. Then John will walk round the corner to his apartment, where Andrea will be waiting for him in the 'her' part of their his-'n'-hers kimonos. And I will lie on the couch with Red Butler and he will read me whatever he has written today and I will tell him about the amorous llamas and how Ellen dances — even when she's strapped into her buggy — whenever I sing the theme song of *The Sopranos* to her and he will reach down and I will reach up and we'll be like two pieces of a jigsaw puzzle, lost for years and then found.

In the photograph, I stand behind this circle of people and I smile. I smile at this family.

My family.

This is not the idea I had for my life.

This has no bearing on any of the plans I made for myself.

No.

It's so much better than that.

Acknowledgements

The postman rang the doorbell this morning. I love when he does that because it means that he's got something that can't be delivered through the narrow mouth of the letterbox. He's got a *parcel*. It was the uncorrected proof of this book. The hefty weight of it in my hands. That gorgeous September smell of New Book. The book that I thought I'd never be able to write. Just because you write one doesn't necessarily mean you can write two, does it? But everyone thought that was a stupid thing to think. So I *parked* that, as the Americans say. And I *applied* myself, as my mother always advises. And I wrote it. And here it is in my hands, smiling up at me like a brand-new puppy. So today seems like a great day to thank everyone who helped me along the way.

A HUGE thank you to all the lovely readers of *Saving Grace* who wrote to me and emailed me and — one woman — who stopped me in my local SuperValu to say how much she *and her husband* enjoyed the book. Readers have no idea how much this means and how grateful I am for all your kindness. Thank you. Thank you so much.

Writing is a solitary profession. It's up there with lighthouse keeping and manning the complaints desk at an Irish beer festival. So it's lovely to have an excuse to get out of the house which I did a couple of times under the guise of 'research'. In this way, I met Caroline McCafferty, a nurse who works in the ICU unit in Holles Street National Maternity Hospital. Caroline took time out from her busy life to show me around the unit and answer my millions of questions. She is one of Ireland's unsung heroes. One of thousands of our nurses who do a difficult job every job and make the time that we have to spend in hospital a little more bearable with their wise eyes and their attentive care. Thank you Caroline, for your time and your patience. Any mistakes that I have made in the narrative are all mine.

There were moments — more than I would like — during the writing of this book when I felt the need to lie on someone's couch and whinge and say *I can't do this*. That person's couch belonged to my brilliant and gorgeous friend Niamh Cronin. She made me tea just the way I like it; in a mug, with chocolate on the side. She listened to me and gave me advice and sent me home with a smile on my face. I am so glad Niamh Cronin is my friend. She is the kind of person who makes you smile.

I once asked Breda Purdue — the managing director of Hachette Book Group Ireland — if I might have a job in her office. It seems like the kind of place I'd love to work. Everyone is lovely and stress seems like a foreign country that people might have heard of but no one has ever actually visited. (Breda said 'No vacancies at this time' by the way.) Special thanks must go to my editor, Ciara Doorley, who *knows* things about writing. Great things. Good things. And the best thing is she shares them with me. Thank you Ciara.

And my agent Ger Nichol. She has enough faith for the pair of us. I love that about her. Thank you Ger. Thank you for everything.

My UK editor, Carolyn Mays and her colleague, Francesca Best. Thank you both for your support and hospitality and all-round loveliness.

I was busy when I wrote this book. First, I was pregnant, then I gave birth to my beautiful Grace, then my husband Frank had a back operation and I panicked and thought I would never get this book written. But I did. Because of people who believe in me and love me. Frank for one. He minded the children at the weekends (once he got over the hump of the back operation, of course) while I escaped to Malahide Library to make stuff up. My stalwart parents, Breda and Don. Who minded my children on busy afternoons while I snuck upstairs to make stuff up. My fabulous sister Niamh, who minded my baby while I sat at a desk and made stuff up. During the writing of *Saving Grace* and *Becoming Scarlett*, my sister gave birth to her two gorgeous boys, Ríain and Finn. She is the kind of mother everyone should have. And even though she is my younger sister by many years, she is the one I look up to. For everything. Thanks to my children — Sadhbh, Neil and Grace — who make me laugh out loud. And smile. And swell with pride. Thanks must also go to my extraordinary brother-in-law,

571

Owen O'Byrne, who painstakingly bound many drafts of this book with an actual needle and thread, just to make it easier for me to read.

Thank you to my kind and gentle sister-in-law, Niamh MacLochlainn. The first reader of this book from start to finish. Every writer should have a reader like you. You'll know what I mean when I say that you are *Gorgio-Armani*.

Thank you to Emma McEvoy who read an early draft of this book and gave me the type of feedback that made me believe I could do it. Thanks also for your emails of support and encouragement. Writing a book is a bit like running a marathon; you need people cheering from the sidelines and handing you bananas along the way. It's the only way you can keep running.

And finally, thank you to our hardworking postman, out in all kinds of weather, with the unenviable task of delivering unfeasibly lengthy Visa bills to our house. But not today. Today he delivered Scarlett O'Hara.

I hope you like her.

We do hope that you have enjoyed reading this large print book.

Did you know that all of our titles are available for purchase?

We publish a wide range of high quality large print books including:
Romances, Mysteries, Classics
General Fiction
Non Fiction and Westerns

Special interest titles available in large print are:
The Little Oxford Dictionary
Music Book
Song Book
Hymn Book
Service Book

Also available from us courtesy of Oxford University Press:
Young Readers' Dictionary
(large print edition)
Young Readers' Thesaurus
(large print edition)

For further information or a free brochure, please contact us at:
Ulverscroft Large Print Books Ltd.,
The Green, Bradgate Road, Anstey,
Leicester, LE7 7FU, England.
Tel: (00 44) 0116 236 4325
Fax: (00 44) 0116 234 0205

WILLIAM WALKER'S FIRST YEAR OF MARRIAGE

Matt Rudd

William is a happy man. He has just married Isabel, the girl of his dreams, and is confidently sailing along on a sea of wedded bliss. Things couldn't be much better. Sure, there are a few bumps in the road, but life on the whole is good. That is until Isabel's 'best friend' Alex starts to intrude on their wedded bliss. And when William's ex-girlfriend Saskia — aka 'the Destroyer of Relationships' — appears on the scene, things go from bad to worse. For marriage, William quickly discovers, has its own set of rules. And though falling in love is easy, staying in love can be a whole lot trickier . . .